UNSPOKEN PASSIONS

"You are wicked!" Lilac said.

The corners of Rejar's mouth curved upward, revealing a devastating little dimple in his left cheek. "I have been told it is my nature."

"To be insensitive?" she sneered. He puzzled her by laughing.

"I can assure you, I am a very sensitive man." Rejar leaned forward, resting his elbows on his knees. By design, the position brought their heads fairly close together.

"You need only test me to find out," he whispered seductively.

Her face flamed and she quickly looked away from his inviting posture.

"I don't like you."

Rejar smiled slowly.

She faced him, nonplussed. "Did you not hear me?"

"I listen to you very well." His eyes captured hers with the methodical gleam of a predator—sophisticated beyond her comprehension and oh-so-tantalizing. "You would be surprised at what I hear."

DARA JOY

Rejar

LOVE SPELL ✦ NEW YORK CITY

TO MY MOTHER, ACE: THE ONE;
THE BEST; THE ONLY.

LOVE SPELL®

February 1997

Published by

Dorchester Publishing Co., Inc.
276 Fifth Avenue
New York, NY 10001

Printed in the United States of America.

"Any time not spent on love is wasted."
—*Tasso (1544-1595)*

Prologue

He was a totally sexual creature.

Handsome as sin, sensual as silk.

His name was Rejar.

He was descended from an ancient, arcane race known as the Familiar; and it was said they walked in two forms. That of human and cat.

Shrouded in mystery, the Familiar were both revered and reviled by those that knew of their existence. Because of this they kept to themselves for the most part—except in matters of casual relations. In that regard, their alliances were legion, their reputations well deserved.

For the males of their species were like no other.

A singular trait of the male Familiar was his ability to completely lose himself in the sensual self. So acute were his senses that he often derived pleasure simply from bestowing pleasure.

Adult males lived for the sensuous. Reveled in it. Became it.

The Familiar's erotic magnetism, once focused upon his prey, was difficult, if not impossible, to resist. Strangely, once roused to passion of any kind, he could be both ruthless and endearing at once. Intrepid predator yet rare delicacy.

And then there was the additional element.

The rumor—the whispered myth the Familiar would neither confirm nor deny.

Legend had it these males possessed a special trait which was peculiar to their species; a physical trait so compelling that it had, at times, caused them to be hunted down and enslaved simply for the possibility that this enticing bit of lore might be true.

It was believed that the male Familiar possessed the physical ability to "enhance" his sensuality during the sexual act.

The fact that this "enhancer" was not visibly present did not stop the tales of its existence. Moreover, if the male Familiar decided to employ this unique ability in his mastery of pleasure-giving, the effect was said to be devastating.

Throughout time, stories continued to circulate of how some of their males were so skilled in the sensual arts that the use of this innate trait combined with their extraordinary felinelike erotica delivered an unparalleled experience.

This was part of his legacy—

But it was well known amongst all Familiar that Rejar ta'al Krue had been gifted with much more.

And his special journey was about to unfold. . . .

Chapter One

London, 1811

"Driver! Driver! I insist you go faster!"

Lady Agatha Whumples turned a harried face to her niece in the somewhat cramped confines of her coach. "Whatever is the man thinking of, my dear? The Duchess will not await us for tea!"

Lilac Devere looked at her elderly maiden aunt and sighed. The woman was peering haughtily up at the ceiling through her lorgnette *and* pince-nez, as if the driver could see her disdain through the walls of the coach. Her aunt was a trial sometimes, but she loved her dearly.

"Auntie Whumples, if you hadn't insisted that society arrive late, we would never have been in this position in the first place."

Lady Whumples fluttered her fan. "Of course society arrives late—but not with the Duchess! Whatever will she think? I hope that dreadful Lord Byron won't be there. Go faster, I say!" She whacked the roof of the carriage with her cane. "That driver has always been the most inconsiderate—"

"He's been in your employ for fifty years!"

"Be that as it may, my child, his impertinence will not stand. It will not stand!" She thumped the seat for emphasis, dislodging several beads from the bodice of her daydress. "And another thing—the man has beady eyes. I don't like beady eyes!"

As usual, Auntie had gotten completely off subject. Lilac patted her hand. "Calm yourself, Auntie Whumples, surely—"

Without warning a brilliant flash of light filled the coach.

It was followed by a low, deafening rumble.

There was a loud *thump!* and the carriage shook.

Lady Whumples was tossed against the window. Lilac braced her hands against the sides of the coach to prevent herself from falling forward.

"What was—" Lilac started but never finished.

At the same time both Lilac and her aunt stared wide-eyed at the opposite seat.

A great black cat sat there, gazing speculatively at them even though his feline demeanor implied that this was *his* coach and that they were intruding upon him.

The strange animal had two different colored eyes.

Lilac's mouth dropped open.

Auntie Whumples's pince-nez fell off.

Then Auntie screamed—a high-pitched, extremely loud wail of pure terror. "It is a beast! A great beast which will surely kill us where we sit! I shall faint! Driver! Driver!"

The driver, with fifty years experience driving for

12

Lady Whumples, ignored her and kept going.

Composing herself, Lilac tried to calm her aunt. "Hush, Auntie! Remember—we are women of logic. The poor thing probably jumped into the coach to get out of this chilling drizzle. It must have been here all the time, hiding under the seat and was just now frightened by the lightning. It's just a cat." A rather large cat. *And those eyes . . .*

"It's a lion, I tell you! It will ravish us!"

As if it understood her words, the cat stared mischievously at Auntie Whumples and slowly licked his chops.

Auntie started screeching again, but Lilac laughed out loud.

It was a lovely trilling sound that pleased the senses. The young woman leaned forward closer to the cat, unknowingly displaying a goodly portion of bosom. "You have beautiful fur, kit, long and thick. It looks so silky. And you're quite the adventurer, aren't you? I like that. Perhaps I should take you in. . . ."

Auntie Whumples gasped. "What are you saying? You can't take that cursed beast into the house!"

The cat focused on Lilac, blinking slowly at her with those beautiful dual-colored eyes and Lilac made up her mind.

"I can and I will. You're coming home with me." Then she made a motion which sealed her fate: she softly stroked the fur behind its *left* ear.

The cat angled his head into her hand as if her touch was ecstasy itself.

"What do you say about that, cat?"

The Familiar known as Rejar closed his eyes and purred.

*   *   *

He was on a different plane of existence.

His senses told him that much. But where? One instant he had been hurtling through the Tunnels, cast about the eddies and currents; the next, a portal seemed to open beneath him (if beneath had any meaning in the space he was in), and he fell headfirst through the opening. In an attempt to protect himself, he had metamorphosed into his cat self.

The conveyance he was in rolled to a stop and the two females exited, with a great deal of fuss from the old one. She banged her walking stick several times, her face turning a fiery red. When the driver opened the door to let her out, she rapped him smartly on the side of his leg with her stick, screeching her way past him.

Oddly, the man only smiled.

The lovely younger one shook her head, muttering something under her breath, before following after her.

He distinctly heard the older one adamantly exclaim that the "beast" would *not* be in the coach on their return. The younger one firmly replied that if it was still in the coach when they returned, she was taking it home.

The "beast" would be here. At least until he learned where *here* was.

Thankfully, he could understand their language—at least most of it. Similar to the language of his brother's wife, it had differences in cadence and syntax that puzzled him. Was he somewhere in Adeeann's universe?

He closed his eyes as he remembered exactly how he had come to be in this predicament.

It had all started with the Shimalee, an ancient Charl icon which had the power to bend space and time. There were twelve Shimalees total, nine of which were linked throughout existence to form the matrix known as the Tunnels.

Now, thanks to him, there was a matrix of *ten*.

He had willingly sacrificed himself for his brother Lorgin's happiness and would do so again. Lorgin had a right to remain with the wife he so loved.

Insistently, he had taken the icon from his brother, entering the Tunnels with it. He released it into the continuum so that it might be absorbed back into the matrix where it belonged.

A violent cosmic storm had resulted and he was flung helplessly about the corridor, lost in space and time . . . and maybe dimension as well.

What would be the effect of this new matrix he had created?

Would it open up more passageways, hitherto denied to them? Was that how he had come into this place; had the additional Shimalee opened up a new portal?

Not being a mystic, Rejar did not understand much in the way of the Tunnels, but, like everyone else, he knew they were a means of transport from world to world.

Provided one had use of a mystic who could call forth the opening.

Unfortunately, he did not have such abilities.

He sighed mournfully.

How long would he have to remain in this unknown place before the great mystic, Yaniff, found him? A week? A year? Fifty years?

There was little help for it.

He knew what he was doing when he had entered the Tunnels in lieu of his brother. At present he would have to bide his time and make the best of the situation he found himself in. For however long, this strange new world was his home.

Best that he see what it looked like.

Sitting up on his haunches, the large, black cat peered over the edge of the open window.

It was raining.

Not a very good sign for the likes of him.

He looked further. Trees! Flowers, grass, and shrubs! This was acceptable. The conveyance he found himself in seemed to be at the end of a long walkway. At the other end of the walkway was a large stone building reminding him slightly of his family home on Aviara.

Rejar decided to investigate further.

Gritting his teeth, he leaped from the coach, scampering quickly through the light rain to the side of the house. Like most Familiars, he detested getting his fur wet—although in his natural human form, he was fastidious about bathing. His kind could not abide uncleanliness. Besides, there was something about the feel of water sliding down his naked skin . . .

His attention was caught by laughter coming from beyond the window just above him. Particularly one soft, lilting laugh, which so pleased his senses.

He effortlessly climbed a nearby tree, lithely balancing himself on a limb close to the window. Several people were sitting in a very ornate room, drinking out of the most fragile-looking cups he had ever seen. It looked as if they were engaged in some kind of social ritual.

His feral gaze immediately sought out the women of the group.

What would he have done if he had come to a world without women? The horrid thought made him shudder. He tried to bolster his flagging spirits. Yes, it could have been worse. Much worse.

16

Women always had a soothing effect on him.

He observed the ones in the room now. They were all dressed in odd costumes. Some of them, a few of the older ones, he noted, wore fake hair upon their heads. Others had unnaturally white complexions. A few were quite stunning.

This looked promising!

His feline sights shifted to the young woman who had been in the conveyance with him. The one who said she would take him in.

He smiled slowly to himself. *Mayhap she would.*

Lilac. The old woman had called her Lilac.

To him, she stood out from the rest of the women in the room. There was a uniqueness about her he had immediately sensed. This one intrigued him.

Minutely, he examined her, fascinated by the little qualities which often go unnoticed by most men, but never by Familiars. The graceful way her hands moved as she spoke. The lambent shine of her eyes when she laughed. Her heightened senses which he knew were arousing as she became more and more interested in the topic being discussed . . .

The siren song of the pulse-flow of her female energy drew upon the Familiar like a magnet.

Here was an extremely sensuous being, he decided. *Just like him.*

Yes, she definitely would be taking him in.

Lilac sat down before the dressing table in her bedroom and began removing the pins from her hair. The long strands fell to her waist in a soft tumble.

Picking up her silver-handled brush, she pulled the bristles through the tangled mass in slow, meandering strokes, closing her eyes to the calming feel of the gentle tugging. *Ah, it felt so—*

An odd feeling suddenly came over her.

The hairs on the back of her neck prickled. *Someone was watching her.*

Her eyes snapped open.

In the large, gilded mirror that graced over half of her bedroom wall from floor to ceiling, she caught sight of the cat sitting square in the center of her favorite chair. He was making himself quite at home!

He stared at her intently with those strange dual-colored eyes of his half shut.

How had he gotten in here?

He certainly wasn't in the room when she had gone into her dressing room earlier to change into her night rail. In fact, she hadn't seen him since they had returned from tea at the Duchess's. As soon as the coach had stopped, he had leapt down, disappearing into the underbrush.

At the time, she was certain she had seen the last of him, which saddened her. Lilac had been so happy to see the animal still in the coach when they returned to it. No matter how her aunt fussed, she had been determined to take the poor beast home.

Lilac had always wanted a cat.

Unfortunately, Auntie had always vehemently refused.

She suspected her poor aunt negated her desire for a cat as a last-gasp effort to prevent her niece from having the trappings of "old maid" hung upon her. After all, she had just turned twenty. An unmarried woman with a penchant for cats often spelled the term "tabby" to the ton—a "no-hope-for-her" old maid.

For some odd reason, today had been different. Today, for the first time in her life, she did not let Auntie have her own way during one of her fits. She had held firm in her desire to keep the cat.

Shrugging her shoulders, she smiled. So, did it really matter how he came to be here? Here the puss was. She turned on the stool to face him.

"You have the most interesting habit of suddenly showing up, cat." She grinned at him.

The cat, of course, did not reply.

Lilac observed the regal black feline, who was sitting on her chair as if he were upon a throne deigning to command his loyal subject! *I guess that would be me,* she mused.

He swished his tail.

There was something about this particular cat that struck a chord within her. Probably its sheer bravado. No one with an ounce of intelligence would dare waste their breath trying to tell this cat what to do. It was obvious he would do exactly as he pleased.

Not like unmarried misses who had to bow to the dictates of society and gossipy women!

The recurring dismal subject depressed her anew. Lilac worked her big toe into the thick pile of the Turkish carpet beneath her feet, sighing wistfully.

She didn't care what her aunt said—what dire prophecies of gloom and doom she claimed would befall her if she stayed on the shelf. She had no intention of ever putting herself on the marriage mart!

And why should she?

As far as she could tell, the woman had nothing to gain and everything to lose. Her property. Her money. Her independence. Her intelligence.

When a woman entered into the blissful state of holy matrimony, she became nothing but chattel. Indeed, men often referred to women as "baggage."

Well, she had no intention of becoming anyone's baggage—even if the alternative was becoming a dreaded "Ape Leader," the charming verbiage used to describe an unmarried woman. So what!

Oh, she knew her aunt meant well by trying to dissuade her from her set course. After all, Auntie Whumples was an Ape Leader herself and was only trying to spare her from the type of censure she had endured for a great part of her life.

But it wouldn't be the same for Lilac; she knew it wouldn't. She was a woman of means, her father's estate having come into her aunt's keeping until she reached her majority next year. She could spend her days following her own pursuits, not existing as someone else's property!

Her quest for knowledge and her penchant for reading already had her labeled as something of a bluestocking. Unfortunately, even that dreaded concept— a woman with a brain—was easily overlooked by avid suitors with an eye to her fortune.

Lilac shuddered. It was just not going to happen!

She would be like this cat here. Master of her own fate. Yes, just like the cat.

Impishly, she grinned at him. "We make strange bedfellows, don't we?"

The cat's blue eye seemed to wink at her.

Lilac snorted at the silly notion, thinking she was sleepier than she realized. Yawning, she stood up to stretch tired muscles. The glow from the fire backlit her, illuminating her nightgown and silhouetting the curvaceous form beneath.

"I'm really glad you've come to stay, kit; I don't think I shall be half so lonely with you for company. I'll have to think of an especially good name for you," she mumbled distractedly as she ambled toward her canopy bed. Throwing back the heavy counterpane, she snuggled beneath the covers.

The Master of His Own Fate watched her with a

predatory gleam in his golden eye. Then, at a deliberate pace, he followed her to the bed.

Lilac was just leaning over to turn down the lamp on her bedside table when she felt the mattress dip. "Oh!" She grinned at the cat. "Have you come to sleep with me, then? I'd like that on this damp night."

She turned down the lamp and burrowed under the covers, smiling contentedly when she felt the reassuring bulk of the animal settle in next to her.

"You and I are going to be great friends," she whispered in the darkened room. "I can tell."

The cat nudged his face against her thigh as if in agreement and Lilac drifted off to sleep. . . .

Like silent lightning, a glow shimmered about the bed and was quickly gone.

Leaning on his side, the naked man gazed down at the sleeping woman beneath him.

Silken lengths of gleaming black hair shifted forward off his powerful shoulders in an unconsciously seductive slide.

If Lilac had been awake and looking at the large mirror on her wall, she would have seen a man in her bed so beautiful as to take her breath away. *He had an eye of blue and an eye of gold.*

Pensively, the man watched her as she slept.

Her skin, he noted, was a mixture of tones: gold, rose, and cream. Inexplicably, he suddenly ached to feel the supple smoothness with his lips and tongue. Thinking he might do just that, he bent closer to her.

A strand of her long hair brushed against his arm.

He examined it curiously. Like her skin tone, it was a tumble of shades: ash, brown, dark blond. He couldn't decide what to name it, which fascinated him all the more. To a Familiar, nothing was so interesting

21

as that which could not be named.

He continued his visual exploration.

Her large, expressive eyes, closed now, were the deepest, darkest green. They brought to mind the leaves of the mystical Towering Forest on his home world of Aviara. The sensitive comparison made him long to brush his lips across the thick gold-tipped lashes, to feel them flutter against his mouth.

The sweet curve of her small ear was most enticing. . . .

His heated gaze drifted across her face.

Ah, those lips! Full and soft, a deep rosy pink reminding him of the sweet inner flesh of—

A low growl of desire rumbled from his throat.

Like most male Familiars, he was susceptible to the female.

In the past, he had never given it much thought, accepting who and what he was; he had simply enjoyed the many pleasures which came his way. Still, he seemed particularly susceptible to this female. Why?

He had seen countless beautiful women before; indeed, he had had them for most of his adult life, but this unusual, delicate beauty beneath him tugged at him in a way he had not experienced in his past.

Moreover, he had sensed it the instant they met.

It was as if there was an essence to her which beguiled him like some intoxicating drug. More potent even than the drugs Oberian slavers used to capture his kind.

He was entranced.

He was hungry.

He was almost powerless to break from the pull of her.

The realization caused a shiver to race down his spine. *Could this woman make a slave of him?* Ensnare him as surely as any captured beast?

No!

She intrigued him more than most, it was true, but that was all. Admittedly, he had been restless for some time, feeling strange and out of sorts. Even before the incident with the Tunnels, he had gone longer than his usual wont without the pleasure of a woman.

Too long.

It would account for his unprecedented reaction to her.

Convinced he was right, that it was only his prolonged abstinence speaking, he shook off the last remaining vestiges of the unwanted premonition. Yet, helpless to do otherwise, he ran his forefinger gently down the length of her exposed arm, testing the texture of her skin.

It was as he expected. Like the finest *krilli* cloth under his touch. So tender! He imagined his teeth barely grazing against—

Lilac's eyelids fluttered but she did not awaken. He withdrew his stroking finger for the time being, his mind made up. Unlike his other past encounters with women, he would relish this particular chase—slowly.

Very slowly.

For the ultimate pleasure, a delicacy must be savored.

It would begin now.

The hunt must start by giving her something of himself.

Deep in his senses, he lay back down next to her, drawing her close to him. *"Rejar,"* he murmured low in her ear as he twined around her. "I am called Rejar."

He slept with the scent of her. Dreaming of capture.

*   *   *

She felt wonderful!

Lilac opened her eyes and languidly stretched beneath the covers. Simply marvelous! She couldn't remember when she'd had such a peaceful night's sleep. For some reason, she had been utterly warm and cozy the entire night, even though it had been terribly cold and damp. It was strange, but she had felt protected, cared for in a way completely alien to her.

During the night, she imagined she was enfolded in a cloak of warm, spicy scent, rather like cinnamon and bayberry and something else totally exotic yet altogether enticing.

An image flashed across her mind.

There was a man.

A dream? When she tried to recall more of the vision, nothing else came to mind, neither who the man was, nor even what he looked like. Now why would she dream about some strange man holding her?

Out of the corner of her eye a flare of movement captured her attention.

Lilac turned over on her side and grinned.

Of course! *The cat.* She had momentarily forgotten about him.

He must've slept beside her all night! No wonder she had felt so cozy. She leaned over to thank the winsome animal for the comfort he had given her throughout the long, raw night.

"Good morning, and how are you this morning?" She scratched behind his left ear.

The big fellow seemed to *really* like it. Would he want his belly rubbed as well? Perhaps when he got more used to her.

"Its a beautiful morning, isn't it?" Sun was streaming in through the open windows, falling across the two of them lying on the bed.

The cat purred his agreement, wedging his head against her hand to coax her into more petting. Lilac didn't even realize she was doing his bidding as she continued to stroke his exquisitely soft fur.

"Let's see what Emmy brought us this morning." Taking the tray from the bedside table, Lilac carefully balanced it across her knees.

Every morning for the past ten years, Emmy had been bringing the same thing to her. A pot of tea, a little pitcher of cream, a biscuit, lemon curd, strawberry jam, and a bowl of sliced fruit. But for her new pet's entertainment she made a great show of examining the contents, holding up each item to his curious gaze.

She suddenly realized he must be very hungry.

Taking the saucer from beneath her teacup, she carefully poured a goodly portion of the cream onto the plate and placed it before him on the mattress.

"That's for you—but be careful; don't spill any on the linens. Emmy would have our heads."

Rejar eyed the plate of liquid warily. He was hungry; it was true. However, he preferred eating in his natural form. Not a possibility at this moment.

Resigned, he began lapping at the rich nourishment, not doing a very neat job of it.

"Oh, my."

Rejar looked up, cream dripping from his whiskers.

Lilac put a hand to her lips, giggling. "You're something of a piggy, aren't you?"

Rejar narrowed his eyes at her.

Unaware of his glowering look, Lilac picked up her cloth napkin. "Would you let me wipe your face?" Very gently, she blotted the cream off, tapping his nose with a linen-covered finger when she was done. "There; you're quite handsome again."

The cat swished his tail.

"You may say thank-you."

Thank-you. Looking slyly up at her, he quickly licked her hand.

"How sweet! You know, I really do need to name you. Let me see . . ." She tapped her chin. "How about . . . Rejar?" She pronounced the strange name: *ray-jhar.*

Lilac blinked. *Where on earth had that come from?*

The cat purred loudly.

Hmm. He seems to like it. What an odd name to think of . . . Well, it seems to suit him. "I guess Rejar it is."

Replacing the tray on the stand, she threw back the covers and walked over to the window overlooking the garden, delighted by what she saw. "Auntie's lilacs have bloomed! Come look, Rejar!"

As if he understood her, the cat jumped down from the bed, crossed the room, and leapt onto the window seat.

Rejar noted the alternating clusters of purple and white flowers blooming on the large bushes which rimmed the walled-in garden. Lilacs. So, she was named for a flower. Would they smell as sweet as she? He doubted it.

"Aren't they beautiful?" She sighed.

You are well named, he agreed.

"Let's spend the entire morning in the garden! You can lie in the sun on your fat belly and I'll read to you from James Weatherby's *Introduction to a General Stud Book.*"

Stud? Adeeann had once referred to him in such a way. Perhaps he would find out what she had meant.

In any case, he would stay close by Lilac until he felt more comfortable with his surroundings, at which point he would begin to explore. Familiars always liked to thoroughly know their territory before venturing forth. Besides, staying in the garden sounded like a good way to—

Fat belly?!

Rejar was incensed. *Did the woman not recognize solid muscle when she saw it?* he grouched, pacing.

Eager to be outside, Lilac dashed over to her dressing room, completely missing the fact that the hair on the cat's back was standing straight up in the air as he padded across the floor.

And his ears were down flat.

Lilac raced down the hallway, book in hand, looking forward to spending time in the garden with her new pet. She sprinted to the stairs. The frisky cat playfully scissored back and forth between her legs.

His frolicsome sport caused her to laugh out loud. *What a tricky little imp!*

She was still laughing when they reached the downstairs hallway, both of them skidding around a corner together.

"Lilac." Auntie Whumples stood just outside the sitting room door.

Discretely wagging an admonishing finger at her niece for her very unladylike behavior, she continued on in a louder voice, "Look who has come to visit with you—it's our Lord Creighton."

Lord Creighton stepped into the foyer from the sitting room.

The smile instantly died on Lilac's face.

"Good morning, Miss Devere." Executing a perfect bow, the obnoxious lordling proceeded to examine her with his ever present quizzing glass.

Lilac frowned. Lord Creighton examined *everything* with his quizzing glass. The insufferable boor!

What was he doing here? She thought she had been quite obvious in denouncing his attentions. Good lord, she had turned down every single invitation the coxcomb had issued to her! What more did it take?

Always in fashion, Lord Creighton was dressed in the blue coat and buff-colored waistcoat that Brummell had decreed was *de rigueur* for gentlemen's morning wear. His mousy brown hair was cut fashionably short with the curls in the front tousled just so over his forehead. His cravat was perfectly tied and so stiff, it seemed he was having trouble seeing over the foolish thing. Lilac sighed forlornly.

Who is this interloper? Bristling, Rejar observed the dandy before him. He snorted derisively at the man's short hair. *What kind of eunuch cut off his hair?* Where was his masculine pride?

He did not seem like much of a man to him.

Did he not know that the hunt had begun and a Familiar had already marked his "prey"? Lilac had taken *him* in. Now she was his to capture.

If the foolish man thought to interfere between a Familiar and his . . .

Well, he did so at his own peril.

Besides, he did not like the way the *flug* was peering at her through that tiny piece of glass!

"And what have we here?" Lord Creighton made the unfortunate mistake of kneeling down to get a closer look at the cat through his quizzing glass.

Rejar arched his back, emitting a low, threatening growl at the man, his blue and gold eyes flashing. Lord Creighton jumped back, his face going deathly pale.

"Zounds! Miss Devere, is—is it dangerous?"

Lilac looked speculatively at her cat. *Hmm . . . Maybe it can accomplish what I apparently cannot.*

She bent toward Lord Creighton in a confidential

mien. "Only if provoked, my lord. You won't provoke him, will you?" She spoke as if frightfully concerned for his welfare.

Lord Creighton's tiny eyes almost popped to normal size. "What—" he ran a finger around his tight collar, swallowing—"what exactly provokes him, Miss Devere?"

Lilac bit her lip as if she were pondering the dilemma. "We haven't quite figured that out yet."

His lordship gulped at Lilac's words but bravely stood his ground. Lord Creighton considered himself a Man of the World. T'wouldn't do to appear squeamish in front of the miss.

Rejar chuckled to himself. So, his little minx was trying to be rid of the *flug. Too obvious, my Lilac. I will have to teach you about subtlety.* He almost purred aloud at the enticing idea.

At that moment, Lilac turned a beseeching gaze to the cat, hoping against all hope that her pet would help her out by being obnoxious to the dandified twit.

You want me to help you with this one? Rejar made a great show of yawning.

Why, oh why, did a cat never do what you wanted him to? Lilac rolled her eyes in disgust. She'd just have to handle the coxcomb on her own. "Lord Creighton, I was just going into the garden—"

"Without your parasol?" Auntie Whumples tittered at her disapprovingly.

"I quite agree." Lord Creighton shook his head firmly. "We wouldn't want to spoil this lovely complexion, would we?" Surprising Lilac, Lord Creighton ran a clammy finger down the curve of her cheek.

Rejar cocked his head to one side. *Ah, so the* flug *believes he has the right. I think not. You give up on me too easily, Lilac. . . .*

The cat suddenly hissed, surprising everyone.

Whereupon he stood calmly watching as his lordship leapt three feet in the air.

Upon landing, Lord Creighton glared at the wretched beast from a safe distance of several feet. Trying to recover his composure, Creighton then affected what he considered a strong, masculine pose, making him look as if he had swallowed a bad piece of mutton.

"We should retire to the sitting room, my dear. I fear the strong sun might be too harsh for your frail constitution."

Frail constitution? Rejar let his expert gaze skim the voluptuous lines of Lilac's curvaceous form. The man was a half-wit. He would wager *this* constitution would go all night long with him.

This time he did purr at the very thought.

Lilac was fuming. She was not going to get rid of him! Her shoulders slumped as she followed "his boorishness" into the sitting room.

Giving the appearance of extreme feline boredom, Rejar made a great production out of stretching before he finally got up to follow.

His blue eye twinkled. This should prove most amusing.

Lord Creighton sat sprawled in the middle of the old-fashioned Queen Anne settee.

To Lilac's irritation, the dandy never failed to sniff disdainfully at the outmoded decor of the sitting room. So what if their furnishings were not "all the crack"? She liked the way the room looked and felt! Bother Lord Creighton and the rest of the ton with their silly expectations!

"More tea, my lord?" Auntie Whumple's voice came from somewhere in the shadows of the room. While proper behavior decreed she must chaperone, she didn't want to appear to be too intrusive.

"No, thank you, Lady Whumples. I'm quite finished." He fastened his small eyes on Lilac. "Miss Devere, I was wondering; will you be attending the Stanhope's soiree?"

"When is it?" As she spoke, Lilac noticed the cat jump onto the back of the settee behind Lord Creighton's head. He settled himself comfortably across the rim, half-leaning against the man's shoulders.

Lord Creighton froze the instant he realized the wretched beast was actually leaning against him. The position brought the animal frightfully close to his throat. He gulped nervously.

"Lord Creighton?" Lilac prompted.

"Ah . . . yes. It's the Friday after next."

The cat began swishing his tail. Up. Down. Up. Down. Lord Creighton gave her a sickly smile.

"I haven't been invited," she replied. *Thank God.*

"Yes, well, that can be remedied, you see, I—" A bushy tail draped across the top of his head, hanging down over his forehead.

Being a gentleman, Lord Creighton was obliged to ignore it.

"I—I thought I might—"

The tail began to seesaw atop his head in an undulating motion. Up. Down. Up. Down.

"That is, if your—"

Lilac tried her best not to laugh. She truly did.

But when the tip of the cat's tail reared up to wave at her from the vicinity of Lord Creighton's eyebrows, she was undone. She clutched her stomach, peels of laughter issuing forth.

"Miss Devere,"—Lord Creighton looked concerned—"are you quite all right?"

31

"Yes, yes, I'm fine." She wiped the corner of her eye, trying to regain her composure. From the corner of the room, she thought she heard Auntie Whumples stifle a few titters of her own.

"You were saying, my lord?"

"Perhaps you would care for some snuff to calm you?" He reached into his coat pocket with his left hand and held a little enameled box out to her.

Lilac detested snuff. She thought it the most disgusting of habits. "No, thank you. I do not partake of snuff."

"May I?"

She waved her hand, indicating he should please himself.

Lord Creighton began to prepare himself for the fine show he was about to perform to impress her.

Carefully, his left hand held and opened the tiny box. With a movement Lilac knew he must have practiced before a mirror for hours to accomplish, he let the dainty lace of his sleeve flutter against his pampered right hand as he ever-so-carefully raised a pinch to his quavering nostrils for a delicate snort.

Rejar was stupefied.

His mouth parted in disbelief as he watched the bizarre ritual. *What was the zorph-brained fool doing?* Did he actually think to impress a woman with this ridiculous display?

Wait. What if the powder had magical qualities of some kind? It could even be . . . *an aphrodisiac.* This required research.

Rejar leaned over Lord Creighton's shoulder to get a better look at the mysterious powder. He stuck his head close to the still-opened box to see what curious secret he would uncover.

Lord Creighton, suddenly noticing a huge cat head

looming over his shoulder, gave an involuntary jump, sending a cloud of snuff into the air and all over the inquisitive kitty's face.

Lilac winced as the poor cat instantly reared off the couch howling and sneezing.

"Oh my goodness!" Lilac jumped up.

Bedlam ensued.

Making a dash, she just missed the sneezing cat as he careened against a side table and sent one of Auntie's vases crashing to the floor.

Auntie Whumples wailed in the background, screeching at Lilac, "Stop that beast!"

Lord Creighton stood by helplessly, uttering meaningless lilting phrases of apology while she chased willy-nilly after the cat, who was snarling his head off.

By the time she had finally cornered him, the poor thing had sneezed himself silly and had collapsed, gasping for breath beneath a chair.

Lord Creighton came running over. "Do accept my apologies, Miss Devere. To make up for my deplorable behavior, I insist that you attend the soiree. I will stop by the Stanhope's this very day to ensure an invitation is sent to both yourself and Lady Whumples."

Ever the opportunist. Lilac grimaced. "That's not necessary, Lord Creighton. If you'll just—"

"Oh, but I insist!"

Leave. Lilac bit her tongue. There was no way she could possibly refuse without appearing churlish. She sighed, willing to say anything at this point just to be rid of him. "Very well, Lord Creighton."

Now that he had gotten what he came for—Lilac's presence at the soiree—Creighton quickly made his farewells.

Exasperated, Lilac plopped into a chair. "Zounds,"

she said imitating Lord Creighton's nasal voice. "What a coxcomb he is!"

The corners of Auntie's mouth twitched. "Be that as it may, child, his lordship did provide us with a much coveted invitation to the Stanhope's."

Lilac looked at her aunt askance. "Coveted by whom?"

"Coveted by me *for you*. It's an excellent opportunity for you to meet all the right gentlemen, my dear. We mustn't waste any opportunity."

"But Auntie Wh—"

"No buts, my child. I have been entrusted with your welfare by your late father, God rest his noble heart, and I shan't fail him. We *will* be at the Stanhope's soiree." So proclaimed, Lady Whumples left the room.

Damn and blast, but her aunt could be stubborn!

Rejar, still gasping from his ordeal with the mysterious powder, listened to the conversation between the two women with interest. This soiree they spoke of seemed to be some kind of social gathering.

The old one had spoken of the men she wanted Lilac to meet.

It was time he began to view more of this new world of his. He would do what Familiars had been doing for the wizards of Aviara throughout the ages; he would investigate the situation.

Rejar decided he would begin immediately. Discretely, he exited the house, heading into the streets of London.

What he eventually saw staggered him.

Chapter Two

It was a world of hideous savagery.

A cooling night wind blew across Rejar's sensitive face while he gazed longingly up at the stars. Lifting the long strands of his hair in gentle wafting motions, the soothing breeze did little to ease him.

He was sitting in the window seat in Lilac's bedroom. A habit of late. Especially in the small hours of the night when the peace of sleep was not to come. His large frame completely filled the seat; he rather liked the feeling of being enclosed on three sides. He supposed it was a carry over from his other self, not bothering to give it too much thought.

His sights flicked over to the bed where Lilac slept.

Even if the light of the full moon had not been illuminating the room, he still would have been able to see her quite clearly, his eyes having the ability of rapidly adjusting to changing light conditions.

Familiars often could sense physical changes in the

body as well; and Lilac's even, measured breathing told him she was deeply asleep. Conversely, any change in her breathing tempo precluded wakefulness, alerting him when to metamorphose back into his cat self.

To his advantage, Lilac usually fell asleep quickly and was slow to rouse. If nothing disturbed her, he knew she would sleep through the night.

If only I could do the same . . .

He briefly closed his eyes, trying to shut out the untenable horrors he had witnessed in the past two weeks. It did little good. Rejar believed the nightmarish visions would forever remain with him:

Mothers begging in the streets for food for their starving children while just a few streets away men and women dined in opulent excess, seeming either not aware of the misery, or not even caring, for that matter.

The streets were full of offal.

People lived in the worst filth and slime he had ever witnessed on any world. Yet there were others, those more privileged, who lived in grand houses with many servants to wait upon them. This wealth in and of itself was not disturbing; it was their seeming indifference to the conditions of those who suffered around them which staggered him.

He, himself, was from a privileged Aviaran family; his father, Krue, was a member of the ruling council, as well as a high-power Charl mystic. Yet no one in his family would ever allow such deprivation to go unanswered.

A more horrifying memory surfaced, causing him to shudder.

One day he had seen a small child run over in the street by a conveyance. The owner merely signaled the driver to move on, not even stopping to see to the injured boy.

Rejar could not believe what he was witnessing.

Still in cat form, he had run to the child, but it was too late. The boy died in the gutter.

Not one person stopped to see or help.

He stayed by the child, curled up to his side for the few moments it had taken the precious life to leave his body. It seemed to him the boy had smiled to him sweetly, just before he . . .

Rejar had gone into an alleyway and thrown up.

Well he would remember the face of the man who owned the coach. It was a face he would never forget, with cruel, dark eyes and sneering lips. He vowed he would find this man, and when he did, make him pay for his heinous crime.

Rejar recalled some of the other injustices he had seen: An old man hung by the neck for stealing food while onwatchers cheered at his suffering. . . . On the streets, a rich man's throat slit just for a few coins. . . . Homeless children wandering aimlessly through the alleys, begging and worse. . . .

It went on and on.

How could he exist in such a world?

He had no qualms about his ability to defend himself and what was his. His father had trained him well, making especially sure his half-breed Familiar son knew how to wield a weapon and how to fight for his own protection.

Against his wife's wishes, Krue had brought his son up an Aviaran warrior. Later, his blood relative, Gian, had taught him the secret ways of the Familiar kill-hunt as well.

No, he had no qualms whatsoever about his physical survival.

But spiritually? This place was an assault on both his Familiar senses and sensibilities. Life seemed not precious at all to these people who squandered their resources so carelessly.

To be fair, in his travels he had seen many planets outside of the Alliance which were equally savage, although none had been quite so ignorant regarding their own savagery. Just the opposite. Such planets had a tendency to revel in their barbarism.

Not this one.

It was curious to note how *civilized* these people proclaimed themselves. They disdained anyone outside their enlightened society; their "ton."

Rejar already knew what he must do to survive.

He must assume the persona of a man of position and means, for this world would never recognize him otherwise, and the alternative was unthinkable.

A position of recognition would also place him above the close scrutiny of others. This was imperative in this particular society whose fears and superstitions could easily turn against him.

He believed he had already found the right man to lead him into his new life. The man had first caught his attention while Rejar was observing a place where men went to wager vast sums of specie, a popular pastime here for men of fortune, it seemed.

Somewhat younger than Rejar, the man had a certain status within the society and his reckless passions perfectly lent themselves to Rejar's purposes. At first, he thought the man's name was George Gordon Noel, but later found out he was called Lord Byron. He was a baron, which Rejar learned was a title of some respect in this society.

Knowing this, Rejar had chosen his new identity with particular care. There was a distant land here called Russia. It was not easily accessible to these people, making it difficult for anyone to check on his story.

He had studied these people well, picking out the nuances which would allow him to appear to blend in with the society. It was a gift of his kind; another trait for which the mystics of the Charl sought out the Familiar.

Furthermore, his new identity would allow him easy access to Lilac; a situation he greatly desired. It was time for the hunt to progress.

His gold/blue eyes drifted to the bed again.

She had become a comfort to him in this strange new world. This house, a small haven from the madness outside.

He was grateful it was her and not another he had first come upon, for she was not like a lot of the other women he had observed here thus far. Lilac was genuinely kind and did not seem to care much for the socializing aspects of her society, preferring to stay at home sitting in the garden with only her "cat" for company.

He rather looked forward to those peaceful hours. With her gentle voice reading to him aloud from some book . . . This Fanny Burney seemed to be a special favorite of hers.

He smiled fondly as he remembered her exuberance for the prose which seemed somewhat melodramatic to him.

From the day he had come to this world, Rejar had held her protectively in his arms each and every night, keeping his own disturbing thoughts at bay. Their scents intermingled, and as the nights wore on she unconsciously began accepting him in her sleep more and more.

He liked the soft feel of her thin night garment next to his naked skin. *Better still, were it skin to skin.*

Such thoughts reminded him of how long it had

been since he had enjoyed intimate pleasure.

Since intimate pleasure was never far from a Familiar's mind, he wondered why he was not bothered more by his forced abstinence. For even amongst the Familiar, whose sexual appetites were legendary, Rejar was often remarked upon.

The truth was, Rejar simply loved women.

All women.

He loved the way they looked; the way they smelled; the softness of their skin; the gentleness of their touch.

Women responded to Rejar on an instinctual level. He was never unkind. He was unfailingly mindful of their pleasure. He was virtually unstoppable sexually, having the ability of ultra energy levels. Not to mention incredibly innovative and commandingly sensual.

Women adored him. And he adored them.

Rejar was often told by his lovers that he did not make love like other men.

If such were true, he could not say.

He knew only that for him, each time he engaged in the act, it was more than an exploration of the senses; it was an immersion of his being. Rejar reveled in textures and tastes; color of hair, skintones, shape of features, expressions of personality . . . in short, women.

He enjoyed them all equally well, knowing without a doubt that no *one* woman could ever be enough for him.

To Rejar ta'al Krue, variety was not only the spice of life, it was the sugar as well.

So, why was he not at all concerned by his abstinence?

He unfurled himself from the windowseat with the unconsciously lithe grace of the Familiar, padding barefoot to the bed. *Where did this restlessness come from? This dissatisfaction?*

Sinking to his knees on the carpet beside the bed, he lightly rested his elbows on the mattress and curiously gazed down upon Lilac's face.

Her generous mouth was slightly parted as she slept.

Rejar briefly thought of dipping his tongue between those enticingly parted lips. He knew he could not do that, of course, so for the time being he settled with just looking at her.

Long gold-tipped lashes covered those forest green eyes of hers. . . .

His little bit of Aviara.

A wave of homesickness washed over him. It was so acute, he could not stop himself from brushing his mouth lightly across her eyelids. No matter how long it took the mystic Yaniff to find him, it comforted him to know he would always have his little bit of Aviara here in Lilac's eyes.

When he felt her lashes flutter against his lips, he pulled back to watch her come awake.

Those expressive green eyes opened, slowly focusing on him. He held his breath as she gazed upon him for the first time, wanting the moment to last; knowing he could not allow it.

When her eyes widened with the beginnings of cognizance, he immediately sent a mesmerizing thought to her.

[You are dreaming.]

She blinked in confusion. Her mouth parted. "I . . ."

He sent the thought again. *[You are dreaming, Lilac.]*

He waited to see if she took his suggestion.

There were some who were immune to this suggestive technique. His father and brother Lorgin, for instance, were impervious to it. But then, most Charls were. You could not tamper with a Charl's mind.

Rejar could not help but smile when he suddenly

41

recalled the first time he had tried it on his own father when he was a young boy. He wanted to see if he could "suggest" his father into forgetting some mischief he had caused. It had backfired on him with predictable results. His father had been doubly furious with him, incensed that he had the audacity to attempt it on him.

He hoped Lilac would be susceptible. He did not think she would respond favorably to the knowledge of his presence in her bed.

Indeed, these past weeks she had often spoken aloud of her utter distaste for the males of her society.

However, she had yet to meet *him*.

"I—I think I'm dreaming." She raised a slender hand to her forehead.

Good. It was working. She was susceptible to him.

Although he had never used this technique in quite this way before, Rejar knew that the greater the physical contact between them, the more she would remember her dream experience. Once he physically entered her, he would completely lose this type of suggestive ability over her.

But then there were many intriguing things you could suggest to someone with their full knowledge.

A slow, feral smile inched across his handsome face. *She would not have distaste for this male.*

Lilac spoke to him, interrupting his pleasant analysis.

"Do I know you, sir?"

"Oh, yes." He rakishly winked at her.

"I do?" She was perplexed. "I think I would have remembered you had we met. You're quite beauti— Why don't you have any clothes on?!"

And would not his father be most displeased with him for this little bit of mischief. Rejar chuckled. What could he do? He *was* a Familiar.

"Do you think I need them?" he asked her not-so-innocently.

She seemed to mull this over for a moment. "I don't suppose so, since this is only a dream; but still, it seems most improper."

Leaning over her, he whispered, "I like being most improper."

Lilac amused him by whispering back, "I think I might like it too."

While under the trance, a subject reacted freely to situations in which normally they might be inclined to be slightly more reserved. However, the true nature of the person always remained. Yes, he chuckled, she was much like him.

Rejar grinned, revealing two roguish dimples. "I have never doubted this." Standing, he lifted the covers to climb inside.

Lilac gaped at him with eyes suddenly gone huge.

"What is it, Lilac?"

"You—you—you don't—you—"

Rejar had no way of knowing Lilac had never seen a naked man before. Even in her dreams. He wondered what was upsetting her so—until his gaze followed the finger she pointed directly at the source of her discomfiture.

He looked down, then back at her, confused. "This?"

"That," she confirmed.

"Why?"

"It's . . . so big!"

Even though it was one he had heard often in the past, Rejar, like any Familiar, preened at the compliment. "If you say."

"Huge, really," Lilac continued, viewing the thing with a mixture of fascination and repulsed awe.

Rejar was starting to feel uncomfortable. Why was

the woman staring at him so intently? Perhaps he was endowed, but she was peering at him as if he were oddly made in some way. Were the men here so very different? If so, it boded well for him.

Indeed, he would become very popular.

"Actually, *enormous!*" she went on, her fingers splaying across her lips in wonder. "I can't believe the size of—"

He was getting annoyed. After all, it was his manhood! "That is enough!" He bellowed. "It is not seemly to inspect a man so intently!"

"Oh. Sorry." Lilac drooped down into the covers.

"Fine."

Rejar settled in beside her, taking her in his arms. Lilac braced her palms against his broad, golden-skinned chest, looking earnestly up at him.

"Why not?" she asked.

"Why not what?"

"Why is it not 'seemly' to examine a man's . . . *part?*"

The corners of his lips curled up. "You may examine my 'part' all you like, sweet Lilac, just do not discuss it as if it did not have feelings."

She did not seem to understand his humor.

"You may touch it, if such is your desire," he clarified. She did not respond the way he had hoped. In fact, for some reason, Lilac seemed quite horrified with the prospect.

"Touch it yourself!"

Rejar stared at her incredulously. What was wrong with the woman? Truly, her reactions were most strange.

Deciding to ignore her outburst, he ran his hands down her back, stopping to cup her rounded buttocks in his palms. They were a nice handful. Soon he would remove this garment she was wearing so he could—

"What on Earth are you doing! Stop that at once!"

Rejar froze. A woman's objection was so foreign to him that he stared at her gape-mouthed. "You do not like the touching of my hands?"

"I most certainly do not! Let me go!" She tried to break his hold on her. Failing that, she glared up at him. The intensity of the glare was somewhat spoiled by the hank of hair that fell over her eyes.

Hmm. He must think on this puzzle a moment.

It was a cosmic truth that woman were not predictable. It was one of the traits which made them so fascinating to the male Familiar—but this reaction of hers didn't make any sense; she was a sensual woman. Unless . . .

"You have been with unschooled men in the past, have you not? Men who do not know how to please you?"

"What— Whatever do you mean?"

Yes, that was it then. It would explain her present attitudes regarding men. Rejar sighed dramatically. How often the male Familiar are called upon to undo the fumblings of other men!

His white teeth flashed in a sudden grin. It was a terrible job, but someone in the universe had to do it.

He patiently removed the strand of hair from her face by smoothing it back behind her brow. *{I will show you what I mean.}*

Lilac gasped. "How did you do that? You spoke without speaking!"

{I can send my thoughts to you.}

"Simply amazing! Why, I never realized how imaginative I am! Now I'll send something to you."

{You cannot.}

"Why not? It is *my* dream, isn't it? I shall do as I please! What did I just say?"

{I do not know. I have explained to you—you cannot do this.}

"I don't see why not." She stuck her chin stubbornly in the air. If Rejar wasn't so exasperated, he might be tempted to laugh.

"I can send my thoughts to you—or anyone for that matter," he said aloud, "but you cannot send your thoughts to me because you are not . . . like me."

"I see . . . it's the rules of the dream world, isn't it?"

"Something like that." He smiled kindly at her.

Lilac yawned. "I'm rather tired; I think I should be waking up now."

"Do you not mean go to sleep now?"

"But I'm already asleep, so if I'm tired, I suppose I need to wake up." She looked confused herself. "How could that be?"

He needed to distract this line of thinking immediately as conscious realization could sometimes cause a subject to break trance.

{Did I not promise to show you what pleases you?}

The diversion worked; she gave him a surprised look. "How do you know what pleases me?"

{I know. Watch . . . } His capable fingers immediately began massaging up and down her back, lightly kneading the muscles into relaxed compliancy.

When he reached her shoulders, he completely enfolded her in his embrace as they lay on their sides. Still gently moving his broad palms in circular motions against her back, he occasionally used just the heel of his hands to augment the soothing kneading action.

"Mmm—that does feel nice." She closed her eyes, enjoying the exquisite sensation of a man giving her a massage.

His hands moved lower to the arch of her waist.

"That feels very good."

Then to the base of her spine.

"Oh yes, that—"

And lower still . . .

Lilac's eyes snapped open. "You shouldn't be touching me there."

He looked at her through half-lowered lids. *{Why not?}*

Lilac frowned. "Because it's just not done! Not even in dreams." Reaching down, she stopped his roving hand.

He gave her a patent look. "And how do men make love here, then?"

Lilac blushed. "I . . . What a question! You must never ask a lady that—it is not—not," she used his own word back at him, *"seemly."*

Rejar exhaled in frustration. This was proving more difficult than he had first thought. It was going to be a challenging hunt; he could sense that already. True to nature, he relished the prospect of an interesting chase.

In any case, it was enough for now.

It would not be wise to test the limits of her trance state. He would continue the sport next eve.

Indeed, the Familiar were noted for their perseverance.

{Sleep, Lilac . . . } He cupped her head close to his chest, resting his chin on top of her head.

"Something is odd here," she mumbled against him, then promptly fell into a deep slumber.

"Yes, definitely," Rejar whispered agreeably.

He brushed his lips across her clean-smelling hair.

The next morning Lilac awoke with a vague sense of some pleasant dream she had experienced. She stretched sinuously under the covers before reaching for her morning tray.

Something licked her ankle.

"Eee!" Lilac frowned down at the huge lump lurking under the covers. "Rejar, come out of there!"

The lump moved sluggishly towards the edge of the counterpane. Two large paws and a nose peeked out from under the blanket.

"You seem tired this morning. Come to think of it, you weren't anywhere to be seen last evening. I suppose you were out tomcatting all night." A tail swished under the blanket. "Shame on you. Serves you right; you'll get no sympathy from me."

The paws and nose disappeared beneath the blanket again.

"Don't sulk. You know very well you're guilty. I can just imagine what you've been up to all night."

Lilac felt a paw playfully swat the lace edging on the hem of her nightgown.

She smiled. "Oh, all right; you're forgiven. I suppose boys will be boys even if they are cats."

Said cat began to purr.

"Come on out and I'll give you some of my cream."

Now there was an enticement. Rejar scooted from beneath the blanket.

Lilac was pouring some liquid into a saucer for him. Oh. *That* cream. He sighed.

Halfheartedly, he began lapping up the thick liquid, thinking it would probably be some time before he could sneak into the room where the food was prepared to help himself. The tidbits he was getting were not enough to sustain him.

And some of them were not to his liking at all.

One day the cook had actually thrown him some kind of water creature's head, beaming at him as if he should be grateful for the disgusting thing! Usually he had to gather his food in the middle of the night, while the rest of the household was sleeping.

Once again, the cream splashed all over his face. He really was not very good at this.

"Just look at you." Lilac shook her head. "You really are a messy puss, Rejar." He stuck his face close to her so she could wipe his whiskers for him.

"There." Lilac settled back against the pillows, drinking her tea. "Now I have to think of some way to avoid that boring soiree this Friday. Auntie Whumples seems so adamant. Perhaps I could say . . . no, that wouldn't work. What if . . ." Lilac's voice trailed off as possible excuses went through her mind, none of them very promising. She spent the rest of the day trying to think of something, anything her aunt would accept.

Several of the excuses that seemed promising she later attempted on her aunt, only to have her hopes immediately dashed when Auntie speared her with her infamous no-nonsense glare that traveled haughtily down her long nose, gaining momentum before it launched itself at the unfortunate victim. Her.

By the time she went to bed that evening, Lilac knew that anything short of getting struck by lightning was not going to prevent her from attending that wretched soiree.

"Oh, it's *you* again."

Lilac opened her eyes to another dream.

The same beautiful man she had seen the previous night in her sleep was back. Only this time he was lying across the top of the covers on his stomach.

He was still very much unclothed.

"*Mmmm . . .*" He rubbed the underside of his chin

back and forth against the top of her thigh while staring impishly up at her.

"I don't know why I'm dreaming about you again."

[Do you not?] Rejar rested his head on his folded arms, letting his index finger lazily trace the outline of demarcation between her night rail and the sheet.

Annoyed, Lilac slapped his hand away. "No, and I wish you would stop touching me in such a forthright manner."

"Ah, you prefer a more subtle approach." His teasing eyes sparkled. "Now, how might I be more subtle, I wonder?" He rubbed his chin as if he were actually thinking it over.

Lilac narrowed her eyes. "I think you're playing with me in some way."

"In *every* way." A rakish dimple popped into his cheek.

He smoothly rolled over onto his back, lacing his hands behind his head before looking lazily over at her. His eyes were dancing with amusement.

For some reason, Lilac got the absurd impression of a cat swishing his tail.

She shook an admonishing finger at him. "You must be nice or I won't allow you in my dreams anymore."

"Very well." He turned onto his side. Propping up his head by leaning on a bent arm, he reached for her with the other.

"What are you doing?" she squealed.

"What you have asked—I am being *nice*."

"You don't look like you're being nice; you look like you're being quite mischievous."

He brought her small hand to his face. "Really. How do I look mischievous?"

"Your eyes sparkle in a certain way and you have these curved lines by your mouth, dimples really, which deepen and—Stop that!" He was running his tongue in a long, slow lick up the center of her hand, straight up to the tip of her middle finger.

"You do not like it?" He spoke around her finger, which was now gently being suckled into his warm mouth. When those thick, ink-black lashes of his lifted to meet her focus straight on, Lilac blushed to the roots of her hair.

"I—I didn't say that."

"Then why should I stop?" White teeth held her finger now and the rogue was laughing!

Before Lilac could think of an appropriate response, he was once more licking the inside of her hand, using his silken tongue to probe in a most intriguing fashion between her fingers where they joined at the base.

Her breath caught with an odd hitch in her throat.

"You do not want me to stop, do you?" His low, resonant voice was partially muffled as he continued to pay the most indecent attention to her fingers.

Who would ever guess fingers could be so—so inspiring?

"I don't suppose"—Lilac cleared her throat—"it would be—I mean, you *might* continue for just a few more moments; seeing as this is a dream and such."

Rejar chuckled deep in his throat, his talented lips moving to her wrist. He lightly scraped her pulse point before pulling up the sleeve of her garment with his teeth.

Lilac gulped for air as his moist tongue slid across the crease on the inside of her elbow.

"You know I don't know how I thought you up, but I think you're exceptionally handsome," she whispered to him in the darkened room.

The corners of Rejar's lips twitched. As a rule Familiars never paid much attention to such compliments. For some reason, women always found them thus. Amused, he stopped to look down at her lying beneath him. "Do you?"

"Oh, yes! Although, I can't see you as clearly as I would like. What color are your eyes?"

Rejar began nuzzling at the collar of her gown. "Blue . . ." His mouth trailed like hot silk across her collarbone. ". . . golden."

Lilac tried not to moan aloud at the feel of the sensual male mouth gliding over her with such devastating effect.

"Which is it?" she gasped.

"What?" His heated breath caressed her skin as he continued his sensual foray.

"Blue or golden?"

Rejar stopped.

It was not an easy thing to do; her skin tasted like the sweetest cream to his hungry lips. However, this was dangerous territory. If he told her the truth, it might jog her awareness of . . . something, the wrongness of his dual-colored eyes to her or, more probably, a connection to her new cat.

No, he could not chance it.

He reined his senses inward, bringing his breathing and body temperature back to normal. The process made him slightly irritable.

His sensual nature needed a release and he had gone far too long without it. He intended to remedy that as soon as possible. The long hunt would have to be momentarily put aside in lieu of a fast conquest.

Tomorrow evening his unaware "sponsor" into society was having a private gathering of his select friends at his country home. Rejar intended to be there.

His entrance into this society would serve a triple purpose: he would be establishing a new life for himself; he would be meeting soon "face-to-face" with Lilac; and he would find somebody on the morrow who could relieve his present condition.

To hope she would have forest green eyes, Rejar acknowledged, would be overly optimistic.

He gazed longingly into those Aviaran eyes and bid them, *{Sleep.}*

Chapter Three

He did exactly what Lilac thought he had done on their first meeting; he hid under the seat inside one of the coaches bound for Byron's country home.

When the inhabitants, two young lords who were already well on their way toward being intoxicated, lurched from the coach, Rejar was not far behind them. His deep coat helped to conceal him in the darkness of night, making it easy for him to find his own entrance through an open set of glass doors that led directly into a deserted library room.

From there, he quickly bolted up a back stairway to the bedroom suites, easily locating the master bedroom with his innate tracking abilities. Once inside he nudged the door shut, purposely striding over to a chifforobe in the corner.

Mirrored doors, which an instant ago had reflected a beautiful, long-haired black cat with blue and gold eyes now reflected a beautiful long-haired man with the very same eyes.

Opening the wardrobe, Rejar riffled though the contents, looking for something to temporarily cover his nakedness while he sought out his host.

Not for the first time, Rejar acknowledged one of the drawbacks of metamorphosing was that your clothes did not change with you. Normally, this did not pose too much of a problem as he usually returned to the same place to change back. However, when he had instinctively transformed himself back in the Tunnels, he had completely lost all his clothing in the turbulent cosmic storm.

Since Byron was a much smaller man than he, his choice was limited to a red silk robe. He yanked the garment out of the closet, securing it around his lean waist with the sash. Then he went in search of his "sponsor."

Every woman in the room and several fops turned to stare agog at the positively stunning man who stood unabashedly in the doorway wearing nothing but a red silk robe.

His tall, powerful frame filled the doorway, yet there seemed to be a certain lithe sensuality noticeable in his movements as he scanned the room, apparently seeking out someone. The silken robe he wore slid sinuously against the obviously nude, muscular body beneath in such a provocative way as to make several of the ladies feel quite faint.

There was a captivating aura of individuality about him, a feeling that this was someone who would either lead or walk alone. Never follow. His regal demeanor proclaimed to all that this was a man who would very much do as he pleased. His presence in a drawing room, so attired, told all he was not in the least concerned about what others thought of him.

Against fashion, he wore his glossy black hair long. The silken mass fell to the middle of his back with the rich, lustrous texture of the finest Russian sable. In fact, his hair seemed softer than sable and there wasn't a woman in the room who didn't immediately itch to feel that hair beneath her hand.

Counter to that gorgeous silken mane, his smooth skin was a tawny golden color; and since the robe gaped open occasionally when he moved, revealing a portion of sleekly muscled thigh, it was evidently his true skin tone all over. Such delectable skin as this invited touching.

But it was his face which captivated even the most discriminating of connoisseurs in the room. For it was a face of such utter sensuality and masculine beauty that many of the women actually gasped aloud.

He was breathtaking.

Madeline Fensley, who had been eyeing the newcomer with a mixture of awe and disbelief, sidled over to her only real competition in the room, Lady Harcorte.

"Darling, is he really there or do you think Byron put one of his interesting surprises in the wine?"

Lady Harcorte blinked at the vision of masculine perfection in red silk. "I was wondering the very same thing myself."

The two women stood side by side taking in their fill of the luscious surprise which had presented itself this evening.

"So, what do you think?" Madeline murmured to Lady Harcorte. "Can he possibly be as good as the wrapping indicates?"

At thirty-five years of age, Leona Harcorte was known throughout the ton as a most accomplished mistress of the boudoir. A widow, her affairs were legend, but while she was indulgent, it was also known she was most discriminating. Men vied for her favors; women sought out her advice. It was said she could accurately assess a man's skill in the art of amour with just a look, and, conversely, ruin his masculinity with just a word.

Leona studied the man intently, noting the fluid, sinuous way he moved, the air of steamy sensuality which surrounded him. There was only one thing a woman thought of when looking at a man like that, she mused. *Sex.*

The man embodied it, dripped it, and probably tasted it too.

"I think, in this case, my dear Madeline, the wrapping is the hors d'oeuvre." Fastening her trained sights on him, she left her rival in stunned silence, already making her way toward him.

Apparently, not having found the person he was seeking, the stunning creature was about to turn from the room when she caught up with him.

"Dressed casually, are we?"

As was his nature, Rejar turned in response to the feminine voice.

She was surprised by his eyes. Rimmed in thick, black lashes, one was a pale glittering ice-blue, the other a heated, fiery gold. They were stunningly beautiful. Eyes that captivated and enticed.

Such eyes promised a wicked passion.

Leona Harcorte had no doubt that by next week every woman in the ton would be talking about those eyes.

He swept her a mocking bow.

"You have me at a disadvantage, madam." His voice was low, melodious, rich.

What an incredibly sexy voice, she thought; *why, it*

almost has a purring quality to it . . .

He had a slight, undefinable accent; or perhaps it was just the cadence of his speech which was a bit different. Whatever it was, it only added to his overwhelming allure.

Leona raised an eyebrow at his facetious reply. "A disadvantage?" She raked his form with an appreciative glance. "An impossibility, I'm sure." His eyes glittered at once with a knowing sensuality.

How exciting! A man who knows exactly how to play the game. He confirmed her opinion by waiting for her to take the next step. She was more than happy to oblige.

"Do you often come into drawing rooms attired in such a manner?" Her hand swept the length of him. To outward appearances the gesture was meant to convey the robe he was wearing; only he felt the tips of her fingers barely graze down the front of his body.

His sensual mouth curved up slightly at the left corner. "I am a man of simple tastes."

His expression conveyed he was anything but.

Lady Harcorte's response was frank and experienced. "Or a man who simply tastes *everything* life has to offer?"

At her provocation, his eyes traveled slowly down the length of her form, revealing more of those lush black lashes of his. When he raised his glance to meet hers, his eyes were twinkling with innuendo.

He did not need to verbally respond.

Leona Harcorte was no novice in the art of seduction, but by comparison his blatant, practiced regard made her feel like an untried country girl. She was suddenly desperate to have him. *Who was he?*

An introduction was definitely in order.

"Countess Harcorte," she said imperiously, using her title in a slight power play.

Rejar looked into her cold yet feverish eyes and knew this woman for exactly what she was. It would never have entered the Familiar's mind to judge her in any way for the excesses of her pleasures. Rejar understood all about excesses of pleasure.

He stood back from her for another reason.

This was a woman who seized power in her pleasures. She did not take joy in the pleasure itself but in something else—something. . . . not good.

All his senses reacted negatively to this and he mentally backed off, shielding himself from her spiritually, if not physically. So his response to her introduction was rather clipped.

"*Prince* Nickolai Azov." He did not feel dishonest in using that particular title. Taking into account his position within his own society, he was probably entitled to it.

She looked surprised for a moment, then gracefully dipped into a curtsy. "Your Highness."

"If you will excuse me, I seem to have misplaced my clothes."

The man might have been discussing the weather, so bland was his voice. He turned and climbed up the stairs without a backward glance.

Misplaced his clothes, indeed.

His words left a searing picture in Leona Harcorte's mind. An image of golden muscular thighs and firmly rounded buttocks. An image of his powerful body with that wildly sensuous pagan hair. An image of his erotically beautiful face contorted with passion as he took her again and again . . .

She must have him.

And in the meantime, what a juicy little tidbit for her

to spread about the ton! Like her, no one would have a moment's doubt as to how the handsome prince had lost his clothes. One only had to look at him to figure it out.

From that moment on, his place and his reputation in society was set.

Rejar found Lord Byron in the upstairs hallway.

The man was slightly swaying from excesses of every kind. This pleased Rejar, for it would probably make Byron more susceptible to his suggestive ability.

"Good lord, man, what happened to you?" Byron peered at him in the dimly lit hallway. "Do I know you, sir?"

{Yes. We met up again late last evening. We went carousing together.} Rejar waited to see if the suggestion would take.

"Wait! I remember now . . . we went chasing a bit of muslin!"

"Yes, we had quite a time with those three women you procured for the night." *{I am Prince Nickolai Azov, a Russian nobleman.}*

"We did, didn't we, your Highness."

"You are most inventive; for a baron, that is." *{We are good friends. You often call me Nickolai.}*

Byron winked at him. "In case I didn't say it last night, it's good to see you again, Nickolai. I say—that robe you're wearing looks rather familiar."

"It should since it is your own."

"Ah, yes! I purchased it last year during my trip to the continent. It is in the Chinese style. But where are your clothes, Nickolai?"

Rejar grinned. "I cannot seem to find them, Byron."

Lord Byron rubbed his chin while he swayed in the hallway. "An amusing fix, to be sure. I'll have my man send my tailor to you at once. After all, we can't have you wandering about the place unclothed." Byron grinned at him in a strange way. "But then again . . ."

Rejar paled. It appeared he had misjudged the man in one way at least.

He began backing down the hall.

"A tailor would be fine. I will await him in this suite." Rejar opened the first door he came to, ducked inside, and slammed the door shut.

Rejar stared morosely into his glass.

His long legs, now encased in tight, thigh-hugging black trousers and Hessian boots, stretched out before him.

Hock, he remembered, *the spirits are called hock.* He leaned his head back against the seat, closing his eyes. Everything is so strange here.

But it was his home now, so he must make do.

He sighed nonetheless. At least he had won the battle with that odd little man who called himself a tailor. He would not wear that ridiculously stiff collar on his shirt known as a cravat! Familiars could not abide tight restrictions about the neck.

Unless it was a woman's arms. Or legs. *That* was different.

Stranger still, all the odd man had to hear was his name and he almost tripped over his own feet to supply Rejar with a wardrobe. He had not given the man any payment whatsoever for his efforts. It seemed his name was enough to satisfy the man—at least temporarily.

This valuable knowledge regarding the power of his name, Rejar could use to his advantage. It appeared this title of "prince" held much magic.

He shifted in his chair.

The restlessness was back. Leaning farther back in

61

the seat, he crossed his legs at the ankles, trying to find a comfortable position. It was useless.

"Why the long face, Nickolai?"

Byron was sitting across from him. The small table between them held several bottles of spirits. And several empties. It was very late in the night.

Since his first evening here, Byron had not made any remarks of a disturbing nature to him, and Rejar, having conveyed his shock at the man's dual inclinations, decided to let the incident go. It was not for Rejar to judge him and, although such inclinations were extremely alien to the Familiar, perhaps this behavior was a common one here. Some of the young men he had met seemed most peculiar with their rouged faces and frilly clothes.

A smile curved through his cheeks as he thought of what the Aviaran warriors would make of that. It would be most amusing.

In any event, he discovered that he genuinely liked the young baron.

"I need a woman." Rejar made the statement with all the honesty inherent between men after imbibing spirits for several days straight.

"Ah. None here to suit your palate?"

That was just it. Rejar could not understand why, for the past two nights, he had not prevailed upon several of the females who had been in attendance here. Especially in his current state of urgency.

All of the women had seemed most receptive to him. In fact, Lady Harcorte had pursued him relentlessly—once even coming uninvited into his chamber just as he was preparing to bathe. He had firmly shown her the door.

His continued refusals were a mystery to him.

Oh, he had *tried*.

One woman was very alluring, yet her hair somehow seemed the wrong shade. Another was enticingly sensual, but the shape of her mouth left him cold. It happened again and again. Just when he thought he had found a good choice *something* would put him off.

It was most frustrating.

"No. None suits me," he responded truthfully. A flash of forest green crossed his dulled mind. He squelched the image immediately.

"Pity." Byron took a long swallow of his drink. "You don't seem like a man who likes to waste much time between his pleasures."

"I am not." Rejar emptied the bottle into his glass, then started another. The drink was not helping alleviate his restlessness, but, then again, it did not seem to concern him so much anymore.

Rejar did not overindulge in spirits often; Familiars generally disliked having their senses dulled. He wondered why he welcomed such a state at this moment.

"Didn't think so." Byron snapped his fingers. "You've given me an idea! 'His manner was perhaps the more seductive, because he ne'er seem'd anxious to seduce.' I believe I shall write about a most interesting fellow; I shall base him on the two of us. Let's see . . . I'll call him Don . . . Don . . . well, it'll come to me."

The room was companionably silent for several minutes as the men continued to drink.

Byron abruptly asked in drunken stupor, "Nickolai, have you ever 'tooled' in a gondola? I have, you know."

Rejar turned bleary eyes to him. "What is a gondola?" He needed no translation for the other term.

Byron waved his glass through the air. "It's Italian— a long narrow boat."

Rejar reviewed his numerous past conquests in his mind. At least those he could presently remember.

"Yes," he said, thinking aloud. "A boat, a sailing vessel, a ship, a raft, a paddle boat, and a supply transport—twice."

Byron seemed surprised. "And here I thought I was the only one to do that." He looked challengingly at Rejar out of the corner of his eye. "How about on a table?"

The corners of Rejar's mouth twitched as he got into the game of one-upmanship. Familiars loved games. "A chair, once on a council seat—when my father was not there—a ledge, a shelf, a bench, and . . . a table."

Byron expelled a breath. The Prince was a challenge. "What about *under* a table?" Byron thought he had him now.

Rejar laced his hands behind his head, affecting a bored mien. "Of course."

Byron narrowed his eyes. "Against a wall?"

Rejar waved his hand, not even deigning to answer.

"Hmm . . ." Byron tapped his fingers against his glass, trying to come up with an even more unusual place where he had succumbed to his passionate nature. "On the stairs?"

Rejar's eyes widened. "The stairs?"

"Yes, the stairs." Byron gave him a comically sinister smile, thinking he had the Prince now.

Rejar grinned slowly back at him. "Which *particular* stair do you speak of?"

The smile died on Byron's face. "You can't be serious?"

Rejar raised one black eyebrow, saying nothing.

"By damn!" Byron slapped his knee. Both men started laughing.

"Will you be taking up Scrope's invitation to stay in his town house?"

Scrope Davies was one of Byron's closest friends.

The congenial man had graciously offered the "prince" use of his home when he found out Rejar intended to seek lodging. Of course, the lodging part was only a guise for his persona. Rejar still fully intended to remain with Lilac.

Especially during the nights.

"I think not. This Clarendon Hotel you spoke of will better suit my purposes." It was vital he maintain his freedom to come and go as he pleased. In the form he pleased.

"Probably wise. Scrope has a bit of a problem with the tables. If he asks you to lend him some blunt, you needn't be concerned—he's a man of honor."

"So I saw." *By Aiyah, what was blunt?* All sorts of alarming possibilities ran through the Familiar's head. From what he had seen so far on this world, it could be anything. Anything at all.

After a while, Byron seemed to become more somber of mood.

"Forgive me for remarking on this, Nickolai, but you are a stunning man; quite the most dashing I've seen. You're intelligent, witty, and as Brummell would say, 'impeccably groomed.' Beau will adore you. I'll wager he'll forgive you for your lack of a cravat. By next week you'll be the toast of the ton."

Byron stared moodily at his glass as if it were portending the future. "Listen well; they'll erect a statue and canonize your name—*then* they'll flay you alive."

Rejar watched him speculatively. "Why would they do this?" he asked quietly.

"Because, my dear beautiful Nickolai, it is such jolly good fun." Byron let his glass slip through his fingers to the floor, a reflective expression crossing his features. Rejar briefly wondered if the man was not seeing a vision of his own future.

From the upstairs landing, Madeline Fensley called Byron to bed. The baron stood up, swaying from the amount of drink he had imbibed. Flicking his wrist in the air, he proclaimed, "The adoring masses await!"

Rejar smiled faintly.

Bowing at the waist a bit unsteadily, Byron exited the room, calling out to Rejar, "Goodnight, sweet prince."

While Byron's wit, in this instance, was completely lost on Rejar, he recognized the man had the soul of an artist whose excesses were born out of a deeper kind of hunger.

A strange world, this. The society that fostered such gifts in a man would ultimately destroy him. Like the Lenark, the famous star cloud of Zynth, Byron would burn bright, but not for long.

However, like that cloud, Rejar knew that once this "star" was gone, his essence would still glow.

It would not be the first time Rejar would regret his inability to read the language of these people. He wished to know the work of such a man.

"Where in the world have you been these past three days?"

Lilac stood in the middle of her bedroom floor, hands on hips, furious with him. He had never been so pleased.

"Do you know how worried I was?" She shook her finger at him. "I thought something terrible happened to you—don't you ever do anything like that again! Bad cat!"

Instead of being properly chastened as he should have been, the cat began purring.

"Oh, all right, you're forgiven—come here."

Rejar padded over to her. He was shocked when she

suddenly sank to the carpet and threw her arms around him, hugging him tightly to her.

"I was so worried about you, Rejar. I thought you were never coming home." She sniffed as she buried her face in his thick fur, making him feel a little guilty for upsetting her so. He hadn't thought about that aspect of it.

Rejar was bone weary from the weekend's overindulgences with rich food and drink; so tired from having to be constantly on guard in this alien world. And exhausted, too, from the sleepless nights of missing her comforting presence next to him.

That evening, he fell into a deep sleep with Lilac tangled to him. He did not awaken until just before she did the following morning.

Some of his strange restlessness seemed to have abated.

For the next several days, Rejar chose not to wake Lilac during the night. Nor did he attempt to seek out other female company when he joined his new "friends" in the evenings.

Despite his state, he decided he would wait until the soiree on Friday. There he would be meeting Lilac face-to-face, man to woman.

That night, he intended to allow *her* to appease his voracious hunger.

The short, choppy motions of Auntie Whumples' fan indicated the old woman's acute displeasure. "Good heavens! Here comes that shallow-pated twit Eleanora Vandershmeer. 'Tis too late to escape her now—she's spotted me."

Lilac tried not to smile at her aunt's irritation as a large overbearing woman bore down on them with a dedicated precision. If Auntie hadn't insisted they attend this boring outing, she wouldn't have had to put up with Lady Vandershmeer. The two of them could be spending a nice quiet evening at home, where they should be!

The only bright spot of the evening had been when she had learned that that idiot Creighton was plagued with a bad case of sniffles and would not be in attendance that night. The fop had probably snuffed himself silly! She giggled to herself.

"Oh, but the woman's constant tiddle-tattle will drive me mad!" Auntie spoke to Lilac from behind her fan, before pasting on a false smile for the ton's nosiest woman. Lady Vandershmeer spread gossip as if she had been divinely called to the task.

"Agatha!" She waved an amaranthus-colored hanky at Auntie Whumples. The cloth had been heavily soaked in jasmine water. Lilac knew Auntie loathed jasmine water.

"Eleanora." Auntie gritted her teeth, trying not to breathe too deeply of the cloying scent. "How good to see you again."

The two women embraced, kissing the air next to their cheeks. Lady Vandershmeer then turned a discerning eye to Lilac, minutely examining her gown and hairstyle before saying, "And here's our little Lilac!"

"Good evening, Lady Vandershmeer."

"How lovely you look tonight, my dear. Why, no one would ever suspect you were *past* twenty now."

Lilac sighed at the woman's snippety implication regarding her unwed state; but Auntie was not inclined to be so passive. "Yes, the Earl of Roxton thought so as well when he complimented her earlier; didn't he, Lilac? Such a refined gentleman. You *do* know the Earl, don't you, Eleanora?" Auntie expertly pinned her adversary to the spot.

Two blotches of color managed to stain Lady Vandershmeer cheeks even through the five coats of rouge the woman wore. To avoid answering Auntie's question (and thereby admitting to such a social dysfunction), Lady Vandershmeer grabbed Auntie Whumples's forearm, leaning closer to her as if she were her dearest friend. A friend with whom she simply had to share something of momentous import.

Her irritating voice rose considerably.

"Have you heard the latest *on-dit*?" Too eager to spread the gossip, she did not even wait for a response. "There is a *prince* here from Russia!"

Lady Whumples did not react in any way to the enticing news, which meant that she hadn't yet heard the rest of the story. Lady Vandershmeer was in Gossip Heaven. In her glory, she breathlessly babbled on.

"Agatha, I simply must tell you! From Tattersall's to Vauxhall—everyone is talking about him! Why, there was even a story about him in the *Morning Post* the other day. It was implied that a certain Russian prince made a stunning appearance in a drawing room . . ."— she savored the denouement—"*sans clothes!* And by all accounts not the least bit concerned about it. Can you believe it? Well, what should one expect? Apparently he's a good friend of Baron Byron."

At the mention of Lord Byron's name, Auntie bristled. She did not favor the young profligate. "And why should that story be of interest to me?" she haughtily replied.

"Because, my dear Agatha, they say he is wildly attractive, rich as Croesus, exceptionally witty, and totally daring. Brummell already adores him! Lady Harcorte, that cyprian, is drooling for him, and rumor has it"—Lady Vandershmeer looked pointedly at Lilac—"he is unwed."

Auntie's eyebrows lifted contemplatively.

She ever-so-slowly smiled at Lady Vandershmeer, lacing her arm through the bothersome woman's. "Come, Eleanora, let us get some refreshment together and you can tell me *all* about this fascinating prince."

Lilac crossed her arms over her chest, exhaling noisily. Bother it! Another sapskull to pester her! Would it never end? A Russian prince. She tapped her foot angrily on the parquet floor. What manner of *beast* would they throw at her next?

Engrossed in her irritation, Lilac did not pay the slightest bit of attention to the buzzing of voices suddenly increasing in volume as a tall, elegantly dressed, devastatingly handsome man entered the ballroom. The words "prince" and "Russia" got whacked about the room like Prinny's croquet balls.

All sights turned to watch the stunning man as he strode purposely across the floor, his lithe, commanding gait causing female hearts to flutter with every step he took.

A hush fell over the crowd.

That the man had an agenda was obvious. He was heading toward someone, but whom? The room quieted, breathlessly awaiting the answer. *Who had attracted the Prince's attention?*

The Familiar stood directly behind Lilac Devere and cleared his throat rather noisily.

A groundswell of sound gathered about the room as his choice became apparent. The Prince was apparently intrigued by the bluestocking, Miss Devere!

This was a juicy tidbit, indeed! He was watching the chit as if nothing on this Earth could distract him. It would be remarked the following morning that the Prince's intensity was almost . . . predatory.

Several of the men, who just moments ago had

ignored the young miss, began to eye Lilac Devere speculatively.

With one gesture, Rejar had made her the talk of the ton.

Rejar's glittering eyes took in everything about her. She was dressed all in white in a high-waisted gown of simple design with short, puffed sleeves. Her long hair had been pulled up into a topknot. Several drooping curls framed her rebellious little face.

Rejar could not help the smile that inched its way across his face as he recalled how the intrepid Emmy had had to chase her around the bedroom earlier, brandishing that thing called a curling iron, with Lilac complaining all the while. It had been most entertaining.

He had spotted her the instant he stepped into the ballroom.

In truth, he saw no other.

He cleared his throat again and, true to his nature, waited ever so patiently for his prey to face him.

Lilac's shoulders bunched in annoyance as soon as she realized that some man was standing expectantly behind her. *What twiddle-head was bothering her now?* Lilac whipped around to confront the pest.

And stopped dead in her tracks.

Much to her dismay, her mouth actually fell open. *Sink me.*

Her second thought was—

He's gorgeous . . .

Followed quickly by the voice of reason.

He's trouble!

The incredible creature made a sweeping bow. Before she could gather her composure, the most sensual voice she had ever heard in her life purred, "Prince Nickolai Azov."

Dara Joy

When he looked up, sharp eyes rimmed in a thick fringe of jet-black lashes fastened on her. She gasped. They were two different colors!

Those eyes . . .

They were positively beautiful. Enticing. Beguiling. With more than a hint of mischief.

She swallowed. *He had the very same eyes as her cat.* How odd.

Curious, Lilac stared at his eyes, instantly falling into their rich allure. He returned her stare and Lilac swore she saw something wild leap into their depths. Reflexively, she stepped back from him, breaking the strange contact.

So this was the Prince. The man the ton couldn't stop talking about. And no wonder. *Just look at him!*

The man unnerved her.

Lilac instantly made up her mind: She wanted nothing to do with him. The way he was staring at her made her feel very uncomfortable. Besides, he was so . . . Well, she just didn't want anything to do with him, that's all.

Her response was intentionally curt. "I don't think this is a proper introduction, your Highness." It was meant to shut him out. It was meant to show him there was no hope for him as far as she was concerned.

So why was he still standing there with that beguiling half-smile on his handsome face?

"Does it matter?" he asked in lazy drawl.

Lilac flustered. What kind of a response was that? This Prince was decidedly spoiled, she reasoned. Well, he'd have to be. *Just look at him.* Standing there beyond devastating, as if he ruled the world and everything in it!

She changed her mind; she didn't just want him to

go away—now she also wanted him to know she disliked his attitude intensely.

The situation called for something special.

It called for the ultimate insult.

Lilac had never used it before and almost gleefully looked forward to testing it out on the overconfident jackanapes.

In a move that would do any Thespian proud, she turned her head away as if he didn't exist and pointedly studied the intricate design on the wallpaper.

The cut sublime!

Several gasps filled the room.

A collective breath was held while the crowd eagerly waited to see how the Prince would handle the spurious insult. It was an outrage! How would his highness respond?

He laughed.

Heartily. Out loud. A rich, rolling sound of devilish amusement.

The ton was captivated. Thirty onlookers made mental notes to send immediate invitations out to the dashing Prince. One young woman swooned.

Lilac turned back to him, stunned. The man was laughing! What did he mean by laughing? It was the cut sublime; How dare he!

Her eyes narrowed. "Sir, you are nothing but a jacka—"

"Lilac Devere, your Highness." A familiar, traitorous voice interrupted from behind her shoulder. "My niece."

Rejar's eyes twinkled with mirth. Two engaging dimples showcased his grin. "And you are, madam?"

Auntie held out her hand, which the Prince immediately took. "Lady Agatha Whumples."

"I am honored. Might I ask permission to dance with your niece?"

Auntie briefly gave Lilac a very displeased look mixed with a good dose of exasperation before replying, "I *implore* you, your Highness."

Lilac flushed red. They were treating her as if she were a naughty child! "Auntie, how could you—"

The Prince interrupted the heated flow of her words by holding out his hand. The simple gesture spoke volumes. He was going to be benevolent by allowing her to save face.

The entire room waited to see what Miss Devere would do. Several of the men watching commented to each other that they had never realized the quiet Miss Devere was such a spirited article. Several more made mental notes to send her their calling cards.

The music began as if ordered up. Which it probably was. Lilac had no choice but to take the rakehell's elegant hand. Before she even had a chance to summon up a particularly nasty retort to him, he effortlessly swung her onto the dance floor and into a scandalous waltz.

There was a singular warmth which enshrouded her in his arms. A heady, sizzling thing that drew on her in some unknown way, tugged on her like a living, seductive magnet. It was if the man possessed some strange ability . . .

The peculiar feeling mirrored the powerful arms, which now lightly embraced her. This intoxicating essence of his seemed to envelop her; an unseen net drawing her inexorably into him. She caught a spicy scent—cinnamon and bayberry and something else, totally exotic.

It was most tempting . . .

Lilac suddenly panicked. What was she thinking?

"Let me go!"

He did not release her. Those incredible eyes, now half-shielded behind heavy lids, calmly regarded her. "Why should I?"

Lilac missed a step, tripping over his boot. No man of her acquaintance would dare act in such an outrageous fashion to a request by a lady. "You, sir, are no gentleman!" she gasped out.

The corner of the Prince's mouth lifted in some private amusement as he gracefully swung her around in an intricate step.

Lilac fumed. How arrogant! Normally she was a very graceful dancer. All right, so maybe she wasn't. What made him think he was so adept on a dance floor?

Lilac had no way of knowing just how fleet of foot a Familiar could be.

When it became obvious the man was going to ignore her words, she counted to ten and tried again. "Prince Azov, I must insist—"

"Call me Nickolai, *souk-souk*." His low voice brushed her ear, sending vibratory tingles down the side of her neck.

Who asked him to send tingles down her neck? She didn't want them! "I will not! Who do you think—*souk-souk*? What is that, Russian?"

Rejar gazed intently down at her. "Do you speak Russian?"

She shook her head. "No."

"Then for your purposes, it is Russian."

What did the Prince mean by that remark? Lilac gave him a strange look. "Well, what does it mean?"

"Where I come from, a *souk-souk* is a soft, little animal which nips at your heels at the same time it desires your attention."

Her eyes flashed emerald fire at him.

He laughed—a low, sexy sound of enjoyment.

Never missing a beat, he turned her in his arms. "It is quite affectionate when stroked a certain way," he murmured teasingly in her ear.

She ground her heel into the toe of his boot.

He smiled. "And quite venomous when it isn't," was the whispered response.

Lilac tried to break his tight hold. The man was infuriatingly playful. "Your Highness!"

"Nickolai."

"Very well," she snapped, "*Nickolai*. I must insist you release me at—*oh!*" His hot hand had dropped to her waist, singeing right through the thin fabric of her dress. Whatever she had been about to say flew from her mind when the large, masculine hand brought her possessively closer to him.

Lilac blinked, not at all sure how to respond to his blatant behavior. The Prince did not react in the expected manner at all. He was extremely unpredictable.

Prince Azov's expert move did not go unnoticed by the avid onlookers. Speculative murmurs were followed by a frenzied round of wagering. The topic of said wagering was not a fit subject for mixed company.

"I will call upon you later, *souk-souk*."

Lilac stumbled again.

Did this insufferable cad actually think she would allow him to court her? "Absolutely not!"

His left hand brushed her waist; a hint of a caress. Small frissons trailed down her spine. "Mmm, *souk-souk*, I agree; it is a waste of time. Your societal customs are exceedingly tedious. I will come to your bedchamber tonight."

Lilac stopped right in the middle of the dance floor.

She stood there in utter stupor, staring in horrified shock at the crude lout. *The man was a barbarian!*

A sharp crack snapped the air with the slap she delivered to his arrogant face.

While leaving the dance floor, she almost laughed aloud at the dumbfounded expression on the Prince's handsome face just after her open palm had connected smartly with his cheek. Lilac patted herself on the back. By his look, she'd wager the man had never been turned down in his life! Well, it was about time *someone* did.

Insufferable arrogance!

Whatever made the sapskull think she would welcome his attentions? Her of all people! His stunning looks? As if that would make a difference to her! She had no use for a man in her life, and she definitely didn't want one in her home. Men had a most nasty habit of making demands.

Lilac had no doubts whatsoever that she had seen the last of the arrogant, albeit beautiful, Prince. The thought brought immense pleasure. It could have been a close call; Auntie had raised her eyebrows—a sure sign of trouble.

Good-bye, your Highness, and good riddance!

Rejar watched Lilac storm off the dance floor and out of the room with a speculative gleam in his narrowed eyes. What was wrong with the woman? The thought that she might not be interested in him never entered the Familiar's mind.

After all, women always wanted him.

It was not vanity on his part, but a fact of his life. And Rejar knew by his senses that this one did too. So why had she reacted to him like this?

It was . . . irritating.

But not beyond repair.

The night had just begun and he fully intended to

make it a long one. For her.

He immediately left the soiree, heading back to his hotel room—a room specifically chosen for his cat self to be easily accessed by a series of outside ledges and windows.

When he left the room again a few minutes later, he was stalking on four paws.

And his difficult prey had the unlikely name of a flower.

He growled.

Chapter Four

Planet Aviara, Star System Tau Hydra, 5187 m.u.

Yaniff, the ancient wizard of Aviara, slowly stepped off the platform lift onto the limb of the enormous tree that his student Lorgin ta'al Krue called home. Deep in the Towering Forest, such trees were of incredible breadth and height, the flat intersecting limbs of this one forming entire levels.

Crystal chimes tinkled in the soft breeze.

In the distance, out of sight, he heard two distinct voices; one deep and coaxing, the other disbelieving— followed by the happy sound of mingled laughter. Lorgin and his wife, Adeeann.

Smiling, Yaniff reached up to his shoulder to stroke the feathers of his winged companion. "We did a good job with that one, eh, Bojo?"

The silent companion ruffled his feathers by way of answer.

"Now we enter into a most delicate time, my friend. A time of great discovery; a time of overflowing happiness and intense sorrow." Yaniff looked off into nothing. "A time of awakenings."

Walking down two levels, following the semicircular pathway, the old mystic stepped through tall, flowering plants into an open glen.

The sight he beheld made him chuckle.

Lorgin and his very pregnant wife were lying together in a hammock. Lorgin had just leaned over to murmur something in her ear as the palm of his hand glided lovingly over the swollen expanse of her stomach. Adeeann elbowed him smartly in the side.

"Did you not see that, Yaniff?" Lorgin laughed over to the old man. "Mayhap it is time to take her into yet another universe?" He joked. "Surely, it would improve her mood."

"I wouldn't be in this 'mood' now if you hadn't kidnapped me from that science fiction convention in the first place." Adeeann, née Deana Jones, formerly of Boston, Massachusetts, shook her head in exasperation. At the best of times, her warrior knight was a handful. She smiled wickedly at the very thought.

"I do not like this face you wear." Lorgin shook his finger at her, spoiling the effect by grinning at her.

"You might get your wish, Lorgin."

The wizard's words stopped him cold. Lorgin's golden head whipped toward his ancient teacher, the smile on his face instantly replaced by intense regard. "You have found him, Yaniff?"

Yaniff inclined his head. "It is so."

Lorgin leaped off the hammock. "Where? Where is my brother?"

"Rejar?" Deana tried unsuccessfully to exit the hammock, her unwieldy bulk making it impossible. "Is he all right?"

They had all been so concerned these many months with the welfare of Lorgin's Familiar half-brother. To finally get some news was something of a shock.

Deana made it to the edge of the hammock again, only to topple backwards toward its center.

"Is he unharmed? How does he fare? Is he—" Lorgin's worried questions were interrupted by the sound of a grunt coming from the direction of the hammock.

"For heaven's sake, Lorgin, get me out of here!"

Lorgin quickly went to the assistance of his wife. Yaniff hid his smile behind his hand.

"Don't keep us in suspense any longer, Yaniff." Standing, she tugged her caftan down over her bulky middle. "Tell us."

"Rejar finds himself in a most unusual predicament. He is, in fact, on *your* world, Adeeann."

Deana gasped. "My world? You mean he's on . . ." Her glance skittered to her husband, then back to Yaniff. She hadn't yet let Lorgin in on the little joke she had played on him when she had first met him and he had demanded to know what planet he was on. Of course, she thought *he* had been joking at the time.

". . . on *Disney World?*" She looked meaningfully at the old wizard, silently signaling him. She rather liked the idea of finally having one up on Lorgin and wasn't about to enlighten her overconfident husband any time soon.

Yaniff's eyes twinkled with mirth. "As I say, on your world, Adeeann. But not your time."

"What do you mean not her time?" Lorgin seemed confused and faintly worried.

"He resides within the framework of your past, Adeeann. In a place called Britain. I believe to refer-

ence it, you would say the year eighteen hundred and
eleven."

"*Regency England?* Why, how fantastic!" She clasped
her hands to her chest as her excitement grew. "Regency England! I've always wanted to—I've never
dreamed I could see—"

Her husband frowned down at her. "You are not going! It is too dangerous for the babe; I will not permit
it."

Deana snorted at the ridiculous proclamation. Number one thousand and fifty-two. "Just try and stop me."

Lorgin threw his hands up in the air. "Does she never
listen to me, Yaniff!" He turned back to his errant wife.
"You are *not* going, Adeeann. And that is final."

Deana waved an irrepressible hand in the air. "Pfft!"

Lorgin strutted back inside the trunk of the tree
which served as their home. "No." He threw the word
at her over his shoulder.

Yaniff bent down, speaking quietly. "If you should
find yourself momentarily in such a place, child, you
may view—but do not be seen." He winked at her.

Deana winked back. No way was she letting her husband traipse off to Regency England without her. No
way.

"Yaniff"—Lorgin stuck his head out a window—"do
you not think it odd that in all the universe Rejar
should find himself on Adeeann's world? And this time
shift, as well."

Yaniff stiffened slightly. Nothing escaped the sharp
eye of this Lorgin ta'al Krue, he thought. In truth, his
favorite of all students. A pity he was not the one. No,
not the one; but close. Very close. *Soon,* Yaniff realized. *Soon . . .*

"Yes." Yaniff spoke no further.

"Strange . . ." Lorgin donned his black cape, adjusting it about his broad shoulders; the golden symbols on the cloak marked him as a Knight of the Charl and a holder of the fourth power. "Once the line of connection was established by my link through the Tunnel, the temporal plane should have remained the same. Is that not so, Yaniff?"

"I have learned over the years never to underestimate your acuity, Lorgin. Once again you do not disappoint me. What you say is true. There are some things you will need to tell Rejar. I will explain it to you at the Hall of Tunnels before you leave."

"Do you mind telling me what the two of you are talking about?" Deana waited impatiently, hands on hips.

Lorgin glanced briefly at Yaniff before responding to his wife. He chose his words with care. "Once the link has been established—"

"You mean like when you came to my world through that tunnel thing?"

"That is correct; the temporal plane was established as well. All other linkages would proceed from that point forward."

"So time would go in a positive direction?" Deana wasn't sure she was understanding this.

"Yes. Even though the Matrix is capable of time shifts, such a Tunnel can be opened only under certain circumstances. This is to ensure the integrity of the temporal continuum."

"I see what you're saying—so paradoxes aren't created, right?"

"Exactly, Adeeann. All of us here in this universe link in the same plane of *contemporal* existence, established when the first contact or link is made with that particular planet."

"So you are all moving forward, so to speak, together in time?"

"Yes." Lorgin nodded. "Even though a time phasing might have occurred during the initial contact."

"But you said the Matrix is capable of time shifts; is there a problem with Rejar being in Regency England?"

Lorgin waited a moment before he responded. "Such time jumping is prohibited by the Guild for the reasons I have mentioned. In any case, under normal circumstances, only the highest level mystic could open such a Tunnel."

"But I thought Rejar didn't have such abilities."

"He does not. When he released the Shimmalee, somehow a new Tunnel opened. I vow, I do not understand it fully myself."

"The matrix weaves a fabric guided by the hand of destiny." Yaniff replied mysteriously.

Both Deana and Lorgin looked at the old mystic. Deana's face showed puzzlement, Lorgin's a wary knowledge.

Lorgin eyed the wizard obliquely. Often it was what Yaniff did not say . . .

He shrugged. Perhaps it was nothing. In any case, he had other things on his mind right now. "Before I leave Aviara, I will go to my parents to apprise them of Rejar's situation. Then I will go to this"—he threw Deana a look—"Ree Gen Cee Ing Land and bring my brother back."

Yaniff, whose eyes were darker than the darkest night, peered intensely at Lorgin. He finally spoke. "You will go to your brother."

Lorgin paused.

Often it was what Yaniff did not say . . .

He hesitated a fraction of a moment more before

turning to his wife, swiftly taking her in his arms. "I will return to you shortly, *zira*." His mouth took hers in a fierce kiss.

With a swirl of his cape he was gone.

London

"He's the most insufferable, overbearing, arrogant cad I have ever had the misfortune to meet!"

Lilac threw her arms up in the air for emphasis as she paced the length of her bedroom. Directly in front of her was the cat, who was resting on all fours by the edge of the carpet.

Said cat's eyes were narrowing more and more with each pass she made; with every epithet hurled from her oh-so-succulent lips. In fact, one could say that the feline's eyes were almost completely shut—except for the odd flash of anger glinting through the slits every now and then.

"What a sapskull he is! Imagine . . . telling *me*,"—Lilac lowered her voice several octaves in an attempt to mimic Rejar's low, dulcet tones—" 'Your societal customs are quite tedious, *souk-souk*. I will come to you this evening.' " She brandished a clenched fist in the chair. "Ha! I'd like to see him try!"

Ears flattened to the back of his head, the cat slapped his tail onto the carpet. Repeatedly. *Thump . . . thump . . . thump*.

"Now, miss, he couldn't have been that bad. There's rumor that says he cuts quite a dashing figure." The ever-stalwart Emmy, as usual, tried to take the edge off Lilac's temper.

Lilac stopped pacing long enough to spin around. "Him? Dashing?" She paused as if she were considering it.

Rejar rotated his ears forward, anxious to hear how

she would respond. Not that he had any intentions of forgiving her! He had no idea what a "sapskull" was, but he did not like the sound of it. It was not . . . seemly. Besides, no one had ever dared to call him one before! Whatever it was.

"He's too cocksure by half!"

The cat's eyes widened. *Does that mean what I think it means?* Well, perhaps he could forgive her after all. . . .

"I tell you, Emmy, he's a nick ninny!"

Nick ninny?

"Well, I don't know, miss, I never heard none call the Prince a stupid fellow." *Thump!*

"In fact," Emmy continued, "just the opposite. Why, Beau Brummell says he's exceedingly quick witted and—"

"Stuff and nonsense! The only thing that fellow is quick about is—"

"Miss Devere!" Emmy gasped.

Chastened, Lilac toned down a bit. "Very well. Just don't mention that irritating sapskull to me again!"

Sapskull! She dares once more! Thump. Thump. Thump.

"I didn't mention him the first time, miss," Emmy shrewdly pointed out while eyeing the young woman. "Seems ya brought 'im up on yer own now, didn't ya?" The maid teased her.

Lilac blushed. "Well . . . if I did, it—it was so you—you wouldn't mention him to me in the future."

"Yes, miss." Emmy smiled conspiratorially at the cat.

Unfortunately, Rejar was too caught up in his own ruminations to catch the maid's private joke. What *exactly* had he done wrong? To his way of thinking, he had not been rude to her in the least. On the contrary, he had approached her in a forthright manner, immediately letting his intentions be known. What did she have to be angry about? Familiars were always direct in their dealings with women.

Well . . . perhaps not *always*, but mostly.

"Good. I'm glad we've got that settled."

"Goodnight, miss." Emmy picked up one of the candleholders to light her way as she left the room.

"If I never see that irritating Prince again, it will be too soon for me," Lilac muttered as she passed by the cat on her way to bed. "Just who does he think he is?"

I will show you who I am.

Insulted, Rejar tossed his head back in a regal feline gesture. Familiars were inordinately proud creatures.

Believe me, you will know, souk-souk.

"*You!*"

"Yes, it is I. Your *sapskull.*"

Rejar lay directly on top of Lilac, holding her hands down to the mattress with his own. He had removed the blanket that had covered her just prior to wakening her.

Unlike the stab to his pride that he had not been able to remove.

"Let go of me! And take yourself from my dream at once! Of all people to dream about—*you!*" It was the dreaded Russian here in her dreams. Egads! "Out! Out, damn spot!" Lilac thrashed beneath him.

Her erratic motions caused her nightrail to slide up her legs. *That* was when she realized her dream Prince was naked. Muscular legs slid heavily against her own; their tougher texture an abrasive heat.

She immediately stopped moving, gasping into his face—a wildly beautiful face, which was very close to her own.

"You—you don't have any clothes on, your Highness!" She squeaked rather lamely up at him.

The left corner of Rejar's mouth curved. "Now Lilac, what do you expect from a—what did you call me—a *nick ninny?*" He smiled down at her. It was not an amused smile. In fact, it was rather . . . feral.

Lilac's eyes rounded. One did not ignore such a smile as the Prince had on his face right then. Especially not if one prided oneself on being a woman of logic. She swallowed convulsively. "I—I wish to wake up."

"I do not think so, *souk-souk.*" He slowly lowered his head.

Ever so gently, the most sensuous of male lips captured her little earlobe. *Whereupon he nipped it sharply with his teeth.*

"Ow! Stop that!" Lilac tried to grab a hank of his long hair, but failed miserably when she realized he would not release her wrists from his powerful grip.

"What do you think—" Lilac sucked in her breath because those same white teeth, which only moments ago had nipped, now nibbled in a light grazing pattern along the rim of her ear.

His agile tongue swirl-teased the entrance to her canal, causing a quivery sensation to run right through her.

"Oh my! I—"

Velvet lips sipped the edge of her jawline, stopping a moment to secretly experience the militant indentation in her chin, before trailing down the front of her throat. She felt herself swallow beneath the debilitating ministrations of this most bewitching of mouths.

"I don't—" She began, only to stop when Prince Azov reached her collarbone. There, he lightly suckled.

Lilac had no way of knowing the expertise that Rejar displayed; the Familiar knew just how strong to draw upon her without leaving a mark on the tender skin.

Despite herself, she shivered.

Rejar acknowledged her reaction with a mischievous, catlike sweep of his tongue. Lilac shivered again.

"I don't like you, Prince Nickolai."

"But I like *you*, my Lilac." His low, soft voice vibrated seductively against the hollow at the base of her throat before his mouth covered the vulnerable spot possessively. She tasted like hot sweet honey.

An unintelligible sound came out of her mouth that sounded like *"Nnnnn . . ."*

Rejar knew exactly what it meant.

He released one of her hands so that he might untie the ribbon bow at the neckline of her garment.

Lilac was so overwhelmed by his sultry actions, she wasn't even aware he had let her go. The strong fingers of his other hand—the one that still captured hers—threaded through her own. Deftly, he untied one bow.

Then the next.

And then the one after that.

In a dreamlike trance for more than one reason, Lilac met his hot-blooded stare reproachfully. "You shouldn't, your Highness."

"I know."

Their mutinous gazes locked for an endless time. Finally he broke the stillness with a response that was very Familiar.

"But . . . I am going to."

Without taking his eyes from hers, he separated the front of her gown, the edge of his hand lightly brushing across the satiny skin. Slowly his vision left hers to rake over her face, her throat.

Her bare chest.

There, he observed her silently for several minutes, his knowing look frank and very male.

Lilac felt herself redden even in the dream.

Then he lifted his eyes to hers. When he spoke, his low voice was a husky rasp of sound. "You are so beautiful, *souk-souk.*"

Moonlight danced off him, haloing him in silver. Lilac could see his dual-colored eyes quite clearly in the dream. The pupils were softly dilated, the lids heavy. An intense sexuality emanated from him.

Like a cloak, it covered her.

Spellbound, Lilac lifted her mouth for the kiss of this Prince from another land.

In a time-stopped moment the Nickolai of her dreams lowered his head to hers . . .

The touch of his mouth never came.

Oddly, at the moment his lips would join hers, he hesitated, exhaling as if in frustration. Lilac watched him, confused. Didn't her dream Prince want to kiss her?

Rejar was indeed frustrated. On all levels. *How could he kiss her without entering that sweet mouth?* Impossible. His lifeforce could not enter her in any way without breaking the trance.

He reflected for a moment . . . There were ways to ignite her without danger of an untimely discovery; he need only be more creative. He smiled wryly at the challenge. In this area especially, he was the son of Krue. *All challenges must be met.* So his father had trained him.

Resolute, he pressed his lips to the center of her chest at the demarcation of her cleavage, letting his tongue slide between the heated, snug crevice there. A long slow lick.

A sound of pleasure issued from her parted lips.

"Something about this seems familiar . . ." Lilac's words were nothing but a breathless whisper in the air.

Rejar chuckled low in his throat at her unintentional

pun. "Everything about this is *Familiar,* Lilac."

"I think I've dreamt this before," she murmured distractedly. "Only there was a different man, a nicer—"

Rejar stopped, not at all liking her words. Or the direction of her thoughts. He wanted her focused—*on him.* "No. It was the same man. I mean *I* am the same man."

Lilac blinked, throwing off the seductive veil he had wrapped her in. "No, it wasn't and you're not," she stubbornly insisted. "The other man was somehow different; he wasn't *you,* your Sapskullness!"

Rejar's brow lowered. A new thing to madden him! Was nothing simple in this strange world? "I tell you, it was I!"

"Ridiculous! How could it be? I didn't even know you then; so there's no way I could have dreamt of you!" She summarily dismissed him. "Please leave. You may tell the other man he may visit if he wishes."

Lilac looked shyly up at him. "I confess, he had the most intriguing abilities with his tongue."

Rejar's irritation instantly turned into humor. His lips twitched as he looked down at her beneath him. Now this was amusing indeed. "Did he?" he drawled.

"Yes." She shook her head in affirmation.

In a beguiling pose, he rested his chin on top of her chest. "Perhaps I could make you forget him?" A dimple curved his cheek as he gazed innocently up at her through a veil of lush black lashes.

Lilac yawned, too tired to spar with this irksome dream image. "Oh, you could try, I suppose."

Rejar smiled. He should not.

He knew he would.

His sights fastened on the beautiful pearlescent breasts which were pillowing him very nicely. How could he not?

He rubbed the underside of his chin in an easy back-and-forth motion. The sweet pink tips beneath him rapidly deepened to rose, protruding right in the direction of his mouth. As if to beckon.

He must.

Inching slightly to his left, lips which had devastated legions of women before her skillfully captured the succulent offering. Gently, he drew on her.

"Oh!" Lilac gasped at both his unexpected action and the new sensation. *What on earth was the Prince doing?* It wasn't decent! It wasn't at all what a young lady should be thinking of, even in a dream! It wasn't . . .

His nimble tongue played the nub inside his mouth. Lilac couldn't breathe.

Rejar intensified his actions, suckling, letting his tongue roll around her, lightly using his teeth as well. She was sweet; he would not forget her taste anytime soon.

Not ever, he realized in a moment of truth.

A small, choking sound of desire issued from her throat, distracting him. The passionate response almost drove him over the edge of his control. Should he continue? Lilac moaned again.

Just a little more . . .

He would stop now.

Soon.

His capable hands—hands that were trained equally well as both warrior and lover—reached around her, between the cloth of her gown, splaying powerfully against the bare skin of her back.

He loved the feel of her in his arms.

Overcome, he reared back, pulling her right up with him. Lilac's head fell backwards, her arms floating helplessly to her sides as the strange, terrifying, *interesting* dream continued and the man (who for some reason looked like Prince Nickolai) feasted on her with a totally improper hunger.

She never thought she would have imagined such a thing, but it did feel so exquisite!

"This is a superb dream," she uttered breathlessly.

Her words reached him. *A dream. She believes this is a dream.* Rejar paused.

He blinked.

He drew in a deep breath.

He did not release her from his mouth, but attempted to talk himself into it. Valiantly, he recited the entire Aviaran alphabet—all three hundred and thirty-three letters.

He called up his father's stern, disapproving visage from his youth.

He pictured the entire assemblage of the Guild, their indignant, righteous expressions more than enough to freeze any man's ardor.

None of it worked.

It was the imagined shock and pain of discovery that would be in those lovely green eyes should he continue that finally did it. He was about to release her when he felt a small tentative hand rest on his head. His eyes widened in panic.

No! *Not the hair.*

Do not let her stroke my hair!

It was too late. Nimble little fingers tangled up in the long strands, ruffling through the silken locks of his mane. He closed his eyes in acute agony. In acute ecstasy.

It was the one thing that completely undid him. The feel of a woman sliding her hands through his hair. Lilac's fingers moved in soft, gentle sweeps, lightly tugging at the strands just the right way.

The way he adored.

Closing his eyes in total bliss, Rejar growled deep in his throat.

He was lost.

And when those same wondrous hands began to massage his scalp, displaying a skill which surely one must be born with—

He fell upon her.

Rejar drained his glass, slamming it onto the table. He glanced at the "cards" in his hand with red-rimmed eyes, not really paying any attention to the game of wagering he was presently involved in. Why should he? He always won these simple pastimes the men of this world seemed to amuse themselves with.

He rested his chin in the palm of his hand and sighed. It was late. Almost dawn. He was tired and yet he knew he would not be able to sleep.

Especially next to *her.*

No! He would not think on it. Absolutely not.

It was not altogether his fault!

Wearily, he closed his eyes, admitting the truth to himself. *Yes, it was all his fault.*

Why was he behaving in such a manner? It was totally unlike him.

He didn't remember exactly what had happened after that red haze of passion had swept over him, but the next thing he knew, they were rolling across the bed together, his arms embraced about her waist, his face buried within her neck. Her scent enveloping him.

He had swiftly rotated her on top of him, his hands wildly stroking and caressing everywhere at once; down her back, her legs, cupping her rounded—

Ironically, it was Fanny Burney who had shocked some sense into him.

In his pleasure-seeking frenzy, his elbow had

knocked into the small table next to the bed; the book Lilac had placed there earlier went crashing to the floor. The heavy thud had snapped his hold on her; she instantly stiffened.

He had only a moment before her confusion focused into full consciousness. Quickly, he flung her from his arms, transforming himself even as he leapt from the bed.

It had been close. Very, very close.

She had not seen him but the abrupt manner in which she had been propelled from his mesmerizing inducement made him sure she would remember much of her "dream."

He would not risk it again. He dare not.

No, he must change his strategy with her now.

This was indeed turning into a challenging hunt. If only he wasn't so restless, he could enjoy it more! The only time he seemed able to get some peace from this strange malady was when he lay beside her. There was something about her presence which calmed him, even as it inflamed him.

Truly, it was most odd.

His desultory gaze scanned the smoky, dimly-lit room of the seedy gambling "hell" in this place called Covent Garden. What was he doing here? He should be out carousing. . . .

Yes, that was it! This was foolishness. Why should he suffer like this? It did not make any sense. No one had asked it of him.

He would find a woman. Any woman. Tonight. They would lie together; he would feel like himself again and then he would proceed with Lilac. It made perfect sense. He would not make the same mistake he had at Byron's; he would choose and that would be it. He would not think about hair color or eye color or any such nonsense. Women were all beautiful in their own way. Equally so to him.

Feeling much better now that he had resolved in his mind what he had to, must do, Rejar gathered the tokens he had just won in front of him. The gentleman on his left grumbled, stood up, and vacated his seat. The man on his right handed him the deck of cards.

Smiling, he began what was called "the deal."

When he finished, he sat back in his chair, briefly glanced at his cards, then let his sights scan the hall. A group of garishly dressed women stood by the stairs on the far side of the room. His blue-and-gold gaze lingered on them.

"Up fer a bit of wenchin, guvna?"

A peculiar man with a weathered face and a contagious smile plopped down on the seat to his left. He was dressed in bright green from head to foot. An unlit pipe dangled out of the corner of his mouth.

Rejar looked back at the women again, then winked at the man in green beside him. "Mmm, most definitely."

The man snickered good-naturedly, elbowing Rejar several times in the side. "That's the way to go fer a youngblood on the town!" Glancing over his shoulder, he eyed the women who had captured Rejar's attention. "Just don't get no pox though," he murmured in an aside, "Be a shame, a good lookin' bloke like you."

Pox? Rejar was confused. "What is pox?"

" 'Tis a cryin' shame to see a man drinkin' by 'isself." The man pointedly stared at Rejar's now empty glass.

Amused and mildly diverted, Rejar motioned with an expert flick of his wrist (perfectly imitating a dandy he had seen earlier) to a server for a glass of spirits for the man. The man gulped it down as if he were dying of thirst. Rejar was momentarily sidetracked by the game.

The man watched the handsome nob place a shrewd bet onto the table. He nodded in approval. *Sharp, he is . . .*

Having placed his bet, Rejar turned to him. "So, what is this pox you speak of?" he innocently asked.

The man sighed loudly, as if to convey there was a difficult job to be done here and "I'm the one who has to do it." Leaning toward his new companion, he draped a guiding arm over the man's broad shoulders. The pitch of his voice dropped theatrically to convey the seriousness of the subject he was about to discuss. "Wot's yer name, lad?"

Rejar threw a bemused glance at the hand resting familiarly on his shoulder. His senses had told him much about this man already. The man had been avidly watching his pile of tokens, but he was harmless; the brusque exterior hid a gentle soul. "I am called Nickolai."

"Nickolai, is it? Well, listen close, Nickolai—the pox is what you get when you lay wit certain wimen."

Understanding dawned. Rejar smiled broadly. "Ahh! We call it the coming. It is most pleasurable."

The man frowned at him. "No, ye bloody sot! 'Tis a terrible affliction!"

The true meaning sunk in. Rejar was horrified. "You mean . . . an illness?" He'd never heard of such a thing.

"Aye, now you've got the size of it."

The smooth brow furrowed. "But—What does it do?"

"Wot does it do!" The man's eyes bulged out so far they looked like they were going to jump from his head. "Why, it shrivels up yer pizzle and makes it fall off, that's wot!"

97

Rejar went deathly pale. He had a sickening idea exactly what a "pizzle" was.

"Of course by that time yer stark bloomin' mad! Yer might not even notice you don't 'ave no pizzle no more."

That would be the day. Rejar rubbed the side of his temple, which suddenly began throbbing. By *Aiyah*, this idiotic world! It would drive him mad! He was fairly certain he would not be susceptible to such an ailment due to his inherent makeup, but the *idea* of it . . .

"You said certain women—which women?" The words escaped from clenched teeth. His head was pounding now.

"Them wimen," The man nodded to the group by the stairs, "is not fer you."

The man noted that the young buck looked disappointed and somewhat desperate. The handsome man briefly closed his eyes and knocked his head against the back of his chair. Twice. *Poor lad.* You might have thought someone had just told him sunshine had been outlawed.

"Ye got a girl, lad?" he asked kindly.

The fleeting expression of horror flashing across the sultry face gave the man his answer. "Go back to 'er then. Wot you want to go lookin' fer trouble fer?"

"You do not understand. She is for later. Right now, I need—"

The man tsk-tsked, shaking his head. "I can see wot you need the guidance of good ol' Jackie boy 'ere. That's me name, Jackie Mulligan." He puffed out his chest proudly, pointing to it with his thumb. "Irish—Cit, I is, and proud of it. Me father and me mither come from Ireland, y'know; but I 'ail from the Cit, chum." The man's speech shifted rapidly back and forth from

Irish lilt to East End twang. Rejar was having trouble following his meaning.

"Who is the Cit?" he asked, totally perplexed.

"Green as me garments, y'are, laddie." Jackie lowered his head tragically at Rejar's lack of worldly knowledge, then quickly raised it to pierce him with a cunning stare. "You, ah, you got someone to look out fer you 'ere?"

"What do you mean? Like a servant?"

"No, I meant a—"

Rejar interrupted him, thinking this might not be a bad idea; the man could instruct him in the hidden ways of this world. "Are you asking to be my servant?"

Jackie hesitated but a second; he swept the battered cap off his head, causing a few wispy hairs to fly out. "Are—are ye lookin' fer a man, sir?"

Rejar's eyes twinkled. The odd fellow was really quite comical. "I suppose I could use someone to help me—it is the custom here, is it not? For men of means?"

"Aye, chum, I mean, sir. That 'tis!"

"Then I will take you."

Tears of gratitude (or was that mirth?) formed in Jackie's eyes. "You ain't jesting me, sir, are you?"

Rejar was offended. "Of course not. I am a son of Krue." As if *that* should answer any doubts the man might have.

Jackie wiped his eyes with a suspiciously shaking hand. "And you would know, guvna. Where can I find you, then, o' kind sir?"

"I am at the Clarendon Hotel. Tell them I said to arrange lodging for you as well."

"But who shall I say wot sent me?"

"Hmm . . ." The magic in the name has worked well enough so far, Rejar thought. In all likelihood it would get lodging for this fellow too. He waved his strong hand imperiously in the air. "Tell them Prince Azov has sent you."

"Blimey, a bleedin' *prince!*" Jackie Mulligan looked as if he was going to faint.

Or burst out laughing.

Chapter Five

It was late morning when Rejar finally made his way back to his hotel suite. Totally weary from his evening of wagering and drinking, he staggered through the door, eyes red-rimmed.

Purposely, he had stayed out past the point of exhaustion in the hopes that he might fall into a dead sleep and thereby forget the unending torment he was forced to suffer in this forsaken world.

Pox! Who had ever heard of pox? What would be the next horror he would have to endure here?

It would probably be something like beautiful, young women forbidden to have sex altogether.

He stopped a moment, snickering at his own imagination gone wild.

No, *that* was too far fetched even for this ridiculous world!

"Here we were all so worried about you; and you, coming in at this hour—after a night of carousing, I wager. Do you have any idea how long it took poor, old Yaniff to find you?"

Rejar came to a dead stop in the entryway, stunned. His brother Lorgin was sitting across the room from him, his booted feet, crossed at the ankle, conquering a tabletop! He was the picture of indolent tolerance.

"Of course," his brother continued blandly, "if you had taken your studies with the Charl, as Yaniff had always hoped, you might have called the Tunnels to yourself and saved him his grief."

"Lorgin!" Rejar's face lit up with a huge grin. He crossed the room in three strides. Lorgin smiled as he stood, embracing his younger brother in a hearty hug.

"I was going to ask how you fare, Rejar, but, as usual, I see you have landed on your feet." He slapped his brother affectionately on the back, then stepped back to grin cheekily at him. "Or, in your case, should I say on your side?"

Rejar wagged a finger at him. "So speaks the voice of his own experience."

Lorgin laughed, then became serious. "We have missed you, brother. Suleila was beside herself with worry; I do not think father has had a moment's peace from her since you were lost to us."

Rejar smiled at the mention of his mother, sorry she had been worried, yet knowing a female Familiar's love for overdramatizing events. "I suppose father enjoyed it, in his own way."

"Mmm. But he was concerned for you, as well, Rejar. Although, he refused to believe any ill befell you. He said he had the utmost faith in his son's abilities."

Rejar raised a black eyebrow. "Did he?" Not his *Familiar* abilities. Rejar exhaled resignedly. Even though he knew his father loved him, Krue had never accepted what he considered to be Rejar's denial of his Charl heritage. His Aviaran father wanted only warrior sons, a difficult path for a child born of a Familiar mother inheriting all the abilities of her race.

Understanding his brother's dilemma, Lorgin placed a hand on his shoulder. "He loves you, Rejar. He wants what he believes is best for you."

Rejar looked down at the carpet for a moment, wisely deciding to let the subject pass. "I know," he finally said.

"Come, let us not think on these things now; I have pleasant news to speak of—Adeeann will soon make you a father of the line." Lorgin crossed his arms over his chest in an arrogantly proud pose. "What say you to *that?*"

Rejar lit up with joy. "Lorgin!" He grabbed his brother in another bear hug, almost causing both of them to topple over. "This is truly the best news! How does Adeeann fare with the babe?"

Lorgin laughed, sharing his brother's happiness. "She is well, though she complains much, as is her nature."

Familiar eyes being what they were, Rejar caught the briefest of movements behind the couch followed by a flash of red hair, quickly hidden. It appeared Adeeann was here and Lorgin did not know of it. The corners of Rejar's mouth twitched in suppressed laughter. *His brother was in for it now.*

He would see to it.

That was what a brother was for.

"Ah, Adeeann did not accompany you, Lorgin?" Rejar asked him innocently.

"Of course not! I would not allow her to take such a risk; she is safely at home, where I have told her she must stay."

Another flash of red, followed by the minutest snort of disgust.

"I see." Rejar nodded slowly. "And she agreed with this?"

Lorgin stuck his square chin out, falling for the bait. "Yes, Adeeann understands she must take my counsel when it comes to certain matters." He waved his hand through the air in a gesture of dismissal. "She is my mate so she does as I bid her."

Two lethal gray eyes speared Lorgin before popping behind the couch.

It was all Rejar could do not to burst out laughing.

Oblivious to the danger he was in, Lorgin leaned against the back of a couch, crossing his arms again. "She wanted to come to see you, Rejar, especially when she found out you had come to her world. But she quickly agreed with my reasoning when I—"

"This is Adeeann's world?" Rejar was surprised. Some of the language similarities he had noticed immediately, but there were so many differences he had assumed he was on a sister planet.

"Yes, Adeeann's world, but"—here Lorgin looked carefully at his brother—"not her time."

The nuances in Lorgin's words passed by Rejar. Lorgin was not totally surprised; after all, his brother was not a Charl mystic and would have no reason to understand the significance of what had occurred.

"I did not know Adeeann was from Earth." At his extempore comment, Rejar heard a slight gasp of dismay come from behind the couch.

"She is not. She is from the Disney World."

"But you said . . . Lorgin, this is Earth."

Lorgin stared at his brother, then blinked once. "I see. I think my wife has some explaining to do."

Rejar smiled before keenly prodding Lorgin. "Perhaps she can explain it to you when you *bid* her to—since she listens so well to you, brother."

Lorgin's brow instantly lowered, proving Rejar had not lost his touch. "That is not humorous, Rejar. In all the months you have been gone, I vow I have not missed your sense of—"

"Months?" Rejar interrupted. "What mean you *months?* I have not been here that long."

"I speak in standard Alliance terms; you have been gone—"

"Lorgin, they measure the passage of time here much as we do." It had surprised him how similar the standard Alliance day, based on the rotation of Aviara, was to this planet's. Though the names were different in his language, Aviaran's also marked day, week, month, and year. "Why do you say I have been gone months? I have only been here a relatively short period of time; perhaps a little more than a standard month—but that is all."

It was as Lorgin had feared; he looked steadily at his brother. "You have been in the Tunnels for many months, Rejar. Almost a year measured by the passage of Aviaran time."

Thinking it was not so, Rejar dismissed Lorgin's words. "It is not possible!"

"After you released the Shimmalee, what happened to you?"

Rejar thought back. "There was an immediate disturbance; a violent upheaval followed . . ." He shrugged. "I was carried along with it, then suddenly an opening appeared and I fell through to . . . here."

"Yaniff thinks that during the cosmic storm, you were buffeted by temporal waves. Somehow the release of this particular Shimmalee back into the Matrix caused vast shock ripples throughout the flux of time.

Since you were still in the Tunnels while this occurred, you rode the waves of the phasing storm, leaping time pulses within the Matrix itself."

Rejar was concerned by this new twist of events. "It does not seem possible. The whole thing seemed like just a brief occurrence to me."

"Perhaps it was." Lorgin paused. "Rejar, Yaniff believes you might have been affected by the experience."

Rejar's head snapped up. "Affected *how?*"

"He was not sure. He wanted me to ask you if you sensed any changes within yourself. Have you?"

Rejar reflected a moment. Except for his restlessness and his penchant for Lilac Devere he felt exactly as he always had. And the restlessness he had experienced *before* he had entered the Tunnels. "No. There is nothing. I am as I have always been."

Lorgin watched his brother closely. "Yaniff believes otherwise. Although he did say that whatever the effect is, it might not be apparent for some time, mayhap not even in your present incarnation."

The Familiar was surprised. "I am years away from my *first* incarnation."

"This I know. There is no need to be concerned now. What will happen has already been set in motion. There is naught to do; best we concern ourselves with your present circumstances. Let us leave now and return home, brother."

Lorgin straightened, preparing himself to open the tunnel.

Rejar quickly forestalled him. "Lorgin, wait!"

"What is it?" Lorgin turned to him.

Rejar's sights flicked to the couch; he sent his thought privately to his brother. *[I cannot leave . . . just yet.]*

Lorgin looked shocked. "But why? Do you not wish to return home?"

"Of course I do, but . . ." He glanced at the couch again. *{There is a certain woman here I want.}*

Lorgin exhaled in disgust, his voice getting louder with every word he uttered. "I vow I cannot believe what I am hearing! Are you telling me that I have left my wife, my *pregnant* wife, to come halfway across a universe after your reckless hide and it is not convenient for you to leave now because you wish to *krnack*!"

Rejar rubbed his ear in sudden embarrassment, trying not to look into the bemused gray eyes that were peeking around the couch. "Lorgin—"

"What can you be thinking!" Lorgin threw his hands up in the air, totally exasperated with his Familiar brother. Then he took a deep breath to calm himself. "Look, Rejar, it is not as if I do not understand these things. Even though I am not Familiar, I can assure you I have had more than my share of exotic encounters on the many planets I have visited. Indeed, a night's pleasure with an alluring alien is something every man remembers fondly—"

"Ah, Lorgin . . ." Rejar thought it was time for him warn his brother. Especially if he ever wanted Lorgin to speak to him again.

"As you know, in the past, before I mated, I had somewhat of a reputation among the Knights of the Charl for my"—he broke off to grin roguishly—"*dalliances*. Indeed, I was—"

Rejar closed his eyes and inwardly groaned. *{Your wife is here, you fool! She is hiding behind the couch listening to every word you speak.}*

Lorgin stopped speaking midsentence, frozen to the spot, his pupils dilating in horror. Slowly, his sights shifted to the left in the direction of the couch.

It was too late.

There his wife stood, hands on hips, eyes narrowed to tiny slits of gray lightning, foot tapping imperiously.

He was a dead zorph.

Lorgin, being the sharp warrior that he was, immediately figured out that the best defense was a good offense. Purposely, he lowered his brow in an intimidating scowl, painting the same ferocious expression on his face that he knew in the past had sent many an opponent fleeing from him in utter terror. His voice was precisely, ominously, low.

"Zira, how come you to be here?"

His little wife did not even flinch.

Instead, she continued to glare at him. *Hmm.* Her stance did not portend well for him. The irritating idea that his brother could have warned him a lot sooner raced across his mind, but he would deal with that later; for now he needed to reassert his authority with his wife and hopefully save his own skin.

"I asked you a—" He began imperiously, only to be cut off by an outraged exclamation of feminine fury.

"How dare you try to bulldoze your way out of this one!" Deana tried to look fierce as she stomped across the room, although she supposed her ungainly waddle took a lot of the bite out of it.

When she came abreast of her husband, she stood on tiptoe and grabbed him by his arrogant, knightly ear. Deana knew Lorgin just hated it. Which made it all the more satisfying to her.

Ear captured, Lorgin glared at her, speaking through tightly clenched teeth. "Woman, do not dare—"

She did. Twisted it for good measure.

"I vow I hate when you do that!" His amethyst eyes flashed down at her, his ear still caught firmly in her grip.

It was all Rejar could do not to burst out laughing.

"Good! Now listen up, Lorgin; I want to know right now if you thought I was one of your exotic dalliances, because if I was—"

Lorgin looked at her aghast, all traces of effrontery gone. "Of course you were not! How can you even speak such a thing? I have told you I have loved you from the moment I first saw you, how I longed for . . ." Lorgin caught the flash of Rejar's white teeth out of the corner of his eye and suddenly realized his brother was a captive audience to this embarrassing display of affection.

And a highly amused captive audience at that.

His jaws snapped shut, a dull flush of bronze highlighting his cheekbones.

Deana, noticing her husband's embarrassment, thought her diversionary tactic was working extremely well. She'd have to remember this one. "Very well. We'll let the matter drop—*this* time."

Unfortunately, Lorgin recovered very quickly.

"No, we will not, *zira*. I ask you once again, how come you to be here?" He lowered his face to hers, his nose nearly touching her own. "After I expressly forbade it!"

Not in the least intimidated, Deana fluttered her eyelashes at him. "I followed you into the Tunnels when you weren't looking." She quickly kissed the tip of his nose.

Lorgin blanched. "By *Aiyah*, tell me you did not! Have you no idea of the danger in such a maneuver?"

Deana dismissed his alarm with a shrug. "Danger, shmanger. I was right behind you; what could have happened?" Lorgin's pupils contracted to pinpoints as he stared down at her, a sure sign he was upset.

"I did not know you were behind me," he said dangerously soft. "When I exited, I could have sealed the Tunnel with you in it."

Deana swallowed, rather sick at the idea. She hadn't thought of that. Her voice came out a tiny little squeak. "Oh."

The small acknowledgement did not seem to mollify Lorgin in the least.

Deana swallowed again. There was going to be Hell to pay for this one; she just knew it. *Change of subject needed at once.*

Quickly, she plastered a smile on her face, turning to effusively greet her brother-in-law. "Rejar! It's so good to see you!"

Chuckling at her obvious diversionary ploy, Rejar threw his arms wide, letting Adeeann run into them for a hug. Holding her hands in his, he stepped back to observe her very rounded stomach. It was all the proof he needed of Lorgin's words. "It is true then; I have been gone for some time."

"And we missed you so!" Deana eyed him appreciatively from the tip of his Hessian boots to the thigh-hugging black pants to the pale gold waistcoat over frilly shirt to the top of his sultry, handsome head. "Look at you! Decked out like a Regency dandy!" *A great hunk of a Regency dandy. The women here must be drooling their coiffed heads off,* she acknowledged to herself.

Lorgin, not liking the way his wife was eyeing the cut of his brother's clothes, decided enough was enough.

"So, you have seen your Ree Gen Cee Ing Land, *zira.*" He took her hand firmly in his, refusing to release it when she gave a halfhearted tug. "Now do we go home."

Rejar stepped in. "Lorgin, I ask you to wait. *[I must*

explain something to you.} The thought he sent only to Lorgin.

"What is it?"

{I cannot return with you now. There is something unfinished here for me.}

"A woman!" Lorgin spat out, causing Deana to look at both of them curiously. What were they talking about?

{Yes, but it is not what you think.}

Lorgin raised a skeptical eyebrow.

Rejar gave him a feral smile. *{Well, it is not totally what you think. I am engaged in a* t'kan, *a special hunt. I can not break off now. I need to—that is, I—}*

Lorgin watched his brother curiously. He had never seen him like this—sure and yet . . . bewildered. And he had unconsciously used the Familiar word *t'kan* but Lorgin knew it did not mean just a special hunt; it also meant a *love* hunt. Was his brother aware he had used that particular word?

Lorgin watched as Rejar began to pace the room. No, he was not aware of it.

The light of knowledge sparked in Lorgin's eyes. So, once again Yaniff was right. His brother would not be returning home with him. At least not now. Lorgin was enough of a mystic himself to know when to stand down.

"Who is she?" he asked Rejar softly.

"Who's who?" Deana piped in.

Lorgin gently squeezed his wife's hand, bidding her to be silent.

{Actually, she is the woman I almost fell into when I was propelled from the Tunnels.} Lorgin watched him silently. *{She is called Lilac.}*

"I see." More than you know, brother, Lorgin reflected.

[It is just that there are . . . unresolved matters between us. It should not take long. Not that I could not leave now, but—]

Lorgin chuckled to himself. His poor brother was really in a remarkable state of confusion. So, he had misread the exhaustion on Rejar's face; Lorgin would wager it was not his brother's usual type of carousing which had put the circles beneath his eyes. In fact, his brother was strung as tight as an Aurlan's bow.

There was only one thing Lorgin knew of that made his brother this on edge. Forced abstinence. He grinned to himself. Now this was a day to be marked!

"And what does this Lilac make of you, dear brother?"

Rejar rubbed his jaw; he did not want to explain to Lorgin the strange situation he found himself in. *[It is somewhat complicated; suffice it to say she curses me by day.]*

"Ah." This was promising indeed! "But what of the *nights?*"

Rejar grinned wickedly.

"As I suspected." Lorgin returned the grin. "I can see you have no need of my assistance for the time being, Rejar. However, if I leave, you need be aware I will not be able to return for you for some time." He nodded pointedly at Deana's swollen belly.

"What's that supposed to mean?" Deana frowned at her husband, wondering if she was missing something. Neither man responded to her question, which made her all the more nervous. If there was one thing she'd learned about these Aviarans, it was: when you least expect it—expect it.

"I understand, Lorgin. Do not be concerned; I have learned to get along quite well in this world. My name here seems to have much magic."

Lorgin just looked at him doubtfully. "Hmm."

In typical Familiar fashion, Rejar ignored the Lorgin euphemism. "Before you leave, Lorgin, tell me of Traed. How does he fare? I have thought much on him since last I saw him."

They all were silent for a few minutes as they each remembered that last, terrible day when they had gone to confront Traed's natural father, Theardar, on a barren Rim world. Traed had suffered terribly that day. Finally Lorgin spoke.

"Traed is . . . Traed. He has taken himself back to the land of Theardar's people—back to the Sky Lands of Aviara. Yaniff despairs for him, although he claims Traed seeks to heal his heart."

"How does one heal such a rent?" Rejar asked.

"I know not."

Rejar knew it was time to tell his brother something that had been on his mind for a long time; he looked Lorgin straight in the eye. "Traed is our brother of the line."

Lorgin surprised him by saying, "I know. Yaniff told me everything. When did you first sense it, Rejar?"

"When we were at his keep."

Now Lorgin knew why his brother had acted so strangely when they had visited Traed on Zarrain. "Did you not sense it when you were a child? He was with us much then."

"No. This particular Familiar ability develops later in life. It is hard to imagine sometimes—that father had a sister and Traed was her son."

"It does take some getting used to," Lorgin agreed.

"Blood of our line; now he is likened to a brother. I do not know if it is a good thing for him to remain long in the Sky Lands, Lorgin. Traed needs to come home."

"I have thought the same. I suppose I will have to go

and drag him out of there." Lorgin did not seem happy with the prospect. "It seems I am destined to chase after the two of you." He gave his younger brother a pointed look combined with a long-suffering sigh.

Rejar's dual-colored eyes sparkled with mischievous humor. "Then I will be sure not ever to disappoint you, Lorgin."

"That is what I am afraid of. Come, Adeeann, let us bid Rejar farewell for now."

"Oh, Lorgin, couldn't we stay here—just for a little while? I would really love to see what this time period was really like. Think of the fun we could have!"

Lorgin shook his head regretfully. "I am sorry, *zira*. We cannot." Deana started to object, but he placed a finger gently across her lips. "Do not ask me to explain; you must believe me when I say we must leave now."

Deana watched Lorgin closely. There was a reason he wanted them to go back to Aviara. Besides being a Knight of the Charl, her husband was also a holder of the fourth power, a mystic in his own right. If he thought they needed to leave, then perhaps they'd better leave. She sighed. She had so wanted to get a glimpse of this fantastic time period in her planet's history.

As if he knew her thoughts, Lorgin took her hand and led her to the window. Pulling back the curtain, he opened the window, saying, "Look, then, *zira*, and see this world that was once yours."

Deana stuck her head out the window and gazed in awe at the street below. It was like a museum exhibit come to life! The coaches and riders, hawkers and venders! The exquisitely costumed men and women! The sights and sounds and—

Deana wrinkled her nose. *The stench in the streets!*

She quickly popped her head in, holding her nose.

"My God! What is that awful smell?"

More than slightly nauseous, she turned to her brother-in-law. "Good grief, Rejar, do you ever get used to it?"

"No, you do not."

"And you still want to stay here? Oh, Rejar, come home with us now."

"It is not always this bad, Adeeann."

"Well, that's a relief." Deana fanned her face, trying to dispel the memory of those noxious odors.

"Sometimes it is worse," he joked. At her crestfallen face, he added, "In certain areas it is not so bad." He remembered the clean, fresh scent of Lilac's home and garden, and the lovely countryside he had visited.

Lorgin took Deana's hand once more. "I will return when I can, Rejar; until then—be well."

"And you, Lorgin." His gaze rested on Deana's stomach, causing him to give a half-smile. "To *all* of you."

With his ability to do so, Lorgin called forth the Tunnel. A small, circular light appeared in the room, growing larger and larger, until a great maw of pulsing, flashing light stood before them.

Deana ran to give Rejar one last hug before she stepped into the portal with her husband. Just before the Tunnel sealed behind them, Rejar heard Lorgin say to his wife, "*Now, zira, you will tell me exactly what you meant by this Disney World . . .*"

He missed them already.

But he had a certain task to complete. A task of the utmost urgency.

He needed to be inside Lilac Devere.

With a vengeance.

Lilac stared at her reflection in the mirror.

She didn't look any different. Same mousy-tan colored hair. Same overly large greenish sloe eyes. Same full lips. Her sights dropped to her chest, lavishly revealed by the square-cut collar of her garden dress. Same embarrassingly *rounded* curves.

She was not exactly what the ton would deem a "diamond of the first water."

So why was she suddenly being pursued by every court card of the Beau Monde? Invitations were arriving by the hour. Would Miss Devere like to attend a little fête I am sponsoring on Thursday the next? Would Miss Devere be available for tea with Sir Geoffry on Tuesday? Would Miss Devere be accepting callers in the afternoons?

No, Miss Devere would NOT!

It was all *his* fault.

That irritating, insufferable, arrogant, spoiled Prince!

And to make matters worse, now she was dreaming of him. There wasn't even an escape for her in the arms of Morpheus! For some strange, inexplicable reason, Lilac had dreamt she was in *his* arms last evening. And the things she imagined he had done to her!

She pressed her palms to her flaming cheeks as vivid, indecent images paraded across her mind's eye. What on God's Earth would make her imagine such shameful things? The Prince without his clothes on! Doing the most wicked things *with his tongue*. And when his mouth actually suckled on—

Did men really do such things?

No, it was too bizarre. What made her dream up such odd behavior? She must have eaten something that disagreed with her last night which had caused her to have the nightmare.

Only it wasn't really a nightmare . . .

Some of it had seemed rather enjoyable.

Foolish thought! Of course it was a nightmare; it involved that—that *Prince!*

Lilac took a deep breath to calm her rising agitation. No need to worry; she would never speak to him again. She had made sure of *that* at the soiree last evening. As for future encounters, Auntie would undoubtedly insist she attend at least some of the invitations she had received; in those cases, if the Prince should happen to be there, she would make sure she avoided him.

In all likelihood he had forgotten her by now anyway and had moved on to his next conquest. She would never have to look into that heart-stopping, beautiful face again.

Fate be willing.

Downstairs, the Face was already waiting for her in the foyer.

Determination was stamped all over its sultry features.

Chapter Six

Lilac's steps faltered on the stairs when she caught sight of the gleaming black hair in the foyer below. *It couldn't be!*

Sensual dual-colored eyes, lambent like a rare smoldering flame, came to focus on her.

It was.

Fustian! Did the man never give up? What did he think he was about? She had slapped him, for heaven's sake! How much more *subtle* could she be?

"What do you think you're doing here?" she hissed from the middle of the stairs.

"There you are, Lilac! I was about to send Emmy up to fetch you. Our nice Prince Azov has come to take you for a carriage ride in the park."

Auntie hadn't heard her, but it was obvious *he* had. He gave her that special little smile of his. The one that curled the hair on the back of her neck.

The one that said "we shall see."

No, we won't see. Behind Auntie's back, she stuck her tongue out at him. It was a childish thing to do, but very satisfying.

The dynamic, commanding look he returned to her almost caused her to trip on the last step. Zounds, but he was a force when he did that! She needed to think up an excuse immediately. The one she came up with was a bit lame, but it would have to do.

"I am sorry, your Highness; I am not up to it." She lifted a limp hand to her forehead. "I have a slight headache this afternoon."

Amused at the thinly veiled ruse, Rejar raised one mocking eyebrow. "Bad dreams?" His deep voice murmured mischievously.

Lilac felt the color drain from her face.

The man was too close to the mark and she did not like his arrogant, knowing look one bit. "Bad memories would be more accurate. I thought I made myself quite clear on the dance floor last evening. If you have come to apologize to me, get on with it and then leave."

"Lilac, your manners!" Auntie was clearly appalled; she immediately sought to placate the Prince for Lilac's breach of etiquette. "Your Highness, please forgive her, I don't know what has come over the chit. Normally she is the most even-tempered, docile, sweet—" Her aunt was definitely overcompensating to this irritating boor.

"Auntie Whumples, stop making me sound like some milk cow put out to pasture!"

The Prince's lips twitched in barely suppressed amusement.

She squinted at the irritant through narrowed eyes. "*You* may leave." In the event the nick ninny had forgotten his way out, she rudely pointed her finger in the direction of the door.

Lady Agatha, horrified that this prime candidate was about to escape her clutches, lost all decorum. As far as she was concerned, he was Lilac's best hope. A prince, for Heaven's sake!

"No, he will not!" Aggravated at her niece's stubbornness, Agatha's stern voice bellowed off the foyer walls, shaking the suspended chandelier in the process.

Lilac stared at her aunt, both amazed at her vehement response and infuriated at her meddling. It was obvious what she was up to—matchmaking. With the sapskull. Not in this lifetime! Auntie Whumples could just think that one over again!

In a rare display of rebelliousness, Lilac put her foot down. Or stomped it down, to be more accurate. "Yes, he will!"

Agatha clutched her heaving bosom, gasping in righteous affrontage. She was a dignified woman who did not put up with such nonsense; the Prince was instantly elevated to cause célèbre. "I've never! You naughty girl! He will not step one foot outside this house until I say so."

Rejar avidly watched the scene unfold before him; it was in the tradition of great entertainment. As if he weren't the perpetrator of the contest of wills, he calmly crossed his arms over his chest and patiently leaned back against a column in the foyer while the two woman fought over him. This, in various forms, he was used to.

Lilac flashed her eyes, lowered her voice, put her hands on her hips, and stared her aunt down. "He goes." She stood firm.

Not bad, Rejar thought, admiring her technique. Still, if he were in a gaming hell right now, he would place his wager on the aunt. She was far more determined, far more bombastic, far more . . . just far more. Not that he had any intention of leaving, no matter what the outcome.

"Lilac *Prunella* Devere!"

Lilac visibly winced at the sound of her hideous middle name—the usage of which rendered her temporarily immobile.

Ah! Rejar nodded approvingly. A very good ploy. The old woman had the skill of a brilliant tactician; first weaken your opponent with a dreaded allusion, then pounce. *Prunella?* He grinned outright at the awful appellation. It was so bad, it was on the border of being adorable.

"I am still your guardian, Lilac Devere! Your sudden display of disrespect—not to mention ill manners— brings great shame to this household." Auntie paused before throwing her trump card. "What would your dear father say if he could hear you now?"

Lilac's shoulders instantly sagged, her head dropping in defeat. Every time her aunt wanted to win an argument, all she had to do was bring up the name of her dear departed father. She sneaked a peek at her aunt. As Lilac suspected, the old termagant was already gloating with victory.

Sensing that the battle was over, Rejar stepped away from the column, chuckling to himself. The Aviaran warriors might learn a thing or two from this old woman. His passing wink to Lady Whumples said "well done."

Agatha surprised him by winking back. "Make sure she does not catch a chill, your Highness. The late afternoons can still be quite brisk."

"You need not worry; she will be in the best of hands—ask anyone." With those cryptic words, he held out his hand to Lilac.

Reluctantly, she took his arm.

"Do not feel too badly, *Prunella*," he whispered softly into her ear as he opened the door for her, "in any case, I was not going to apologize."

Lilac glared up at him.

How could she not gape at the driver of the open-topped landau?

Instead of being properly attired as any decent coachman would be—in white leather breeches, striped waistcoat, and dark tailored coat—the man was entirely bedecked in bright, garish green. An unlit pipe dangled from the side of his mouth. Odd wisps of hair flew out from beneath a moldy cap, also green. He looked like a walking fir tree.

"In y'go, colleen."

While she continued to gape at him in a stupor, the man actually had the audacity to place his palm on her backside and shove her into the vehicle! When the Prince settled himself beside her, she turned an incredulous face to him.

"Is that *man* in your employ?" she asked.

"Yes." She is impressed, Rejar thought.

Lilac's eyes widened in disbelief. Shaking her head, she stared pointedly out of her side of the landau, ignoring his Highness.

"Where to, yer princeship?" The green thing from the front asked.

"I believe it is called Hyde Park; is it not, Lilac?"

"I suppose so," she muttered.

"Hyde Park, 'tis! Gor, this oughta be a treat, seein' them nobs strut about like they's all fine and dandy!" He cracked the whip in the air and the horses bolted as if the hounds of hell nipped at their shins.

The sudden momentum caused by the forward

movement almost toppled Lilac over the back of the carriage. Her derriere slid off the seat and her legs flew up in the air, sending her dress spiraling to her thighs. Several sections of her hair broke free of her ribbon to drape cozily over the Prince's leather-clad thigh, sliding intimately down between his long, powerful legs.

Lilac clenched her fists and stared at the top of his black boot.

Said boot was now level with her face since she was sprawled across the bottom of the coach. Lilac tried very hard to recall Mrs. Chapone's instructional letter on The Government of the Temper.

Gritting her teeth, she reached up to yank the traitorous strands of hair away from his person. Throughout all of this, the Prince remained suspiciously silent. The insufferable jackanapes was not even offering to assist her back up onto the seat!

"Are you going to help me up or not?" She spat at him through clamped jaws.

"Not, I think," he drawled.

Furious with his blatantly rude behavior, she gazed up into his face with all the contempt she felt for him.

Rejar knew he would not forget this picture for a long time. Half of her hair had come undone and now was hanging over one side of her face. He glanced down her body. . . .

This was indeed humorous.

Eyes brilliant with laughter, Rejar nodded his head in the direction of her lap.

Afraid of what she'd see, but knowing she must, Lilac slowly looked down. Her dress was hiked up somewhere around her hips, exposing most of her pantalettes and *all* of her white silk stockings.

Lilac did not move, did not blink, did not say anything for a full minute. Finally, she gathered what was left of her composure.

She spoke to the floor in a ridiculously righteous tone. "A gentleman would not look."

Rejar placed one elbow up on the side of the coach, resting his head on his curved palm so that his index finger resided indolently against his temple.

Unquestionably, he continued to enjoy the tantalizing view.

"So you have said." He threw the implication back at her.

"You are wicked!"

The corners of the Prince's mouth curved upward, revealing a devastating little dimple in his left cheek. "I have been told it is my nature."

"To be insensitive?" she sneered. He puzzled her by laughing.

"I can assure you, I am a very *sensitive* man." Rejar leaned forward, resting his elbows on his knees. By design, the position brought their heads fairly close together.

"You need only test me to find out," he whispered seductively.

Her face flamed and she quickly looked away from his inviting posture.

"I don't like you, Prince Nickolai."

Rejar smiled slowly.

She faced him, nonplussed. "Did you not hear me?"

"I listen to you very well." His eyes captured hers with the methodical gleam of a predator—sophisticated beyond her comprehension and oh-so-tantalizing. "You would be surprised at what I hear."

Bewitched by those gorgeous eyes despite her resolve, Lilac almost fell under his spell. Blinking, she broke free of his strange hold.

"Come." He held out his hand to her, waiting patiently for her to take it.

There he sat above her in the coach, like some fairy-tale Prince—handsome beyond measure. Her mouth parted as she looked up at him, affected for all her self chastisement by his sheer masculine beauty.

Knowing she needed his help to regain her seat in the rocking carriage, she tentatively placed her hand in his, noting how his powerful, well-formed hand completely engulfed her small one.

The way he would engulf all that she was, if she let him.

The sober thought brought common sense back to her; and as he easily helped, almost lifted her one-handedly, back onto the seat, she resolved that she *must* remain aloof from this man. He was far too dangerous.

The landau entered the park, picking up a well-used, popular path in its circuitous route, passing many other carriages and riders.

Lilac noted that every time they passed by a member of the ton, as soon as they were supposedly out of ear-shot, the whispers began. She looked for a reasonable place to hide, but other than under the Prince's long hair, no such retreat was forthcoming. Oh, Auntie Whumples would pay for this!

"Coo, don't this 'ere one look like she's suckin' on a lemon?"

Lilac threw a disgusted look at the driver's back then cringed as she spotted that infernal gossip, Lady Vandershmeer. She was coming right toward them. Of all the terrible luck! Her impromptu outing with the Prince would be all over the ton by this evening.

"Lilac Devere! And his Highness." Lady Vandershmeer tapped her chin with her fan. "What an interesting development this is."

Lilac tried desperately to contain the damage with an invented story. "Prince Azov is new to our city, Lady Vandershmeer. He—that is, a friend of his—is a mutual acquaintance of the family, who asked us, my aunt and I, if we might show him about town."

"A mutual acquaintance? And who might that be?" Lady Vandershmeer was plainly disbelieving.

"Prinny," came the deep voice beside her, shocking both the women.

Lady Vandershmeer dropped her lorgnette. "The Prince Regent?"

"Why are you surprised? I am a Prince and he is a Prince; should we not know each other?" Rejar stared the irritating woman down.

"Well, I suppose so, your Highness." Lady Vandershmeer was clearly flustered by Prince Azov's commanding demeanor.

"Lilac and I must continue with our"—he glanced at her, then back to Lady Vandershmeer—"tour. Good day." He waved his hand imperiously in the air. The driver immediately lurched the coach forward.

But not before Lilac saw Lady Vandershmeer's mouth drop.

Outraged, Lilac turned to the Prince. "What possessed you to use that name?" she demanded. "Now you've ruined everything!"

"Prinny?" Rejar was confused. "I assure you, I have met this ruler you speak of at an engagement I attended with—"

"No, you twit! *My* name. You called me Lilac in front of her!"

Rejar leaned back lazily into the corner of the landau. "What was I supposed to call you—Prunella?"

Lilac winced. "Don't you ever speak that name again. I detest it!"

"Really?" He made a great show of yawning, reminding Lilac of . . . someone. "What a revelation."

"You are so aggravating! You know very well I am referring to your usage of my first name, which, by the way, I have never ever given you permission to use."

"It is your name." He shrugged as if he were not very interested in the topic. "Why should I need permission to use it?"

The man was an idiot! "Because, you were too familiar!"

Rejar chuckled low in his throat at her unknowing play on words: too Familiar. Not yet, but he intended to be.

His laughter was the last straw. The man was insufferable and strangely obtuse; it was time to end this charade of an outing. "I wish to go home. Immediately."

"Why?"

Why! *Let me count the reasons.* She already knew enough about this man to realize she was going to have to convince him. Unlike any proper gentleman who would bring her home simply because she had stated it was her wish. The mutton head.

She reached for a good excuse. "It's getting chilly."

"It is not."

Lilac pursed her lips. "I tell you, it is!" She rubbed her hands briskly up and down her arms. "Look, I'm shivering. Brrr . . ."

A mischievous dimple popped into his cheek. "Let me see."

Before she realized his intent, he leaned forward to run the pads of his long, well-shaped fingers down her arms, leaving a trail of molten heat in the wake of his touch.

Lilac froze.

He was almost embracing her! In public! Caught within his powerful hands, she stared wordlessly up at him.

The aggressive hunter within him met her motionless, captive look with candid sensuality.

At once, a languid veil of warmth enshrouded her, followed by the spicy tang of cinnamon and bayberry and something very exotic. Something provocative.

She shivered in truth now, but not from the cold.

Rejar's sights fastened on her full mouth, parted for him exactly the way he wanted.

"Do you not like to shiver a bit, *souk-souk?*" he murmured, very close to her luscious lips. His sexual scent surrounded her.

"Your Highness," she squeaked. "Please, don't—"

"*Make me shiver,*" he whispered before his mouth came down on hers.

His lips were silk and velvet.

They came over her mouth in a fiery possession. Lilac could feel his breath against her mouth, sweet and hot. And, somehow, acquainted. The Prince tasted of sultry, forbidden dreams.

There was something about the way his mouth took hers; the way his determined hands laced through her hair to hold her to him in a particular way that bespoke of a mastery and artistry that even her unschooled self could recognize. She whimpered beneath the gifted, virile mouth that wreaked such havoc on her, an act of passion that she suspected was in its simplest form for him.

The tip of his hot tongue delicately sampled her bottom lip as if savoring the moment before the feast.

Then it began to slide suggestively between her parted—

Fear and desire tumbled up inside her, confusing her. She jerked away from him.

"You—you cad!" she spat out, wiping the sleeve of her arm across her mouth in a deliberate display of revulsion. "How dare you! Accosting me in public! You're—you're vile and indecent; take me home at once!"

Rejar was not at all surprised by her behavior; he suspected she would react in such a way, although he couldn't figure out exactly why. After he had gotten her into an actual embrace, he had hoped she would feel differently.

Some male Familiars had the ability to bring a woman to peak by their kiss alone. He had done so himself countless times in the past to the immense pleasure of the women he had bedded. Only Lilac had pulled away from him before he had the time to introduce her to that particular expertise of his.

It had been hard for him to stop.

The taste of her still sizzled along his nerves and it was all he could do not to tell Jackie to find a secluded area in the trees and lose himself for a while. Solely by Lilac's present reaction, he supposed it would wiser to wait.

He crossed his arms over his chest and gazed down at her speculatively. "It is a big reaction you show for such a small act. I wonder why that is?"

Lilac's cheeks reddened. "What—what do you mean?" she sputtered defensively.

He looked at her coolly. "I think you know what I mean."

Lilac swallowed. Scared and embarrassed, she yelled to the driver, "Coachman, I insist you turn this vehicle around and take me home!"

The Prince immediately countered her order. "Jackie, you will continue riding around this park until I say otherwise; is that clear?"

"Clear as me pockets, yer Princeship."

Lilac clenched the jonquil material of her dress, hopelessly wrinkling it. "What do you hope to gain from this, your Highness?"

Rejar rested his head back against the seat. "Everything," he said mysteriously, closing his eyes.

While Lilac sat staring stonily at the scenery they passed, Rejar did some serious thinking. It had been a mistake to kiss her, he acknowledged. The timing had been wrong.

He couldn't recall one instance in his life when that had ever happened to him. Was he losing his skill?

Ridiculous! A Familiar's skills were inherent; they could not be lost. So, why, in Familiar terms, was he snarling up everything with her?

Every time he tried to take one step forward, it seemed he had to take two steps back.

He yawned.

He was very tired; he hadn't been able to sleep for two days. After Lorgin and Adeeann had left, he had tried to rest in the hotel room but was unable to. Finally he had given up, going in search of Jackie.

Now that Lilac was next to him, he felt more at ease.

He yawned again.

She had the most calming affect on his restlessness. It was really very strange.

Lilac felt a nose poke into her neck.

"What are you—" She stopped. It seemed the Prince was fast asleep. Good. She wasn't the least insulted. Now she could tell the driver to bring her home and finally rid herself of this boor.

"You there—driver!"

"Me name's Jackie, Jackie Mulligan, yer mistress."

Thank god no one could hear this excuse for a servant call her by such an appalling name. "Yes, well, Jackie, your master has gone and fallen asleep. It appears thinking has overtaxed his brain. You can take me home now."

"Sorry, yer mistress. I'd not be doin' that now."

"What do you mean you won't? I just gave you a direct order! I insist—"

"Insist all y'like, girlie, but I takes me orders from 'is Princeship and 'is Princeship tells Jackie to ride 'round this 'ere park lessen 'e says otherwise and tha's what I aim t' do." That said, he stuck his pipe in his mouth, indicating that as far as Jackie Mulligan was concerned, the discussion was over.

"Well, I have never, in all my life—"

"Tha' was clear to king and shepherd when 'e kissed you, yer mistress." Jackie Mulligan was one to call it like it was. No bloomin' clankers on him.

Lilac's entire face went crimson at his crude reference. She knew when she was up against a stone wall; she crossed her arms close to her chest and stared moodily out at the passing trees. In a silent huff, she simmered.

So, they circled the park.

Afternoon turned into early evening. Early evening gave way to nightfall. The moon came up. Stars dotted the sky. Round and round they went.

Still the Prince slept.

Cozy as a kitten, he wrapped his arms around her waist, contentedly holding her close while his sultry face snuggled into her throat.

She wouldn't have been surprised if the beast purred.

* * *

Agatha Whumples sat in her favorite chair in the parlor, trying to read a book on one of her favorite subjects: the mysterious effluvia. It was a secret hobby of hers; Agatha Whumples had a passion for the unknown.

However, tonight she could not concentrate on the fascinating text of Dr. Lopidori. She looked one more time at the ormolu clock on the mantelpiece. It was past ten in the evening! She was more than worried. The Prince should have brought Lilac home hours ago. This was a potentially scandalous situation. Where were they?

Just as that last worried thought passed through her mind, she heard the front door bang open and slam shut, followed by the angry tap of ladies' half boots marching in a huff towards the foyer stairs. A second bang of the door quickly followed with the decisive, swift step of a man's Hessian boots.

"Lilac, wait!"

That was the Prince's voice. And highly agitated, too. Agatha rose from her chair to see what was afoot.

"I do not want to *speak* to you; I do not want to *hear* you; and I do not want to *see* you ever again!"

Agatha's cap-covered head peeked around the doorway. Lilac was balanced halfway up the stairs, glaring angrily down at the Prince. The Prince placed one booted foot on the steps.

Lilac glowered at him. "Don't you dare."

Agatha noted that the Prince stopped but at the same time left his foot exactly where it was. A good, strong character; she approved of that in a man.

Rejar studied Lilac reflectively. He was somewhat embarrassed; Familiars did not tend to fall into a dead sleep in the presence of females they wished to consort

132

with. It was not considered a romantic plus. He knew he must make every attempt to appease her. "Lilac, I do apologize for this. I have never before—"

There was no sense in trying to explain *that* part.

He gazed up at her beseechingly. "I did not know Jackie would listen to me so . . . exactly."

His change of subject did not escape her. Just how many times would he find himself in similar intimate situations with women? Zillions, by the look of him. She was incensed! "Do you have any idea how many times we circled that wretched park?" She stamped her foot to emphasize his faux pas.

Rejar took a deep breath. "I can imagine."

"It was awful! That—that man you call a servant, he—he ignored me!"

"I am sorr—"

"Just refused to listen to me!" Lilac was venting spleen now—six hours of it.

"I know how—"

"And you"—she pointed the finger of outrage at him—"you, cozy as a kitten, not caring one fig how I felt about it!"

Cozy as a kitten? Rejar smiled to himself. Well, he was at that. "Please." he held out his hand to her, giving her his most winning expression. "Forgive me?"

To her dismay, Lilac discovered she was not immune to his beguiling entreaty. Which made her all the angrier. The scapegrace. Well, he could have his own medicine back! She smiled sweetly at him.

Rejar smiled back, his other foot coming onto the second step.

Before he could take another step, she dropped the fake smile. "I don't think I shall." She showed him her back and flounced up the stairs.

Rejar stood there, dazed at the sudden about-face.

Stunned, he watched her strut up the stairs, dismissing him completely.

Women never did that to him.

Who did she think she was dealing with? He was a son of Krue! How dare she treat him in such a cavalier fashion! If she thought—

"Your Highness, might I have a word with you?"

Irritated, Rejar spun around to gaze down at Lady Whumples. The elderly matron stood firmly planted in the hallway below, reminding him of several grumpy Guild members he had faced in the past. A stern expression crossed her weathered features and although she had phrased it as a question, its tenor was command. *What now?*

When the old woman saw she had gained his full attention, she pivoted about, marching directly into the parlor.

He had no choice but to follow her; as his elder she was deserving of his respect. She stopped in front of the fireplace and faced him.

"Close those doors behind you, young man."

Rejar did as she bid, sliding the doors shut with a snap of his wrist.

"Now you will tell me what you have been doing with my niece till this ungodly hour!"

Rejar watched her before he spoke, not entirely sure what she meant by her inquiry. "Doing? I told you my intentions earlier, Lady Whumples; I took Lilac for a ride in your Hyde Park."

"Come, come, my boy, no one rides in the park at this hour. What were you about?" The old woman suddenly picked up a folded fan from the side table, wielding it like a small weapon.

Speechless, Rejar could only stand there and watch as she rapped him smartly on the shoulder.

"Tell me, I say!"

Rejar gaped at her.

He had no idea what she was seeking. Had he done something to offend their customs? "It was as I say— I took her to the park."

"Then why are you returned so late? Was there a problem with the coach? Why was my niece so upset?"

A dull flush of bronze highlighted his cheekbones. "I fell asleep," he admitted, reluctantly. If his brother ever found out about this, there would be no end to the teasing.

It was Lady Agatha's turn to gape. "You—you *fell asleep?*"

A muscle ticked along his strong jaw. "Yes," he gritted out.

Agatha hid her grin behind the fan.

"It was . . . an unfortunate occurrence which I am at a loss to explain."

"Perhaps my niece bores you, your Highness?" she shrewdly prodded.

Rejar emphatically shook his head. "On the contrary, she captivates me."

Excellent, Agatha thought. All she had to do now was find a way to keep it going. "You realize Lilac is very put out with you."

"I believe so." Rejar exhaled, purposely putting a forlorn expression on his face. He did not know why, but he sensed the old woman might be willing to aid him in the hunt.

"Show some spirit, boy!" She whacked him with the fan again. "Are you prepared to give up?"

Rejar looked down at her, his white teeth glinting in a steady smile.

"I didn't think so. You have your work cut out for

135

you; presently, she won't be very accommodating toward you."

"I can overcome such feelings." His bold statement held all of the cockiness years of successful dealings with women had brought to him.

In the past, Lilac had proven most resistant to any unfortunate young blood who came to call. The Prince's positive attitude gave Agatha cause to examine him more closely through her pince-nez. *Demme, but the buck was an out and outer.*

"I do believe you can, your Highness." She met his eyes. "My niece has often expressed a desire to view Week's Mechanical Museum in Haymarket. I think tomorrow would be a good day for such an outing for the two of us. If you should happen to be there the same time—say, two o'clock—well, t'would be fate, wouldn't it?"

Rejar grinned; she was going to help him. "It would indeed, madam."

Lady Agatha grinned back.

Neither suspected that when it came to Lilac Devere they each had very different things in mind.

He returned to her room within the hour.

Lilac was already in her night garment, sitting on the edge of her bed staring out into space.

She is probably thinking of new ways to torment me, he acknowledged ruefully.

He jumped onto the bed beside her.

"Rejar! Have you come to comfort me? What a good cat you are!" Lilac petted his head, scratching behind his left ear.

Purring, Rejar stretched towards her, rubbing his face along her jawline in a sweet feline caress.

Won over, she kissed the top of his head. "I won't

think about him anymore." She spoke to the cat as if he knew exactly what was on her mind.

Which he did.

"Come to bed now." Lilac scooted under the covers.

Rejar padded over to her, lying against her exactly the way she liked. Lilac snuggled her face into the soft fur and instantly fell asleep.

If sometime during the night she had a crazy dream that it wasn't fur she rested against but the naked skin of a male chest, she was able to dismiss the nonsense from her mind in the clear light of day.

However, the exotic cinnamon-bayberry scent, which seemed to be all over her person, truly puzzled her.

Chapter Seven

The skin on the back of her neck prickled.

No, it must be her imagination. They had just walked into Week's Mechanical Museum, an outing Lilac had been looking forward to for some time.

It was quite crowded that day. Several of the ton had apparently had the same idea as her aunt. There was one exhibit in particular which—

There it was again . . .

That odd feeling on the back of her neck.

Lilac looked over her right shoulder. Her green eyes momentarily widened, then took on the light of fury. "I don't believe it!" she exclaimed in an angry undertone.

"What is it, my dear?" Auntie said distractedly; she was already peering at the first exhibit through her lorgnette.

"It's that awful Prince—he's here! Of all the rotten luck!"

"Prince Azov is here?" Auntie dropped her lorgnette, whipping around to survey the room. "Why, yes, there he is." Lilac stood helplessly by, watching as her aunt waved her fan in the Prince's direction. "Prince Azov, over here!"

"Why did you do that?" Lilac hissed.

"Don't be foolish, my dear; he is a friend of ours."

"Since *when*?" Auntie wasn't listening to her, she was too busy attracting the Prince's attention. Blast it!

"Lady Agatha, Lilac." Rejar cordially greeted the two women; one looked supremely happy to see him, while the other looked supremely furious. Purposely, he let his eyes gleam with the flash of victory simply to annoy Lilac. A roguish smile spread across his face when she promptly turned her back on him. He so loved to play with her.

"Why, Prince Azov, what a nice coincidence." Agatha winked conspiratorially at him. "Do join us as we tour the museum."

Dismayed, Lilac spun back around. "Auntie!"

"Thank you, Lady Agatha." Rejar watched Lilac from under heavily lashed eyes; it appeared his blue-and-gold regard was unnerving her. "I believe I shall do just that."

"Excellent! We've just begun." Agatha pointed out the first exhibit. "Now this, I believe, is a reenactment of the Battle of Alexandria."

Rejar knew a museum was a house of artifacts. The concept did not greatly excite him. He meant to briefly glance at the scene, then turn his full attention onto Lilac, but what he saw made him look twice.

Tiny metal soldiers were moving about a small battlefield!

This was sorcery!

He quickly looked around, viewing the room for the

possible culprit. No one appeared suspicious. He examined the walls—nothing there except some old metal swords and a few banners. Where was the source? Surely, this was the mark of a powerful wizard! Instinctively, he edged closer to the two women to protect them.

"Why do they move?" On guard, he spoke in a low voice behind Lady Agatha. "Are they spellbound?"

Agatha tittered. "How amusing, your Highness. One would almost think so, they look so lifelike."

Rejar was captivated by the scene before him; he curiously watched as the tiny warriors marched about the mock battlefield. The universe he came from was based on the Laws of Magic, but the mechanical men completely mystified him. "I do not understand this," he murmured abstractedly.

"Quelle surprise." Lilac dripped sarcasm.

At her condescending tone, Rejar shifted his sights from the strange exhibit to return her contemptuous look with one that plainly said, *I am not amused.*

I'm trembling, her answering look said. She batted her eyelashes at him, pasting a superior little smile on her face.

He quirked his eyebrow, this expression saying, *I will be tolerant for now, but there will come a time . . .*

So, the tone was set for the rest of the tour.

Agatha was delighted; Rejar was baffled by the moving figures, patiently tolerant of Lilac's mood, and Lilac was suffering the Prince's presence, but not in silence. She made it a point to toss verbal insults his Highness's way whenever the opportunity presented itself. This occurred often, since, as far as she was concerned, the Prince made a wonderful fool.

In fact, Lilac was having such a good time making

mincemeat out of the Prince, she almost didn't mind his company.

Almost.

The only thing that worried her the teensiest bit was that every time she lambasted him with one of her jibes, he gave her *the smile.*

The one that said, *You may play all you like but I will win the game.*

The one that said, *We shall see.*

She absolutely hated that smile.

"Prince Azov, I was just thinking of you! What a co-incidence!" The three of them turned at the wispy sound of a woman's voice directly behind them. By her gasps for breath, it sounded as if she had run a race to catch up with them.

Rejar stared down into the covetous face of Lady Harcorte and felt annoyance begin to overshadow his pleasant mood. This was a complication he did not need. "Lady Harcorte," he cooly replied.

"Here to see our famous museum? And with our lovely Lilac Devere." Leona Harcorte gave Lilac a brilliant smile, completely winning the younger woman over. Agatha, being older and wiser in the ways of the world, stuck her Whumples nose in the air and sniffed haughtily.

"Agatha." Leona purposely used the grand dame's first name to irritate her. "You do look marvelous to-day—for your age."

Agatha, never one to be outdone, immediately retorted, "I was just thinking the same of you, Leona."

Only the slight blink of Lady Harcorte's right eye let Agatha know she had hit her mark. It was well known that the Cyprian was impossibly vain and consumed with the fear of loosing her looks. Although, Agatha grudgingly admitted to herself, the woman had no real concerns in that area—she was truly a beauty. A *hungry* beauty.

Agatha shrewdly edged herself between Rejar and Leona, placing a proprietary hand on the Prince's arm. "Come, your Highness, let us view this exhibit." She wisely left Lilac and Lady Harcorte to follow.

Leona resigned herself to enjoying the view. She eyed Rejar's backside appreciatively. "He is really the most stunning man." Lady Harcorte spoke to Lilac as if they were the best of friends sharing confidences.

Lilac had no idea what Lady Harcorte found so interesting. She raised an eyebrow, carefully examining what Leona appeared to be examining. Mmm. It was rather nicely shaped. She cocked her head to one side—firm-looking yet round and tight. "You really think so?"

"Oh, yes. Let me give you a clue, my darling; the more he reveals, the better he gets."

The meaning behind Lady Harcorte's scandalous words registered abruptly. Lilac's face flamed. "You don't mean—"

"Of course I do. He's quite gorgeous in a bathtub, nearly took my breath away. We met at Byron's country estate; need I say more?"

So, he was a libertine and a rogue as well as a mutton head. Did she doubt it for a minute? It was obvious to her that Lady Harcorte knew the Prince intimately. Very intimately.

Not that she cared. She didn't care one whit. Not at all.

Rejar choose that ill-fated moment to speak to her. "Lilac, look at this," he gestured to the exhibit of tweeting mechanical birds, smiling boyishly.

Just look at that innocent face! At once, he represented to her everything duplicitous she found vile within the ton. Oh, how she detested him! "Go to the devil, you scapegrace!"

Rejar's mouth dropped. What had brought this on? He glanced over at Lady Harcorte who was smiling like . . . well, like a cat. It was a smile he understood very well. He took Lilac's arm, drawing her aside.

"What did she say to you?"

"Let go of me!" Lilac tried to squirm out of his hold.

Rejar had no intention of letting her go. "Tell me." He speared her with a very serious look.

"She just told me the truth, so you needn't be surprised. I certainly wasn't! I know you for the scoundrel that you are! What I don't understand is why you persist in annoying me; I have already told you I am not interested in your pursuit." She stuck her stubborn chin in the air.

Rejar raked a hand through his hair. Somehow—he wasn't quite sure exactly how—he was snarling up with her again. "Whatever she told you, Lilac, it was not the truth."

"You didn't meet with her at Lord Byron's country estate? In your bath?" Caught, Rejar opened his mouth to explain but she cut him off. "I thought so! You look as guilty as sin. In fact," she said, eyeing him insultingly up and down, "you look like sin."

"This is foolish! I tell you, there was nothing!" As if he had to explain to her what he did! Or didn't do. The thought of it alone was enough to trigger his annoyance. Not to mention his restlessness. "And why do you show such an interest?" he shot back. "If you are not, as you say, interested in my pursuit?"

His smug expression really aggravated her. "Oooh, I detest you!"

Standing tall above her, his heated gaze focused on

her delectable mouth. "That is unfortunate, *souk-souk,* since I intend to have you."

Under his burning regard, her lips parted; she was suddenly quite breathless. "Wh-what do you mean by that?"

His flashing dual-colored eyes silently spoke volumes to her: *Exactly what you think.*

Lilac blanched. Placing a hand on her heart—which had suddenly begun beating erratically—she said in a reedy voice, "Never."

That slow, feral smile inched its way across his utterly sensual features. "Soon," he promised.

Their gazes locked and held.

Lilac swallowed; the rogue meant it! She could see it in the determined thrust of his jaw, the set expression on his face. What had she ever done to get this man so—so excited over her?

She couldn't think of a single thing. It had to be an aberration on his part. Lilac was about to try to get through to him one more time when feminine screams from the next exhibit interrupted her line of thought.

What foolish thing was causing this ruckus?

Lilac poked her head around Lady Harcorte's elaborate hairdo to get a better view. It was the large mechanical spider!

She smiled broadly. This was the exhibit she had so wanted to see; she had heard it was very lifelike and that the craftsmanship was extraordin—*What was that sapskull doing now?*

Rejar, alerted by the feminine cries of fear, chivalrously placed himself in front of the ladies and tried to send a mental *flicker-warning* to the multi-legged creature coming towards them.

The creature did not respond to his signal to back off in any way, just continued to advance. It was strange, but he could not sense any life within it. How could that be? Was it a sorcerer's animus? If so, it could prove to be deadly.

He quickly scanned the room looking for something to defend themselves with should the creature continue its aggression.

His sights lit on the old swords tacked to the wall by the battle exhibit. They were crude, but they would have to do. His power to call to all beasts was failing him here; he needed a more conventional protector.

He strode directly over to the wall. With a powerful twist of his arm, he yanked one of the swords free of its mooring. Testing its heft and balance within his grip, he pivoted about. Without thought, he placed himself as shield and protector before Lilac and her aunt. In battle stance, he confronted the multi-legged beast.

For that moment, he became an Aviaran warrior. His father's son.

Expertly, he scalloped the sword about his hand, carefully monitoring the track of the creature. With the lithe grace of movement characteristic of his kind, and the warrior skill honed into him by Krue, Rejar challenged the aggressor with circular, taunting movements of his blade.

His aim was to distract the beast away from the women. If it should prove to be an animus, an instrument of a maligned spell, it could change form at any moment, becoming a towering, deadly menace.

Lilac could not believe her eyes. "What is that long-haired idiot doing?" she hissed to her aunt.

"Hush, dear." Auntie trained her lorgnette on the Prince so as not to miss this thrilling Theatre of the Absurd.

The Prince engaged the spider.

The spider backed off, spun around on its clicking legs three times and advanced once again.

The Prince made a quick lunge with the sword.

The spider jumped back a couple of feet, faltered slightly, but stoutly advanced.

Several of the women spectators were still issuing little shrieks of alarm as befitted ladies faced with such a horror as a mechanical spider; although most of them had paused to watch the dashing Prince wield his blade with such a fluid line. The supple masculine movements distracted even the faintest of hearts from the dire threat of the automated arachnid.

On the other hand, the men, who at first wondered what Prince Azov was up to, were now kicking themselves because they had not thought up the amusing prank themselves. This innovative, dashing act would be talked about and toasted for days throughout the gaming hells and private clubs of the beau monde. Prince Azov was a buck of the first head! They avidly watched his movements.

The Prince made a bold lunge; catching the spider on the tip of his skilled blade, he adroitly flipped it onto its back.

The spider, legs whirring ceaselessly, let out a hideous shriek of grinding gears.

A Hessian boot came stomping down with powerful force. A loud crunching sound was followed by bits and pieces of metal rolling across the floor.

The spider walked no more.

A huge cheer went up from the male members of the viewing audience, eager to get in on the fun. They eagerly surrounded the Prince with huzzahs all around, slapping him on the back.

Lilac watched the scene in total disbelief. *The mutton head!* Did no one, save her, see that he was not acting a charade? The birdbrain actually thought he was in a duel with a windup toy! She scanned the adoring crowd in disgust, her sights meeting her aunt's.

Lady Agatha knew.

The sharp look she returned to her niece was proof of it. Lilac raised her eyebrow in a mocking gesture meant to tell her aunt she had been right about the man all along.

Agatha shook her head slightly, her steel grey eyes piercing into her niece's. "You're wrong, you know. 'T'was a very gallant thing to do. This I tell you, Lilac—were it a small menace or a fifty-foot beast, he would have acted the same. He is a courageous man; one who would willingly give his life to protect those he cared for."

Lilac disagreed. "Nonsense! He is a buffoon."

"No." Agatha slowly lowered her viewing glass. "Every time we have met, I have watched his demeanor very closely. He is not like these shallow-pated bucks of the ton—disrespectful, empty, stiff collars hiding behind their dandy ways. His outward appearance cloaks a man of substance. Mark my words."

Lilac regarded the Prince consideringly. Her aunt was a very astute judge of character; it was the main reason she had never wed—she had refused to compromise on character. *Had* she been wrong about him?

Unfortunately, at that precise moment, Rejar threw back his head, laughing at something Lady Harcorte had whispered in his ear. Lilac's brows lowered. In this case, Auntie Whumples had judged wrongly. She stood by her initial impression: There was a lamp burning in the belfry but no one was home. The frosting was sweet but the cake beneath had no flavor.

A great wail of dismay interrupted her ruminations. Apparently Mr. Weeks had just discovered the fate of his beloved spider. In a rare display of pique, he tossed everyone out of his museum and slammed the doors shut, presumably to weep over the destruction of his star creation.

Lilac was just happy to be released so expeditiously from the Prince's company.

It was a happiness that was to be short-lived.

The following weeks it seemed that no matter where she went, there he was. It was almost as if the man possessed some uncanny ability to predict her movements. How did he do it?

At the Pantheon, he coincidentally had a seat next to them.

At Hatchard's Book Store, he just happened to run into them (although he didn't seem the least interested in purchasing any books).

At soirees and fêtes and routs she attended, he was always there. Demanding a dance. Sitting by her side at supper. Monopolizing her company. His single-minded pursuit became the talk of the ton.

What's more, small gifts started to appear outside her bedroom door each morning. Odd tokens, really; a length of pretty hair ribbon; a set of shiny carved buttons; an intricate lace handkerchief; and once, a choice selection of sweet meats wrapped in a napkin.

When Lilac questioned the servants, no one would admit to doing the Prince's bidding; although she was sure he was behind it.

And if, by chance, she chose to remain at home on a certain day, he miraculously appeared on her doorstep to visit, to have tea, to bring her sweets, to insist she join him for a walk in the gardens, to beseech her to read aloud to him. Basically, to annoy her.

Thankfully, he had not repeated the embarrassingly

forward behavior that he had displayed on their disastrous ride in Hyde Park.

Instead, he seemed merely to observe her as if she were some mysterious puzzle he needed to solve. She could only wonder when he would figure out whatever it was that so perplexed him.

Maybe then he'd leave her the bloody hell alone!

She did not make a very good enigma.

The sooner the man realized it, the sooner he'd be on his way.

Rejar gazed up at the underside of the canopy covering Lilac's bed.

Not that he was really paying attention to the small winged figures of chubby, naked children who, for some unknown reason, cavorted across the bizarre fabric with tiny bows and arrows.

He sat back against the headboard, one arm thrown negligently over a raised knee, hair trailing down his back. There was much on his mind.

The hunt was progressing at the slowest of paces.

This was irksome to say the least.

Over his outstretched arm, he idly gazed at Lilac lying beside him. She was curved into his hip, sleeping comfortably away without a care in the world. He sighed disgustedly.

There was not going to be any relief from that quarter in the near future.

Why was it taking so long?

He had put his best effort forth to entice her into a liaison with him. Lilac was proving to be an extremely difficult quarry. He was frustrated with the hunt, among other things . . .

It had been too long for him.

Familiars did not go this long without their pleasures; at least, he did not think they did. Not having been raised on the Familiar world of M'yan, he could not say he was positive of it, but it seemed to be an accurate assessment. In the times when he had visited his mother's people, he had not noticed anyone there depriving themselves of pleasure for very long.

This was especially true of his older blood relative Gian Ren, who appeared to be most proactive in seeking out his enjoyments. Indeed, one season when he was visiting with Gian, they had spent entire weeks doing nothing but carousing.

It was expected of younger male Familiars.

And when you found something especially enticing, it was good to play with it awhile. Every Familiar knew this.

His sights shifted to Lilac again. He had played here a long time, yet there seemed to be no prize forthcoming.

He exhaled noisily.

The idea that he might give up on his quest with Miss Devere did not even enter into his Familiar mind. What he did ponder was why he wasn't pursuing other women in the interim.

He drummed his fingers on the bed cover.

There had been plenty of likely candidates these past weeks; women who had made it quite plain to him that they would welcome his sexual advances. Yet, he had done nothing. Or more to the point, his body had done nothing. The uncomfortable thought caused him to impatiently toss his hair back over his shoulder.

Perhaps the reason he did not was that he could not.

It was a horrifying theory. Was there something physically wrong with him? Trying to overcome his apprehension, he gazed down at himself.

It *looked* normal, but who could tell?

Many strange things had happened to him since he had come to this wretched world.

There was only one way to be sure.

He nodded to himself, convinced he was on the right course. Difficult though it may be, he would have to test his theory out. The dual-colored eyes strayed speculatively to Lilac.

He had promised himself he would not do this again, but this was a dire situation. By *Aiyah*, he was grateful she had broken off from his kiss before he had entered her mouth! If she had not, he would not be able to attempt this now. Then where would he be?

How could he pleasure women if he was useless? And what good was a Familiar who could not pleasure women! It would be a most terrible thing. So terrible that even Lilac might approve of his decision if she could understand the great service she was about to render . . .

In the span of five minutes, the Familiar had not only made a case for a little seduction but managed to altruistically rationalize it as well. If his brother Lorgin had been there to witness it, he would have laughed his head off.

Before he could talk himself out of it, or, more accurately, see reason, Rejar quickly woke Lilac up with a nudge to her backside with his naked hip. As soon as her eyes opened, he entranced her.

"Your Highness," she said sleepily, yawning, "what are you doing in my bed?" In her present state it seemed like a perfectly normal question.

Rejar brushed his mouth against her creamy cheek. "At least call me Nickolai, *souk-souk*."

"Mmm . . ." Responding to his caress, Lilac nuzzled against his face, breathing in the accustomed cinnamon-bayberry scent. In her sleepy entranced state, he was as warm and snuggily as her favorite old quilt.

"You feel so nice, Nickolai . . ." She cuddled against him, slumberously wrapping her arms about his neck.

It was a well-known fact that Familiars were excellent sleep-mates—being affectionate, cozy companions.

But he did not want her cozy just yet.

He removed her arms from around his neck. "Not now, Lilac."

Gathering both her wrists in one hand, he rolled partly over her. "I must conduct a test. It is a very serious thing, so you must be willing to help me." His heated sights fastened on her full lips. "Will you?" he whispered.

Lilac stared up at him, captivated by his molten look. "Yes," she breathed, secure in the knowledge this was only a dream. "I believe I shall."

Rejar released the breath he held.

Lilac wondered at his tenseness. Then, as if he could not help himself, the Prince dropped his head and skimmed her mouth with his own. His loving action caused his hair to slide forward; the long strands teased at her breasts. Lilac decided she liked the feel of it sliding against her; she enthusiastically waited to see what would follow.

She did not have to wait long.

With his free hand, Rejar began to undo the front ties of her nightrail, his dexterous fingers making fast work of the task. When he was done, Lilac was uncovered to her waist.

Rejar wholly examined the milky white skin, the beautiful full breasts with their small pink tips, the graceful curve of her waist.

A tremor raced through him. It was a good sign.

Before he had the chance to think about what he was

actually doing, he grabbed a fistful of the material gapping at her waist. With one powerful tug the material split down the center, revealing her fully to his gaze.

She was exquisite. Even more beautiful than he had imagined.

A second tremor raced through him.

His lips found the tender plane of her stomach first. There, he lingered in reverent acknowledgement, rubbing his face against the smooth, silky skin.

The gentle touch of the Prince's mouth upon her flesh made Lilac flinch. It was a bit ticklish, she thought, bemused. However, when his Highness began a litany of tiny kisses and started to lick her with fluctuating sweeps of his wet tongue, she relaxed, sighing in delight. Nickolai was making her feel tingly right to her toes. For once she was not irritated with him. She had found something in her dreams that the Prince excelled at. In fact, he was outstanding.

Her enchanted response was exactly what Rejar had been hoping for. This was proving an excellent idea! Not only was he testing himself, he was also inflaming her. Moreover, as far as his own supposed problem was concerned, he need not have worried. *That* fear had been laid to rest almost immediately.

There was absolutely nothing wrong with him.

He grinned against her stomach, giving her a little love bite.

Nothing wrong at all.

Rejar continued with his enjoyable meanderings. He was confident now that she was so attuned to him subconsciously, her arousal would carry over into her waking state. And he definitely wanted her to consciously associate him with arousal. So, he teased her navel with a swirl of his tongue. Then, using just the moist tip, he prodded the small indentation delicately.

Lilac was enchanted with the provocative caress. When she lifted her hips slightly to give him better access, she felt the vibration of his low laugh against her skin.

It was working. Rejar nibbled the underside of her plump breast. All she had needed was a little time to adjust to him, he marveled. Lilac made an approving sound in her throat and impatiently rubbed the plane of her torso against his face.

Perhaps it was working too well.

He could only continue to inflame her so long as he could control the situation. It was important she understand this. Rejar stopped his love play to look up at her with narrowed eyes.

"You will *not* touch my hair, *souk-souk*," he warned her sternly.

"If you say so, Nickolai." She all but panted her response.

Satisfied she understood his direct decree, he nodded curtly to her before resuming.

He pressed his lips against the curve of her upper thigh, following a path to the inside; here he hesitated briefly, noting the small, kitten-shaped birthmark. His lips curved upward at the delightful surprise.

He could not help but cover it with his lips, taste it with his mouth, love it with his tongue.

His free hand glided seductively up her leg, over her rounded hip, and aside, to softly stroke the small of her back. The sensitive spot responded well to his expert touch; she tried to bring herself closer to him.

Consumed with the taste, touch, feel, and scent of her, Rejar, poised at a very enticing crossroads, took a chance and very slightly opened his special sensual senses to her. It was something he had avoided with her in the past for obvious reasons.

Ah, but she was so sweet!

She was like the rarest of treats, like spun crystal!

She was . . . *untouched.*

Rejar froze.

It could not be! Yet, it had to be—Familiar senses did not deceive. She had never been touched by the hand of another man! Never been kissed or stroked or petted or . . .

He shook his head to clear it. She was an adult woman—who had ever heard of such a thing? He remembered his facetious jest many weeks ago concerning women on this planet not engaging in sexual play, and he wondered if he had somehow jinxed himself.

What was he to do now? He released her hands from his hold.

Beads of perspiration dotted his upper lip. There was more.

Much more.

When he had opened his sensual senses to her for the first time, he had also discovered something else. Something totally unexpected.

She was his.

There was no denying it. What he had been blind to these many weeks became crystal clear. She was his mate.

How could he have not known? Familiars sense their mates, always. It was a hidden ability inherent in their kind. Still, he had never suspected . . .

It must have been his trip through the Tunnels. Somehow his mating senses were affected.

Or, did the Tunnels bring him to her? Totally ignorant in the mystic ways, he suddenly missed the advice of Yaniff, whose wise counsel he could definitely use. Odd, but he suddenly realized how much he had always relied on the old man in the past; he remembered clearly how the old wizard was always there for him.

Now, however, Yaniff was not here and he had a big problem to solve.

Untouched! It explained much of her behavior toward him. But, what was he to do with an untouched woman? Him, a Familiar! It was ludicrous.

Wait a moment.

There might be something special here, something he had initially overlooked in his horror of the situation. While it was true she was inexperienced, it was also true she had not yet developed a taste for likes or dislikes.

Hmm . . . This could be interesting.

He could *teach* her about the sensual journey; show her what pleased him and, in turn, pleased her. She would have no preconceived notions coloring her willingness to experiment with him. He could awaken her fully. *To everything.*

The concept stimulated him.

And when it sunk in that no man had ever been intimate with her, that he would be the only one to claim her, he became downright passionate over the idea.

While Rejar was having his amazing revelation, Lilac was wondering why the Nickolai of her dream had stopped dispensing pleasure. Still in the throes of the raging desire he had aroused in her, she sunk her hands into the luxuriant strands of his hair.

Rejar almost choked on his own breath. "Lilac . . . stop!"

Emboldened by the very nature of the dream she was having, Lilac flatly refused. "No. This is my dream; I will do as *I* please—not the other way around." Purposely, she massaged his scalp, stroking through his silky mane with a ruinous intent.

156

Rejar was caught completely off-guard by her rebelliously amorous behavior, so at odds with her past demeanor. On the one hand, he was proud that he had been able to move her so; on the other hand, he was rapidly loosing his control. He was already lying naked between her thighs.

She was entwining his Familiar senses, which were now completely vulnerable to her. Soon he was incapable of distinguishing their separate scents, breaths, textures. Her scent mingled with his, became their scent; her taste the only woman's taste he could remember; her feel, a texture so unique, it belonged to him alone.

From henceforth he could conceive of no other.

He was hers.

But not this way. "You *must* stop." He closed his eyes to draw strength of purpose. It was difficult; he was throbbing against her and could not believe the hint he was getting of the feel of her.

There was a danger of him turning feral.

He captured her hands again, holding them down by her sides. Unexpectedly, she wiggled beneath him, causing him to loose his balance. He fell on top of her. Lilac quickly turned her head and captured his earlobe with her small teeth.

Now, she was truly making him shiver. He moaned out loud. "Li-*lac* . . ."

Her maneuver appeared to be successful; Nickolai was trembling against her. She darted her tongue in his ear in a teasing, sliding motion.

Rejar gritted his teeth. This must end—*now*. "*Stop it*," he bit out, clamping her wrists. "Stop this now, Lilac, or we will both be sorry."

The tone of his voice frightened her. She went still beneath him.

Rejar drew in great gusts of air in an attempt to still his pulsating body. It was not working. There was only one thing left for him to do.

"Close your eyes, *souk-souk*."

Lilac looked up into his face, so near to her own. "Why?" She, too, was gasping for breath.

"Do as I ask." He groaned in agony, "I beg you."

Lilac immediately shut her eyes. "For how long, Nickolai?"

"For a few of your minutes . . ." His voice was already trailing off.

There was a flash of light and the dream was no more.

Lilac found herself awake, in the middle of the bed. Her night rail was split in half and hanging from her in tatters. Scared by the strange, terrifyingly real dream, hurting from unfulfilled desires she did not understand, she burst into tears.

Soon the bed dipped and she felt whiskers nudge her face, consolingly.

"Oh, Rejar!" Wrapping her arms around the sweet cat, she cried herself out for the next half hour. His steady, gentle purring finally lulled her back to sleep.

The knowledge had been revealed to him.

Like a Guardian of Old, Rejar stood close by her side throughout the night. It was part mystical, part superstition. It was a rite of passage and it was obligation. It was duty and it was desire. It was always a sacred trust. Sometimes, it was destiny.

His father's people called it *Chi'in t'se Leau*.

Chapter Eight

That very afternoon, Rejar stood before Agatha Whumples in the grand dame's study. He had chosen his time well, carefully coming to call when he knew Lilac was not at home.

Earlier in the day he had sought Jackie out. He had questions he wanted answers to. Questions as to why Lilac would still be untouched at her age and what the proper procedure was in this society to make her his.

Jackie had been most informative before his language became most colorful. There had been a lot of suggestive winking and elbowing into his side from the odd man. It seemed some gestures transcended the language barrier. He chuckled to himself—one could say some male gestures were universal.

But he got the information he needed.

Rejar intended to "marry" Lilac Devere.

And not just by the customs here. He intended to take her as his *real* mate. In order to accomplish this,

159

he must first follow the dictates within her own society—just for show, of course. The true ceremony, as far as he was concerned, would follow.

He had some trepidations.

It was highly unusual for a Familiar man to take a mate before his first incarnation. *Never* had a male Familiar mated outside his own kind. There were good reasons for this, but Rejar believed he could overcome the problems inherent in such a match. In any case, he did not have much choice; they belonged to each other.

He would simply have to teach her to adjust to his . . . To adjust.

Appetite, he reasoned, can be a learned behavior. Consequently, she would have an excellent tutor. The very model of patience. Albeit, a perfectionist. If the situation warranted, he could patiently instruct her for hour upon hour. Gian had always told him a male Familiar was not finished until he was good and finished.

He smiled wickedly.

Remembering Jackie's bizarre instructions, he faced Lady Whumples. "Lady Agatha, as Lilac's only living relative and guardian, I ask permission from you to marry your niece."

Lady Whumples's mouth dropped. Obviously, she hadn't been expecting this so soon. It was too soon, in her opinion. Despite her mechanizations, Lilac was barely tolerating the man.

Seeing her hesitation, Rejar pressed his suit. "I realize this is sudden, but I assure you I am sincere. I am a man of means as well as . . . a certain title; you need not fear for her welfare. I intend take care of both of you, if you will let me." This, Rejar spoke from his heart.

Once he mated with Lilac, he would be responsible for the care and protection of the two women; his family. In his universe, it was a responsibility no man, Aviaran or Familiar, took lightly.

"B-but what does Lilac say? I was under the impression she still couldn't tolerate the very air you breathe." Agatha peered at him through her lorgnette. "You will forgive me my bluntness, your Highness, but the chit is rather outspoken."

Like her aunt. Rejar smiled wryly. "Be that as it may; it changes nothing. What say you to this arrangement?"

Impertinent! The man was impertinent. Agatha peered at him through her lorgnette again. And damned handsome . . . Of course, it would be Lilac's decision—she wouldn't take that away from the girl. If the twit refused this magnificent specimen before her it would be her business!

In her personal opinion, such would be the act of a Bedlamite.

She reluctantly dropped her looking glass. "Your Highness, I'm afraid the decision is up to Lilac."

Rejar frowned. This was not what he wanted to hear. Jackie had told him that as Lilac's guardian, ultimately it would be Lady Whumples's decision, which suited him fine. He knew he could win over the aunt; it was Lilac who was going to prove more difficult. That is, until he could show her how loving a Familiar man could be.

Before he could respond, there was a brief commotion in the foyer, followed by the angry swish of skirts and the purposeful stride of pounding shoes. He guessed correctly that Lilac had returned early from her outing and the butler had informed her of his presence in their drawing room. She would be annoyed over his unannounced visit.

Lilac entered the room, all blazing eyes and clenched

fists. Rejar briefly glanced at her, then purposely turned his attention to adjusting the cuff of his jacket. He knew his insolent action would so aggravate her that she would be speechless for a moment. A moment he needed to press his advantage.

He gave Lady Agatha a bland look. "I'm afraid it has gone too far for that."

Lady Whumples sat straight up in her chair. "Whatever do you mean?"

"I have compromised your niece." The absurdity of the statement suddenly struck him. A Familiar compromising a woman! It was difficult for him to contain his laugh, but he managed it.

Lady Whumples did not see anything humorous in the statement; on the contrary, she was aghast. *"What?"*

"What?" Lilac said at the same time. She threw him a furious glare and started walking over to her aunt, who was fanning her face, her shallow breath coming in short gasps.

"I'm afraid I did not hear you correctly, your H-highness," the old lady stuttered, "wh-what did you say?"

Rejar cleared his throat and succinctly repeated in a loud voice, "I said, I have compromised your niece."

"He's lying!" Lilac hissed. She knelt before her aunt. "The despicable rogue is lying! He's made no secret of the fact the he wants to . . . well, you know, Auntie."

Agatha brushed away Lilac's words, turning to the Prince. Her low authoritative voice bellowed throughout the room. "What is the nature of this compromise?"

Rejar's gaze flicked to Lilac's furious expression. "We have been intimate."

Lilac stood, her fists clenching. "Oh, he lies!"

Agatha looked back and forth between the two of

them. Her sharpened gaze rested on Prince Nickolai. She relaxed. He was clever, she'd give the young blood that.

"What am I to do, young man?" Agatha slyly said, stressing certain words so the Prince would get the point. "She denies your statement. Quite vehemently I might add."

Rejar rubbed his jaw in thought, suddenly piercing Lilac with a smug look. "She has a kitten-shaped birthmark on her thigh." His eyes flashed with devilish mischief as he whispered, *"Her inner thigh."*

"I shall faint!" Aunt Agatha began fanning herself vigorously. This was a bit much!

Lilac flushed. *How had he known?*

Sensing that the chase was all but over, Rejar artfully sprung the trap. "Yes, I have quite 'ruined' your niece." As if a woman could be ruined by such a thing. Again he tried not to let the vagaries of this race make him laugh out loud.

He turned to Lilac, blinking slowly, as if something of momentous import had just occurred to him. He recalled a line from a joke Byron had once told him. "And there could be a child to think of, sweetings."

"I shall faint!"

Aunt Agatha had said it, but Lilac did it.

"I shocked her." Rejar took the moistened cloth from Lady Agatha and gently laid it across Lilac's forehead. After she had fainted, he had scooped her up, carefully laying her on the settee. She still had not come to.

"She's not the only one whom you shocked, your Highness. Tell me, was it unwise of me to place my trust in you? Did you debauch my niece?"

The Prince was seated on the edge of the settee, observing Lilac, concern etching his features. He stopped watching her to look past his shoulder at Agatha. Smiling faintly, he shook his head no.

Agatha nodded approvingly; her assessment of him as a man of honor had been correct. "I didn't think so. Now tell me, my boy, how *did* you know about the birthmark?"

Lilac moaned as she regained consciousness. Rejar fixed the cloth on her forehead.

He gave Agatha an intriguing smile. "You would not want me to reveal all of my secrets, would you, Lady Agatha? I believe a woman such as yourself needs a mystery to solve every now and then."

Agatha snorted at the silly statement; but she was chuckling when she said, "Better leave before she wakens to see you here. Best leave it to me to lay down the law to her. After all, what else can I do? She's been compromised!" Grinning, she showed Prince Azov out the door.

Lady Whumples let out a sigh of relief. Lilac would be wed.

Through the years, the girl had always kept her company, but it had been a great fear of Agatha's that, should something happen to her—as it inevitably would, she being an old woman—her niece would have no one to care for or about her. She would be all alone in the world.

In a society which could be extremely cruel to unprotected women, Agatha wanted more for her beloved niece.

Now her fear was laid to rest. By the look of the strapping Prince, Lilac would soon have her own family. If Agatha was any judge of character, Prince Azov would take care of her very well. She had not missed the look of tender concern on his sincere face when Lilac had fainted. The lad was besotted.

It was a better start than most marriages of the ton, she reasoned prosaically before steeling herself for an argument she had no intentions of loosing. Her niece would be wed.

She was engaged.

Lilac wasn't sure how the bounder had managed it, but he had.

There wasn't much she could do about it; her aunt had been adamant. She would brook no refusal. Lilac had ranted and raved, pleaded and begged. Auntie Whumples crossed her arms over her ample chest, flatly declaring that the honor of the family was at stake; the matter was closed.

Well, he may have tricked her into marrying him, but she'd be damned if he was going to get any satisfaction out of it!

She adjusted her leather glove with a short, angry pull. Through happenstance (and several coins passed to a bellman at the Clarendon) she had been able to ascertain the Prince's whereabouts this afternoon.

It had been reported that he was seen with the bow window set at White's Club. Weeks later, Brummell was still delighted with the Prince's lark at the museum and had invited the Prince to join him at his favorite pastime—being on display to the ton at the bow window of White's.

Had the young lady heard of the Prince's amusing prank? asked the kind bellman.

Gritting her teeth, Lilac assured him she had.

Lilac stood on tiptoe and peered through the bow window into the famous establishment. A man his size should be easy to spot. . . . There he was! Right between Brummell and Alvanley.

White's was exclusively a male establishment; there was no way she could go in there and drag him out by his perfectly shaped ear. Lilac knew she would have to wait for him to look her way, then try to lure him out under false pretenses.

She had an itinerary. Not only was she going to tell him exactly what she thought of this farcical marriage of his, she also intended to set him straight on matters of the boudoir! At least, as much as she understood of such things, which admittedly wasn't all that much since she lived with a maiden aunt who *never* broached such subjects.

While Rejar sipped his tea and chuckled over something Brummell said, his thoughts strayed to the love-mark he had discovered this morning during his bath. It was just above his left breastbone; a small darkened spot where Lilac had drawn on him with her mouth.

A little passion gift from Miss Devere.

He smiled with the memory. Women often gave him such marks but this one was special to him. It denoted a sensualistic passage.

Idly, he gazed toward the window, surprised to see the object of his ruminations smiling sweetly at him, gesturing for him to come outside. Excusing himself, he immediately went to her.

Like calling a puppy, Lilac thought.

As soon as he came through the door, she launched into her prepared speech, all pretense of sweetness gone. "I wish to speak to you, your Highness."

Her sudden change of demeanor wasn't lost on him. He viewed her obliquely. "Yes, Lilac?"

"Since it seems I am forced to comply with this farce of a marriage, I insist on a marriage of convenience." There, that was to the point.

Rejar blinked slowly. "A marriage of convenience . . . What, pray tell, is this?"

Lilac blushed; the man was irritatingly obtuse. Surely a man of his proclivities should have a clue. The sapskull. "A marriage of convenience sets aside . . . intimacies."

It took Rejar a full minute to completely comprehend what she was saying—so bizarre was the suggestion. When he did, he threw back his head and laughed; a rich, throaty sound. He grinned wickedly at her. "Do I look like the type of man who will set aside intimacies?"

No, he didn't. Lilac swallowed. Somehow, her prepared speech was not going the way she imagined. Damn the man, anyway! He never did what was expected!

"I—I must insist—"

Rejar narrowed the distance between them.

Lilac froze as his hand came up to casually brush a stray lock of hair from her forehead. As if he already owned her and had every right to do so! His fingers slid lazily across her skin, a smooth, sultry stroke.

Taking his time, he bent forward to lightly graze his chin against her cheek in an action that was almost feline.

Silent, he held her to the position.

His deep, silky voice teased against the folds of her ear. "I will not leave you alone, you know. *Not for a minute.*"

It was several seconds before the true meaning of his words pierced the lulling quality of his gentle actions. When Lilac grasped what he was actually saying, she stepped back from him in horror.

"You're despicable! I will never allow—"

His powerful hands captured her. Clasping her

shoulders, he brought her firmly against him. "Not for a minute, Lilac. I will be at you morning, noon, and night. In fact, I intend for you to forget what it feels like to not be entangled with me."

She paled. "Let go of me!"

He ignored her, pressing his sensuous, velvet lips against her heated forehead. "And what is more, my Lilac, you will love every minute of it. You will crave my touch, my kisses, my . . ." he paused meaningfully. "Well, I think you get the idea."

"You delude yourself! You are arrogant beyond belief, your Highness—why, your conceit knows no bounds!"

"It is not conceit. My kind have no need for false promises."

"Your kind? What—libertines, rakes, and rogues?"

He only grinned the grin that never failed to make her nervous.

"You will find out."

Aviara

Yaniff climbed the rocky pathway that led inexorably upward. For an old wizard such as himself, it was an arduous journey. Wind constantly grabbed at his crimson robes, pulling them this way and that, its sound a low, mournful dirge through the crags and peaks of the Sky Lands of Aviara.

Some journeys were not of one's choosing, he acknowledged philosophically, and not for the first time. Nevertheless . . . He rounded a bend in the path.

There on a promontory, perched on the edge of two worlds—sky and land—sat Traed ta'al Yaniff. His son.

Captured in silhouette, Traed seemed a part of this wild, turbulent land. Yaniff could see a certain symbolism in the way Traed gazed out over the horizon, his booted legs hanging dangerously over the edge of the cliff, his sights inward. Normally tied tightly back, his waist-length hair now flew unrestrained on the keening moan of this Sky Land wind.

The powerful emotions he kept under such tight control found some kind of ally here in these raw, untamed peaks. Even though Traed was not facing him, the old wizard knew his eyes were closed.

Yes, wild and turbulent. The real Tread kept well hidden from others. A man of deep passions.

It said much to Yaniff, who watched silently some distance away. This kind of son let the wind speak to his spirit.

By Aviaran law, Yaniff had claimed Traed to his line just before the disturbing death of his natural father, Theardar, a powerful mystic who had turned renegade. In his madness, Theardar had disowned Traed.

Not only had Traed been the victim of his father's twisted desires and hatred, but Theardar's rash actions had set into motion events which could well affect the lives of generations of his people.

They were headed for busy times.

Yaniff stopped to rest. He leaned heavily on his staff, his thoughts more weighty on him than the difficult journey. Traed would not yet know of his approach.

"Why do you come here, Yaniff?" Traed's sure voice carried to him above the keening.

He sees.

Yaniff had suspected but now he knew. *Traed's power is strong. How long did he think to hide it from me?* From the Guild. Traed's sire had been a sixth-level mystic. There were not many who achieved that level.

Yet, Traed had always believed it was his father's power which had driven Theardar mad.

And power often flowed in lines of descent.

So, too, Traed believed, did madness.

It was a gift that tortured him.

The situation was as complex as the man; Traed denied his heritage as well as his power. He condemned the Guild of Aviara for their actions against his father, actions that in turn had unwittingly punished him.

Yaniff could not totally blame him for his attitude. Though he would not speak it out loud, the old mystic thought Traed had just cause. The boy had suffered greatly at the hands of his cruel father.

The repercussions of the Guild's unthinking actions were coming home to roost. Traed refused to acknowledge their entreaties to take his rightful place within the Charl.

Yaniff sighed. Should the Guild discover the extent of Traed's power, they would force the issue. A power such as this was extremely rare. They would never allow such a gift to lie fallow.

It was a situation that, if left alone, could cause much grief.

Traed was not one to be forced into anything. Better the man make his own discoveries.

"Can I not choose to visit my son without a reason?" Yaniff narrowed the distance between them.

The corners of Traed's mouth lifted very slightly. He knew Yaniff too well. The old wizard never did anything without a reason.

He opened his eyes and stared at Yaniff standing above him. "What would you have of me?" he asked, casting aside pretenses.

Yaniff chuckled, a dry, raspy sound. "I think I am getting too transparent in my old age." He sat next to him on the rocky ledge. "Interesting view."

"You did not make this climb to speak to me of scenery." Traed was direct, if nothing else. His was the blunt honesty of a man who walked alone for most of his life. Under the present circumstances, it was a trait which worried Yaniff.

"No, I did not." Yaniff replied truthfully. It was best to approach Traed directly. "You must go to Rejar."

Traed's pale green gaze shifted to the vista beneath them. "Why?" he asked calmly.

Patience had always been one of Traed's finer points, Yaniff thought. An important quality for a high-level mystic. Especially for a high-level mystic who refused to acknowledge his abilities. "You are *Chi'in t'se Leau* to Rejar."

Traed looked at Yaniff inquiringly.

"There is danger around him. His kind heart will lead him into trouble."

Traed's expertise with the lightblade was well known. He had been called an artist of the blade. But others could make the same claim. "Is there no one else?"

"It must be you," was all Yaniff would say.

Traed did not relish the idea of leaving his mountain retreat. He was not sure he was ready to; as far as he could tell, he had come to terms with nothing. When last he saw Krue there had been shadows in the older man's eyes when he looked upon him—the man who, by right of law, would have been his father had the Guild not interfered. Their ruling, made well before Traed's birth, forbid Krue to acknowledge him as his son of the line.

It pained Traed for he loved Krue greatly.

Hence, for Krue and Krue alone, Traed said, "I will go." For the first time in his life he would wear the cloak of his family's honor. Ironically, the unacknowledged son would protect a favored son. As was his wont, Traed reflected on this aspect dispassionately.

"I expected no less. Guard him and guard him well, Traed. *Nothing* must happen to him. If it comes to it— your life for his."

Traed nodded curtly. For Yaniff to ask such a thing was enough for him to know.

"I hear you, Yaniff, though I do not know if it falls to me, as you say. I will not be the cause of further disruption in the house of Krue—I will consult with Lorgin first."

"Do so. The outcome will be the same."

Traed stepped off the platform into the gardens of Lorgin's home.

It was place of uncommon beauty. The peaceful surroundings filled him with a rare serenity. Sounds of enchantment surrounded him: crystal chimes, *trilli* singing in the trees, a gentle waterfall.

He walked over to the open doorway; there did not seem to be anyone inside. Was anyone here?

Since no one could observe him, Traed closed his eyes, concentrating on his inner vision until he saw a picture of Lorgin seated on a bench. He was behind the main trunk, several levels below by the small pool.

Traed made his way there.

Lorgin, concentrating at the task at hand, did not hear him approach. Traed had never seen him so absorbed. "What is it you are doing?"

At the sound of Traed's voice, Lorgin looked up, a huge smile on his face. "Traed! When did you return from the Sky Lands?"

"I have only just arrived, Lorgin. You need not prepare yourself to rant at me for failing to visit with you."

Lorgin grinned. "Actually, I am glad you have come

back on your own. Now I will not have to drag you out of there."

Traed's raised eyebrow said, *as if you could.*

"I vow, Traed, you choose the most inhospitable regions in which to lose yourself." Lorgin teased him. "First Zarrain, now the Sky Lands . . . Perhaps next time, you can take pity on me and go to a place more amenable. Mayhap an island in the Placid Lagoon?"

Traed snorted. "That is not humorous."

"Come, Traed, if you must torture yourself, at least think of me." He gave him a patent look. "The one who is always sent to retrieve you."

Traed looked up at the canopy of leaves overhead, his green eyes glittering with suppressed amusement. Usually it was Rejar who had this effect on him. When Rejar set his mind on mischief, there were few who could resist his beguilement. One corner of his mouth curved. "I will think on it."

"Ah! Then mayhap I will sleep tonight!"

Traed actually chuckled. "So what are you doing?" He nodded to the small piece of wood in Lorgin's hand. It looked as though Lorgin was carefully mutilating it with the blade of his Cearix.

"It is called a *toy*. Adeeann says the children of her world play with such." Lorgin lopped off a chunk from the bump at the top. "It is for the babe."

Traed stared at the lump of wood. "What is it supposed to be?"

Lorgin proudly held up the piece. "You of all people should know since you lived on Zarrain so long! It is a *prautau*."

"A *prautau*?" He squinted, trying to see a shape in the hacked up mess. "Where is its head?"

"Here." Lorgin pointed to a protrusion bulging out on one side.

Traed was skeptical. "Then where are the feet?"

Lorgin pointed to six misshapen spindles sticking out from the other end.

"*Prautaus* do not have spindly little legs like that! Give it to me." Lorgin gingerly handed over his creation. Traed removed Yaniff's Cearix from his waistband and began to expertly whittle away at the wood. "Why a *prautau*?"

"Let us just say it has a special meaning for Adeeann and me." Lorgin smiled slowly at the fond memory.

Traed paused briefly to look over at him, then resumed carving. "Where is Adeeann?"

"She went with Suleila to the village." Lorgin leaned back against the trunk of the tree, lacing his hands behind his head. "She will be back for the evening meal. You will join us."

It was a Lorgin invitation: one part request, three parts command. Traed nodded.

They sat in silence for a time; Traed working at the carving, Lorgin watching him out of the corner of his eye. Waiting.

Finally Traed spoke. "Yaniff has asked me to go to your brother."

"Then you will go."

"In your stead. I realize you cannot leave your *zira* now when she is so near her time. As your friend, I—"

"No." Lorgin was going to put a stop to that type of thinking immediately. "In *your* stead. You have a responsibility to Rejar as I do to you. You are his brother of the line. If need be, you must stand for him. This is your place, your honor. *You are his brother.*"

Traed exhaled noisily. "Krue does not acknowledge me as such."

"He cannot. But *I* acknowledge you. And so does my

brother. We know who you are. In our minds and hearts, we are your family."

Traed was deeply moved by Lorgin's words. He could not speak.

Lorgin gazed into the pool. "I vow Traed, this request of Yaniff's unsettles me. Rejar is well equipped to defend himself. In some respects, because of his Familiar abilities, he is more able than either you or I. The danger to him might be of the kind one cannot touch. This concerns me."

"I would heed your words, Lorgin. There has always been truth in them."

"Good—then I say you will go."

They both knew Traed could not refuse the sacred trust. He was bound to go. Still, Lorgin had always had the ability to manipulate a situation to his liking.

Traed ran his finger down the edge of his blade, saying softly, "Since when did you get the idea you could order me about?"

Despite the ominous tone, Lorgin caught a glimmer of a smile on Traed's face.

He raised a regal eyebrow. "Since I discovered I am the *elder* brother. Now, let me see what damage you have done to the babe's only toy. . . ."

Chapter Nine

London

She had no intention of "finding out," as Prince Nickolai had so crudely put it.

Lilac gave herself one last cursory glance in her floor-length mirror. It was her wedding day.

The guests were below awaiting the bride's entrance. Leave it to the Prince to get a special license! The banns hadn't even been read. It was rather scary, the speed in which he moved. Once his Highness had made up his mind to be a groom, he was like a stampeding bull.

The analogy made her cringe.

No sense thinking of *that*.

No sense at all—because it wasn't a white lacy veil she stuffed a stray strand of hair back under, but a moth-eaten cap.

Turning to view her backside, she looked over her shoulder at her reflection.

The stablekeeper's son's clothes fit her perfectly. Thank god the jacket was so loose—no one would suspect she was a woman in this getup. Except . . . did her hips look a bit rounded? Come to think of it, she had never seen a boy with such a curvaceous posterior. Lilac bit her lip.

"Oh, miss! I do wish y' would reconsider!" Emmy stood behind her, wringing her hands. "Where will ya go? What will ya do? 'Tis a bad business, I tell ya!"

"Oh, hush, Emmy! I'm just going to disappear for a while." Lilac was hesitant to tell even Emmy where she was going for fear the Prince would worm it out of her. It was only a pure stroke of luck and an unusual visit from Lady Harcorte last week that had saved her.

Seeing Lilac's distress, the kind woman had offered to shelter her for a time. "Until this ghastly mess blows over," she had said. Lilac was extremely grateful. To throw off suspicion, Lilac herself had invited Lady Harcorte to the wedding—much to Auntie's horror.

She was downstairs at this very minute, ready to carry out the ruse of consoling the Prince when he was left standing at the altar. Lilac thought it had been a very clever plan of Lady Harcorte's and commended her on it. Lady Harcorte had smiled, calling her a lovely, naive little girl, who was much too sweet for the Prince.

There wasn't much time left. She threw the sash on the window up and gingerly grabbed for the wide limb of the oak tree outside.

Lilac had never actually climbed a tree before, but how hard could it be? Her cat, Rejar, did it all the time. With one last push, she launched herself out the window.

A strong hand grabbed her ankle.

"Emmy, what are you doing?" she whispered frantically. "Let go!" She tried to tug her foot free from the powerful grip. Instead of being set loose, she was inexorably being drawn back into the room.

There was only one person she knew of who was that strong.

She clutched at the windowsill, refusing to let go. Unfortunately, by this time, she was back in her bedroom in a rather horizontal position, parallel to the floor. "Unhand me at once!" she ordered.

"If you say so," the deep voice drawled. He released his hold on her and she fell in a sprawl to the carpet.

Throwing him a venomous look, she sat up, rubbing her backside.

Rejar knelt down on one knee beside her. He reached up, removing the lopsided cap from her head. Her hair tumbled down in total disarray, strands flying every which way. A smile quirked his sinful lips.

"I like this outfit you wear to your wedding." The dual-colored eyes flashed with more than amusement. Lilac could swear she saw a hint of anger blossoming in the depths of those blue and gold eyes.

She looked away for a moment, worrying her lip. Just what would he do if he got really angry? Would it be better to push him into finally loosing his temper outright with her? He might call off the wedding then. Or, should she . . .

She wasn't going to have the chance to do either, for Prince Azov simply stood up and tossed her over his shoulder.

"Ahhh! Put me down! You crude lout! You barbarian! Do you hear me?"

The entire assemblage heard her.

Lilac screamed and ranted down two flights of stairs, bouncing on the Prince's broad shoulder.

Every head looked up to watch this unprecedented spectacle.

It appeared Miss Devere was to arrive at her wedding with her backside bouncing in the air, wearing a lad's clothing, and shouting like a dockside whore.

The Prince, on the other hand, calm and collected, appeared impeccably groomed in a black cutaway coat, black pantaloons—which, the ladies noted, clung snugly to his muscular limbs—and a white frilled shirt protruding from the deep V of his gold waistcoat. As was his style, the Prince was without his cravat. His gorgeous hair, of course, hung free.

The scene in its entirety was more than the spectators could have hoped for. Invitations for the wedding had been zealously coveted amongst the ton. It appeared his Highness was not going to let them down. *This* wedding would be talked about for ages.

"Don't know why she picked him over me," Lord Creighton sniffed.

Leona Harcorte glanced at the gangly lord out of the corner of her eye. "Incomprehensible," she murmured in a sarcastic undertone that was completely lost on the obnoxious lord. She knew for a fact it had been the Prince who had done the choosing, but she had no intentions of sharing that actuality with anyone. Not that she would need to—anyone with a decent set of ears could plainly hear Miss Devere's viewpoint on the subject.

Everyone except the nitwit next to her.

As Rejar passed by with Lilac howling from his shoulder, Creighton waved his lace-edged hanky in the air, affecting a laissez-faire attitude. *"C'est la vie!"* he shouted merrily at the pair. He thought the gesture combined with the fashionable french verbiage displayed him to great advantage.

Lady Harcorte snorted behind her fan.

When she regained control, she eyed Prince Nicko-lai's broad back with interest. He was hefting the girl about, barely exerting any effort, holding the chit firmly with one well-placed palm. Leona sighed at the sheer beauty of the masculine picture he presented. Ah, well, she reasoned, it shouldn't take long for a man like that to get bored to tears with his provincial little wife. And when he did, she would be there—to rein-state excitement into his poor, passionless existence.

Leona Harcorte would have been mightily depressed if she had a glimpse of what was on Rejar's mind at that moment. Rejar was thinking he *liked* his soon-to-be mate thrashing wildly against him; it signaled to him exactly how passionate Miss Devere was going to prove herself to be.

In just a few short hours, she would be thrashing *under* him. And alongside of him. And on top of him. And in front of him . . .

Rejar displayed a wicked smile.

Flipping her upright, he deposited her before the minister, positioning her to the appropriate place with a guiding clamp of his hands to her shoulders.

She was still reeling from the sudden change of per-spective when he clasped her hand solidly in his own and took his place beside her.

Rejar nodded to the minister, a small, shadow of a man.

The minister swallowed once, then reluctantly began the service. In all his days, he had never seen such a spectacle as this. It didn't appear the lady was quite willing. Perhaps he should . . .

One searing look from the towering foreign Prince with the two different colored eyes and the minister speeded up his recitation of the vows. In fact, he was going so fast, no one could understand him. The guests turned bewildered faces to each other. Whispers of "what did he say?" flew about the room.

Agatha briefly thought of telling the gudgeon to slow down, but remembering her niece's mutinous face, reconsidered. Best this was over with quickly.

When Rejar's low, fluid voice said, "I will," Lilac came to her senses. She threw Prince Azov a fulminating glare of disdain. *Does he really think I'll agree to this?*

Rejar watched her speculatively from under lowered lids. The man who was marrying them had asked Lilac the question Jackie had warned him about—the question which must be answered in a positive manner for the ceremony to be completed. What an annoying requirement! he brooded. The men of his world would never tolerate such a loophole.

Lilac clamped her lips together, remaining stonily silent.

Unperturbed, Rejar's eyes flashed with sudden mischief. Anyone who knew the Familiar usually became instantly wary when he displayed that particular expression. It meant Rejar was up for some sport.

While smiling innocently to the minister, he sent Lilac an offer she could not refuse in the form of a thought.

{Do you wish me to put a stop to this?}

Lilac, who had been staring straight over the minster's head, naturally assumed the Prince had spoken out loud to her. "Yes, I do!" she yelled, stomping her foot in outrage.

"Then by the power vested in me," the minister droned, "I now pronounce you man and wife."

Lilac's mouth dropped. "I wasn't talking to you! I was talking to him!" She nodded in the Prince's direction, but neither man seemed to be paying any attention to her. The minister dutifully told Prince Azov he could kiss his bride. Lilac tried to tug her hand free from his powerful grip.

He turned to her.

She was relieved when he released her hand, but her relief quickly turned to apprehension when his large hands cupped the sides of her head. Strong fingers sifted through her hair to commandingly tilt her face to his.

She expected his kiss of ownership.

What she did not expect was that she would become captivated by the arresting look in his beautiful, compelling eyes.

Those spiky, long lashes . . . His eyes seemed to capture her into their spell until she did not think she could turn away even if he should let her. She stared up at him wordlessly, caught by his intense regard in a spellbinding moment.

All of a sudden, his scent seemed to envelop her, the cinnamon-bayberry scent she had come to associate with him. And that other more exotic hint underlying the overtones. The wild, provocative subtlety that sizzled her blood and heated her skin.

He lowered his face close to her own.

His spicy warm breath drifting across her, he spoke almost against her lips. The words he proclaimed seemed to vibrate with his personal eroticism.

"This Familiar takes you
And discards all others.
This Familiar will give himself only to you
And no other.
This Familiar unites with you now forever
For him there is no other."

His strange, enigmatic eyes dilated. The silken lips parted slightly and descended in a what seemed to her, captured and captivated by him, a ritual of some kind.

Her eyes widened as those softest of male lips pressed lightly against her own.

And took her breath from her.

She could not breathe! Panicked, she clutched his shoulders, not sure whether she meant to throw him off or bring him to her. But he held her immobile beneath him, his mouth to hers. She grew faint in his arms from lack of air; black spots swam dizzily before her eyes. She thought it likely she would die of asphyxiation right then and there.

Then he breathed into her mouth. A warm, surging gush of air. Filling her lungs with life.

And somehow she knew in her deepest heart that this breath he gave back to her was not her own.

Lilac stood in her bedroom staring at the oak tree outside the window with a woebegone expression.

It had seemed such a perfect plan. What had gone wrong? How had he found out? Come to think of it, how did he find out everything about her? Where she was going, what she was doing, who she was with, what *birthmarks* she had. It was uncanny.

The meal had been a nightmare for her.

Byron held court at one end of the table, Brummell at the other. Each tried to outdo the other by spewing forth questionable remarks and obscure references regarding the forthcoming wedding night. Most of their meaning was lost on her, thank goodness, but others at the table found them wickedly amusing, snickering into their cups as they looked knowingly between her and the Prince.

On top of this, that idiotic fop, Creighton, had

snuffled his way through the meal, inappropriate French phrases dropping from his lips like *je ne sais quoi;* while Lady Harcorte barely took her eyes off of Nickolai.

The worst, worst part of it was having to sit next to her hus—*him* the entire evening while he made a great show of being ever so solicitous of her needs. Filling her plate with the choicest morsels. Inquiring if she would like more wine. And when no one was looking, placing his hand on her thigh under the table in blatant ownership, his challenging, laughing eyes meeting hers.

When she finally had been able to excuse herself, she had rushed headlong back to her room only to find that her only refuge had been marred by the sheer, white, lacy nightgown Emmy had left draped across her bed. It waved at her like a white flag on the battlefield of defeat.

Lilac had tossed it out the window and proceeded to don her heaviest night rail. It dragged on the floor and buttoned up to her chin.

Lilac eyed the door to the connecting room warily. She had no intentions of sleeping with the lout even though he had informed her earlier that he had no intentions of sleeping in the connecting room. Uncivilized oaf! Who ever heard of a man and a woman sharing the same room! *The same bed.*

Well, she just wouldn't do it!

He had tricked her! She hadn't figured out how yet, but she would. Her shoulders slumped. Lilac honestly admitted to herself that she had sorely underestimated his capabilities. The man was exceedingly clever. It wasn't sporting of him to hide all that cleverness under that beautiful facade.

His stunning looks had thrown her off; she wouldn't

make the same mistake again. As soon as he showed himself, she intended to toss him out—right on his taut, compact little rump! Lilac slapped her hands together as if the distasteful job was finished. She had worked herself into a fine lather. Just let him try to—

He stood in the connecting doorway.

He was leaning against the frame, arms crossed over his wide chest, idly watching her while she paced the room muttering to herself. A red silken robe and nothing else clung to him.

My word.

Irrationally, she fumed at how good he looked. There wasn't a woman on the entire planet who could deal with that! The thought that he might be wearing the infamous robe written about in the *Morning Post* flickered across her mind before sanity returned. Under the circumstances, an offensive attack was best.

She whirled on him.

"You have what you want now—my property, my things, my house! Get out!"

Rejar viewed her calmly.

"I have no need of your property, your things or your house. But you are right"—his eyes did a slow survey from the top of her head to the tips of her pink toes peeking out from under the voluminous gown—"I have what I want."

His blatant action made her blush to her pink little toes. Lilac threw her arms up in the air. "Why are you doing this?"

Because I cannot look upon another woman without seeing your face; because your scent follows me even into my dreams, because I want you beyond everything in my life. And because, my wife, you belong to me as I belong to you. He only replied, "I told you before—I have my reasons."

As an answer, Lilac deemed it insufficient. A vase came hurtling towards his head.

He didn't even blink.

Pottery crashed against the wall not two feet from his head. Not one muscle in that sculpted physique moved.

This infuriated the woman of logic all the more.

She clenched her fists. "I don't understand you! I don't understand any of this! How did you know all those things about me?" She gritted her teeth to ask the unaskable. "How did you know of the birthmark on my . . . thigh?"

His eyes sparkled devilishly. He blinked twice, those ridiculously long lashes fanning his cheekbones. A dimple curved his left cheek. *"Meow,"* he whispered to her.

Lilac hesitated. Was he mocking her? Making light of her upset? How dare he! Another vase crashed against the wall followed by a screech of outrage.

Downstairs, Emmy raised her eyes to the ceiling. "Cor, what a racket! Is that 'er cat a screechin' like that?" she asked Jackie.

"Naw—'t'is the mistress-ship 'erself."

"Is 'e killin' 'er then?" Emmy worried.

Jackie snickered. "Yes, but a 'little death' ne'er 'urt no one, eh, Emmy?" He elbowed the plump maid in the side.

Emmy smiled knowingly at him. "Listen—it's gone quiet up there now."

A first edition of *Lady of the Lake* sailed by him, landing on the carpet with a dull thud.

Rejar was getting tired of this particular game. It was

time to enlighten her on the facts of life and move on to the next level of play.

"Have you ever wondered why you have never seen your 'precious' cat around me?" He asked in a detached mien. "For that matter, why you have never seen us together? And why do you suppose it is that we both have the same eyes—one of each color?"

Lilac's brow furrowed. What did this have to do with anything? "Not really. I will admit when I first met you I thought it an odd coincidence that you both had similar—"

"Not similar. Identical."

"What are you saying?" she asked sarcastically. "That you knew my every move because you have some kind of strange communion with my cat?"

"No. I am saying, my Lilac, that I *am* your cat."

She laughed hysterically. "Are you ill? I have never heard such a ridiculous tale in my life. Think up a better one, your Highness."

He gave her The Smile.

A chill raced down her spine. If ever there was a man who reminded one of a . . . She paled. "I am a woman of good sense and sound judgement! I cannot credit such a wild story. As I say—try again."

The red silk material pulled taut over the muscles in his crossed arms. His long black hair slid forward to curtain his face as he inclined his head, patiently in wait. "Really?"

Lilac faltered for a moment. The picture he made was of an utterly sensuous man. An utterly untamed man. She tried to regain her composure. "Positively. Next you'll tell me that the dreams—" She stopped abruptly, realizing what she almost revealed to him.

His head snapped up. With a sardonic grin, he abandoned his casual stance by the door and began a deliberate pace towards her. "Those dreams—my sweet, sweet Lilac—were not dreams."

Her mouth parted in surprise. Did he know about the dreams as well? Her face flushed. How? "I don't know what game you're playing, but I do not find it amusing! You may leave." She waved her hand as if to brush the debris out.

He stopped in front of her and pierced her with a steely gaze.

She swallowed convulsively. The Prince could be most intimidating.

Lifting his hand, he insolently ran the tip of his finger down the side of her face. He stopped his motion long enough to rub the pad back and forth over the sensitive spot in front of her ear. Excited nerve endings instantly sizzled to his expert touch.

Somehow, it did not surprise her that he knew this about her as well.

He continued to trace his fingertips lightly along the underside of her jaw to her chin. With a simple upward flick of his thumb, he positioned her mouth to his liking.

"Stop," she whispered nervously.

"I think not," he murmured.

Lilac watched those sensual lips coming near and her breath stopped in her throat. Odd—the small indentation below his slightly full bottom lip fascinated her. It was as if she somehow knew exactly what pleasure that sultry lip could deliver. She stood transfixed like prey caught in the hunter's sight, feeling the heat of him, his warm breath drifting against her mouth. Poised to capture.

He lowered his mouth to hers very, very slowly. He was through waiting.

Instinctually, just a hair's breath from touch, he hesitated. It was the false reprieve of predator to prey that signified the end of the chase.

Then he was there.

Covering her mouth with his own. Filling her with his taste, his scent, his velvet warmth. He was fluid, damp, expert. He enticed while he demanded. He mastered while he claimed.

It was the kiss of a conqueror.

This time he insisted on entrance to her mouth, seizing his right as her bonded mate to take possession of that which belonged to him and him alone. His swift tongue dipped between her lips, shocking her into clutching the lapels of his robe. He stroked inside her. Tasted her. Swallowed her.

The Familiar unleashed her control with one sweep of his gifted tongue.

In this one area, at least, she never stood a chance. He knew it. And now she knew it too.

Lilac closed her eyes tightly. He was going to have her. She could not stop him. With this sure knowledge came fear . . . and something else. She began to shake, from exactly what she could not say.

Rejar sensed her fear—a lot of fear. But under the fear . . .

He spoke low in her ear. "You cannot hide what you feel from me, Lilac; I sense your desire."

A small sound issued from her lips. He stared deeply into her frightened, expectant eyes. Their breaths sounded in the quiet room, a complimentary cadence. The *mating kiss* he had given her earlier was syncopating their life rhythms.

When she inhaled, he exhaled.

When she exhaled, he inhaled.

It was the awakening sound of building passion.

His arm went securely around her waist, bringing

her snug against him. Lowering his head, he began to sip on the skin of her neck and throat, his movements as graceful and sophisticated as an artist's. Rejar entered into the trancelike state which preceded the ancient mating dance of the Familiar. The nearer he came to the spot in the curve of her throat where her neck met her shoulder, the more his blood pulsed. His breathing became deeper, slower. Desire pounded in his veins, thick and hot.

He had never experienced the mating trance before. It was a drugging sensuality, at once enervating and electrifying. Surrendering to his passion, he opened all his senses to her completely, letting her seep inside him. She was a rich viscous honey. Each pore of his being filled with everything that was Lilac; her essence hummed inside of him, vibrating a complimentary pitch to their now synchronous breaths.

It was the most extraordinary experience of his life.

Without conscious thought, he shucked off the robe he wore. It slid to the floor in a puddle at his feet, forgotten. In the same beat, he began to undo the small pearl buttons going down the front of her nightrail.

Lilac closed her eyes tightly, too ashamed to look upon a naked man. In her fear, her hands clutched his powerful shoulders—in some strange way the cause became the anchor. *What terrible thing would he do to her?*

His lips followed the descent of his hand, laving what he revealed between the heavy folds of the material. She felt the heat of his mouth, a line of fire trickling down her belly. The masculine hands at her waist began to inch up the fabric of her gown while his lips and tongue worked their magic on the narrow band of soft skin. Her eyes opened a slit.

The buttons stopped just below her belly button.

Down on one knee now, Nickolai paused to look up at her before leaning forward to press a possessive kiss on the slight swell of her stomach. Then he stood, his hands taking the bunched cloth in his grasp and lifting it over her head.

He tossed the ugly garment into the fire. It would no longer come between them at night.

"My gown!" She could not evade his embrace to save her night rail from the fire. Greedy flames licked at the cloth. In seconds it was consumed by the inferno. She viewed Nickolai out of the corner of her eye, catching a smooth expanse of golden-tan skin. *Consumed as I shall be.* A little whimper escaped her.

Rejar had no way of knowing that a great deal of Lilac's fear was in not knowing exactly what he was going to do with her. She knew it involved some mysterious exchange but no one had ever told her what that exchange was.

His hands came down on her shoulders, turning her in the direction of the expansive floor-length mirror which hung against the wall. Lilac took one look, saw something very large, and shut her eyes. She heard his low chuckle . . . behind her?

Maybe they were just supposed to stare at each other naked in the looking glass. That seemed pretty risqué—a very intimate thing to do. Yes, that must be it. How long would he want to look at her? This was terribly embarrassing. No wonder women dreaded it! This was—

His velvet lips touched her shoulder. The edge of his hand brushed her hair forward to the right side of her throat, exposing the back of her neck.

Strong arms came around her waist from behind, pulling her back against heated skin.

Those same arms crossed in front of her, imprisoning her, each hand cupping a breast to massage and knead and rub. His thumbs flicked her nipples, making them protrude and tighten. It made her feel edgy and wanting.

Muscular male legs stroked sinuously against the back of her legs and derriere.

The erotic things he was doing to her made her shiver. *I think it's not just looking in the mirror.* Lilac began to shake with a combination of fear and desire.

Growling, his heated lips opened on the curve of her neck, wildly drawing on her as his arms tightened about her waist. Lilac's breaths were ragged now, catching in her throat at his almost animalistic action. It was the Nickolai of her dreams! How? How?

"Put your palms against the mirror." His low snarl was an order.

By the sound of him, she did not dare refuse. She braced herself against the glass. A powerful thigh forced its way between her legs. She could feel him against her now, enormous. The broad head of his shaft was at the entrance of her feminine core. He wasn't going to . . . !

She had only a second to panic before he sunk his teeth sharply into the nape of her neck and simultaneously pierced her maidenhead in one powerful thrust.

Lilac screamed.

She kept her eyes squeezed tightly shut as the pain flowed through her in waves, making her aware that he was embedded in her to the hilt. A tear slipped out of the corner of her eye.

Rejar knew he had hurt her. There was no help for it. Her maiden state combined with the position of the ritualistic first *mate-bond* of the Familiar made it in-

Thrill to the most sensual, adventure-filled Historical Romances on the market today...

FROM ⬛ LEISURE BOOKS

As a home subscriber to Leisure Romance Book Club, you'll enjoy the best in today's BRAND-NEW Historical Romance fiction. For over twenty-five years, Leisure Books has brought you the award-winning, high-quality authors you know and love to read. Each Leisure Historical Romance will sweep you away to a world of high adventure...and intimate romance. Discover for yourself all the passion and excitement millions of readers thrill to each and every month.

Save $5.00 Each Time You Buy!

Each month, the Leisure Romance Book Club brings you four brand-new titles from Leisure Books, America's foremost publisher of Historical Romances. EACH PACKAGE WILL SAVE YOU $5.00 FROM THE BOOKSTORE PRICE! And you'll never miss a new title with our convenient home delivery service.

Here's how we do it. Each package will carry a FREE 10-DAY EXAMINATION privilege. At the end of that time, if you decide to keep your books, simply pay the low invoice price of $16.96, no shipping or handling charges added. HOME DELIVERY IS ALWAYS FREE. With today's top Historical Romance novels selling for $5.99 and higher, our price SAVES YOU $5.00 with each shipment.

AND YOUR FIRST FOUR-BOOK SHIPMENT IS TOTALLY FREE!
IT'S A BARGAIN YOU CAN'T BEAT! A Super $21.96 Value!

⬛ LEISURE BOOKS A Division of Dorchester Publishing Co., Inc.

GET YOUR 4 FREE BOOKS
NOW — A $21.96 Value!

Mail the Free Book Certificate Today!

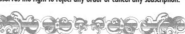

Get Four Books Totally FREE – A $21.96 Value!

PLEASE RUSH
MY FOUR FREE
BOOKS TO ME
RIGHT AWAY!

Leisure Romance Book Club
P.O. Box 6613
Edison, NJ 08818-6613

AFFIX
STAMP
HERE

evitable. He could feel her trembling against him, around him.

He remained motionless inside her, allowing her to adjust to him. The pain would soon be over and the pleasure would begin. His action mirroring his thought, Rejar licked her tear away.

When he felt her ease around him, he spoke low in her ear. "Open your eyes and look at me, my beautiful wife."

Still shaken, Lilac remained as she was, eyes tightly closed.

"I want you to see me when I first move in you," he whispered against her. "I want you to look on me and know that I am inside you. Open your eyes, *souk-souk;* we are joined. Right now—this moment. We are like one being. Look . . ." he coaxed softly.

She opened her eyes slowly. Great luminous green pools gazed up at him through the mirror. Innocent, beautiful eyes that tugged at his heart. Aviaran eyes.

"N-Nickolai . . ." She turned her head to look up at him. There was wonder on her face. Wonder and soon, he hoped, desire.

He bent his head at an angle, sweetly capturing her lush lips. "Watch . . . in the mirror." He moved a fraction of an inch. Her eyes widened. Her lips, still dewy from his kiss, parted in surprise.

He withdrew halfway and slid into her. She gasped. Again.

"My god."

And again.

"*Nickolai.*"

He made a low husky sound against her neck. "Mmmm . . ."

His mouth laved her neck and throat, kissing, licking, as he hugged her close to him and began a steady, vigorous rhythm.

His spicy scent surrounded her, steaming her hot. Little mewing sounds issued from her throat. He acknowledged them by catching her earlobe in his teeth with a quick, tugging motion. Watching him in the mirror, Lilac could not prevent the moan that escaped her lips.

The rhythm he set became a harmonic chant to his pagan saturnalia.

He excited, he touched, he moved, he awakened.

Each thrust came more powerful than the last. She bit her lip to stop herself from screaming out loud. He was a raging storm.

The tempest of his sexual fury called forth her latent passion. Longing flared up from deep within, burst through her and, in turn, him. He fueled their hunger higher and higher with every yearning stroke, then, like his kind, mastered the ferocity he unleashed.

His hands came over hers on the mirror, his strong fingers interlacing with hers. She could feel the sinews of his muscular arms slide along her own, straining and bunching with his erotic movements. The fiery heat of him covered her like a second skin. He thrust and thrust and thrust.

She couldn't catch her breath! Torrid sensations spiraled through her, wave upon wave . . . the pleasure, she would surely die of it!

"I . . . I can't . . . I—" was all she could seem to utter. Her head fell back against his chest. She was near to swooning.

He bit her shoulder.

"Have mercy! Have mercy, Nickolai!" she cried out.

With a final thrust that nearly lifted her off her feet,

he growled savagely into the nape of her neck, "*Rejar.* I am Rejar."

Then everything exploded around her and within her.

Including him.

Chapter Ten

She collapsed into his arms.

Rejar easily scooped her up. Walking over to the bed, he tossed back the covers and carefully laid her down. Lilac's eyes fluttered open. Dazed, her pupils were still dilated with her recent desire. Catching sight of them inflamed him anew.

She watched him silently, her lips gently parted. There was wonder on her face as well as apprehension and shock.

He stood beside the bed, letting his gaze trail a possessive path down the length of her body. He flinched slightly when he spotted the splatters of blood on her thighs.

Embarrassed, Lilac tried to cover herself.

His hand shot out, clasping her wrist. "No."

She turned away too shy to look at him. "I need to wash; let me—"

"Leave it for now." His lids lowered halfway. "The sight of it stimulates me."

Lilac didn't think he needed any more stimulation. She purposely threw him a scathing look to dampen that line of thinking. "Proof of how you hurt me? Does that make you feel good?"

He shook his head. "Proof of how you belong to me alone. Where I come from, it is not a common sight. I apologize for the pain I gave you; although, I must admit, I savored the rarity of the experience."

Lilac blushed red as a beet. She didn't want to think about what he had done to her. Well, it was over with now. She had survived the encounter. It was time to put it behind them and go on about their lives. The Prince had gotten what he wanted. He could go his merry way.

"How nice for you, your Highness. Now, if you'll just—*What do you think you're doing?!*" she yelped. Nickolai had come down full length on top of her.

Rejar chuckled low. "What do you think I am doing?"

"You can't be serious! We already did it! I have no intentions of standing up to lean against that mirror again!"

Rejar threw back his head and let out a roar of laughter.

"I fail to see what you find humorous in the situation. I—*oh!*" He slid into her completely, the moistness from their previous encounter easing his entry. "This way too?" she squeaked.

His deep laugh rumbled against her.

"Every way, *souk-souk*." He nipped her bottom lip.

"No, Nickolai, you mustn't!"

He grinned down at her. "I am afraid I must." He started to move in her, then suddenly stopped when he remembered her untried state. Raising his head, his face was intent on hers. "Does it hurt?"

If Lilac had been thinking more clearly she would've

realized that if she responded in the affirmative, he would have stopped immediately. As it was, her honest nature won out. "Not now . . . it's just that I thought you were done with this"—she wiggled against him—"business." Her squirming movements made him flex deep inside her. A little sigh of enjoyment escaped her lips.

Rejar smiled knowingly. "As long as I am breathing I will never be done with this 'business.'" One black eyebrow lifted. "You will just have to *suffer* through it, *souk-souk.*" So saying, he dropped his head to capture her nipple.

On hearing his prognosis, her lower lip pouted mutinously. "But Nickolai, I don't like you!" She moaned as his white teeth grazed the peak of her breast.

"It is all right, Lilac. You do not have to like me to do this—you just have to *want* me." He pressed in on her and Lilac shivered in response.

Rejar had no way of knowing how his casual words would later come back to haunt him. Distracted by their passion, he proceeded to give her a small taste of what it meant to be the mate of a Familiar.

At close to one in the morning, she began to shyly whisper her encouragement to him.

Around two, she started moaning in ecstasy.

At three o'clock, she was screaming her pleasure.

And by four, she was begging him for it.

Lilac was in a dead sleep.

She lay curled against him, her cheek resting against one side of his chest, her fingers splayed against the other side. Their legs were tangled up and every now and then her little toe twitched against the inside of his ankle as it did now. Rejar kissed the top of her head.

For her sake, he had held back.

Lovemaking was very new to her and he thought it best to introduce her only to the basic essentials this first night.

Even so, it had been a surprisingly satisfying beginning.

The memory of it was enough to get him started all over again, and if Lilac was not so exhausted he might do just that. The palm of his hand unconsciously rubbed her back. A Familiar woman would not be so tired. Then again, a Familiar woman would not be in a maiden state by this age. The one thought led to another . . .

The primary reason Familiar men stayed close to home when it came time to mate was that they believed a non-Familiar woman could not satisfy them over the long term. Rejar disagreed. In his travels, it had been his experience that passion was contagious and tended to rise to its highest form, whatever that form may be. He would simply have to guide Lilac to his own level of physicality.

Already his very existence had set a precedence in the Familiar race, being the first child conceived of Charl and Familiar. Now he was setting a second precedent as the first Familiar male to take a non-Familiar wife. An untouched woman. He smiled. *Perhaps it is my destiny to forge new pathways.*

He chuckled at the incongruous idea. He was a man who cared little about forging pathways; he just liked to enjoy life.

Temporarily sated, Rejar's thoughts drifted pleasantly. He never would have believed introducing a woman to her sensuality could be so erotic. Never would he forget the look in her eyes when he first moved in her; the wonder on her face when she experienced the beginnings of feminine desire; the joy in her eyes when he gave her her first release. These were gifts to him alone and he would carry them with him in his heart forever.

Much of his restlessness was gone.

But not all.

There had been no Transference.

Despite his Familiar blood, he had wondered whether it would occur. Aviaran men had a tendency to spark when they made love. And when they mated, they *really* sparked. The Charl, of course, by their nature, were high sparkers.

Even though he did not outwardly display any of his father's Aviaran characteristics, Krue still insisted on teaching his Familiar son the ways of the Transference when he was but a boy.

Nevertheless, Yaniff had been wrong; there was not the least bit of Charl in him.

The fingers of the hand which held her to him traveled up her back under her hair to lightly stroke the soft skin at the nape of her neck. Still, it had been an unparalleled experience for him.

Unparalleled.

He gave a short purr before he, too, fell asleep.

She was ravaged.

Completely ravaged.

He was like a wild, pagan beast!

After the second time, he just kept going. The third and fourth times blurred together. She didn't want to think about what he had done to her the fifth time.

Images of the way he had looked filtered across her mind: those astonishing eyes of his teasing her, luring her, tempting her—blue and gold flashing with desire, then softening with satisfaction; that sultry, silken mouth—smiling with delight, seducing with a caress, softly sipping as if she were the finest delicacy; his head thrown back—eyes clouded with passion—the cords of his neck straining with the strength of his fire.

Yes, that was him: teasing, tempting, laughing, and igniting. It appeared her new husband was a sensual storm of considerable tenacity.

With every loving stroke, he had worn her down.

With every hot kiss, each slow lick of his tongue, he had reduced her to a moaning, quivering creature as wild as himself.

It was . . . an unexpected bonus.

Perhaps this marriage business wouldn't be quite the horror she had imagined it to be.

Lilac sneaked a peek over her shoulder. Nickolai's face was burrowed into her neck. He was sleeping like a baby. She remembered the last time he had fallen asleep next to her; it was in the carriage during their ride through Hyde Park.

It seemed the Prince had a penchant for sticking his nose in her neck.

She giggled as he gave a little lap to the soft skin under her ear.

He had done it three times already in his sleep during the night. She had noticed that at those times when he seemed particularly comfortable, nestled cozily into her, and she had decided to change her position, he gave her a small lick in his sleep to quiet her movements down. It was really rather sweet.

Odd, but it seemed to work for his benefit—it *did* calm her.

"Does that little laugh mean that I have pleased you, *souk-souk?*" he purred sleepily, snuggling against her.

"Nickolai." She placed her hands over the strong arms which were encircling her, watching him over her shoulder.

"Yes, you have pleased me." Realizing what she had said, she quickly faked a yawn in case he was thinking of getting frisky again. It wouldn't do to give in too easily. Not that she hadn't already demeaned herself the previous night by downright begging for him.

"I am glad." He kissed her shoulder. "Now you can please me by calling me by my true name—*Rejar*."

Lilac stiffened. "Please don't tease me, Nickolai. I thought we could begin anew this morning since we probably have to spend the rest of our lives together." The irritating thought did not put her in the best of moods. She still wasn't quite able to figure out how he had maneuvered the situation.

"I am not teasing you, my heart." His cheek caressed her own. "Did you not understand what I was telling you last night?"

Lilac turned in his embrace to face him. "That nonsense about you being . . ." She couldn't even say it, it was so foolish.

Rejar frowned. "It is not nonsense—it is the truth. The cat and I are one and the same!"

He seemed to believe what he was saying.

Oh, dear. This was worse than she thought. The man was delusional. If anyone should hear him speak this way, they would take him to Bedlam! Just the stories she had heard of the horrible place made her shudder. Even though he wasn't her favorite person, the thought of him there—suffering who knows what kind of torture—made her inexplicably ill.

She placed her fingertips gently against his well-shaped lips. "Nickolai, you must never, ever, say this again."

He looked down at her through lazy-lidded eyes. "You do not believe me."

"Of course I don't believe you! What person in their

right mind would believe such a—What are you doing?" He had rolled away from her. Throwing the covers aside, he jumped from the bed.

"Watch," he said, standing before her.

"Really, Nickolai, I wish you would—" *A strange aura seemed to be shimmering around him.* No—*from* him.

Lilac watched in astonishment as arcs of *light* began twirling around and through him, faster and faster, like a dance of sparks, illuminating his entire form in a halo of brilliant glimmer. The pulsating light entirely engulfed him; it was so bright, she almost had to shield her eyes from the intense glare. What was happening?

As quickly as it started, the light display faded. Nickolai was gone and there, on the rug, *was a cat.*

A black cat with two different colored eyes.

Her cat.

Lilac fainted dead away.

Her eyelids fluttered opened slowly.

Nickolai was leaning over her, concern and a half-smile on his face.

"It seems I am forever shocking you, *souk-souk.*"

It all came back to her—the strange, flashing lights, Nickolai no longer there. *The cat.*

Terrified, she scrambled back toward the headboard in a vain attempt to put distance between them. "Stay away from me!" She put her arm out to ward him off.

"You are being foolish. Let me explain—" he reached out to her.

"Don't touch me!"

He ignored her words and clasped her shoulders. "Stop this. I want to tell you—"

Caught within his embrace, Lilac panicked and began screaming at the top of her lungs. "Help! Help! I'm in here with a beast!"

*   *   *

"Help! Help! He is a beast! A beast!"

Downstairs Emmy gave one look to Jackie, grinned, and continued with her dusting. Jackie's eyes rolled, but his gaze went speculatively to the ceiling.

"You are letting your fears and superstitions overwhelm you!" Rejar shook her slightly in an effort to bring some sense back to her. It did not work. At a loss, he shut her up the best way he knew how—with his mouth.

"Mmgf!" She pounded against his back to no avail. When she finally realized he wasn't going to release her until she quieted down, she went limp in his arms.

He lifted his lips from hers.

Lilac immediately wiped her mouth with the back of her arm. At the insult, his blue/gold eyes narrowed. Her eyes flashed back at him. "What are you?"

"I am a Familiar. I come from a race—"

My god, a familiar! She had secretly read all about them in one of the books Auntie thought no one knew about—the books she kept hidden behind the davenport. "I will not hear this!" she covered her ears. He was a *witch!*

He pulled her arms down. "You *will* hear this."

"I—I don't believe—I'm a woman of good sense! There is no such thing as witches!"

Rejar sighed. This was not going as he had thought. "I have no idea whether there is or there is not. In either case, it has nothing to do with me."

"You—you're not a witch?"

He shook his head in disbelief. Laughing, he replied, "No. I am a—"

"Then you must be a sorcerer! I—I saw you—I saw what you did! Why, you cast some kind of a spell on me! That's why I behaved as I did! You made me wanton and—and—breathless!"

He revealed a lazy half-grin. "Did I?" his deep voice rolled in his throat.

She bit her lip and nodded.

Rejar exhaled. She was being serious. "Lilac, I am not a sorcerer!" He paused a minute. "At least I do not believe I am."

"What do you mean?"

Distracted, Rejar unconsciously sent her his thought. *[Yaniff thinks . . . never mind, it is not important. I am only confusing you further.]*

He spoke in her mind! She gasped. He had unearthly powers! Just like in her dreams! *Only, they weren't really dreams.* Somehow he had come to her in the night. Come to her and—and *played* with her! Wove some kind of enchantment about her.

Why did he have to pick on me? Well, what did one expect from someone coming from such an outlandish place as Russia? It wasn't at all civilized like England.

Lilac was petrified. What should she do? They were married. My god, she had *consorted* with him! It was too late. She must talk some sense into him before the situation came down around them! Frantically, she clutched his arms.

"Do you know what they could do to you? To all of us if they find out? You must give this up, Nickolai!" she beseeched him. "Renounce these black arts! It was not so long ago that—why, we could all be burned at the stake!"

Rejar snorted, exasperated. "Do not be ridiculous. Your superstitions are overwhelming you."

"No, Nickolai! You must never, ever do this again!" Tears streamed down her cheeks.

"Lilac." Rejar took her in his arms. He had not realized she would react like this. Women always loved Familiars. Who could have predicted this reaction? It was not his intention to upset her so. She was nearly hysterical. "Shh. It will be all right." He soothed her.

"Pr-promise me, Nickolai! Promise me you won't!" she cried into his chest.

He kissed her forehead. He could not make such a promise. "We will not speak of it now, *souk-souk.*"

"You—you won't ch-change again, will you?" she sniffed.

Not unless I want to. It never ceased to amaze him how quickly she could go from woman to child. For all her bravado, she really was very young, he realized. And very inexperienced.

He shook his head at a loss. What was he to do but temporarily appease her? "Not now," he answered ambiguously.

The vagueness of his reply passed by her. She accepted his words at face value. "Good." Her tear-streaked face gazed up at him. "It shall be our secret then. No one need ever know of it."

He brushed the tears from her cheek with the indulgent hand of a husband. "You are right; no one need know of it." He sighed to himself. How was he going to overcome this unforeseen barrier? He could not. For the time being. However, there was one thing he could make clear to her.

He met her pleading look with a commanding one of his own. "You are my wife. Do you understand me?"

Lilac swallowed, then looked away. "Yes."

He caught her chin with the crook of his finger, turning her back to him. "Then I accept your challenge."

Krue's second son lightly pressed his mouth to hers, sealing the exchange.

*   *   *

Emmy walked through the foyer, took two steps into the parlor, and remembered she had left her dust rag in the dining room. She immediately turned to retrace her steps. And walked into something very solid.

There was a tall man standing in the foyer.

Emmy gave a startled jump and backed up a few steps. "Beggin' yer pardon, sir! I didn't see you standing there."

Cool green eyes assessed her. "Think nothing of it."

Cor, but he was a looker! And that hair! Tied back in a queue and down to his waist, it was. Must be a heathen Scotsman. Emmy straightened her apron. "I didn't hear you come in."

"No."

What did the bloke mean by that? "Can I help ya then, sir?"

"I am looking for Rejar. Do you know his whereabouts?"

"Her ladyship's cat? What would ya want wit' him?"

Not one iota of expression crossed the man's handsome features. "Perhaps you can tell me who lives here."

This was decidedly queer, she thought. But then, nabobs were always peculiar in their way. "Why, there's Lady Whumples, her niece, Li—"

"Males?" He interrupted her.

"Well, if you mean the new master, that would be his Highness."

That brought forth a small expression. The man quirked a mocking eyebrow. "His *Highness?*"

"Yes, Prince Azov."

"Does this prince you speak of have two different colored eyes?"

"How'd ya know that?"

The corner of his mouth lifted ever so slightly in the

semblance of a smile. "No one else would have the *kani*," he murmured to himself. "Tell 'his Highness' Traed is here to see him."

Emmy did not even think to question an order given in such an authoritative tone. "Very good, sir."

Rejar blankly stared at the bookcase in front of him. His mind was not on the tomes before him. In view of the fact that he could not read in this language, his stance was a measure of his distraction. He linked his hands behind his back, pondering the best route to take with his recalcitrant mate. A brief knock at the study door interrupted his thoughts.

He looked up. "Yes?"

Emmy stuck her head in the door. "Beggin' yer pardon, yer Highness, but there's a Mister Trey Ed to see you. Shall I show him in?"

Traed? Here? By *Aiyah*, as if he did not have enough problems! So who shows up on his doorstep but Traed! His dour brother-of-the-line. The man Adeeann affectionately refers to as "Mr. Levity." He sighed. What was he doing here? "Send him in, Emmy."

"Yes, sir." Emmy hesitated.

"Is there something else?" *Do not let there be something else.*

"No, yer Highness, it's just that—well, I didn't *hear* him come in, sir."

Rejar smiled faintly. "No, you would not."

"Sir?"

"He moves quietly, Emmy. Show him in."

"Yes, yer Highness."

Emmy returned a few minutes later. "Mister Trey Ed, your Highness!" she loudly announced to the room, causing Rejar to start. It was not very often she got to announce a visitor. Do it up nice and right, she

did. She closed the door softly behind her after the re-
remarkable gentleman had entered the room.

Traed watched her leave, then turned to face his ca-
pricious brother-of-the-line. "Your *Highness*," he said
dryly.

"It suits me, does it not?" Rejar preened, comically
throwing back his head with a regal, feline finesse.

Traed exhaled in a great gust of air as if to convey
the measure of his unerring patience at having to put
up with these antics.

Rejar broke into a genuine smile. Strange, but he
actually was glad to see Traed. Sort of. "So, tell me, to
what do I owe the pleasure of this visit?"

Traed's pastel eyes gleamed in what could only be
called gratification. His brother-of-the-line was not
completely successful in hiding his discomfit over his
sudden appearance. "Yaniff has sent me here to visit
with you for a while. I think I am getting on his nerves."

No doubt. "I did not know Yaniff had nerves."

In a rare show of whimsy, Traed replied, "Perhaps I
conjured them up for him. You think he would thank
me?"

Rejar grinned. "That would be a sight worth seeing."

"Indeed."

Rejar tried not to sound too dispirited when he in-
quired, "So . . . you will be staying a while?"

Traed strolled over to the window that Rejar was
standing in front of. With two fingers, he carefully
moved the curtain aside and surreptitiously glanced to
the street below. Satisfied no one was lurking about,
he said, "Yes."

The pupils of Rejar's dual-colored eyes momentarily
kindled. How was this not going to complicate his
problems with Lilac? Mated one day and a brother-of-
the-line shows up the next! To stay. *I will kill Yaniff.*

"Good." His voice did not hold much conviction. He cleared his throat and tried again. "That is . . . good."

"Mmm." Traed sauntered over to the French doors in the corner, swiftly yanking them open. His steely green gaze scrutinized the garden area beyond before reclosing the doors.

"Traed, what are you doing?"

"Doing?"

"Yes, you are behaving most strangely." *Even for you.*

"Why do you say this?" The doors of the large cabinet in the corner were snapped open with a flick of his wrist, the contents scanned.

"What are you searching for?"

Traed paused after a considering glance at Rejar. It was not going to be an easy thing to watch over the Familiar without his knowledge of it. Even as a child, Rejar had been extremely bright. A scamp, true; but a sharp scamp. "I am viewing this world you have come to. What else would I be doing?"

"I do not know." Rejar gave him a speculative look. "If you wish to know of this world, you need but ask me."

"Very well." Traed plopped onto the couch, hooking his booted feet over a small serving table. He crossed his arms over his well-defined chest. "Tell me," he commanded.

I will kill Yaniff. Rejar sighed, resignedly—he was honor-bound not to refuse his brother-of-the-line anything. Especially an elder brother-of-the-line. "We are in a place called—"

"Ree Gen Cee Ing Land. I know, Lorgin told me." He waved his hand impatiently bidding him to "get on with it."

Rejar's nostrils flared in annoyance. Traed was not the easiest person to have a conversation with. "It is a strange place, ugly and savage."

Traed leaned his head back against the cushions, closing his eyes, his expression conveying acute boredom.

"At first I thought it the most barbarous of places . . ." Rejar's eyes narrowed, then gleamed mischievously, "much like your Zarrain, Traed." He gibed.

The barb hit. Traed's eyes opened a slit. "I am listening."

"But there is beauty here as well. Incredible beauty." His sights drifted to the ceiling above, where he had left Lilac not too long ago, then back.

"You must see the art they produce. And the writings! There is a man here I know called Byron. He has recited some of his work to me. It is brilliant. But it is the music—Traed, the music! Like none I have ever heard! It fills the soul; it transcends boundaries, taking one to new levels of awareness."

Despite himself, Traed leaned forward, caught up in the Familiar's enthusiasm.

"Mozart! You must hear Mozart. His is a wondrous layering of sounds of such exquisite majesty that there are no words to describe it."

"Truly?"

"Yes, truly."

Traed seemed to think about this a moment. "Hmm. I will meet this Mozart."

Rejar smiled faintly. "You cannot, Traed; he is from their past, but you can know him from his music. I will take you to a place called the Pantheon where you may experience it."

Despite his aloof demeanor, Rejar could tell Traed was interested. So he was not surprised when the green-eyed man said, "Tell me more."

Rejar walked over to the liquor cabinet and poured

out two tumblers of whiskey. He handed one to Traed, then took the chair opposite him. "Try this—it is called 'malt.' "

Traed viewed the amber liquid speculatively then downed the drink in one gulp. "It does not have much life to it. Surely this is not a warrior's drink!"

"Give it time, Traed." Rejar poured him out another glass, thinking that if he could keep Traed in a constant state of inebriation during his stay it might not be so bad. This might have merit.

A mellow Traed?

Rejar snorted, dismissing the foolish notion. With one such as Traed, it would probably take a great deal of malt. More malt than he could reasonably acquire. And even then there might not be any visible effects. The man was stone-clad iron.

Surrendering to the inevitable, Rejar eyed Traed's Aviaran garments. "I will have to get you some proper clothes."

Green eyes narrowed to dangerous slits. "And what is wrong with the clothes I have on?"

As if struck by lightning, Rejar got a brilliant idea. Now this might work. . . .

"Nothing—to me." He shrugged nonchalantly. "However, I have found the people here to be most sensitive about their mode of dress."

"In what way?" Traed took a drink of his malt.

"Well . . ." Rejar rubbed his jaw, "You will have to get some *tracas* made out of a . . . a red silken cloth. They are called pantaloons."

Traed raised his eyebrows over the rim of his glass.

"Over this goes a bright green shirt . . . with frilly ruffles about the sleeves." He gestured with his hand so there would be no doubt as to the amount of frills required.

Traed stared at him stonily.

Unperturbed, Rejar continued, "And you must never leave the place where you reside without artificial hair upon your head."

"Artificial hair." Traed's even voice drawled. He placed his empty glass down, gesturing to Rejar to refill it.

"Yes, white artificial hair in fact, hanging tubes all about your head. It is the fashion." Rejar laced his hands behind his head, affecting a knowledgeable air. "Here, in Ree Gen Cee Ing Land you will find that fashion is *all*. I have a friend named Brummell who has told me this." Traed would refuse to be attired in such a manner and thus would be forced to leave. Honor would be satisfied and he could completely focus his attentions on instructing his wife in the art of Familiar love.

"I see." Traed lifted his glass slowly to his lips. The pale jade stare pierced the younger man. "Are you telling me that you actually believe I will go about dressed in this manner?" he murmured in a low, sardonic tone.

Rejar's eyes drifted to the left. Perhaps it was not such a brilliant idea after all. "I suppose not."

Since Rejar was looking at the wall, he missed the slight twitch of amusement of Traed's lips.

What else could he come up with? The Familiar ran a hand distractedly through his long black hair. Well, there was always *that*. Even for one such as Traed. He looked at him shrewdly, then refilled the other man's glass to the rim.

"The women here are very amenable." He picked up his own glass as if the topic were of no concern to him whatsoever, and, as a service, he was simply imparting an interesting tidbit of trivia.

Traed was not fooled for an instant. He knew exactly

213

what the scamp was about; he wished to sidetrack him. Traed exhaled noisily. Shaking his head slowly back and forth, he intoned, "Rejar. Rejar. Rejar. What am I to do with you." It was not a question.

Which was just as well because Rejar had a reply he was sure Traed would not appreciate.

In an irksome manner, Traed tapped his fingers against his glass. "Please do not feel you must curtail your . . . activities on my account. Feel free to do as you have always done, Rejar. Carouse to your Familiar heart's content."

Rejar frowned. Traed could be most irritating.

"I will even accompany you," he offered magnanimously. "To observe your astounding technique."

Rejar began to wonder who was toying with whom. "You will not."

"I insist." At the fulminating look on the Familiar's face, Traed smoothly added, "Surely you do not begrudge me. How did you put it on Zarrain? A night of *entertainment.*" His glittering green gaze riveted on him. Why was Rejar trying to be rid of him? He was hiding something.

Rejar was through with the game. He stood up. "It is for you to go out carousing!" he bit out. "I do not *wish* to go out carousing." He all but snarled.

Then he began to pace. Not a good sign. Familiars had to be watched when they paced.

"Why not?" Traed took an infuriating sip of his drink.

"Because I am mated!"

Coughing, Traed almost choked on his drink. "You are *what?*"

"You heard me—I am mated." It was one of the few times Rejar could ever recall seeing true shock cross

Traed's face. He just stared at Rejar for several moments, utterly stunned.

The impossibility of the words won out over his stupefaction. Rejar mated? It was laughable. The Familiar was playing with him. "I do not believe you."

Rejar bristled. "What do you mean you do not believe me?"

"Just as I say. You may cease this Familiar game, Rejar, it is not working."

"It is no game! I am mated, I tell you!"

Traed stood, placing his booted feet in front of Rejar. "Forgive me if I sound disbelieving but I find this hard to credit. It was not so very long ago that you availed yourself of half the female population in my keep!"

"Yes, but I—"

Traed faced him, arms akimbo, looking very much the Aviaran warrior. "So you will understand when I say that I have known you most of your life and that I have yet to see any indication that there is a modicum of the seriousness such a state would entail. Do you get my meaning? So what game are you playing?"

Rejar's eyes flamed with the feral light of anger. It was not a state one would necessarily want a Familiar to get into. That is, unless one could adequately defend oneself.

"Then you know me not," Rejar said softly, dangerously. "Guard your tongue."

Traed hesitated. He had never seen Rejar like this. Perhaps it was time he reexamined this younger brother-of-the-line. It appeared there was more here than he ever let on. *More than Yaniff let on.* Traed watched him obliquely.

"Very well. I believe you. Now tell me; who is this paragon who has mated herself to you?"

Traed's jesting words served to settle Rejar down. He

smiled slightly, relaxing his stance.

"She is—"

The door to the study crashed opened.

Lilac stormed in, hands on hips, ready to do battle. "Nickolai! What is the meaning of this?" In her fury, she did not even notice the tall man standing to her right.

"Emmy tells me you have instructed her to move your belongings into *my* room! Well, I will not have it!" She stomped her foot and shook her finger at him at the same time. "It is just not done! I have told you that I will not share a bedroom with you! And furthermore, just because I have to—to *consort* with you does not mean—"

A slight movement out of the corner of her eye captured her attention. An exceptionally good-looking man with light green eyes and long dark hair watched her with an amused intensity.

"Who the blazes are you?" she blurted out.

Rejar stepped forward. "Lilac, this is Traed. He is my . . ." How do you explain the intricacies of Aviaran relationships? There was no equivalent to a brother-of the-line here. The term cousin did not even come close. "He is my brother."

Surprised, Traed looked over at him. An expression came over his face suspiciously close to pride.

"Your brother?"

She should have known that anyone who looked that good had to come from her husband's family. She scrutinized him carefully, noting the lean, muscular build, the tall frame, the chiseled features, and the glittering eyes. She could come to only one conclusion.

"What does he turn into—a wolf?" she sneered, before storming from the room.

Rejar shrugged apologetically to Traed, a sheepish look on his face.

Hmm, Traed thought. This may prove an interesting journey after all. An idle, decidedly "wolfish" grin materialized on his enigmatic face.

It did not sit well with Rejar.

Not at all.

Chapter Eleven

Lilac leaned back against the rim of the tub.

The water was good and hot. Maybe it would help to alleviate some of the achy feeling she had. It was the second bath she had taken that day and it was only the late afternoon. Still, muscles she didn't know she had yesterday were sore today.

It felt good to be in the privacy of her dressing room. Emmy had balked about placing the tub in here instead of in the bedroom in front of the fireplace but Lilac had insisted. She was feeling terribly sorry for herself and had every intention of enjoying her displeasure. Alone.

Nickolai.

The autocrat.

After she had stormed out of the study, she had raced back to her room demanding that Emmy remove his things.

Emmy had gone back downstairs to check with his

Highness. If anything could point out the difference in her station from yesterday to today, that was it. Her orders didn't count anymore. *He* had last say. The interloper! It was infuriating.

However, she did feel a tad badly about the way she had treated his brother. For all she knew, the poor man could be completely ignorant of Nickolai's errant behavior. And she had promised Nickolai she would keep his secret. She supposed she would have to apologize to his brother at dinner.

But she would not apologize to *him*.

Naturally, Nickolai had countermanded her instructions to Emmy, telling the maid to do exactly as he had said. He had moved into her room lock, stock, and barrel. Just as he had moved into her life.

He was odious!

A barbarian!

Unbidden, the words *a rather cute barbarian* popped into her head. Despite herself, the corners of her mouthed twitched as she remembered the little lick he gave her in his sleep this morning. The Prince was very angelic-looking while he was sleeping. Too bad it didn't carry over into his waking state!

She settled down into the warm water, closing her eyes in bliss. She could feel herself drifting into a doze. Mmmm, the water felt so nice. . . .

Soft lips sipped gently up her arm . . .

"Nickolai?" she mumbled sleepily.

"It better be."

Lilac opened her eyes. Nickolai's blue-golden stare met her look. He was sitting down on the stool by the tub next to her. "I must have fallen asleep." She yawned, then gasped as she realized she was stark naked and wantonly displaying herself to his view. In broad daylight. "What are you doing in here?" She was outraged.

"I was looking for you."

"For what?"

Ever-so-slowly, his fingers walked up her arm. Those ridiculously long lashes of his lifted languorously, revealing eyes gone incandescent with a certain heat. A heat she was beginning to recognize.

"No."

"Yes."

Lilac pouted. "I don't wish to."

One strong finger reached out to flick her nipple. It went pebble-hard instantly. He bent down, taking the nubbin gently between his lips to suckle. A little sound suspiciously close to pleasure escaped her mouth.

"No?" he whispered against the peak of her breast.

"I—I don't think—" His perfect teeth bit down on her. She groaned his name.

It was enough of a consent to him. Powerful arms reached under her in the tub, lifting her body out of the water and across his lap with impossible ease. Water dripped all over him and onto the floor, soaking through his garments, but he didn't seem to mind.

"You shouldn't do—"

His mouth closed over her own.

In a heated press, his lips demanded a response and the fiery penetration of his tongue received it.

Lilac clutched the open collar of his shirt, moaning at the fierce sliding motion of his tongue inside her. She could taste him, feel him, rich in her mouth.

He would show her a small portion of a Familiar's special talent. . . .

The palms of his hands slid along her damp body, reheating the water-cooled skin stroke by sensuous stroke as he continued to ruthlessly plunder the hot, damp well of her mouth. Lilac shivered at the sheer mastery of his kiss.

He withdrew to suckle sweetly on her lower lip, teasing her with small nips of his teeth, laving her with refined sweeps of his tongue—only to suddenly plunge into her again in a strong, powerful thrust. He drank of her.

As if he willed it, her breath started coming in short gasps.

Into his mouth.

Rejar took the gift of her breath, giving it back to her intermittently between his measured strokes and sweeps. Blood, like a savage, beating drum, pounded through her veins as he gave vibrant life to her senses. She writhed against him, prisoner to his skill; and she realized she could not take any breath except that which he deigned to give her.

She became captive to his rhythmic prowess. Avidly seeking his next breath, stroke, slide. *His.*

A tiny waterfall of pleasure spasms trickled over her body, increasing with each deliberate surge of his mouth against her. With every licking plunge into her. Nickolai effortlessly ignited her to sizzling point with just the talent of his lips and tongue.

No match for his expertise, Lilac thrashed wildly under him. "More," she begged. She had to taste more. Have more.

So he opened his lips on her and gave her what she wanted. He *purred* into her mouth.

Lilac burst into a thousand flames. Vibrations flared unendingly through her; it was a long, hot blaze of completion. When it was finally over, she sagged against his chest.

The Familiar had brought her to peak with his kiss alone.

When she lazily opened her eyes in the aftermath and gazed up into the sultry, beautiful face above her, Lilac did the only thing she could.

She wound her arm around the strong column of his throat and brought that incredible mouth firmly back to her own.

Nickolai ran his hot, damp mouth over her throat.

She didn't remember him carrying her to the bed. She didn't remember him disrobing. She didn't seem to remember much of anything.

She only knew that he covered her now like a feverish, throbbing blanket; that his palms securely clasped her shoulders; that he rubbed the head of his erection seductively between the folds of her nether lips.

A low sough of satisfaction rustled from his throat.

Words in a language she had never heard before were whispered huskily against her skin.

"K'mata ninqué shateer . . ."

Like an exotic spice, the mysterious words fell upon her, enhancing his torrid movements, making her want to savor him slowly, infusing her with the tangy promise of what he could give her. . . .

How had he gotten her like this?

Wild and wanting?

Maybe those enticing phrases were more than just words. Maybe they were sorcery. Surely no conventional man could do this to a woman?

"Nickolai." She placed her hands on either side of his face, raising his head to her. "You must not cast any spells over me—remember your promise? You must—" She panted as he slid along the outside of her cleft, gently nudging a very sensitive spot with his shaft. "You—you must give up the magic. . . ."

"Which magic do you speak of, *souk-souk?* This?" he

whispered hoarsely, as he licked around her aureola. "Or this?" He laved just the very tip of her jutting nipple. "Or *this* . . ." He penetrated her slowly, letting her feel him sink into her forever, inch by blessed inch.

"Ohhh—Nickolai . . ." Her legs went around his waist. It appeared her husband possessed a talent that was completely natural.

When he had gained entrance to the hilt, Rejar moved that little fraction more to let her know real magic. Then he lifted his head, tossing back his black hair. His eyes sparkled down at her, teasingly.

"Kiss me, quick," he whispered.

Without thinking, she did.

Her new husband showed her how much he approved the innocent touch of her mouth on his. He proceeded to give her a loving she would never forget.

"Good heavens, Emmy! That isn't enough food to keep a child fit, let alone a man like this! Put some more on his plate!"

"Yes, mum." Emmy dutifully ladled another dollop of potatoes onto the green-eyed man's plate.

Rejar expected Traed to lift one supercilious eyebrow and stop that nonsense from continuing, but he surprised him by graciously nodding his head at Lady Whumples and excepting the extra helping.

For a reason no one at the table could quite fathom, Agatha Whumples had immediately taken to Traed ta'al Yaniff.

In the short span of fifteen minutes, she was already referring to him as "my boy." While she also referred to Rejar in this manner, it was not quite the same. For one thing, Rejar never expected Traed to put up with it. For the second, it was difficult to conceive of anyone referring to an Aviaran warrior, especially one like Traed, as "my boy."

If the truth were known, Traed was somewhat at a loss as to how to deal with the elderly woman. Never having known the kindness of a mother's touch, he was completely out of his depth with the display of caring concern from Lady Whumples.

In typical Traed fashion, he decided to tolerate it until he understood it better.

"Prince Nickolai tells me you are his brother, yet you do not go by a title. I find this very confusing. I'm too old to be purposely confused, my boy—I don't take well to it."

Traed raised an eyebrow at Agatha.

"Well?" Agatha pierced him with one of her "you must answer" expressions.

Lilac recognized it as such immediately and hoped Nickolai's brother was wise enough to heed it. The ramifications if one did not were too unspeakable to bear. It appeared the brother was no fool, for he set his wineglass down on the table to answer her straightaway.

"*Nickolai*"—Traed turned to give Rejar a pointed look—"and I do not share the same father. I do not use a title because it does not suit me to do so."

Agatha knit her brow. Did that mean he had a title or not? "Yes, my boy, but are you entitled to a show of respect by a proper title?"

"Is not everyone?"

The man was very circumspect. Agatha tried to worm her way around his answer. "But . . . are you Russian?"

"Russian?" he looked perplexed. "No, I am not Russian."

Patience at an end, Agatha bellowed, "Where do your father's people come from?"

"The Sky Lands of—"

Rejar coughed loudly, interrupting Traed's words.

"The Highlands?" Agatha asked, mishearing him over the Prince's sudden coughing fit.

"I knew it! He's a heathen Scotsman!" Emmy mumbled loudly to herself as she cleared away a plate from the table.

How could he be a Highlander if his brother was a Russian Prince? Agatha was confused. It was very difficult to get a straight answer out of the man. He seemed to keep his business to himself. Still, he seemed honest enough in his answers, almost to the point of bluntness.

Well, she liked him nonetheless. There was something there . . . a certain gentleness he tried very hard to conceal beneath a tough exterior. He probably succeeded in fooling most—but not her.

When it came to people, Agatha had insight.

This man had a good, decent quality about him, denoting strong character. Her sights went proudly to her new nephew sitting across the table from her.

And why shouldn't the man be of good stock? Just look where he came from—now here was a specimen! She winked secretly at the Prince. Grinning, he covertly winked back.

Throughout the meal, her niece appeared slightly flustered. Lilac and Nickolai had been late coming down to dinner and when they did finally arrive, Lilac had a nice, rosy flush on her face. Agatha noted that her niece did not seem quite so acetic to his Highness now. On the contrary. Her niece could not seem to look at him without blushing prettily.

Agatha let out a sigh of relief. She had done the right thing.

After the meal, they all retired to the drawing room.

Lilac recalled that both men had given her aunt the strangest look when she asked them if they would like the ladies to leave the room so they might partake of some port. Nickolai had then turned to her aunt asking her if she would like some of this "port." Auntie Whumples had tittered that she had often been tempted, before she apparently came to her senses and suggested they all go into the drawing room.

The brothers just looked at each other with foggy expressions.

Lilac supposed the men of Russia did not indulge in port. One could not speculate what the men of the Highlands did, being Scotsmen. She made a mental note to ask Nickolai's brother about a lurid rumor she had heard regarding something called *haggis*.

She was not surprised when Nickolai sat right next to her on the couch. For some reason, he always liked to be near her. It was very . . . She swallowed. *Catlike*.

No, she promised herself she would not think about it. Determined, she squelched the allusion.

Auntie asked Nickolai something about how he was settling in so Lilac took the opportunity to speak to Nickolai's brother. He was about to sit across from her on one of Auntie's few odd purchases—a Greek Revival chair. She noticed him curiously examine the chair's winged paw feet, only to throw a speculative glance at his brother.

Lilac smiled. "Nickolai had nothing to do with it. I'm afraid it wasn't a very good shopping day for my aunt."

"Ah." He sat down in the chair, although she couldn't

say he actually relaxed. He did not seem like a man who ever truly relaxed.

"I believe I owe you an apology. You must think me terribly rude. It's just that I was . . . was . . ." How did she explain it?

"You were angry with . . . Nickolai." He finished for her. "He had upset you in some way. I understand this. There is no need for you to apologize."

Lilac was surprised at his comprehension of the situation. Then again, being Nickolai's brother, he was probably well acquainted with how irascible the man could be. It was curious—every time he said Nickolai's name, he appeared to have trouble with it—almost as if it were choking in his throat. In any event, it seemed obvious to her that he knew nothing of his brother's questionable activities with the darker arts. In fact, the brother seemed most . . . pedantic.

"That is so kind of you . . . May I call you Trey? Since it seems we are now related?"

Traed stared at her. Her innocent words had a profound effect on him. Yes, they were related. Rejar had mated with her. She was blood to him now. His oath of *Chi'in t'se Leau* would cloak her as well. And he supposed that by association, he would have to watch over the "aunt" too.

He frowned absently. When he started out on this journey, he had no idea what Yaniff was getting him into.

Rejar's mate watched him expectantly, her large green eyes open and guileless. How had this innocent ever fallen into the hands of his Familiar brother-of-the-line? There was no doubt in Traed's mind but that she was untouched. Or at least, she had been.

It was certainly an unprecedented event.

Everyone knew a Familiar's tastes usually ran to those

more . . . sophisticated. So how had Rejar come to this passage? And would it not be interesting to press him to find out? A brief wily smile flashed across his face.

"I believe you are mistaken about my name. It is Traed. Traed ta'al . . ." he hesitated here, never having referred to himself as anything but Theardar's son. However, like everything else in his life, that name had been taken from him. ". . . Yaniff," he concluded.

"Then I apologize again for my second offense, Traed ta'al Yaniff." She smiled prettily at him.

Traed nodded graciously, uncharacteristically moved by her sweet entreaty. He caught Rejar's sights above Lady Whumples's head. *You do not deserve her,* was what his visage plainly related to the younger man.

Rejar's eyes gleamed mischievously. For the first time in his life he intruded upon the older man's privacy by sending him a thought. *[Of course I do.]*

Traed did not even flick an eyelash. He just looked at Rejar speculatively for a moment. Then quirked that eyebrow.

Rejar grinned flippantly before answering something Lady Whumples had asked him. He decided that since he had to deal with having Traed as his brother, Traed was going to have to deal with having a Familiar as his.

Now I have him in my head. Traed exhaled a long-suffering gust of air, in that moment resembling his other brother-of-the-line, Lorgin.

"Tell me, my boy"—Agatha faced Traed—"have you seen much of our London Town yet?"

"I have seen nothing," Traed replied more than truthfully; he had not even stepped out the door of this abode.

"We shall have to remedy that, won't we, my Nickolai?" Agatha patted Rejar's arm.

Lilac wondered if her elderly aunt wasn't having the time of her life thinking she was commandeering these two robust men about like a small gray-haired general. But did her aunt realize they were *allowing* her to do it?

"Yes," Rejar agreed. "Tomorrow I will take you to a place called White's Club and introduce you to—"

"Nickolai, you can't!" Lilac was mortified.

Rejar turned a questioning glance at her.

"We . . ." she fidgeted with her dress, "We just got married," she whispered to him.

His eyes sparkled down at her. "I have not forgotten. Do not worry," he said sotto voce, "I will not leave you alone for too long, *souk-souk*. You will not have time to pine for me."

As if she would pine for him. "You nick ninny," she hissed. "If it were up to me, you could stay away the whole week for all I care! The point is, one does not marry one day and show up for a rousing good drink with the lads the next! It is just not done!"

Rejar placed his arm around her, bringing her close to him. He bent down to murmur in her ear. "What do you mean by these words?"

"It is just—not—done," she reiterated. "It would be a terrible insult to me. Couples who marry do not show themselves in public for a respectable amount of time."

"Why?"

"Because it is done that way! Most newlyweds have a 'going away' after the marriage ceremony."

"Where do they go?" he whispered back.

"I don't know! Somewhere. We did not do that—so we must stay here and not show our faces for a time."

"This is the most foolish society I have ever . . ." Rejar took a deep breath. "Very well. I will not 'show my face.' "

Dara Joy

"Good." She nodded approvingly.

"Except to you," he added playfully. "Which face would you like to see this eve?"

She blushed.

"And Lilac?" he murmured in her ear.

"Yes?"

"Do not call me a nick ninny again." He ended his whispered words with a small lick to her ear.

"Have the two of you finished your little . . . discussion?" Traed asked wryly.

"Yes." Rejar stood to make an announcement. "Lilac and I have decided not to show our faces. We will begin immediately by going to our bedroom and remaining there until such a time as we can either show our faces again or we have vigorously expired ourselves."

"Nickolai!" Lilac was twice mortified.

Agatha tittered behind her palm.

Taking Lilac's hand, Rejar urged her to her feet. "Lady Agatha, I will leave my cherished brother in your capable hands. Be gentle with him."

"*Nickolai!*" Lilac trailed after him, dragged along by his firm clasp to her wrist.

"I am only doing as you ask, *souk-souk*. You may thank me properly in a few minutes."

"Nickolai . . ."

Lilac's voice faded away as Rejar closed the door firmly behind them.

Agatha looked at Traed.

Traed looked at Agatha.

Traed snorted; Agatha snickered. They both burst out laughing.

Traed shook his head, grinning. Rejar had always had a certain way about him. . . . Not that he would ever let the scamp know it.

* * *

230

He had a certain way about him, she'd grant him that.

In fact, Nickolai had just positioned her naked self to sit atop him without a hint of apology.

She looked at him lying prone beneath her and cocked her head to one side. "And just what am I supposed to do now?"

"What do you think?" He shifted his hips beneath her to give her a clue. The throb of his swollen shaft between her thighs seemed to punctuate his suggestion.

Lilac's eyes widened. "Really?"

"Would I mislead you?" he asked silkily.

Lilac decided not to answer *that* question. "But how?"

Rejar sighed theatrically; it seemed a mentor's work was never done. "Sit—on—it."

Sit on it? How could someone do that? It would tear her asunder like a hare on a spit. "I don't think so!" she scoffed.

"Lilac, put your palms against my chest and lean forward."

She was skeptical, but when Nickolai used that special, sexy, rumbling tone of voice . . . she did as he said.

"Now . . . move back until you feel . . . that is it, right—*there.*" Rejar clasped his hands to her hips. "Now sit."

He guided her down with practiced precision.

"Oh!"

His eyes gleamed with satisfaction. "Come forward."

"I—Can I do that?"

A lopsided grin tilted his mouth. "You need not worry; I am fairly resilient. I will try not to break beneath this terrible pressure."

"I was not referring to you," she quipped, but gingerly leaned forward just the same.

He immediately took her breast in his mouth and began to draw on her. She felt his suckling motions all the way down to her toes. Lilac decided then and there that even if he did break, she was damn well going to stay right where she was.

"Fine, now, *souk-souk*"—he flicked the pearl of her breast with his tongue—"*pump*."

Lilac went stock still. What did he mean, pump?

A hot stream of breath gusted across the nipple. "Like this." He showed her exactly what he meant by several upward thrusts of his hips. Lilac blinked at the delicious sensation.

"Oh, like this?" She wiggled down on him, bounced up, and slid down again. Nickolai clenched his teeth.

"By *Aiyah! Yes . . .* "

Lilac decided she liked it and instantly became more enthusiastic. "This is quite stimulating, isn't it?" There was something about being on top . . . Perhaps there were other ways just as stimulating?

"Nickolai?" She squeezed his lean hips with her thighs. Her husband groaned something about her being an excellent student.

"*What?*" he gasped, massaging her breasts as she continued to move boisterously on him.

"How many ways are there to do this?"

Silence.

"Well?"

"Shh . . . I am counting."

But his hands were caressing. Especially those rounded thighs which were wringing him so perfectly. *This deserved a reward.*

He hooked his arm around her neck, bringing her down for his kiss. At the same time, he lunged up and met her downward motion.

Lilac thought him most inspired.

"Five thousand, three hundred fifty-two and three-quarters," he panted against her mouth.

"Five thousand three hundred and fifty-two?" That stopped her for a minute.

"And three-quarters—not counting certain combinations." He pulled her down tight against the base of his shaft. Both of them groaned.

"You're making that up!"

"I am not." He nipped her chin.

"You are!"

"Let us find out, shall we? We will start next with number two hundred thirty-three."

Lilac playfully slapped him. His white teeth showed in a grin in the dimly lit room. Then he surged swiftly into her.

Lilac closed her eyes in ecstasy and started to say something to him, but he placed a long tapered finger against her lips. "I know what you wish to say."

"What?"

" 'More, Nickolai, more.' " His low voice held more than a hint of amusement.

Lilac made a face at him. Dropping her voice several octaves, she tried giving him his own medicine by imitating his low, dulcet tones. "How much more, *souksouk?*"

Familiars adored such games. A mischievous dimple popped into his cheek.

He whispered the words she had cried to him earlier that afternoon. "Harder, faster."

Despite herself, she blushed. "Stop that!"

"Deeper," he teased relentlessly.

"You are terrible, Nickolai."

Rejar laughed, surprising her by grabbing her around the waist and rolling over on top of her. "Is this what you meant before?" He embedded himself in her to the hilt.

Lilac gasped and clutched his powerful shoulders.

"Is this what you wanted?" He moved in her hard and fast.

Lilac began moaning the words in earnest. "Nickolai . . . more . . . more . . ."

He responded to her passionate mood, at once becoming serious. Intently, he gazed down at her beneath him. "Yes, my Lilac, yes," he avowed against her lips. "I will give you everything . . ."

And he did.

He freed his Familiar passion, driving into her with a ferocious intensity. Lilac, as caught up in the storm as he was, urged him on. When she began to claw at his back with the intense desire he had aroused in her, Rejar almost lost all control. *She was becoming a Familiar mate.*

So, he did what a Familiar man should; he growled wildly against her and bit her properly in the shoulder.

When their culmination finally came, it was simultaneous and meteoric.

Rejar reached up to brush back a lock of his hair.

He was lying flat on his back next to Lilac. Both of them were still trying to regain their breath after the tumultuous lovemaking session they had just shared. He closed his eyes, thinking he might drift off for a quick, revitalizing nap.

"Nickolai?"

"Mmm?"

"Have you been with a lot of women?"

He opened his eyes, all trace of sleepiness gone. He turned on his side to face her. "Yes."

Lilac expected the answer, even applauded him for

his honesty; but, for some reason, it made her feel . . . bad. "By a lot," she cleared her throat, "do you mean, for example, ten women?" She didn't know where she got the nerve to ask.

This time he did not answer; he simply gazed squarely at her.

"Twenty?"

He remained silent.

"Surely not more than *forty?*" Her voice went up in pitch at the end.

Rejar exhaled deeply. "I have been with many, *many* women, Lilac."

She swallowed the inexplicable lump in her throat. "I see."

There was something in her voice which troubled him. "Why does this bother you? Do you not benefit from my knowledge?" His hand reached over to cup the side of her face.

"I don't think you understand."

He smiled slightly. "I understand. But you must understand as well—my people are very different from your own."

Lilac thought of the rakehells of the ton. "Not so very different."

Rejar watched her expression change. What was upsetting her?

"I suppose I will have to catch up with you," she said.

His brow kinked. "What do you mean?"

"Well, it's only fair. You shouldn't mind, should you? I understand it's quite an acceptable practice in the ton." A practice she despised. Lilac had no intention of doing what she was implying, but she was curious as to how he felt about it.

Rejar saw through her ploy immediately. "You will not find one to please you as I do," he teased her.

Although she knew that was probably true, she replied, "I only have your word for that."

Was she serious? "You will not." He stated very firmly.

It didn't seem to sit too well with him. Lilac had recently discovered that her new husband was quite something when he was inflamed. Perhaps she should scratch his back, so to speak, and see what developed. It might prove interesting.

She lifted her leg as if she were stretching, rotating her small foot in the air. Out of the corner of her eye, she noted Nickolai avidly watching her sinuous movements. "Mmm, perhaps . . . sometime."

Lilac got more than she bargained for.

Nickolai suddenly laced his fingers through her hair and pulled her up against him. This was one game he did not like. Anger leapt in the depths of his blue and gold eyes. *"Not ever."*

"But you will," she flung back.

The real reason behind her game was at last surfacing.

The corners of Rejar's lips curved upward. *She was becoming possessive of him.* This, he liked. She was indeed becoming a Familiar wife!

But did she not understand the mating ways? The oath he had taken for her? The *mating-kiss* she had given to him? He would make sure she understood.

He lowered his head to hers.

"Not ever," he promised against her lips, covering them with his own. "You are my only Lilac. Therefore, I intend to keep you in a constant state of bloom."

Nickolai always meant what he said. Appeased, she smiled at his endearing play on words. He was probably too often in Byron's company—Nickolai was starting to sound much too romantic.

The impression was whisked away when he sweetly kissed her. A perfumed sublety of cinnamon and bayberry wafted around her.

She blissfully inhaled the intoxicating scent.

This marriage business was nowhere near as awful as she had thought.

Chapter Twelve

During the time that Rejar and Lilac were "not showing their faces," Agatha Whumples took it upon herself to introduce and escort Prince Nickolai's brother about the ton.

It did not take Lady Whumples long to discover that Traed did not have any clothes with him except what was on his back. Traed did not think it prudent to enlighten the elderly woman that the clothes he wore were of the finest Aviaran cloth—which meant they came with a self-cleaning spell put on them by the weaver's guild wizard. He did not need any other clothes.

Since the man had no belongings with him, Agatha erroneously concluded that all of his baggage had been lost in transition during his travel from there (wherever *there* was) to here.

Unlike Rejar, Agatha would brook no refusal, insisting on bringing in a tailor for the man.

Traed proved most resistant to certain suggestions made by the tailor, choosing modestly styled, dark clothes with absolutely *no* frills about the sleeves and collar. When the tailor had balked at this, Traed had simply tossed the man bodily out the door.

At the time, Agatha had looked up from her reading to see the tailor sailing through the air, a stream of French invectives spewing from his mouth.

After the ordeal with the wardrobe was completed, Agatha then took the reluctant Traed to Madame Tussaud's Wax Museum, then on to Duchess Street to view the various rooms of treasures, followed by Westminster Abbey. It was not often Agatha had such a male at her disposal and she intended to make the most of it.

Traed seemed fascinated by the Egyptian Room and Grecian Temple in Duchess Street and particularly interested in the Rosetta Stone at Westminster, asking Agatha what mystical properties it displayed.

Agatha was not at a loss to answer and set into a lively discussion of the mysterious effluvia. Obviously the lad had a curiosity for the unknown. She set about to enlighten him.

Confused by her erroneous knowledge, Traed listened intently to Agatha's words, causing her to believe she had found a person of similar interests.

And, in a sense, she had.

The two of them formed a strange alliance. Agatha doted on the man she called "my boy" while Traed stoically put up with her antics.

Everywhere they went, Lady Whumples made it a point to introduce Prince Nickolai's brother to the ton. She was very proud of these new in-laws of hers and saw no reason not to show them about to her advantage.

Somehow, a story had sprung up that the Prince's

brother had been on his way to the wedding when his party was attacked by bandits. His baggage was stolen, everyone in the traveling party was killed except the brother—he was left for dead on the road—and he had missed his beloved younger brother's wedding by just one day. The ton had great sympathy for the man who was the tragic hero of such a romantic gesture.

If Traed had heard the ridiculous tale, even he might have laughed.

On meeting the Prince's steely-eyed brother, however, the story was immediately changed to: The brother had killed all of the bandits except the one who ran off with his baggage.

Traed, not being a Familiar like Rejar, had a more difficult time fitting in with the culture of Regency England. When Agatha tried to explain some little nuance of the society to him, Traed simply waved her off. In his fashion, he decided to ignore the rules and go about his own way as he had always done.

Instead of putting off the ton, his uncompromising behavior and steely-eyed glances at the goings on about him only served to elevate his status. He was referred to as an obvious "man of the world."

The Prince's enigmatic, brooding, darkly handsome older brother, who did not bear the Prince's family name of Azov, intrigued the ton. He gave nothing of himself away—which made him all the more interesting. Whispers and rumors followed him wherever he went.

He was a Highland Chieftain; he was a brother of the blade.

He was a common Scottish reiver; he was the son of a Duke.

By his bearing there was no doubt in anyone's mind

that he was of noble blood. *Just who was he?*

It was the question on everyone's lips.

While Agatha was merrily dragging Traed about London Town, Rejar was introducing his new wife to the joys of Familiar love.

So far, the explanations, while spirited, were still in the beginning stages. As he had always suspected, Lilac was proving herself an apt pupil, her innate sensuality coming to the fore with his expert tutelage and guidance.

For the first time in her young life she was exploring her sexuality and it was a heady tonic to the Familiar.

He could not get enough of her.

In fact, just that morning, he had decided that they had better start "showing their faces" soon because she was starting to look decidedly wan.

When he had spoken of it to her, she had hesitated, delightfully biting her lip as she pondered on whether she wanted to leave the exclusivity of his bed just yet.

At his chiding laugh, Lilac had come to her senses and, face flaming, had leapt out of bed.

Even if she did not want to admit it, he knew how much she enjoyed their lovemaking. Did she somehow think he wondered whose lips breathlessly moaned in his ear all night? Whose nails scored his back? And who did she think tightly clamped him in the throes of completion?

He chuckled, shaking his head at the sometimes illogical behavior of women.

Then again, such behavior was one of the reasons Familiar men so adored the female. It was that unpredictability which so appealed to their feline senses.

Standing in the dressing room in nothing but a shirt, he stared at his choices of apparel. Lilac had gone below earlier while he had lingered in his bath. She had come up once, a while ago, to tell him that Agatha had suggested that for her first outing as a married woman, she accept an invitation to Lady Whitney's for an afternoon of embroidery.

Looking rather adorable, she morosely informed him, "I am not very good at embroidery." The idea of spending the afternoon engaged in this pastime quickly irritated her. She suddenly gave him a disgusted look, declaring, "It's all your fault!"

Rejar had been somewhat surprised at her mercurial change of mood. Only a few short hours before she had been mewing contentedly in his arms. Her attitude was not unlike that of an overly indulged child.

He would have to see what he could do about that. It appeared Lilac needed to be enlightened in ways other than intimacy.

Begin as you mean to go on, Krue had always told him.

Remembering his father's advice, Rejar sternly advised her, "Since this is all my fault, I will personally see to bringing you to Lady Whitney's." He intended to go out for the afternoon with Traed and he intended to know her whereabouts at all times. He had told her, "You will wait for me there until I fetch you."

It was no surprise that this decree did not sit well with her; she stormed out, slamming the door behind her.

Under normal circumstances, he might not have made such an outrageous decree. Besides the fact that she had goaded him into the display, there was something about her going around unescorted, without his protection, that made him uneasy. To his way of thinking, it was too dangerous a world. In this savage place, he had seen a man get his throat sliced simply for the few tokens in his pocket.

Lilac was much too vulnerable. Especially now that it was believed she was the wife of a prince.

The truth was, she was the mate of a Familiar. A unique Familiar. Whose sire was a high-level Charl warrior and one of the ruling council of Aviara. There were times in his own worlds, as well, when heeding the words of your mate could mean the difference between life and death.

The Familiar practice was an aid to their survival and an important lesson for her to learn—a lesson which might not be wise for him to put off.

Lilac marched with a determined stride through the bedroom toward the dressing room.

It was still chilly in the late afternoons, and she thought it best to bring a shawl with her to Lady Whitney's.

She had no intentions of waiting for Nickolai to bring and fetch her like some treasured possession. Who did he think he was?

Your husband, a little voice said.

She ignored it.

Flinging open the door to the dressing room, she stepped inside. Her hand reached for her green woolen shawl on the shelf nearby. She didn't see him until it was too late.

At first his back was to her.

He was standing there wearing nothing but his white lawn shirt. The gleaming length of black hair seemed all the glossier against the snowy material. Strong thigh muscles flexed as he easily stretched for a pair of boots on a shelf which would have taken a ladder for her to reach.

The movement lifted the hem of his shirt.

Two perfectly shaped globes of male backside proudly displayed themselves.

Lilac sighed. She understood perfectly well now what Leona Harcorte found so enticing. They were a lively handful. Nickolai must have heard her soft exclamation, for he smiled at her over his shoulder.

Until his sights drifted to the shawl in her hand.

The smile died on his face.

Instantly, the pupils of his blue and gold eyes flared once in what she was coming to recognize as a warning signal of his anger. Nickolai knew exactly what she was about.

He turned to face her.

That was when she realized his shirt was unbuttoned; it hung open, revealing a tantalizing glimpse of . . . everything. All that golden-tan skin was enough to give anyone pause.

A muscle ticked in his jaw. Not a good sign.

Lilac's hand went to her throat.

"Close the door, Lilac," he said softly.

Not stopping to question his order, she did as he said, shutting the dressing room door behind her. After all, he was standing there almost in the nude; one of the maids might walk in, although that was unlikely.

His burning gaze flicked to her shawl. "Put it down."

So, he wasn't concerned about someone walking in; he was furious with her planned act of rebellion. Lilac thought about not doing it, but one look into those glittering blue and gold orbs made her change her mind. She wisely walked over to the shelf near the door, replacing the shawl.

"Come to me." His voice was quiet and deadly serious.

This time she did balk. Nickolai looked a wee bit too

angry. She shook her head silently.

"Come here, Lilac."

Such a tone required some response. She slowly approached him, lifting her chin defiantly when she stood directly in front of him.

Her defiance abruptly vanished at his shocking words. "Lift your dress," he ordered.

"What?"

"Did you not hear me?"

She heard him all too well. "I will not!"

"Charming world, this," his eyes flashed a warning, the silk and velvet of his voice at complete odds with the expression in their depths. "From what I understand, a wife must obey her husband. Is that not so?"

Lilac's nostrils flared. She reluctantly lifted her skirts.

The dark, sooty lashes drifted downward. Nickolai eyed her lacy pantalettes dispassionately. "Remove them."

She sucked in her breath. "Nickolai, I—"

"Do it."

Holding the material of her dress in one hand, she reached over to untie the ribbon at her waist. The cottony material slid down her legs, gathering about her ankles in a soft puddle. Exposing her totally to his view. Lilac wished she could hide her face. Among other things.

"Step away."

Looking at a spot somewhere to his left, she did as he bid, gingerly stepping out of the undergarment.

He took one step forward.

She took one back.

The corners of his mouth curved mockingly. She did not like the look on his face. He took another step, forcing her back against the door.

"Nickolai, I don't think—"

Strong masculine hands reached down, cupping her derriere. Without any visible exertion, he lifted her up, high against his chest. "Enclose my waist with your legs," he hissed.

When she hesitated, he braced her against the door with one hand and easily positioned her to his liking with the other. She was completely open to him now. Poised on the tip of his masculinity.

He stared down at her—all male fire and smoldering heat.

Passion and fury mixed equally on his sultry face. Despite her apprehension, Lilac could feel her dewy moisture slicken the head of his manhood.

By the narrowing of his eyes, he felt it, too.

Nickolai was very angry. She had flaunted his words in his face, outwardly defying him. What would he do to her? There was something almost feral about him.

"Nickolai, don't! I'm afraid, I—"

He sunk ruthlessly into her.

A cry somewhere between alarm and ecstasy escaped her lips.

He withdrew, then fiercely plunged into her again.

Sliding her hands beneath his shirt, Lilac gripped his shoulders. She didn't know whether to yell in outrage or bliss. This was aggrieved ecstasy! It amazed her how fast her husband could turn from sweet to savage. Nickolai was definitely inflamed.

And he was inflaming her in a way he probably didn't intend. The sight of that remarkable masculine face, jaw tensed, eyes flashing, struck her with a powerful surge of desire.

Bracing her against the door, he thrust into her with a steadfast, ironclad rhythm. No words came from his lips; the upward motion of his thighs gave him all the power he needed to get his point across. And not just sexually.

Lilac moaned over and over, senselessly; burying her face into the skin of his warm, sweat-damp throat. The position he held her in would not allow her to escape his masterful impalement. Even if she wanted to. The door rattled against the hinges with his constant, ramming strokes.

Still, he pounded into her.

She shivered and screamed at the exquisite torture. "You're killing me! You're killing me!"

But they both knew what she was really saying.

His hot, racing breath fell across her face. "Who am I to you?" he ground out between teeth clenched with his exertion and, although she did not know it, his control.

"My—my husband," she sobbed against his neck.

"Yes." He drove up into her. White-hot flame shot through him; exploded in him.

Lilac began to climax with him, tasting his blood as she bit sharply into his lower lip in her frenzy.

Rejar sagged heavily against her, pinning her between him and the back of the door. Trying to catch his breath, he spoke raggedly in her ear. "Do you understand me?"

She nodded, rubbing her forehead against his chin. With very few words, he had expressed himself remarkably well, had sharpened her awareness of him and what he was to her. There would be no taking herself off to Lady Whitney's. Her husband expected her to consult with him in such matters and heed his advice.

"Good."

She thought his lips brushed her hair, but when he released her curtly and coldly turned away, she realized she must have been mistaken. This was an untamed side of Nickolai and she never wanted to see it again. Lilac swiftly grabbed her pantalettes off the floor and fled the room.

After she had gone, Rejar yanked on his clothes with precise, irate movements.

He was still concerned about her safety; she was headstrong and youthfully rebellious. These attitudes, while charming in their way to him, could cause significant problems between them. In his anger, he had almost turned feral on her.

He was worried about that.

Lilac would not be able to handle him if he turned feral. She was too inexperienced with his kind—with any kind.

A Familiar woman innately understood her male. This unsophisticated woman did not.

Rejar rolled his shoulders to release some of the tension there. Familiar males had a way with their mates which was never questioned. The female knew that her mate always had a reason for his behavior, often an instinctual reason. Consequently, she knew he would never request anything from her without a strong sense of necessity. To do otherwise was not their way.

Female Familiars trusted their mates in all things; for they knew the male cherished and protected his family, even at the cost of his own life.

Lilac knew nothing about instinctual reasons.

He licked his lip, tasting the blood. He remembered her wildness and smiled halfheartedly. Well, she certainly had the passion to become like a Familiar woman. Maybe in time, she would come to understand him.

Before leaving the dressing room, he thoughtfully retrieved her shawl, bringing it with him downstairs. The weather had a habit here in Ree Gen Cee Ing Land of turning raw.

She would need it when he escorted her home from Lady Whitney's.

His dutiful wife was waiting for him in the parlor when he came downstairs.

The picture of abject misery, she sat primly in her chair, back straight, hands folded in her lap, staring straight at the wall. Rejar shook his head disbelievingly at the tragic melodrama portrayed before him.

Agatha and Traed entered the room from the doors which led out to the garden. Agatha was adjusting her pince-nez as she expostulated on some topic, while Traed walked at her side, hands clasped at the small of his back, listening to her with a patience only he possessed.

"Lilac! I've been looking all over for you."

In keeping with her role as the pitiful martyr, Lilac sighed dolefully. "Yes, Auntie Whumples; what is it?"

"Why, did you not hear it? There was a terrible racket! It appears there is a shutter loose somewhere on the house—the banging was dreadful! Traed and I just went out to investigate, although we couldn't find anything loose."

Lilac turned scarlet.

She risked a glance at Nickolai. *Did he realize just what banging noises Auntie had heard?*

Blue/gold eyes twinkling, her rogue of a husband slowly ran his tongue over the little red spot she had nipped on his lip. Abashed, she turned away from him.

His low laugh just reached her.

Oh, how she detested him!

Traed came alongside Rejar. Glancing knowingly at

the Familiar's lip, he murmured facetiously, "Have you been to battle, Rejar?"

He grinned, sending Traed a cocky look. "Mmm."

Traed's eyes danced with sport. "Perhaps there is some Aviaran warrior in you after all."

"Only in certain parts," Rejar mouthed to him as he walked over to fetch his wife.

Traed coughed.

"It is a little early in the day, but what do you think, Traed?"

Traed ta'al Yaniff gazed around the smoky interior of the gaming hell at 77 Jermyn Street. Everywhere he looked, men were engaged in various kinds of wagering.

"This is what the men here do for a pastime?" he asked in disgust.

"Yes. Sons often wager entire family fortunes."

Traed chuckled. "Krue would knock your head against a wall, Rejar."

"Only if I lost."

Both men grinned at each other.

"What is this game here?" Traed walked over to a green baize table.

"It is called hazard."

"What are the rules?"

"Do you see those two cubes with the spots on the sides? They are called dice. A caster throws the dice until he scores spots numbering five, six, seven, eight, or nine. This score is called 'the main.'"

"Then what?"

"Then he throws again. If his second score equals the main, he wins all the tokens. If he throws anything other than his main, he continues to throw until he gets the main—here he loses—or he gets his second score, in which case he wins. However, if he throws a two or a three, it is called 'crabs' and he loses at once."

Traed was not impressed. "Where is the challenge?"

"Ah! That is called 'hedging' or knowing the odds. Someone good at hedging can ensure his victory by the bet he places."

"Show me."

Rejar placed a bet on the table after the caster had thrown his second score. By carefully watching the throws, he was easily able to figure out the odds in his favor. So he was somewhat surprised when he lost his tokens.

Traed looked at him.

Rejar rubbed his ear. "I meant to do that . . . to show you how the game is played."

"Of course you did." Traed glanced at him out of the corner of his eye.

The caster "threw out" and the dice were passed to Rejar. He picked them up, weighing them in his palm. The hazard table at 77 Jermyn Street was notoriously crooked. Rejar, with his Familiar abilities, could tell at once that the cubes were not balanced.

He leaned over and spoke in Traed's ear. "The dice are askew. The game is set up for a loss."

"Do not play."

"I believe I can compensate for the imbalance in my throw."

Traed raised his eyebrow. Familiar's had an excellent sense of balance and coordination; he probably could. Traed swept his hand, palm side up, in front of the table, indicating to Rejar he thought this was an excellent idea. "By all means, *brother.*"

Rejar grinned at him.

He threw a main of 8. His second throw was also an 8.

Shouts of, "By God, he nicked it!" ran throughout the hall. Soon, the area was swarmed with players converging on the table.

"I've got some blunt on you, my man. Don't disappoint me—deliver the ready."

At the insidious voice coming from across the table, Rejar looked up.

And went stock still.

The man, avidly watching his tokens, did not notice Rejar's stance. Traed did. "What is it, Rejar?"

"This man—I will destroy him."

Instantly, warning bells went off in Traed's mind. "Why? What has he done to you?"

"Nothing—to me. He killed a child in the street."

Traed's features went to stone. "How?"

"He ran over him with his conveyance. I was too late to save the boy. He did not even stop."

"Are you sure it is him?"

"It is a face I will never forget." Traed could understand that; the man had a cruel, evil look about him.

There was one thing Traed could not abide and that was mistreatment of any living thing, especially a weaker life form. His arm went to the hilt of the retracted light saber he had concealed within his waistband.

Rejar's hand on his arm stopped him. "He is mine."

"Take my blade, then."

Rejar shook his head. "I will do this the Familiar way."

Traed did not approve. "Challenge him and be done with it."

"There are worse things than death to a man such as this."

"Such as?"

"It will not be today, but over time, I will make his

worst nightmare become his new reality. Watch . . ."

Traed was surprised at Rejar's insight. The words he spoke were wise. Wise beyond his years. There was more here than he let on. . . .

Rejar spoke to the man, a sharp smile carving the planes of his handsome face. "I will do the best I can. To whom do I give the pleasure of winning?"

"Lord Rotewick. And you'd best be winning me a great deal. I've had a nasty day; I'm not in the best of moods."

"Uh-oh. That be Rotewick 'is-self." Traed looked down, surprised to see Jackie at his side. They had left the man outside by the coach.

"Best tell yer brother to watch 'is step; the man is a fencing master, 'e is. Killed twenty men. Rumor what 'as it 'e once skewered a man dead for spilling white wine on 'is red coat only to later quip white wine ne'er went none with red—warn 'is Princeship, sir."

"Do not be concerned, Jackie, my brother can fend for himself."

"That may be true, but an extra set of peepers ne'er 'urt no one."

Traed smiled. "I will watch over him. What are you doing in here? Did we not leave you by the coach?"

Jackie grinned sheepishly. "I got a yen fer the hells sir. I met yer brother in one. 'Tis my ruination and that's a fact."

Traed nodded prosaically.

Rejar shook the dice in his palm. "Leave it to me. Your mood is in my hands, *Rot Wick*."

"That's Rotewick. Rote rhymes with smote, my dear fellow."

"Rhymes with *fot*." Traed murmured in an aside to Rejar, causing the Familiar to grin. *Fot* was an Aviaran word referring to a certain recess in the body. The description fit Rotewick perfectly.

"In my country, my dear fellow, we say Rot Wick." Rejar managed this straight-faced, even lifting his midnight eyebrow arrogantly at the end.

"And what is this country?" Rotewick disdainfully took some snuff.

"Russia. Allow me to introduce myself, I am Prince Nickolai Azov."

Rotewick clicked his heels together, nodding a bow. "Forgive me, your Highness." The pompous man was fuming.

Traed's peridot eyes danced with suppressed mirth. Rejar was at it.

"Nonsense, Rot Wick. *I* have nothing to forgive you for." Rejar threw the dice, scoring a 5. His second throw garnered a 9.

"Anything but a two, three, five, eleven or twelve, yer Princeship!"

Rejar threw a look at Jackie, who had somehow muscled up to the table to place his own bets. "Who is watching the coach, Jackie?"

"Got that covered—don't ye worry 'bout nothin' 'cepting throwing that nine, yer Princeship."

Rejar rolled his eyes and threw the 9.

The crowd cheered.

Traed took his elbow. "What are you doing?" He nodded Rotewick's way.

"Give me some time, Traed. Leave a hunt in the proper hands."

Traed stood down.

For the rest of the afternoon, Rejar threw and nicked it.

Lilac stared petulantly at the stitches stretched across her hoop.

The sampler was supposed to say "A Happy Home Is Blessed" but it looked more like "A Naddy Momc Is Piffed." She sighed. She was not very good at this. Perhaps Nickolai would not ask to see her creation. Shoulders slumped, she attempted a little lilac flower on the edge, oblivious to the women's comments around her regarding their husbands and marital duty.

If Lilac had been paying more attention to the conversation, she would have realized just how revealing the ladies were getting. With each stitch they took, the bolder they got.

The circle eyed the new Princess Azov with unabashed curiosity. Everyone was dying to know about the Prince. How had the handsome buck performed? Was he as promising as he looked? It was noted that the new bride, while reticent, had a becoming bloom to her cheeks which had not been there previously.

Lady Whitney gave a knowing look to Lady Hallston and started the conversation by saying, "Philip"—Phillip was Lady Whitney's elderly husband—"is a once-a-weeker at best. But I can always count on him after a rousing hunt; it seems to get his juices going."

"Lord Whitney has juices?" Lady Henry quipped, causing a round of snickering.

"Well, he thinks he does." Lady Whitney smirked. Philip Whitney was twice her age and three times her weight. She had been taking lovers for years.

"What I can't stand is when they paw you to death." Lady Hallston took the helm.

"Oh, I know!" Lilac stopped stitching for a moment. Even if she couldn't sew, she could at least try to join in the conversation. "And that business when they *lick* you all over . . ."

Twelve needle-baring hands froze in midair.

Preoccupied, Lilac attempted a French knot, continuing on, "And then there's that thing they do with their teeth . . ."

All needlework was immediately cast aside.

The women avidly leaned forward, eager to hear whatever choice bit the new bride was unwittingly giving out.

"Thing they do with their teeth?" Lady Sugarton prompted.

"You know—when they nip you like you're a choice morsel or something! Or that other thing . . ."

"*What* other thing?" Lady Whitney asked breathlessly.

"When they clamp their teeth on the back of your neck to hold you in place so they can . . . well, I'm sure you know what I mean."

Several of the women, eyes glazed, gasped.

"I swear I must have Nickolai's teeth marks all over me." She didn't—Rejar had been very careful with her tender skin, but Lilac didn't know that.

"Men do have their odd habits, don't they?" That gorgeous hell-born rogue of a Prince bit her? All over. Lady Whitney began fanning herself vigorously.

"Mmm, they certainly do." Lilac frowned as the French knot unraveled. Attempting another, she added distractedly, "Why, when I finish—"

"Don't you mean when *he* finishes, my dear?" Lady Henry interrupted, from the lofty viewpoint of years of experience with the opposite sex.

Lilac waved her hand. "Goodness, no! Nickolai takes *forever* to finish."

Twelve pairs of eyes bulged at the very thought.

"Sometimes," Lilac blithely went on, "I finish four or five times before he does."

Virginia Hallston's scissors crashed to the floor.

At that precise moment, the door opened and the butler announced, "Prince Azov—here for his wife."

Rejar walked into the Whitney drawing room.

Every female eye turned to stare at him with a such an intense scrutiny that his step momentarily faltered. What was this all about?

Briefly, he surveyed the room with a questioning expression. The women just kept gawking at him.

Spotting his wife in the far side of the circle of women, he said, "Lilac, are you ready to leave?"

"What? Oh, Nickolai, I didn't hear you arrive."

The twelve sets of eyes shifted to Lilac, incredulously. How could she be married to this magnificent specimen of a man and be so unaware? Several of the ladies present wanted to seal her up in the Egyptian sarcophagus which graced the center of Lady Whitney's drawing room.

"Um, yes, I'm ready." Lilac quickly stood, stuffing her erstwhile project into her bag. She said her good-byes to everyone, thanking Lady Whitney for inviting her.

Nickolai draped something around her, his hands lingering at her shoulders. She looked down. It was the green woolen shawl. Still within his embrace, she looked up at him.

"I do not want you to get cold." He spoke in a very intimate voice.

The shawl and his tone of voice brought to mind what had transpired between them earlier that day. Lilac's cheeks got noticeably rosier.

They stared at each other for an endless moment.

Even to the casual observer, the regard they had for each other was fraught with sizzling sensuality.

Then Prince Nickolai took his wife's hand and, saying farewell, left with her.

Several women began fanning themselves at once, and Virginia Hallston rang for cold drinks for the ladies.

Ice cold, she informed the butler.

Chapter Thirteen

Upon their return, Lilac decided to retire to her room to read until the evening meal. They had all elected to stay home that evening, which suited her just fine. It was chilly and damp outside; it would be a perfect night for reading by the fire.

She went into the library, picked out a few books, and carried them up to her room. Nickolai was already seated in the large chair in front of the fireplace.

Thinking his presence was an indication he might like to nap awhile, she asked, "Will I be disturbing you, Nickolai?"

Rejar looked at her. She always disturbed him. "Of course not."

"Oh. I thought you might like to . . ." This was not coming out right. Her speech faltered.

"Like to what?" A dimple curved his sensual mouth.

"Never mind. Would you like one of these books to read, then?"

He shook his head. "Let me see what you were doing with the threads at Lady Whitney's."

Her shoulders sagged. The last thing she wanted him looking at was her hideous creation. "It was nothing. Really."

Rejar wondered why she was being so reticent about it. With his honed instincts, he sensed some intrigue here. Grinning, he crooked a beckoning finger at her. "I want to see it."

"Very well." She sighed. Resigned to the fact that her husband usually got what he wanted, she tromped over to her bag and pulled out the disaster. He better not laugh. She peered surreptitiously at it. He was sure to laugh.

Warily, she approached his chair, clutching the fabric to her bosom.

Nickolai patted his lap.

Gingerly, she perched on his thigh.

"Well?" He held out his hand.

"Very well—here." She almost flung the scrap at him.

Rejar looked down at the piece of linen. Since the letters had no meaning to him, all he saw were the tiny stitches and dainty needlework. "It is beautiful, Lilac."

So, he was going to make sport of her! Her chin notched up. "Don't tease me, Nickolai."

"Tease you?" Rejar was genuinely surprised. "Why would I tease you? Rarely have I seen such intricate workmanship. The colors of the threads are woven perfectly—here." He pointed to a spot where she had jumbled up the strands.

He didn't seem to realize the section he found so colorful was a dreadful mistake. Lilac chewed her bottom lip. "The floss sort of knotted up there."

"And over here"—his tapered finger traced the fabric—"a little lilac."

She twisted her head sideways as she stared at the clump of purple knots. "You can tell?"

"Of course. I will treasure it always."

Lilac was stunned. "You want it?" No one had ever wanted anything she had made before. Especially her embroidery.

He raised an eyebrow. "And why would I not?"

"Because it's . . . it's . . ."

"Beautiful. Like you, *souk-souk.*"

Lilac's face lit up. "Nickolai! You really like it, don't you?"

"Have I not said?" He smiled sweetly at her.

Lilac was so moved by the gesture that she unwittingly took his gorgeous face between her two hands and kissed him soundly on the lips.

Rejar was so moved by *her* gesture that he almost made the mistake of taking over the embrace. He stopped himself just in time. This was probably a measure of gratitude and not emotion on her part.

Something about the thought troubled him deeply, but he squelched his concerns. They would not be mates if they did not have the capacity for great affection for each other.

Lilac simply needed time to adjust to the change in her life. When she did, she would come to realize how much she meant to him. How serious he could be. How much he . . .

Why think of it now? There were better ways to spend the late afternoon in Ree Gen Cee Ing Land than worrying needlessly about such an obvious thing. They *were* mated. Her breath had become his. She belonged to him.

Abruptly standing with his mate in his arms, he grabbed one of the books off the side table as he made his way to the bed. Depositing her gently on the mat-

Dara Joy

tress, he handed the book to her.

Plopping down on the bed near her feet, he instructed her, "Read to me."

"Now?" Lilac was surprised by his behavior. And a little disappointed. By the way his eyes had lit up when she kissed him, she thought for sure he was going to . . .

"Yes, now." He smiled at her.

"And you want me to read this?" She looked down at the book he had given her; it was *The Tempest* by William Shakespeare. Not exactly the type of subject a man might ask a woman to read aloud. Most men would choose a romantic sonnet. It was an odd request.

Nonetheless, he gestured with his hand for her to begin.

"Very well." Leaning back against the headboard, Lilac opened the book and began to read while her husband lounged across the foot of the bed.

After a while, Nickolai began tickling her ankles. With his mouth.

Lilac looked up from her page. "Stop that or I shan't continue."

He grinned at her, but motioned for her to proceed.

She read, " 'Full fathom five thy father lies . . . ' "

Nickolai lifted the bottom of her skirt and began to kiss her leg through the thin cottony material of her pantalettes. Soon his dark head completely disappeared under her skirts.

"Nickolai."

"Go on, I am listening." Came the muffled voice.

She was skeptical, but continued on, " 'Of his bones are coral made . . . ' " His damp open mouth blew a puff of heated breath against the gauzy material on her upper leg. "Nickolai, what are you doing under there?"

262

"Keep reading." The voice ordered from beneath her skirts.

" 'Those are pearls that were his eyes . . . ' Oh!"

His hot tongue wiggled the slit of her pantalettes at the juncture of her thighs. "I believe I am about to find my own pearl."

Lilac swallowed.

"Read, *souk-souk*."

" 'Nothing of him that doth fade . . . ' Nickolai, what are you *licking?*" His tongue swept along the vertical, open seam in a long, slow lap. "Oh, my God! Stop that at once!"

He did not, of course.

{Would you not give me what I desire, my Lilac?}

She was so unnerved by what he was doing to her that she didn't even realize he had sent her the thought. If she had paid more attention, she would have immediately noticed he couldn't possibly be both speaking and doing what he was doing at the same time.

She tried to regain her faint voice. "What is it you desire, Nickolai?"

{Just a taste of what I crave . . . from your sweetness.} His nimble tongue darted through the slit. Lilac's whole body shuddered.

"N-Nickolai . . ."

{Continue with the story, Lilac.}

She made an attempt. " 'B-but doth suffer a sea-change into something rich and strange . . . ' "

There was a man beneath her skirts—between her legs—that changed into something rich and strange.

An exotic, wildly handsome creature who knew how to use his tongue.

Lilac gave up all pretense of reading the play when his tongue slid inside her with a delicious stroke. Only to wriggle about in a most sensational way.

"Sto—Ohhhhh."

{I agree. What say you to this?} He swirled around his "pearl," flicking the hidden nub repeatedly with the tip of his very talented tongue.

"Ohhhh . . ."

{Mmmm—I thought you might say that. And this?} He suckled on her.

"Oh! Oh! Oh!"

{Do you like my poetry, Lilac?} He licked her over and over. *{Is it metered and rhymed to your delight?}*

Lilac was beyond answering. She moaned incoherent phrases.

{When you are ready, I want your release against my mouth, souk-souk, so I can feel your pleasure on my lips.}

If those words weren't enough to do it, his next action certainly was. His tongue slipped inside her and he *pur-r-r-ed.* . . .

Lilac did exactly as he asked.

Unable to withstand his intense erotica another moment, she burst into a thousand fragments. And every one of them had his name on it.

There was a rustle of her skirts and Nickolai's tousled head popped up. Looking rather like the cat who swallowed the family canary, he quirked a raven eyebrow at her.

"Nickolai . . ." she gasped, still trying to regain her breath.

"Lilac." He said her name with an upward tilt of his mouth. A teasing, knowing sound of utter deliberation.

Against her better judgement, her lips twitched. "So," she said, picking up the book, "do you want to hear the rest of this?"

Rejar let out a roar of laughter. Smiling seductively down at her, he said, "By all means. Let us see what the next page holds, shall we?"

As Lilac began to read and Nickolai began to do something extremely interesting with the pads of his fingers, she couldn't help remarking on how much trouble her pantalettes had gotten her into that day.

Rejar whispered in her ear that it was not the pantalettes.

By that evening word was all over the ton about Lilac's enticing "tell all" at Lady Whitney's.

Leona Harcorte heard the story at a rout she was attending. Even though she had suspected the Prince knew his way around the sheets, the bride's story of the groom's prowess went beyond all expectations.

It was time for her to begin laying her foundational trap.

A man of his proclivities would not stay satisfied long with his innocent little wife. Leona intended to be first in line when the Prince let loose. It was always best to catch these rogues while they still had plenty of energy left.

She immediately decided she would throw a small, impromptu dinner party the next evening for some of their mutual friends. On exiting the rout, she headed back to her home to write out her invitations.

Leona decided to send a personal note of friendship along with her invitation to Lilac. The kindhearted, gullible chit would definitely accept, bringing her sensational husband in tow.

Perhaps she should include the brother as well?

Leona had heard some amazing reports about him; her curiosity needed satisfying. She quickly jotted his name on the invitation.

The following morning Lilac received the invitation along with the personal note. As Leona had predicted, she immediately accepted. Much to her husband's and Lady Agatha's displeasure.

"She is my friend, Nickolai. If you do not wish to attend, then don't."

There was no way he would let her attend any function Lady Harcorte sponsored by herself. He had seen Lady Harcorte in a disturbing light at Byron's country home. "I will accompany you, Lilac, but Leona Harcorte is no friend of yours."

"Believe as you like." She turned to Traed. "The invitation was extended to you, Traed. Will you not join us?"

Traed had no intentions of doing anything else; he needed to keep a close eye on Rejar. "I will definitely be there."

Rejar looked at his brother-of-the-line, surprised by his ready acceptance. Traed normally was not one to socialize with strangers. With any, for that matter. The man was typically a loner.

Lilac turned to her aunt, ready to offer up an apology; Auntie Whumples was not included in the invitation. Before she could speak, however, Agatha forestalled her.

"Do not even ask me as I will not step foot into that Cyprian's house!"

"Very well, Auntie; if that is your wish. We shall miss you." Lilac's eyes twinkled with a private amusement. It did not go unnoticed by her husband.

They arrived at Lady Harcorte's town home just before eight in the evening. There were about twenty-five people present for this small, impromptu gathering of the *beau monde*.

Rejar had already warned Traed that the evening meal in a gathering such as this could last from three to four hours. Rejar did not think Traed believed him. Well, he would find out soon enough when plate after plate arrived with no end in sight. He groaned inwardly. Much of the food here was not particularly to his liking.

Since dinner was called for eight, there would not be too much time to socialize before they were ushered from the drawing room into the dining room.

Just before dinner was announced, Leona Harcorte strategically angled her way over to the Prince's party. When they were called to table, she intended to have Prince Azov escort her.

Leona hesitated slightly when she caught sight of the man next to the Prince. He was almost as tall as Prince Azov and just as well built. But the physical resemblance ended there.

This was no sultry, sensual creature she faced. There was something about this one which gave her pause.

He was dangerous to his core.

She approached the darkly handsome, enigmatically brooding man and waited while Lilac introduced her.

Tapping him lightly on his arm with her fan, she smiled coquettishly up at him, several carmine plumes fluttering in her hair. "And what does Prince Nickolai's brother think of our little group?"

Glittering green eyes flicked down at her in cool appraisal. He scanned the guests, paying particular attention to the mode of dress of several fops. The corners of his etched mouth curved sardonically. "Otherworldly," was all he said.

In honor of the Prince, Leona had donned a clinging dress, which she had naturally dampened. The sheer, wet material was not much of a covering, yet this contained man seemed not even to notice the enticing style. It irritated Leona.

Dara Joy

When the butler announced dinner was being served, her annoyance prompted her to loop her arm through the older brother's. "How nice of you to escort me, Mr. Yaniff."

Traed watched her knowingly. "Traed."

Leona, thinking he was giving her permission to use his first name, responded, "Then you may call me Leona." She fingered the strand of pearls at her throat, "Please take care not to tread upon my dress—for nothing is under it but my modesty."

His mocking jade glance raked over her. "I do not believe your modesty is to be found . . . under there. *Lee-oh-nah.*"

Her pretty brown eyes flashed with annoyance at the subtle insult as he briskly marched her into the dining room.

As Rejar had predicted, course after course was presented to the table.

Lady Harcorte had taken to the Continental custom of sending footmen around with the dishes. In this way, everyone had a chance to taste everything, not simply those dishes which happened to be at one's end of the table. Such munificence made Lady Harcorte's table a well-sought-after one.

The first course started out with mulligatawny and turtle soups. This was followed by salmon and turbot surrounded with smelts.

Lady Harcorte, at the head of the table, addressed Rejar, who had been seated by design to her right. "Russian caviar, your Highness; I procured it expressly for you." She nodded at the footman, who placed a spoonful on his plate.

Rejar looked at the black lumpy mass and swallowed the bile rising in his throat. *By* Aiyah, *what was it?*

"Thank you; that was most thoughtful of you, Lady Harcorte." Gingerly, he followed her lead, spreading some of the gooey mass on a hard, flat biscuit.

Lilac, seated next to him, watched him curiously out of the corner of her eye.

Taking a deep breath, he popped the noxious stuff into his mouth. He blinked. *It was hideous!* Forcing himself to swallow, he smiled rather sickly to Lady Harcorte. "Delicious," he managed to croak.

Lilac dabbed at the corners of her mouth with her napkin to hide her blossoming grin. It was obvious to her that her husband could not abide the vile stuff. An impish light imbued her green eyes. "Oh, then do have more, Nickolai! I can see how much you love it." She snagged the footman bearing the caviar and plopped a large spoonful onto his plate.

Nickolai privately sent her a fulminating glare.

She batted her eyelashes at him, then quickly turned to engage the person on her left in conversation. Lilac tried not to giggle when she heard him mutter something foreign under his breath. The Russian Prince was forced by politesse to take another bite of the Russian caviar.

With the serving of the first course, a curious phenomenon seemed to settle about the room. As soon as the first spoonful of soup lifted to waiting lips, a constant thirst arose out of nowhere, afflicting all of the guests at once. Port, sherry, hock, ratafia, and claret were liberally poured to stave off the malady.

And continued to be poured throughout the long feast.

This naturally led to an ambiance of geniality, which, over the course of several hours, led to total stupefaction.

The second course was served.

There was roast hare, roast pheasant, roast turkey, Bolognese sausage, Laplander reindeer tongues, Westphalian ham, pistachio cream, burnt cream, roast woodcock, collared pig, and stewed mushrooms. Then came the French dishes, potatoes, cauliflower, Spanish olives—the platters kept coming.

Traed caught Rejar's eye. Neither man could believe the lavish amount of food spread before them. On Aviara, feasts were customary, but not on this scale. Rejar could not help but think of the hungry people begging for food that he had seen wandering the streets of this savage world. In light of that, this display seemed almost obscene to him.

The various aromas mingled, filling the room with scent of gluttony.

[Did I not tell you?]

Traed inclined his head slightly, acknowledging Rejar's thought.

"Your Highness," Lord Wolfston, seated across the table from Rejar, addressed him, "do you think it likely Napoleon will invade your homeland?"

Rejar paused in the act of picking up his wineglass. "Who is this Napoleon?" he blandly asked.

For a tension-fraught moment the table went completely silent. Whereupon, Beau Brummell, seated at the far end of the table, burst out laughing. "Marvelous wit!" he declared, setting the tone for the rest of the diners, who immediately broke into laughter and saluted Rejar with their glasses.

The words "who is this Napoleon" echoed around the room as if it were the cleverest of jests. Lilac gave her husband the oddest look. She believed he meant exactly what he said: He had no idea who Napoleon was. Yet these people thought him a marvelous wit. She gnashed her teeth. Oh, the irony!

"Prince Azov," Wolfston chuckled, "may I pirate your *bon mot*?"

Rejar, having no idea what a bon mot was, replied, "If my wife does not object to its loss, you may pirate it."

This caused another round of raucous joviality.

Lady Harcorte rested her hand on Rejar's arm. She lifted her lashes slowly in a blatantly seductive motion. "You are a sly boots, aren't you?"

Lilac leaned forward, taking note of their hostess's personal gesture with her husband. For some reason, it bothered her immensely. She instantly took affrontage. Why was that woman's claw on Nickolai's arm?

To make matters worse, Nickolai bent close to the woman and said something in an intimate tone to her. Fuming, Lilac kicked him under the table.

Rejar paused, blinked once, then finished what he was saying to Leona Harcorte. He turned to his wife.

Lilac did not like the twinkle in his blue eye one bit. Instead of being properly chastened like any normal husband would be, he seemed greatly amused.

In fact, the expression on his face as he regarded her might be interpreted as delighted.

"Something upsetting you, *souk-souk*?"

"Don't *souk-souk* me! Stop speaking to that woman in that tone of—of face!"

He grinned at her, making her realize her faux pas. "Are you possessive of me, my Lilac?"

"Don't be silly! I—I just think that you should be more—more circumspect in your dealings." She stammered defensively, trying to cover her idiotic display.

Smiling triumphantly, Nickolai's arm curved around her shoulders, his hand going up to her topknot to give it a little tug. He purred sexily in her ear. "I hate your hair."

Her mouth rounded into a surprised O.

Taking advantage of her combination of shock and dismay, he whispered softly, "Let me release it, *souk-souk*, so I can see it spill down your back and I will remember how it feels as it flows over me at night like the finest *krilli* cloth, streaming down my chest, across my hip, feathering my—"

"Stop that!" Lilac turned beet red.

Chuckling low, her husband turned away to answer a question from across the table.

He was odious! Why couldn't he be more well-behaved like his brother? Her sights went across the table to where Traed sat, quietly eating his meal.

The guests on either side of him had attempted to engage the stony-eyed man in conversation, but on receiving only monosyllabic replies from him, they soon turned their attentions elsewhere.

Even in a room full of people, Lilac noted that Nickolai's brother seemed secluded and apart. She wondered why that was. On the occasions when they had engaged in conversations, she had found him to be attentive, interesting, and extremely intelligent. She was sure his present behavior was not due to reticence, for his persona was almost bold in nature.

With his captivating looks, she would have thought he would have chatted up several of the women by now. By the coveted glances some of the female guests had been sending his way, they certainly hoped he would do just that.

Yet, there he sat, patiently apart. Solitary.

Despite this, there was a quality about the lone, handsome man that evoked her compassion toward him. He was something of an enigma.

As if he read her thoughts, he looked up suddenly from the forkful of food he was about to put into his mouth, catching her eye. She smiled gently at him.

He returned her smile with a small one of his own.

She read his look exactly. Unlike Nickolai, who seemed to be at ease wherever he went, neither Traed nor she really belonged here at this garish outing. It was something she had in common with Nickolai's brother and at that moment a special, silent bond of understanding formed between them.

Plates were cleared once again and desert arrived.

Ordered up from Messrs. Grange, the dessert was, again, an extravagant affair. Fresh strawberries, exotic hothouse fruits, all manner of pies, and confections. The selections seemed endless.

Leona addressed Alvanley, "Your favorite apricot tartlet, my lord." Lord Alvanley beamed. In spite of the outrageous expense he had an apricot tartlet every day.

A footman placed a slice of apple *tarte tatin* in front of Nickolai. His dual-colored eyes lit up. Lilac had long suspected her husband had something of a sweet tooth. She was proven right when he took a bite, saying to her, "Mmm, what do you call this?"

Strange, but he was pointing to the apple, not the tart itself.

Lilac looked at him askance. Was he jesting? Who didn't know an apple when they saw one? Surely they had apples in Russia.

"A kumquat," she replied drolly. Lilac had never actually seen a kumquat, but she had read all about the little orange fruits from China.

He looked boyishly confused. "A come-kwat?"

She nodded, hiding her grin.

"Ah. It is good." He slowly licked the filling off his fork with the edge of his industrious tongue.

Lilac's wide gaze riveted to that hardworking, swirling tongue of his.

Rejar watched her knowingly from beneath thick lashes.

"Have you been to Ireland or Scotland yet, your Highness?" Leona leaned forward, her deep cleavage threatening the tensile strength of her dampened gown. "The hunting and fishing there are marvelous. Perhaps you would like to join a group of us next time we go—you do hunt?" The innuendo in her throaty voice was unmistakable.

Rejar's glance fell to his wife. "On occasion," he murmured cryptically.

"Excellent! Then you must join us!" Leona was already making her plans.

It did not go unnoticed by Lilac that she did not seem to be included in the invitation.

Nor by Traed.

His pastel gaze shifted speculatively from his plate to Lady Harcorte.

After dinner, Madeline Fensley cornered Lilac in the drawing room while the men were still in the dining room enjoying their port.

"Is it true?" she asked her breathlessly.

Lilac furrowed her brow. "Is what true?"

"Did he really lick you all over?"

Lilac paled. Her hand went to her throat. "Who told you that?"

"Why it's all over the ton, my dear girl!"

She suddenly felt rather sick. Whatever possessed her to trust those women? What could she have been thinking of?

It had just seemed so nice to be able to confide in other women for once.

Everyone seemed to be talking intimately about the same subject. Why had they chosen her words to bandy about? Surely, they had all experienced similar things.

Madeline Fensley nudged her out of her reverie. "Come now, Lilac, why so shy?"

The dining room doors opened and the men rejoined them.

Lilac put a hand to her perspiring forehead. What would she do if Nickolai found out? She hadn't meant to be so indiscreet. "What?" she whispered distractedly.

"I said, cat got your tongue?"

At that precise moment Nickolai came up beside her. "Mmm, most definitely." He winked smartly at Madeline, her unknowing pun amusing him.

Lilac blanched.

She had to get rid of Madeline right away! Before the woman alerted Nickolai to her indiscretion. "You know what they say, Madeline." She stared pointedly at the woman, trying to give her a clue. "Curiosity killed the cat."

Nickolai's eyes widened slightly.

"Yes, darling." Madeline was not going to take the bait. "But t'was information which brought him back."

What a humorous tenet, Rejar thought, not understanding a thing that was going on between the two women. He must remember to tell it to his mother.

Lilac was beyond repartee. "Please . . ." she almost begged the other woman, her eyes filling with tears.

"She's such a sensitive little thing, your Highness." Madeline smirked, pitiless.

Rejar's brow furrowed. Concerned by his wife's sudden distress, he ran his finger tenderly down her smooth cheek. "What is it, Lilac?"

A single tear slipped out of her closed eyes.

"Would you excuse us?" It was not a question. It was

a royal command. Madeline Fensley immediately left them alone.

Rejar guided her into the darkened alcove to his right. "What troubles you so, *souk-souk?*"

"I didn't mean to, Nickolai. I swear I didn't!"

Rejar frowned. "What did you do?" He prepared himself for the worst.

"It was just that I thought I could trust them not to say anything—we were all talking about our husbands . . ." She bit her lip.

Had she given his secret away? This could be serious for all of them. She was not ready to accept the consequences such a disclosure would entail. "Tell me exactly what you told them." His hands cupped her shoulders.

"I told them how you liked to . . . do I have to tell you, Nickolai?" she sniffed.

"Yes," he ground out. "You must tell me, Lilac. Now. Perhaps I can undo this damage you have done."

"I—I told them how you—you lick me." Her voice dropped off at the end.

He was stunned. This was not what he expected to hear. *"You what?"*

She nodded dismally. "And how you like to use your teeth . . ."

His lips parted. He just stared at her. "Is that all?"

She looked at his booted feet. "And how you take forever . . ." She twisted her dress. "This is terribly embarrassing," she mumbled into her chest.

The humor of the situation got to him. A dimple curved his twitching mouth. Since Lilac was still looking at the floor, she missed his expression, hearing only the sternness of his voice. "So, you would discuss me to others."

Her head snapped up. He quickly lost the dimples.

Lilac grabbed his lapels, her tear-streaked face beseeching him to understand. "I would never do that, Nickolai! I wasn't paying attention—not really. I was embroidering!"

"Ah. That explains it. It is difficult to think and do such intricate work at the same time." He teased her.

She looked down again and sniffed.

His arms came around her. "Do not worry about it, Lilac. There is no harm done." He kissed her forehead.

"Do you mean it?" Her sweet, imploring face tugged at his heart.

"Have I not said? Best we go back into the room before we give them more to gossip about." He tugged her topknot, smiling to himself when it listed to the side.

Unaware that the bun on the top of her head was lopsided, she rejoined the group, taking a seat on a couch next to Lady Hendrake. The elderly woman, dying for an ear to gossip to, dived into a tedious story about some earl's son who had run off with a baker's daughter. Lilac listened silently, pouting at the boring tale.

With her pouting mouth and sagging hair, Rejar thought she had never looked more adorable.

Taking a glass of claret from a passing waiter, he sat behind her, in a chair near the wall.

Truthfully, he was getting tired of the evening's excesses. He longed to go back to the house, back to Lilac's bed. His sights sought out his brother, Traed. He was surprised to see him talking with Lady Harcorte.

Traed spoke in a low, commanding voice to his erstwhile hostess. It was time to inform her that her game with his brother was finished.

"If you desire to hunt, I suggest to you, Lee-oh-nah,

that you have a care for your choice of prey."

Leona was not easily intimidated. At the veiled threat, her eyes instantly narrowed. No one told her what to do. Ever. "I see." She ran the lip of her fan mockingly down his chiseled cheek. "And what prey would you suggest?"

Traed watched her from beneath lowered lids. The woman was overly bold. "Never play with something unless you know the danger of its bite," he said quietly.

Instead of dampening her interest, his words of warning only served to entice her. "Perhaps we can discuss this dangerous bite later, hmmm?" Not giving him a chance to answer, she left him, her steps seeking out Rejar's location.

Traed's green eyes watched her from across the room.

He would have to shift her focus. He did not like the unhealthy interest she was showing in his mated brother. As Rejar's *Chi'in t'se Leau* it was up to him to protect him—from any threat.

In his opinion, this woman could cause much trouble for his brother. Traed had noted the hurt look on Lilac's face when she had not been included in the woman's false invitation to hunt.

Traed smiled sardonically.

Familiars were not the only ones who had a talent for the sport. Aviaran warriors were known on occasion to engage in the pastime.

Rejar settled back in his chair to watch his mate.

He noticed every tiny nuance of her.

The texture of her skin, the shape of her hands. The curve of her ear, the softness of her skin. Her smile.

He loved to see her smile.

Feeling suddenly frisky, he decided to share his provocative thoughts with her. *{Do you know what I am going to do to you when I get you home, souk-souk?}*

Lilac looked up at the opposite wall, hunching her shoulders. She had received his message.

{I am going to lick you all over, exactly the way you told those women. Lap you up like sticky spun crystal . . . }

Still looking at Lady Hendrake, Lilac pushed her sagging topknot to the crown of her head with a shaking hand. Nickolai was speaking in her mind! Lilac responded to the chattering elderly woman with an ashen smile.

She would kill him! He had promised to stop that naughty behavior!

He continued relentlessly. *{I will scrape my tongue across your velvet skin so I can feel every curve, every ripple, every little nuance of you . . . }*

Lilac broke out in goose bumps.

She glanced over her shoulder at Nickolai. His seductive, lazy gaze bore into her from over the rim of his wineglass.

Deliberately, he watched her while he gradually sipped at his wine.

Taking his sweet time, he dipped the tip of his tongue into the glass, moistening it with the wine. He stroked his tongue delicately around the rim. Just to torment her.

Lilac fidgeted in her seat. Rejar smiled.

{Then, when you are ready, my beautiful little wife, I will give you that special kiss we both know you like so well. I am going to glide my tongue right between your—}

"Stop it! Stop it! Stop it!" Lilac stood up.

"Excuse me?" Lady Hendrake was appalled.

"Forgive me, Lady Hendrake. I'm not feeling well this evening."

"Perhaps we should leave." Her husband came up behind her. There was a satisfied smirk on his handsome face. Once again, he had gotten what he desired.

Lilac was tempted to stomp on his arrogant foot.

Ignoring the darts her eyes were throwing at him, he took her hand and, collecting Traed, said good night to their hostess.

Leona Harcorte stared out at the cloudless night before pulling the draperies shut.

The night had not gone as she had hoped.

The Prince was not yet ready to accept her blatant offer. It was painfully apparent by the smoldering glances he kept sending his wife that the rogue was still enamored of her. Consequently, she was alone this evening. *How utterly boring.*

Standing before her boudoir mirror, she plucked the carmine plumes from her hair, releasing it from its intricate style. The soft brown waves cascaded about her shoulders. She ran her fingers through the tangled mass.

A movement in the mirror caught her attention.

"Who's there?" she called out, hoping her strong voice masked her trepidation. Leona never allowed herself to show fear.

The Prince's brother stepped boldly out of her dressing room.

She was surprised. Immensely pleased but surprised.

"However did you get in here? I saw you leave with your brother and his wife."

Tread crossed his arms and leaned against a wall. "So you did."

Leona raised her chin. The man was arrogant. Albeit captivating. She would have to nip that annoyingly arrogant attitude in the bud before sampling the dangerous delicacy. Her men always danced attendance on her—not the other way around.

"You are a bit presumptuous, don't you think? I don't recall inviting you to my bedroom." Not in so many words, at any rate.

"Do you not?"

His cool appraisal unnerved her; the brooding handsomeness was really rather alluring. It struck her clearly that this was a man who would always do as he pleased. Both in and out of the boudoir. There would be no "nipping" with this one.

A sizzle of excitement raced through her. *It would be different . . .*

"Should I leave?" He raised a self-assured eyebrow, already knowing what her answer would be.

It would not do to play with him, she realized. Dropping her false outrage, she smiled seductively while sashaying provocatively towards him. "Why be hasty?"

"Why, indeed," he murmured.

Leona stood on tiptoe, reaching behind the strong column of his neck. She released the queue which held back his midnight-mahogany hair. The waist-length strands shifted to fall about his shoulders.

Lord, he's stunning, she thought. Positively stunning!

A rumble of thunder sounded above, interrupting her impression. *Funny, the sky had looked clear just a few minutes ago. . . .*

As if to belie her observation, an arc of lightning flashed, illuminating the room; it silhouetted the arresting, masculine face before her. The sight of those intense, chiseled features alight with the passion of the storm made Leona's breath still in her throat.

Eyes of the clearest green surveyed the length of her. When he raised his dark lashes, she could have sworn those pastel eyes were *sparking*.

She shook her head, thinking herself the silliest of women; it must be the lightning making them appear that way.

"The weather seems to have changed." She stated the obvious in an attempt to regain normalcy in a situation which seemed to be going completely awry.

"Consider it atmosphere." The corners of his mouth curved enigmatically.

There was a wealth of secrets in that smile. He really was exciting her. However, Leona preferred to be the one in control.

In a typical power play, she stepped back from him. "I think I should like a drink. There are many questions I have about your—"

A strong arm came around her like a band of iron; the fingers of his hand splaying against her scalp. Without delay, he pulled her head back, exposing the arch of her throat to him. "Yes or no," he whispered against her lips.

The string of pearls around her throat snapped, scattering and rolling across the bedroom floor. Overcome, Leona clutched at his powerful shoulders. "Yes," she breathed.

He took her to bed.

She begged him to stop. She begged him not to stop. Lady Harcorte knew not which.

Traed ta'al Yaniff, Aviaran warrior, did not pay the least attention to her passionate entreaties one way or the other. He simply proceeded.

After all, she had been warned.

Chapter Fourteen

Aviara

"Lorgin! Lorgin, wake up!" Deana shook her husband's shoulder. Normally the lightest of sleepers, tonight of all nights, he seemed to be in a dead sleep. Probably because I've been keeping him up all night, every night, she reluctantly admitted.

Well, these last months were no picnic, and why should she have to suffer alone? It was his fault to begin with! Not telling her how the Transference *really* worked . . .

She punched his arm.

"Mmm . . . I am not hungry." Lorgin tried to burrow under his pillow.

"Who cares if you're hungry? Lorgin ta'al Krue, wake up this minute!" She pounced on his broad back.

"I am up." The resigned voice came from under the pillow.

"Good, because I want you to go into the village and get the healer."

His golden blond head rustled out of the bedcovers. He turned on one side to face her. "The healer? Are you ill?"

She whacked him with her pillow. How could such a brilliant, magnificent warrior be so dumb? "No, I am not ill! It's *time*."

His brow furrowed. "Time for what?"

Time for what! "Time to have the baby!" A dull pain gripped her lower back. "Please hurry, Lorgin!"

Lorgin came instantly awake, all peripheries working. He leapt out of bed. "You are sure?"

"Of course, I'm sure—now go!"

"Let me see." He ran his large palm gently over the swell of her stomach. He looked at her. "You are right, Adeeann. The babe is ready to come."

She knew that . . . but how did he know that? Chocking it up to another Aviaran oddity—and they were legion—she motioned for him to leave.

He grinned. "You do not need a healer, Adeeann."

"Are you nuts? And who's going to deliver the baby? You?"

"Yes."

Deana's mouth gaped. "Stop trying to make me laugh—this is serious, Lorgin."

"Very serious," he agreed.

A sweat broke out across her brow. When Lorgin had that look, he usually meant what he said. Oh no. "Don't do this to me now, Lorgin. Go get the healer."

Lorgin sat on the edge of the bed, taking her hand in his. "There is no need to be concerned, *zira*. It is a time-honored tradition. Aviaran fathers teach their sons how to birth their children into the world. I will bring forth the babe."

Deana stared at him, stunned.

"Does this not make you happy?" he asked sweetly.

She started screaming her head off like a woman possessed.

"I want a doctor, do you hear me! I want a hospital! I want people wearing scrub suits around me with masks!" A particularly sharp pain gripped her lower belly. *"I want morphine!"*

Lorgin's eyes widened; he backed off from the bed—carefully.

"But, *zira*—"

Deana would later swear that her head turned one hundred and eighty degrees just like the kid in *The Exorcist.* Surely that deep, inhuman voice which came from her mouth was not her own. "GET THAT HEALER!" said the voice from hell.

Lorgin stood transfixed in the middle of the bedroom, gaping at the changeling that was once his lovable wife. He swallowed, trying to figure out how to deal with this zealous creature. It would not do to provoke it.

"Are you having some difficulty, Lorgin ta'al Krue?" The amused question came from the bedroom doorway.

Lorgin gratefully greeted the visitor. "Yaniff! Why does she act this way? Our custom is one in which wives find much joy. Surely she misunderstood me?"

Yaniff chuckled. "I think not, Lorgin. Things are much different in her world." His sights went to the corner of the room where their tree had already grown a small connecting room for the babe. Over time, Yaniff knew, many rooms would be added to this house and they would all be filled with happiness.

A loud wail came from the bed, followed by a scary roar of outrage.

Lorgin paled.

"I will speak to her. Perhaps I can ease your path."

"Thank you, Yaniff." Lorgin ran his damp palms down his thighs. He was so concerned, he had not even realized he was standing in the middle of the room stark naked.

Yaniff found this extremely humorous. Lorgin was their finest warrior; in the past he had faced down countless enemies, not to mention dangerous beasts of all kinds. Yet, here he stood like a youth in his first battle. Truly, he loved his wife.

"You may wish to put on some *tracas* while I speak to her. She may feel more comfortable giving birth into the hands of a man who at least has on some *tracas*." Yaniff's eyes twinkled.

Lorgin looked down, surprised to see he was completely unclothed. He stormed over to a cabinet and, pulling out a pair of black leather pants, slipped them on.

Yaniff approached the bed. "Adeeann."

"Yaniff!" She grabbed the old wizard's hand. "Help me! You said you would send me back when ever I wished—well, I want to go now! You may deliver me to a place called Mass General. The front door will be fine."

Lorgin came up to the bed. He had overheard her words and he was blazing with anger. "Yaniff, what does she mean when she says you will send her back whenever she wishes? Think you I would allow such a thing? I forbid—" Yaniff motioned him behind his back to be silent.

Due to his *zira's* condition, he stood down; but he fully intended to straighten Yaniff out about that ridiculous idea of his wife's.

"Adeeann," Yaniff began calmly, "what is all this

commotion about?" He sat on the edge of the bed.

Deana started to cry. "I'm so scared, Yaniff. I really do think I need a hospital—with lots of professional people and tons of medicine."

"There, there." The old man patted her hand. "I can assure you Lorgin will do fine; Krue has trained him. He knows what to do to help you. Think of the beautiful experience it will be for the two of you to share such a momentous event together. The life you have both created will take its first breath surrounded only by the love of its parents. It is the Aviaran way."

"But I'm not Aviaran." Her lower lip quivered.

"Nonsense. You became Aviaran the instant you accepted Lorgin's troth." He leaned over, speaking quietly near her ear. "Would I leave you in less than the best of hands?"

Knowing Yaniff as she did, she had to acknowledge his words. "No, I know you wouldn't."

He squeezed her hand. "You see? Everything will be fine. You have my word on it."

Deana instantly relaxed. If Yaniff said it, then it would be so.

"Do you trust Lorgin?" he wisely asked her.

"More than anyone in my life," she whispered.

"Than you have spoken for yourself. I will leave the two of you now." He kissed her forehead, then nodded to Lorgin, who was standing by the door. "Walk with me, Lorgin. I believe your *zira* is inclined to the Aviaran way now."

Before Lorgin walked the old mystic down the stairs to the living level, he paused, turning back to Deana. He met her wide-eyed, frightened look with a level one of his own. "I will be right back, *zira*."

Deana nodded nervously.

Downstairs, Lorgin said what was on his mind.

"What is this nonsense of you returning Adeeann to her world should she desire it?"

Yaniff smiled. "Do you see her desire it?"

"That is not the point and well you know it. You can not interfere with an oath couple! What were you thinking to promise her such a thing?"

"The illusion serves her well. So long as she believes she has the power to return to her world, the more comfortable she feels in remaining."

"I do not like it."

"Come now, Lorgin, surely a warrior such as yourself can keep his woman happy enough so she would not want to return to her old home." Yaniff was being his usual sly self.

Lorgin was not to be misled. "I would have your oath, as well, Yaniff," he shrewdly demanded.

The ancient wizard watched him. "And what oath could I give you that would still honor my oath to her?"

"You can honor your oath to her, but *only* with my permission."

Yaniff snickered. "You have always been an excellent student, Lorgin."

He smiled. "So, you agree?"

"How can I not?"

"Good. I best return to Adeeann."

"She will be fine."

"I am relieved to hear you speak thus, Yaniff. It eases my mind."

Yaniff nodded. "This one will not give you any trouble."

Lorgin blinked. "*This one?* What mean you by that?"

Yaniff's eyes gleamed with amusement; he cuffed Lorgin soundly on the head. "And what mean you by asking your Charl master questions you know he will not answer?"

He laughed at the expression of sheepish chagrin on the younger man's face.

"Go back to your *zira;* I will visit with you on the morrow's eve after you have all rested. By then, there will be a new life for me to welcome—a most favorable addition to the line of Lodarres. A proud moment, indeed." Yaniff placed his hand on Lorgin's shoulder.

Before the wizard had reached the platform, Lorgin was already by his wife's side.

Throughout the long hours that followed, Lorgin showed her the true measure of a great Aviaran warrior. In constant control, despite his own inner trepidation, he was a tower of strength by her side.

His calm, coaxing presence was a balm to her fraying nerves. Through each phase of her labor, he patiently and lovingly guided her. And when the pain became severe, he took her hands in his own, sending her wave after wave of his power. The transferring of his strength to her somehow acted like a prophylactic, taking away her discomfort and renewing her vigor.

It was a long labor, draining them both. After several hours, when Lorgin took a moment to carefully clean the blade of his Cearix, Deana endeavored to joke, "I don't want to know why you're doing that."

He smiled faintly. "Good, then I will not tell you."

The birth of the child was imminent. A tremendous pressure seemed to grip her belly. "Lorgin!" She called out his name. He quickly returned to her side, giving her even more of his powerful strength.

He was starting to look quite wan himself, Deana realized. Dark circles ringed his amethyst eyes. His normally vibrant golden tan skin tone had a pallid, gaunt cast. *He would give me his last shred of vital force if he felt he had to. . . .*

At that moment, Deana felt so much love for him

that she thought she would burst of it.

"No more, Lorgin, it's enough," she managed to gasp, worried now for him.

"You are sure?" He watched her, a drawn look on his face.

"Yes, yes I'm sure." she tried to stifle a groan as a tremendous urgency seized her.

The crystal chimes outside all started to chime at once from a sudden breeze. What a beautiful melody, she thought amidst her exertions.

"The babe comes, Adeeann!"

Their child slipped into his waiting hands.

Lorgin was silent for several moments. When he looked up, there were tears in his eyes. "A daughter, Adeeann. We have a beautiful daughter."

"A little girl?" Deana's face lit up with joy.

Speaking in a strong voice, Lorgin intoned the traditional Aviaran words of birthing with the overwhelming emotions he was experiencing.

"I give to you my power, my wife,
And you return it to me—
The most precious gift of generations."

He then cut the cord with the Cearix that had seen the birth of sixteen generations of his family.

"The line is cut
And so begins anew;
The line of Lodarres continues."

He reverently handed their child to her.

Deana looked down at the baby in her arms, her own eyes filling. "Look what we did, Lorgin—it's a miracle."

Moved, he kissed her softly on the lips.

Deana tasted one of his tears on her tongue. Yaniff was right; it was an incredible moment, one she was glad to share only with Lorgin. The Aviaran custom was a good one. Fathers must teach their sons well here.

"What is it?" Lorgin noticed the speculative look on her face.

"I was thinking about your custom and I suddenly realized that Theardar must have loved Traed; how couldn't he after experiencing the same thing you did?"

Lorgin looked away. "Theardar could not do it, Adeeann. You see, he knew that Marilan would die with the birth of his child. It was a terrible thing, unheard of, for an Aviaran father not to bring forth his own child. It was Krue who brought Traed into this world."

"And watched his own sister die?"

"Yes."

Deana gazed down at her own precious baby. Little bits of red hair fuzzed her head. Amethyst eyes stared adoringly up at her. Who could not love a baby? Remembering the beautiful tinkling of the chimes at the moment of her daughter's birth, she lovingly stroked the downy-soft cheek. "Melody," she said.

Although it was traditional for Aviaran father's to name their firstborn, Lorgin whispered to his wife that it was the perfect name for a child conceived in harmony with so much love.

London

Lilac opened her eyes.

It was still night, the room dark, although a pale glow of moonlight filtered through the windows. Nickolai always left the drapes undrawn, favoring the room "open to the night" as he slept.

He seemed to like the first light of dawn awakening him as well—even if he often drifted back to sleep. Several times, she had been awakened to his passionate lovemaking in the early hours of daybreak.

It suddenly occurred to her that Nickolai seemed particularly active at dawn and dusk. *Just like a cat* . . .

Lilac buried the awful thought immediately.

It was a part of Nickolai she simply could not deal with. Already, she had half-convinced herself that she had imagined the bizarre transformation the morning after her wedding. The sorcerer's tricks.

She had never believed such things possible—even as a child. It was silly, the stuff of fairy tales. Maybe it wasn't possible; maybe her husband was very skilled at mesmerizing.

It was the only reasonable explanation for what she had seen.

There was no logical way, however, to explain exactly *how* he was able to speak in her mind.

When she had questioned him about it last evening, Nickolai had told her that it was a naturally occurring trait among his people and she must not fear it.

Maybe it was true; maybe some of his people did have this ability. Strange abilities like this were not unknown; she, herself, had heard stories of Gypsies who seemed to possess the ability to foretell the future. So perhaps certain tribes of people in Russia could speak without speaking.

Then why didn't his brother seem to have this ability?

Well . . . Traed did say they had different fathers. That could explain it. Yet, there was something altogether *different* about Nickolai. Different even from his curious brother, Traed, who did not appear to her to quite fit in either.

Something beyond foreign differences . . .

Maybe there wasn't a logical way to explain this.

Fear rose up in her. Who was Nickolai?

What was he?

Lilac swallowed the butterflies in her stomach. She promised herself she would not think about this! And she would not. It had no place in their lives. No place at all.

They seemed to be getting by; everything appeared to be going smoothly. Why look for trouble?

As long as she never acknowledged this . . . strangeness of his, it would not have to exist openly between them. Over all, Nickolai seemed to be doing very well.

In fact, he had surprised her on many counts.

After her initial apprehension for the marriage bed— and he had proven himself most patient with her in that regard—he had shown himself to be gentle and kind with her. Even that one time in the dressing room, when his anger had almost overridden his passion, she had sensed that he had held back for her sake.

He was constantly teasing her and caressing her and . . .

He always seemed concerned about her welfare.

She was loath to admit it, but Nickolai, against all expectations, was proving himself to be a very good husband.

In a labyrinthine twist, the thought almost irritated her.

Aggravated at this bizarre victory of his, she looked down at the source disgustedly, and immediately lost her displeasure with him. It was difficult to sustain anger against a man who looked so beautiful when he slept.

Nickolai was lying over her, arms wrapped around her waist, his legs tangled with hers, and his face burrowed into her throat. Fast asleep, he looked as innocent as an angel, his thick, black lashes crescents against his golden skin.

Bemused, Lilac shook her head. The man slept in the strangest positions draped over her! She sighed. In a small movement, she turned her head toward the window, idly wondering if she should get up; she wasn't very sleepy.

A little lap caressed the underside of her ear.

She smiled. Well, yes, she supposed he was very comfortable. Without thinking, Lilac pressed her lips to his smooth forehead.

A low roll of contentment resonated in his throat. Nickolai gathered her closer in his sleep, insinuating his thigh snugly between hers. He continued to doze, softly purring against her.

Awake, Lilac continued to hold him in her arms.

Something was bothering him.

Just what it was, he could not say.

A touch of that odd, restless feeling had returned. It niggled at him below the threshold of irritation. Most of the restlessness had abated when he mated with Lilac and he had thought it gone for good after that first night with her. Only here it was again.

It was different now. Changed. It seemed to be . . . *beckoning*.

Beckoning to what?

He knew not.

It was odd; while he was occupied sexually with his mate, the feeling dissipated—or else his senses were too involved to notice it.

Sex, however, did not seem a viable solution to him.

As much as he would like to keep Lilac immersed in that activity, he did not think she was physically up to the challenge. And it would not be right of him to wear her out simply because of his unrest.

If he was going to wear his mate out, he wanted it to be for the right reasons!

Besides, he could never think straight when he was sensually engaged.

Something was building in him.

What he needed was a good hunt. Predatory challenge would clear his head.

He sought out his brother Traed, asking him if he would like to accompany him. The Aviaran readily agreed.

Together, they combed four gaming hells before finding the selected quarry at Pickering Place. Their Lord Rotewick was holding court at a far table, apparently fleecing the other players soundly at cards.

"There." Traed indicated the Familiar's challenge.

"I will finish him tonight."

Rejar sat down at the table to play the game known as whist.

"Good evening, Prince Azov." Rotewick gloated in a cavalier manner. "Since you were so lucky for me the other night, I will return the favor by warning you. You might wish to sit somewhere else this eve."

Rejar speared the supercilious lord with a cool look. "And why would I do that?"

"My dear man," he gestured to the high pile of counters before him. "I cannot lose."

A small smile tilted Rejar's mouth. "We shall see. Rot Wick."

Rotewick's glacial eyes narrowed.

A voice whispered rather loudly behind Rejar, "Cor, what is 'e sittin' there fer?" Neither Traed nor Rejar were overly surprised to see Jackie.

"I take it you have secured our coach, Jackie?" Rejar asked dryly.

"Tha' I'ave, yer Princeship." He leaned in to speak in Rejar's ear. "This ain't an idea, sir. Pick another spot fer ol' Jackie. 'E's a mean one, 'e is." He nodded in Rotewick's direction.

Rejar smiled slowly. "I am counting on it."

The cards were dealt.

"Sir?" Jackie tugged on Traed's sleeve.

"Yes, Jackie?"

"I warned ye about 'im, I 'as. 'E's the devil's own at cards. 'E'll fleece yer brother clean 'e will. And if 'e don't . . ." Jackie shuddered.

Traed was attentive. "What happens if the man loses, Jackie?"

" 'E never pays up is all I known. After a few days, 'e'll call yer brother a cheat and then challenge 'im to a duel. 'E's done it before. A master with the blade, the rotter is. Dead men don't be collectin' no gambolin' debts, iffen you get my drift."

"I hear you." Alert, Traed watched the play very carefully from behind Rejar's shoulder.

The Familiar possessed a clear head and a remarkable memory. He was able to make dispassionate judgments quickly and soundly. Consequently, several rounds went his way.

However, Rotewick was also an excellent player. He, too, possessed a certain lethal skill for the game.

As the night progressed, wins and losses going back and forth between the two of them, the stakes began to escalate rapidly. It wasn't long before the men were wagering upwards of twenty thousand pounds a hand.

Word spread quickly and patrons crowded around the table to watch the exciting match. As the stakes grew, so did the animosity between the two men. Rejar remained cool and contained. Rotewick, however, began to jeer at the younger man in an attempt to throw him off stride.

"Your wife is quite a pretty little thing; although I must admit she never interested me much. I have a more sophisticated palate, so to speak. The suit is diamonds."

Rejar lifted his sights from the cards to capture the man in his steely regard. "Your throw," was all he said.

Rotewick discarded in a seemingly careless move. "Of course, now that she's been broken in, one can't help but wonder what kind of ride she delivers." Several of the spectators sniggered at the crude innuendo.

Traed's hand went to the light saber in his waistband. Jackie's hand on his arm forestalled him.

A muscle ticked in Rejar's jaw. He said nothing, throwing his card onto the table.

"Smooth or in the rough style? . . . Thirty thousand." A gasp went up from the onlookers at the enormous bet. Rotewick discarded with a flourish of lace.

Rejar calmly matched his bet, also discarding.

A speculative demeanor graced Lord Rotewick's face. He hadn't expected the Prince to match his bet. The man had more mettle than was healthy for him. How far would the young blade go? he wondered.

"Now let me see . . ." he tapped his pointed chin as if entertaining a mildly interesting thought. "For this next wager, perhaps a diversion for her Highness?"

The area went silent.

What would the Prince do? It was not unknown for men in the heat of gambling fever to make outrageous bets. Would he accept? Would he offer up his lady's services?

Rejar's dual-colored eyes pinned the man to his chair

297

with a predatory intensity. Just seeing the look on the Prince's face made several of the onlookers squirm nervously. He was likened to a wild animal preparing to spring. In contrast, when he spoke, the measured voice was chillingly low.

"I will rip the heart out of any man who seeks such a diversion with my wife."

By the man's savage intensity, no one doubted it. To say the Prince did not take well to the idea was an understatement. The man looked ready to kill.

The corners of Traed's lips twitched. *Rip out his heart?* Familiars could be so excessive.

The last thing Traed needed was an enraged Familiar defending the honor of his mate. It would take days to clean up the mess.

He bent over, speaking quietly in his brother's ear. "Come, Rejar; a slice across the throat with the saber is that much easier."

Traed's ploy to lighten the tension worked.

Smiling faintly, Rejar glanced at his brother behind his shoulder. *[But not as much fun.]*

Traed nodded sagely. "True."

Turning to face his adversary across the table, Rejar spoke in a bored mien. "What is your wager? You are wasting my time."

Lord Rotewick's face flushed with anger. No one spoke to him that way. No one. The man was as good as dead. "So I won't be wasting your time—fifty thousand pounds."

A murmur of disbelief raced through the crowd. Fifty thousand pounds! Would the Prince match it? Could he match it? He did not have enough counters before him to cover it.

Rejar lifted an imperious hand, signalling the proprietor for paper, pen and ink. Traed's eyes widened.

Rejar could not write in this language—what was he doing?

Rejar took the quill, dipped it into the inkwell, and scribbled something across the page. He threw the scrap of paper onto the table. Rotewick picked it up.

"What the devil does this say?" He held the paper up, facing it towards Rejar's side of the table. No one could make heads or tails out of the elaborate swirls and symbols.

Except one man.

Surprising everyone, the Prince's taciturn brother burst out laughing.

Blinking innocently, Rejar stated, "It says that in the event I lose, I owe you fifty thousand pounds."

That was not what it said. The Aviaran words were quite explicit in instructing the man what he should do with a *prautau* beast.

Rotewick turned to the proprietor. "Is this acceptable?"

The proprietor was not about to offend a prince. Especially such a well-placed prince as this. He quickly gave his approval. "It's more than acceptable." He nodded, smiling affably at Prince Azov. "It is in the Prince's native language of Russian, which I have had an occasion to study in my youth."

Traed looked sideways at the man.

"You see?" Rejar gestured with the hand not holding his cards. It was a subtle Zarrainian gesture of insult, which complimented his written words nicely. Behind him, Traed gave a low chuckle.

Rotewick stroked his jaw. It would nearly bankrupt him if he lost. But he was not going to lose. One way or the other. He would nick it. And bury the upstart Prince.

Rotewick threw down his last card. The eight of diamonds.

There was only one card in the suit of diamonds not accounted for above the eight. Did the Prince have the ten? The crowd held its collective breath.

Rejar paused, staring at the eight of diamonds. No expression showed on his handsome face. Then he gazed up at his adversary. Slowly, he flipped his card onto the table.

"Trump," he said blandly.

A great cheer rang through the crowd. Even Traed slapped him on the back. Jackie, however, was not overly happy.

He muttered sadly under his breath, "I not be knowin' whether ta cheer fer ya or not, yer Princeship."

Traed overheard him. "Have no worry, Jackie; you and I will keep a close watch on his 'Princeship.'"

Which was just as well because Rotewick was already making plans to kill him.

Despite his victory over Rotewick, Rejar returned to the townhouse late that evening in a disquieting mood.

He stood in front of the window in his bedroom and gazed out at the moonless night. Lilac was already sleeping. He did not know whether to feel anger at her for blithely going to sleep without knowing his whereabouts, or pleased because she trusted him so. A Familiar wife would have hit him over the head with a *zooplah* for daring to come in this late.

He rubbed the back of his neck.

A Familiar wife would have been more open to accepting him for who he was. The insidious words wrapped around his brain.

When was Lilac going to accept him? The troublesome issue was followed by another. How could she begin to accept him if she would not even listen to who and what he was? He had a life outside of Ree Gen Cee Ing Land. He had a home and a family. . . .

Yaniff would say he was being too indulgent. The Aviaran way would be to simply conquer.

He supposed the Familiar way was much the same except more subtly done. His Familiar kin, Gian, would tell him, "Snare first, then pounce."

Rejar did not think either of those approaches completely appropriate in this case.

Since the day he was hurled out of the Tunnels, this mating danced to its own tune. It was unique. There were no guidelines for him to follow. No fatherly instructions. No Charl platitudes. No Familiar ken.

The simple truth was, he was mated to a woman who came from a primitive culture. A culture who had never heard of life on other planets, Tunnel travel, or Familiars. At least, not his kind of Familiar.

He padded over to the bed.

Standing there, he watched Lilac as she slept. She was lying on her back, hand thrown innocently over her head, fingers curled into her palm. Sheltered and not much more than a babe.

He smiled gently. She was so unprepared for him.

Shedding his clothes, he climbed into bed with her. She immediately rolled into the warmth of his arms.

He hugged her to him, running his mouth along her hairline to the tip of her ear. She mumbled something incoherent in her sleep and snuggled into his chest.

The dilemma which most preyed upon his mind came to the fore.

When would she open her heart to him?

Chapter Fifteen

When he thought back on it, Rejar would remember that the terrible thing he had done was precipitated by a simple comment from Lady Agatha.

"Lilac, I haven't seen your cat about for ages," she had said.

They were seated for the evening meal. Just the four of them.

Rejar had been feeling on edge all day and had thought a quiet evening would settle him. He intended to ask Lilac to read to him after the meal, by the fire in the parlor. Sometimes, her gentle voice had a soothing effect on him. Traed had elected to remain in as well.

"'Tis a pity," Agatha said, going on with her fateful topic, "but I must admit I had grown rather fond of him."

"Yes, Auntie. It appears Rejar has left us for good." Lilac took a bite of food without looking up at her husband.

In silent anger, Rejar toyed with the stem of his glass. "Do not say that." He took a sip of his wine. "He might show himself again."

Lilac glanced up from her plate. This was not an issue she was going to back down from. Nickolai had given her his word. Hadn't he? She glared at him. "No, Nickolai; I am sure he won't."

"Cats are unpredictable, Lilac. You, of all people, should know that."

"I think I understand *this* one and he is *never* coming back." Lilac stared at Nickolai pointedly.

Traed looked back and forth between the two of them, concern etching his chiseled features. Something was brewing here. Something powerful and dangerous.

Rejar's golden eye twitched with the raw emotion he was containing. The reality of the situation struck him. She was nowhere near to accepting him! He was not Traed; his patience only went so far. Her blind stubbornness inflamed the feline in him.

"I do not believe you understand him at all."

Lilac blinked back the sudden dampness in her eyes at Nickolai's harsh words. She shouldn't care what he thought. *But she did.* "Perhaps you are right. If you'll excuse me?" Not waiting for his reply, Lilac stood and left the room.

"My word!" Agatha sputtered. "I knew she was fond of the beast; I should have realized how upset she would be over his disappearance."

Rejar thought Agatha's statement ironic, since his wife's actual upset was over the possibility of the cat's reappearance. "It was not your fault, Lady Agatha."

"I still feel terrible; she seems so distressed. Should I get her another, do you think?"

"I do not believe so, Lady Agatha." Rejar got up to

follow the path his wife took. "I am sure one 'beast' is all she can handle."

He closed the dining room door behind him.

The door to the bedroom opened, then shut.

Standing by the bed, Lilac looked up at the sound of the ominous click. The fierce expression on Nickolai's face made her grab the bedpost for support. His sensual dual-colored eyes were leaping with fury. In fact, he seemed rather wild.

What should she do? They had an agreement; he was not the wronged party. She made a conscious choice to meet fire with fire. "What do you have to be angry about?" she flung at him. "I'm the one who is angry!"

It was the wrong tactical decision. He said nothing but that small muscle ticked in his jaw. Resolute, she squared her shoulders.

"We have a bargain, you and I! No more of your hypnotizing foolishness! No more of your silly games! No more of these little mind tricks of yours! If you mean to break your word and go on with this reckless pastime of dabbling in the black arts, then I am afraid I can no longer live with you as your wife!"

That did it.

Something snapped inside of Rejar.

The Aviaran in him was completely cast aside as the untamed Familiar rose up. The female never, *never* threatened her mate with removal from his presence. To do so invited the wild, spitting, roaring heart of the cat to unleash.

Rejar unleashed.

In two strides he was by her side.

He grabbed the bodice of Lilac's dress and, with one yank of his clenched fist, ripped it in two.

"Stop it!" Lilac pounded his chest with her fists to no

avail. He did not even seem aware she was doing it. Nickolai tore the clothes right from her body.

So caught up in his outrage was he that he did not accord himself the privilege of removing his own clothes. Not wasting any time, he simply transformed himself back and forth in the blink of an eye; thereby rendering himself completely nude. In an instant, his clothes lay in a puddle on the floor behind him.

Lilac screamed. He did not seem to hear.

She was still trying to get over the shock of seeing that wretched *change* when he advanced on her. While it was true Lilac was naive, she was not stupid. On the contrary, she was an extremely intelligent woman. She immediately turned and prepared to run toward the door.

Familiar reflexes being what they were, he overtook her before she completed the pivot. His strong arm came around her waist from behind to bodily lift her off the floor.

"Nickolai, put me down!" She kicked, thrashing naked in his arms.

Rejar gave her what she wanted, but, perhaps, not in the manner she expected. He tossed her down on the rug before the fireplace and immediately covered her with himself.

Splaying her hands against his bare shoulders, Lilac pushed at him in vain. The muscles of his powerful chest rippled in the firelight as he clasped her wrists, one in each hand, to bring them down over her head. Effortlessly he pinioned her by interlacing his fingers with her own. It was a sexual stance of Nickolai's that Lilac knew well.

He was inflamed.

Remembering what had happened to her on the previous occasions when her husband had been so

Dara Joy

inflamed, Lilac ceased her thrashing. She hesitated, thinking quickly. Nickolai was quite something when he was inflamed. . . .

Those incredible eyes of his, narrowed with fury, shot blue and gold fire at her. His sable hair hung about his face, tousled and silken. Those velvet lips of his were compressed in anger but it only accentuated their firm, sensual curve. Lilac thought he had never looked more beautiful.

All rational thought flew out of her head. What was she fighting him for? She wanted him. Lord knew he was exciting her!

Unfortunately, blinded by the splendid picture above her, she was missing his very real ferocity.

"What did you say to me?" he hissed, a hint of white teeth showing.

She grabbed a handful of his hair and made the terrible mistake of saying, "I want you."

Women had been saying that to him his entire adult life.

Her unthinking words enraged him anew. He did not want her to just want him; he wanted . . .

With a growl, he speared her with a smoldering look. "Do you? Then far be it from me to not give you what you want." His mouth crashed down on hers claiming her mouth in an overpowering abduction.

Rejar was out of control.

He pressed forcefully against her lower lip with his tongue, using the expert technique to gain entry into her waiting mouth. There, he swept inside, demanding all that he touched.

Kissing her over and over, he claimed her mouth as he intended to claim her. Thoroughly. There was no conscious thought to his movements, only a cloud of primitive passion.

Employing the Familiar technique of the *silken sting*—using two teeth on a small portion of her skin—he nipped the corners of her mouth and the center of her lower lip. The bite was designed to kindle selected points of feminine sensitivity.

He continued the technique along her jawline, delivering the silken sting in a devastating line to key spots of her collarbone.

With the carnal onslaught of that merciless mouth, Lilac couldn't help but moan. Nickolai's mouth. A mouth that could deliver untold ecstasy. Her cry of passion escaped lips that pressed against his heated brow.

In his haze, Rejar continued his path, not even realizing he was starting to introduce her to a multitude of methods Familiars had with the loving bite. He moved to her breast, capturing it in his open mouth to administer the *waiting haven,* a bite particularly suited to his task.

By her choking sounds, Lilac agreed.

After paying equal attention to the other breast, he traveled down the plane of her torso, intermingling several different bites: the *kitten's taste,* the *fluttering wing* . . . On and on he went, leaving a trail of acutely aroused nerve endings in his wake.

When he reached the joint of her thigh, he ruthlessly delivered the *sting of honey,* arrowing along the dainty crease. Male lips and teeth came together in an unparalleled combination.

The highly erotic bite brought shivers to his wife.

Tossing back his black hair, he moved up the length of her, only to demand in a low, husky voice the question which would be her downfall. "What is my name, Lilac?"

Passion-dilated eyes glazed back at him. "N-Nickolai," she whispered.

He held her within his embrace. "No. It is Rejar. Say it, Lilac."

So, that was his game, she thought, some of the passion-fog leaving her. Well, it wouldn't work! He would not bend her to his will with his sensual expertise. "I will not call you by that ridiculous name! It is a cat's name, not yours."

Rejar's eyes glinted, a muscle in his jaw pulsed. "Gifted," he said quietly.

"What?" she bristled.

"Gifted. My name means gifted in the language of my mother's people." It was a name he carried with pride, a name his mother had given him in the time-old Familiar tradition of using the senses to name one's child. It was a name she had given him with great joy when she realized that despite Krue's Charl blood, she had birthed a Familiar babe.

It was a name his wife would not speak.

As if echoing his perception, she said, "I will never call you by that name, Nickolai."

He did not take the news well.

His blue/gold eyes became slits of ice and fire.

In a dreadful decision to lighten his darkening mood, Lilac smiled tremulously. "But you may try to convince me how 'gifted' you are."

"Do not play with me, Lilac, lest you are ready to deal with the consequences."

It came over Lilac then. A heretofore undisclosed mulish streak. She hadn't even known she possessed one this strong. The fact that it was horribly ill-timed escaped her.

She reached up to run her fingers through his luxuriant hair, for she knew he particularly liked it. "If you play with me, then I shall play with you . . . *Nickolai*."

He did not react as she would have hoped.

Her playful action combined with the blatant use of the name Nickolai seemed only to make him madder. Too late, she realized her mistake. Eyes widening, she vainly tried to scoot out from beneath him.

His full weight came down on her.

She felt rather like a squashed bug. "Nickolai, get up!"

He raised up on his elbows, taking some, but not all, of his weight off her. "Think you we will not resolve this tonight? What manner of man do you believe me?"

After what she had seen, she really couldn't say.

"I ask you now to acknowledge the truth. What is my name?" He was barely controlling the fire in his blood. A fire that had its roots in the restlessness which was somehow, in some way, connected to all of this.

Defiance rose up in her. Her chin notched up in the air. "It is Nickolai. Nickolai! Nickolai! Nickolai!"

With his first thrust he set the tone for what was to come.

It was powerful, raw, untamed.

With every one following, he went deeper, surer, stronger.

Poignantly, he stared down at her as he moved inside. Their eyes met and held. Then his rhythmic movements began building. And somehow Lilac knew he was just starting.

His hands released hers to cup her face, and he brought her mouth up to meet his own.

"Say it."

This stubborn side would not back down. "No, I will not!" she gasped defiantly against his mouth.

His eyes flashed; the cords of his neck stood out.

It was a nonverbal roar.

Lilac's eyes widened. Now she had done it! For the first time since Nickolai had come into the room, Lilac was starting to have second thoughts about inflaming him. It appeared she had awakened a sleeping lion!

Nickolai is lost to reason! Lilac had the moment's lucid realization before she was swept away by the sensual storm invading her.

Beyond cogent thought, Rejar fiercely covered that stubborn mouth with his own.

And *enhanced*.

She felt . . . something . . .

It sizzled through her from the place where they joined, radiating outward to every point of her body. A burning vibration of raw, sexual energy. Awakening the tiniest of sensory nerve endings.

Each and every part of her body seemed to become instantly erogenous as the effects of this alien augmentation magnified the sexual sensations she was experiencing.

In the midst of this overpowering skill, Rejar's provocative mating scent, like an exotic spice, covered them both.

Lilac writhed beneath him, scattering kisses all over his face—his eyes, his lips, his nose, his jaw.

Reputation withstanding, the Familiar had made her wild.

With Lilac's fervid response, he growled something indecipherable. Then he bit her shoulder.

Without realizing it, Rejar began the rhythm of the Nine Hundred Strokes to Love.

It was the sacred ceremony of Familiar incarnation.

His thrusts followed an ancient incremental pattern: eight shallow, one deep. The compelling movements were not actually counted but were measured against a mnemonic device Gian Ren had taught him when he entered his maturity.

With each measured stroke, Rejar's breathing and concentration increased, his love-thrusts emulating the fire building inside him. It was a fire Lilac was not prepared for and a fire which he should not be experiencing for years.

Lilac begged him to stop even while urging him to continue between breathless moans and pleas.

He was beyond hearing her.

Rejar was in the throes of a highly explicit mating—ritualistic and savage. He had turned completely feral.

Lilac lost track of time, of herself, of where she was. Only his endless thrusts had any meaning to her. In what way, she was not sure.

She only knew that she hugged him tightly to her and cried out his name over and over.

It was not the name he wanted to hear.

He glided the edge of his hand along the seam of her mouth. Nudging her lips apart with the side of his wrist, he snarled, *"Bite!"*

Lilac searched his glazed eyes. He wanted her to . . . ?

She sunk her teeth into the spot he indicated on the back edge of his wrist.

Rejar groaned aloud. It was an old Familiar trick to increase sexual stamina in the male. The secret spot was a pressure point in direct connection to his erotic senses.

It brought him to another level.

He reared back on his haunches. Clasping her waist, he brought her halfway up his thighs.

He grasped her right ankle. Tormenting her with his innate ability, he scraped his nails along her responsive instep before lifting the leg over his shoulder. Carefully, he bent forward to support the back of her neck with his left hand.

The creative position allowed him to thrust very deep.

Lilac shattered.

Before her convulsions had even stopped, he withdrew from her.

She had not even regained her breath when her left leg joined her right over his opposite shoulder. Nickolai had situated her so he could replace his manhood with his mouth.

With her legs dangling over his back and Nickolai intent between them, Lilac came again.

"What is my name?" he murmured, his mouth hot against the delicate inner folds of her femininity.

"N-Nick-Nickolai," she stuttered, barely able to speak.

"Wrong answer." He scraped his teeth over her, making her cry out at the exquisite torture. Then he rolled across the floor with her in his arms, entering her anew.

The tempo continued.

And so it went to the small hours of the night until Rejar finally came to his senses and ended it. By that time, Lilac had screamed her releases so many times that she simply fainted dead away.

He lifted her in his arms and carried her over to the bed.

Depositing her beneath the covers, he angrily seized his pants from the floor and yanked them on.

Barefoot and bare-chested, hair flying about him, he stormed downstairs to the study.

The dark room was lit only by the fire in the fireplace. Rejar strode over to the liquor cabinet, slammed down a glass, and poured himself a brandy. With a shaking

hand, he lifted the glass to his mouth and downed the
contents in one swallow.

He had brought his wife to the first tier of the incarnation ceremony. He had meant only to *enhance!*

Enhancing was an accountable trait for a man to
possess and for this reason Familiars used it very cau-
tiously. There were many reasons for it to remain
shrouded in myth and cloaked in secrecy. The mating
rhythm, however, was something he should not have
felt the need to attempt for years. What had happened
to him?

Disgusted, he threw the empty glass against the fireplace.

It shattered into a thousand pieces.

Like his heart.

A voice came from behind the high-backed chair in
the darkened corner of the room. "What troubles you
so, Rejar?"

Traed.

Drained, Rejar sunk into the chair near the fireplace.
He heard Traed approach.

This newfound brother stood before him, his back
silhouetted by the firelight. The odd thought, Why does
he have his back to the fire? filtered through Rejar's
mind. *Traed needs to face the light. . . .*

Rejar shook off the unsettling insight.

With the patience he was famous for, Traed waited
for his brother to speak.

When Rejar finally looked up, there was intense sad-
ness in his blue and gold eyes. "I have mated with a
woman who does not love me, Traed."

"What foolishness is this? Lilac—"

"No."

"Why do you speak thus?"

Rejar uttered words the meaning of which he never

thought would matter in his life. Words, the essence of which, in his carefree youth, would have been more than enough for him from *any* woman. Prophetic words that came back to haunt him.

"Lilac does not love me; she only wants me."

"Surely not!" Traed was not certain what to make of this development. It did not make sense to him; the two of them were mates, therefore . . .

Rejar must have perceived the situation wrong.

"It is so, my brother." The enormity of his recent feral act confronted him. "What have I done?" Overcome, Rejar bent forward in the chair, covering his face with his hands.

Compassionately, the elder man placed his hand on Rejar's shoulder. The fraternal gesture was new and alien to Traed. "Tell me."

"I cannot speak of it."

"Cannot or will not?" Traed asked this with some alarm. What had the Familiar done?

Rejar looked up at him, eyes shining with moisture. "I cannot, Traed. It is something Familiars do not speak of—to anyone."

"I understand." Traed crouched down before him, meeting him at eye level. For the first time in many, many years, Traed was acting the older brother. "I am not of your kind . . . but I have had some experience with women."

This bizarre disclosure was almost enough to snap Rejar out of his mood. He peered at Traed curiously. "You have?"

Traed gave him a look. "Yes."

A tiny line of perplexed disbelief appeared between Rejar's brows. Like most Familiars he was born inquisitive. "What kind of experience?"

Irked, Traed waved his hand. "That is not important!

What is important is that I might be able to guide you from a non-Familiar viewpoint."

"What good would that do me?"

Traed took a deep breath. Guiding this younger brother was not an easy task! When he got back to Aviara he would have to commend Lorgin on his superb tolerance all these years. "You are looking at this situation through the eyes of a Familiar." He choose his words carefully. "Perhaps you need to give Lilac some time to realize—"

"I have given her plenty of time. It does not seem to do much good." Rejar leaned back in the chair, wearily closing his eyes.

"I do not mean that."

Rejar opened his gold eye. "Then what do you mean?"

Traed stood, placing himself before the fire. "I mean you should allow her to know you without . . ." He let the sentence drift off meaningfully.

Rejar was completely perplexed. "Without what?"

"Without *krnacking*, you fool!" Traed bit out through clenched teeth.

Rejar leaped out of his chair. "You expect me to sleep next to my mate and *not* touch her? I am a Familiar!" He slashed his hand through the air in a gesture Traed had seen Lorgin do many times. "I cannot."

"You are also Aviaran. Lodarres' blood runs through your veins. Both our veins."

It was the first time Rejar had heard Traed readily acknowledge his Lodarres bloodline. It also reminded him that he was obligated to give credence to the advice of an elder blood relative. Not that he was bound to follow it. Still . . .

"Why do you believe I should do this?"

Finally. Rejar was listening to him. "My father made

a terrible mistake with my mother. I do not want to see you do the same with Lilac. Your mate is young and inexperienced; she knows nothing of our ways or the ways of men."

Rejar rubbed his jaw. "This is true."

"I do not know what transpired between you, but I can surmise it was something physical. Did you hurt her?"

"No."

Traed raised an eyebrow. "There was a lot of noise, Rejar."

"I am a Familiar." As if that explained a woman gasping and screaming and sighing for hours.

Well, come to think of it, it did. "Hmm. Very well; then mayhap you have frightened her with your . . . zeal."

Rejar exhaled heavily. "I am sure of it."

Traed nodded. "Let her become comfortable with you again before you touch her. Let her discover how she misses you."

"You believe this?"

"I know it."

Rejar sat wearily back in the chair. "Even so, she might come to accept me again but she still will not love me."

"We shall see." His assessment of the situation was quite different from his brother's. Traed had noted the way Lilac watched her husband when he was unaware of it. But Rejar had more than this on his mind. Traed patiently warmed his hands in front of the fire and waited.

{Traed?}

"Yes?" He did not turn around.

{There is something else.}

He stared into the flames. "What is it, Rejar?"

{I have a restlessness I cannot name. It seems to call me and I have no peace.}

Traed watched the fire greedily consume the wood with its embrace. A prickle went up his spine. No expression showed on his chiseled face.

{What could it be?}

Traed closed his eyes. He was beginning to suspect that Yaniff had not told him the entire story when he named him Rejar's *Chi'in t'se Leau.*

Now he was positive of it.

There was more here than Yaniff let on.

Lilac brought her clenched hand to her mouth.

She was weak and could hardly move—so she lay where he had put her in the bed. She watched the shadows of the firelight flicker against the wall. *What does he expect from me?*

She had given him what he demanded and when he demanded more, she had given him more. She had given him all that she had. Yet, it did not seem to be enough.

Maybe it was not enough. . . . Maybe *she* was not enough.

The disturbing notion made her feel inexplicably ill. Was she doing something wrong? Nickolai had always been pleased before tonight.

Something had happened between them. He seemed to savor her and yet he did not appear satisfied.

What if I am not enough for Nickolai?

Would he seek out other women? He told her he would not, but . . .

Why should she care if he did?

He would leave her alone then. He would stop waking her all night long with his erotic demands. Stop his constant caresses and tender kisses. Stop calling her "my heart" in the dark of night while he held her tightly to him. Stop giving her little laps under her ear in his sleep when he wanted to settle her down and stay cozy.

Lilac sniffed.

She didn't care! She didn't care at all!

I'm losing him.

She didn't know why she began to cry. The tears just started trailing down her cheeks of their own accord. Soon she was sobbing uncontrollably. Rolling over onto her stomach, she clutched her pillow and cried into it, the intense emotions of the entire evening a jumbled brew.

She was not aware of the door opening and softly closing.

Rejar stood beside the bed, gazing down at his sobbing wife. Drawing all the wrong conclusions. *What have I done?*

He reached out his hand to touch her shoulder to offer comfort. His hand hovered in the air above her; he could not bring himself to do it. After what he had put her through, he fully expected Lilac to shrink away from his touch in horror.

Such a thing he could not bear to see.

Walking around to the other side of the bed, he quickly shed his clothes and got under the covers. Remembering Traed's advice, he was careful not to touch her in any way, moving close to his edge of the mattress.

Lilac felt the bed dip and raised her tear-streaked face from the pillow. Nickolai's naked back was to her. Solid. Hard. And indifferent. He had never slept that way before. Always, he took her in his arms, wrapping himself around her warmly.

She buried her head in the pillow and wept anew.

Rejar stared at the wall facing him and tried to block

out the sound of her tears. He could not. Each one was a blade in his heart.

Summoning up his Aviaran willpower, he did not soothe her.

He prayed he could endure the night.

"Psst! Sir, might I'ave a word wit' you?"

Traed felt someone tugging on his sleeve. Drowsily, he opened one eye. Jackie was leaning over him, a concerned expression on his comical face. "What is it, Jackie?"

"Ya been ta bed yet, sir?"

Traed yawned. "Hmm?" He glanced at the windows in the study. Daylight streamed in. "Is it the morrow?"

Jackie chuckled. "That 'tis, sir. Seems like y'fell asleep in this 'ere chair."

"So I have."

Jackie cocked his head, watching him knowingly. "Do that a lot?"

Traed glanced swiftly up at the man. "What do you mean?"

"Well, seem ta me y' be one that don't be sleepin' so easy. I seen yer lamp in the wee hours of the morn. Got the insomnia, do ya?"

The green eyes narrowed slightly. "Some."

"Aye." Jackie stroked his chin, his accent suddenly becoming Irish. "I got a cure fer that! Me father learned it from 'is father who learned it from a leprechaun."

Traed was puzzled. "A what?"

"A leprechaun, laddie. Y'know, one of the little people." He gestured expansively with his pipe as if to indicate they were everywhere.

Traed jumped out of his seat; his hand going to the belt at his waist for a weapon.

"Now there's no need fer that. It's not like y'got a

leprechaun askin' ta do ya a favor, lad. Besides, it wouldn't do ya any good—what y'need is a big club about yea big—"

"Jackie . . . what did you seek me out for?"

The odd man went serious in an instant. If one could call lowering shaggy brows and bulging out one's eyes serious. "There's word about that Rotewick is planning on calling out yer brother. I warned y' about 'im, I did."

"When you say calling him out, what exactly do you mean?"

"First 'e'll start a rumor that yer brother somehow cheated at cards the other night. Gossip bein' the delicacy it is, the story will be devoured quick-like. Some will believe it, some won't. Either way 'is Princeship's honor is at stake."

"I see. Rejar will be compelled to challenge him."

"Who's this Ray bloke?"

Traed waved him to continue.

"Well now, Rotewick's a fencing master, so 'e'll be sure to challenge 'im to a duel with the blade. And what are y' smiling like that fer?"

"You did say the blade, did you not?" The jade eyes gleamed.

"Aye." He chewed on his pipe stem.

"Tell me, Jackie, where is this man now?"

"I can show y' where 'e lives."

"Good. Take me there."

Jackie's eyes bulged out further. "Now? Before I had me bangers and biscuits?"

"Yes. I vow I look forward to it."

Indeed, Jackie noted there was almost a spring in the normally solemn man's step. *Must have a yen for the danger.* "All right then. But don't y' want ta know the cure?"

"Cure? What cure?"

Jackie blew out a breath of exasperation. "The one fer insomnia!"

Traed raised his eyebrow skeptically. "Ah, yes, the remedy from the—what did you call them? The little people."

"Aye. 'Tis a simple one."

Traed sighed. The man was not going to let it be until he told him. "Very well, what is it?"

"First y' got to find out what it is what keeps y' from sleepin'."

"This is brilliant," Traed said dryly.

Jackie lanced him with a you-just-listen-now look.

"Very well—I find out what keeps me from sleeping; then what?"

"Why, then, lad, *you confront it.*"

The Aviaran looked at him out of the corner of his eye. "Mmm." He put his hand on the back of Jackie's neck, steering him out the door.

Chapter Sixteen

"I am sorry, sir, Lord Rotewick is in the garden for his morning practice. He is never disturbed at this hour."

Lord Rotewick's butler attempted to look down his nose at Traed. Since this was impossible due to the man's impressive height, he settled for a sniff of disdain. No one of decent breeding would call at this ungodly hour of the morning!

"And what practice would that be?"

The forbidding man had a look that could freeze ice. It effectively put the butler in his place. "Lord Rotewick fences in the morning hours, sir."

A chilling smile etched its way across the green-eyed man's face.

"Mmm, which way is the garden?" Traed strode boldly into the house, Jackie trailing behind.

"Sir! You can't barge in here like this! I tell you his lordship is indisposed!"

"Not yet," Traed murmured, heading in the direction of the back of the house.

It did not take him long to find the doors leading into the back gardens of the house. Standing on the terrace, he easily spotted his "lordship." The man was engaged in a practice match of the blades.

Traed noted both men wore protective masks over their faces. He chuckled to himself, shaking his head. An Aviaran warrior would never wear such a device. Where would be the challenge?

He continued to stand on the terrace watching the men fence. Traed carefully observed Rotewick's moves. The man was good, he would give him that. His moves were quick and fluid, and he had a tendency to be clandestine in the strikes he delivered. Precisely as Traed would have expected from a man of his nature.

There was no doubt in Traed's mind that Rotewick was aware he was standing there.

"I told ya 'e was good." Jackie spoke under his breath. "Do y' think y'can take 'im?"

"If you are asking me if I think I can disarm him, the answer is yes. Although it will take me a few moments to get used to this kind of weapon."

Jackie almost swallowed his pipe. The man began coughing uncontrollably.

Traed slapped him on the back to clear his air, the casual blow sending the poor fellow halfway across the terrace.

"Cor, are ye sayin' ye ain't fenced before?" Jackie tried to speak between wheezes. "Are ye daft, man? 'E'll skewer ye through 'ere y'can say jack rabbit!"

Traed snorted at the foolish statement, waving Jackie's words aside.

Worried, Jackie grabbed his sleeve. "What are ye thinkin' of, lad? Ye cannot fight a man wit' 'is skill! And you not bein' a swordsman!"

Traed inhaled deeply as if to indicate the measure of

his patience. "I did not say that, Jackie." The match suddenly ended victoriously with Lord Rotewick delivering a touché directly over his opponent's heart.

Before Jackie could object, Traed stepped forward.

Rotewick pulled off his mask. The two men met eye to eye. Traed did not cloak what he was there for by any softening of his expression.

Rotewick raised his eyebrows. He had not expected this brash cheek from a man who up to now had remained silently impassive in the face of his flamboyant brother's activities. The Prince seemed a reckless, dashing type; it was one of the reasons Rotewick had accepted the outrageous bet. He knew that if he lost, he could always call the rogue out; youth was often impetuous.

This cool-headed brother, however, might prove irksome.

"Ah, yes, here to safeguard the little Prince." Since Rejar surpassed even Traed's impressive height, it was a rather ridiculous statement.

"That must get tiresome for you." He wiped the sweat off his forehead with a lace handkerchief. "Do you have to fight all of your brother's battles?"

"Only the unimportant ones."

The barb hit its mark. A stain of red flushed his cheeks. Lord Rotewick suffered from a surfeit of vanity.

As a titled and privileged member of the crown, he naturally assumed the world revolved around him. It was not very wise of this upstart to imply otherwise. Up until that moment, he might have considered letting the man live.

"There is a lot of rumor floating about the ton concerning you. Some say you have a title but refuse to use it; others say you are the bastard son of a Scottish chieftain. Doesn't say much for the Prince's mother, does it?"

Traed's green eyes flicked over him in cool dismissal.

"Of course there is no doubting that the two of you are brothers. You both have a certain . . . *look* about you." Rotewick swaggered back and forth, the lace trim on his sleeves fluttering with his expansive hand movements. He slowly paced a circle around Traed, looking him up and down. "Although my money is on the colonies."

"The colonies?" Traed's voice was evenly modulated.

"Um, yes, you do have that rough-around-the-edges look to you. Who is your tailor? Never mind—where was I? Oh yes, the colonies . . . it's quite obvious to me."

"And why is that?"

"Why, you have no respect for your betters! You seem just the type to revolt against your parent country in the name of some nebulous quest for independence."

Something flickered in Traed's eye. It did not go unobserved by the sneering lord.

"Yes . . . I see I have guessed it after all."

Not quite—although Traed was intrigued by the reference, making a mental note to ask Jackie about these "colonies" the man spoke of. He might want to see for himself a place that had the courage to throw off the yoke of its past to start out anew. Yes, it would be most interesting.

"Are we done for the day, your lordship?" The man who had been fencing with Lord Rotewick approached.

"Yes, Herr Schimmer, that will be all. You may go." The man turned to leave. Traed forestalled him.

"A moment, Herr Schimmer." The man turned, curious. "Might I borrow your fence?"

The man appeared confused. "My fence? Ach, you refer to my sabre! Ya, of course." He handed him the heavy dual-edged sword.

"This is not the *salles d'armes*, Mr. Yaniff." Rotewick did not try to hide his condescension. "We do not use foil or épée here."

Traed tested the heft and balance of the blade. His sights went to the metal blade, comparing it unfavorably to his own deadly light saber. He frowned. The weight would slow down the speed of action and re-action. "It does not seem like much of a weapon."

Rotewick sneered. The sabre was a weapon which required enormous strength, fast reflexes, and considerable skill to wield. "Is that so? Would you care to test it out? Unless, of course, you can't handle a sword . . ."

Not bothering to answer, Traed expertly sliced the blade through the air, testing the strength and length of the weapon to the parameters of his movements.

Then he faced Rotewick and calmly motioned to him that he was ready to begin by arrogantly circling the tip of the blade. "Are you just going to stand there Rot Wick, staring at the flowers?"

Jackie started choking again. "Sir, perhaps ye oughtta think on this once again—"

"Listen to your servant. My quarrel is with your brother, not with you."

Traed shrugged. "Where is the difference? We are family—I am the elder. His quarrel *is* my quarrel. However, I will return your *benevolence* with my own. Do not think to 'call' my brother out; pay him that which is your fair debt, and I will walk away."

"You think to toy with me? Your brother is a cheat. Soon he will be a dead cheat."

Rotewick's threat had a meaning to Traed his lordship would never have guessed at. *This must be the danger to Rejar that Yaniff had foreseen!* The reason he had been sent here as *Chi'in t'se Leau.*

"My brother is a man of real honor, something you know nothing about. His victory over you was a fair one."

"If what you say is true, why send you in his stead? Only a coward stands behind the shield of another."

Traed's eyes flashed with private amusement. "He did not send me; in fact, he does not even know I am here. This is very lucky for you, Rot Wick."

"Lucky?" Rotewick scoffed. "Forgive me if I fail to see your allusion."

"Best be glad it is me you face."

"And why is that?"

"Because if he so desired, my brother could kill you in the blink of an eye. You would not even be sport to him. At least I will let you 'strut' a bit before I finish this. You should thank me for the privilege."

If Jackie didn't know better, he'd swear his Princeship's solemn brother was making a jest. What a time to pick to expand one's humorous side! Did the man not know he was on the threshold of danger?

Jackie scratched his head. *Look at the way those light green eyes of his are flashing!* And isn't the lad just enjoying this. He snickered. Well, even at his age, Jackie supposed he could still be surprised by a thing or two.

"I hate being annoyed before my midday meal. It absolutely ruins my mood." Rotewick assumed the *en garde* position. "Better say goodbye to your handsome face; I intend to carve it up some."

The corners of Traed's lips lifted slightly. "Your blade will never get near my face," he stated very softly.

"No?" Rotewick began circling in an attempt to get Traed facing into the sun. "Say goodbye to the ladies.

After this, they'll never look at you again." In a light-ning-quick move he extended his arm chest-high, ro-tating his hand so the blade cut vertically down Traed's right cheek.

Except it was not flesh which met his lordship's blade but thin air.

Traed, anticipating the move, had feinted to the left and parried.

"I would not want to say farewell to *all* of my many women," Traed intoned drily, delivering a point thrust. "By *Aiyah*, they would be beside themselves." His self-mockery was lost on the vainglorious lord. Traed ef-fortlessly met the next lateral cut.

"That's a fact, sir!" Jackie loyally piped in, although, truth be told, he had never actually seen the man with any women. The Princeship's brother was a quiet type, he was. And deep as the Thames.

Rotewick disengaged, then lunged. The sabres met in a series of lightning-fast clashes. "You are better than you let on . . . but not good enough."

"We shall see." Traed easily parried a half-lunge.

Rotewick feinted, then closed. Traed stopped him with a bind, seizing his opponents blade strongly—high then low. The move gave him access to Rotewick's arm. He neatly sliced a piece of Rotewick's shirt, and drew first blood.

The battle heated up considerably after that.

Both men became deadly serious as the snap and whoosh of their blades charged the morning air. Their duel took them across the landscape as each tried to get the vantage point of the other. Both Jackie and Herr Schimmer raced after them to watch the intense swordfight.

Aggressive in his stance, Rotewick lunged forward again and again, attempting to strike a hit. Traed, on the other hand, waged a subtle battle, feinting, parrying, and moving lithely; it was almost as if he were simply biding his time.

Rotewick looked for any opening; the man did not give him one. He was being difficult—staying just out of his reach. And there were certain *moves* the man executed that he had never seen before. Rotewick attempted a riposte. Traed countered and parried.

But Rotewick had finally succeeded in turning Traed into the sun.

Rotewick saw his chance and lunged. The Aviaran gracefully leapt on top of the stone bench behind him, swung around, and delivered what might have been a fatal lateral cut if Rotewick hadn't leapt back in the nick of time.

Traed smiled slowly. "Forgive me," he mocked, throwing the lord's previous words back at him. "I only wanted to see how quickly you could move. Not bad—you are not as slow as you look."

Rotewick turned purple. "You bastard!"

Traed actually grinned.

The blades crackled in a fierce encounter.

Traed met Rotewick thrust for thrust. Rotewick was starting to get winded; Traed was not even breathing hard. They broke apart near a wall bordered by potted plants.

Gasping, Rotewick lunged. Traed neatly parried.

"Have you had enough, Lord Rotewick? It is a simple matter. Fifty thousand of your pounds; no disparaging words against my brother. We can end this now."

"Oh, we will end this, but not in the manner you suggest!" The deceitful lord suddenly grabbed a handful of dirt out of a nearby pot and flung it in the other man's face.

Traed tried to step back but he was hemmed in by

the wall on one side and a shallow pond on the other. The dirt hit him square in the face, temporarily blinding him. Rotewick took advantage of the opportunity. With a straight thrust, he lunged right for his heart.

"Sir!" Jackie started to run toward them, not stopping to think what he would do when he got there. Herr Schimmer trailed behind, swearing in German.

Vision impaired, Traed managed to turned away from the fatal blow. The blade caught him in the fleshy part of his shoulder. It pierced his sword arm deeply. A dark red stain immediately soaked into the cloth of his white shirt.

Wounded, vision impaired, Traed staggered back, falling into the shallow pond.

The water at least helped to clear the debris out of his eyes. Rotewick was advancing. He tried to defend himself, but he could not seem to lift his sword arm.

Rotewick stood over him, gloating. "I think you are finished."

Traed lay sprawled in the water at Lord Rotewick's feet. He looked up at him, droplets of moisture clinging to his black lashes.

For someone who was about to die, there was not a hint of emotion on his handsome, chiseled face.

Rotewick could have stopped the duel then and there.

Instead, he brought the blade to bear, preparing for the kill. "It is over," he sneered, starting his descent.

Gritting his teeth against the pain, Traed rolled to his right, in the direction of his injured shoulder. His vulnerable stance in the water had been designed to test the villainous lord, to give him one last chance if there was any decency left in the man. Rotewick had failed miserably.

At the same time, Traed's *left* hand grabbed his

sword and he lithely rose to his feet. "No, it is only just begun."

This time, Traed did not hold back.

The blade scalloped about Traed's left hand, his *true* sword arm, zinging through the air in a blur of movement so fast as to be almost undetectable to the naked eye.

In an astonishing show of artistry, Traed advanced.

Eyes widening, the "fencing master" began backing up while trying to fend off a blade that was everywhere at once. *Where had he learned those moves?*

Pale green eyes narrowed, and, glittering with his cold fury, Traed showed no mercy. In one continuous catlike spring, he broke into a full run, launching an Aviaran version of the flèche. It was a risky maneuver that always had to be executed perfectly; for if not, it put the attacker at the mercy of his opponent.

Traed's flèche was exactly on the mark.

In short order, their positions were completely reversed. Rotewick lay at Traed's feet, his sword having been flipped from his hand by Traed's blade, only to rest seductively a few feet to his right.

Traed rested the tip of his blade against the man's bobbing throat.

He tossed back several strands of the waist-length, midnight hair that had come loose from his ponytail during the fight. "And now I have a dilemma, Rot Wick."

Rotewick watched him, fear causing a drop of sweat to trickle down his nose.

"I dislike killing, you know. It does not sit well with me."

A sudden gleam came into Rotewick's small eyes. Traed did not like it.

"However—" he nicked the tender skin of the man's

throat, drawing a bead of blood. Rotewick's eyes bulged. "—if I let you go you will undoubtedly cause grief to someone else. A man like you has a tendency to prey on certain people, especially those less able to defend themselves." The jade eyes hardened. "Like children."

Rotewick went a shade paler. How did the man know about that? Had he somehow learned of his special fondness for inflicting pain? He thought he had been very discreet—in fact, ever since the day he had purposely run over that pretty little street urchin just for the pleasure of it, he hadn't . . .

Traed interrupted his meandering thoughts.

"There is the chance you might start feeling ill-used and come after my brother again. Something about him particularly appeals to your sickness, I think. What is it?" Those pale green eyes narrowed, scanning Rotewick intently. "Do you take pleasure in destroying beauty?"

The man gulped nervously, and Traed knew he had seen his awful secret. The green eyes hardened and Rotewick truly feared for his life.

"I—I will not!" he managed to stutter out. "You—you have my word as a gentleman!"

Traed sighed. He slowly lowered his blade. "Very well. I will take you at your word."

Traed had no sooner turned around when Rotewick lunged for the sword lying to his right.

Jackie saw exactly what was going to happen. Alarmed, he yelled out a warning. *"Traed!* Your back!"

"Mein Gott!" Herr Schimmer echoed.

They needn't have worried. In a seamless move, Traed whipped around, sword arm up. He knocked the blade from the other man's grasp.

"I had hoped you would not." He ran him cleanly through the heart. "But I *knew* that you would."

Rotewick stared up at him as if he could not believe the man had the audacity to defend himself. He died clutching his chest. Before his midday meal, which must have really ruined his mood.

"Y'had 'im figured out, y'did." Jackie came up beside him. "Knew 'e would go fer that blade! Did y'leave it lying there next ta 'im on purpose?"

Traed nodded curtly. What he had said to Rotewick was the truth. While he reveled in the battle itself, killing did not sit well with him.

Unfortunately this was one of those times when it became a necessity. He could not allow this man to continue hurting innocent people when it was in his power to stop him. Traed had known something besides the fact that Rotewick would go for his sword. He had known that the man had *intentionally* slain that boy in the street.

He had seen the evil in his eyes.

"Look at ya!" Jackie brought him out of his reverie. The servant made a fuss over Traed's filthy, torn clothes and sodden hair, giving him a thorough inspection. "How's tha' arm? Is is 'urt bad?"

Traed covered the spot where the stain was with his palm. "It is fine."

"Sir!" Herr Schimmer approached. "I have observed this entire duel—his lordship acted in a most dishonorable fashion! I will inform them at the house what I have witnessed."

Traed nodded.

"You are an artist with the blade; it was a privilege to watch you. There were some things that you did that I have never . . . May I ask who taught you?"

"My fath—" Traed hesitated, shocked by what he had

almost said. "His name is Krue."

"A true master," Herr Schimmer remarked with respect for the unknown man's extraordinary technique.

"Yes."

"Come now, lad." Jackie proudly led Traed away. "Emmy will arrange a nice, hot bath fer ya, she will."

"That would be most welcome."

It would take some doing for them to heat the water. Such things often took a very long time here in Ree Gen Cee Ing Land.

But he did not mind.

There was a certain comfort in simplicity.

"Jackie?"

"Aye, sir?"

"What do you know of a place called 'the colonies'?"

"Oh, you'd not be wantin' to be goin' there, sir! 'Tis a heathen place, full up wit' barbarians. I 'ear men there actually *fight* fer what they believe in. . . ."

Something seemed to change in Nickolai after that night.

Lilac didn't know when she had finally fallen asleep. Although she was sure Nickolai had to have heard her tears, he did nothing to bridge the gap between them. It had made her all the sadder.

When she opened her eyes, he was already dressed. She had just caught him leaning over the bed, presumably to check on her. He hesitated when he saw she was awake.

Lilac gazed up at him in a beseeching way; lips slightly parted.

A muscle ticked in his jaw but he turned away.

She was crestfallen. It had always worked before. Whenever she gave him that particular look, Nickolai would give a little moan deep in his throat just before he pounced, kissing her senseless.

He was loosing interest in her.

The notion took hold of her and wouldn't let her go.

She had come to expect Nickolai's attentions. Not that she had feelings for him, it was just that . . .

You did not have feelings for a man like him! A man so skilled, so sultry, so damn beautiful. True, he was generous at providing pleasure, but to how many women before her?

He's kind, a small voice said.

He was overbearing with a terrible streak of arrogance!

He has a marvelous personality . . .

He irritated her beyond belief with his strange ways!

He could be so sweet . . .

When he was sleeping!

He could touch a woman's soul when he made love.

There was no answer to that. Lilac could get no peace from her self-inflicted torture.

To ward off her troublesome thoughts, she threw herself into a frenzy of activity around the house. She even rearranged the furniture in the drawing room, much to Auntie's horror—the displaced davenport revealed Auntie's wealth of hidden books.

Agatha immediately directed her niece to safer territory by casually mentioning an orphanage which could use some donations. Might she like to weed through the clothes in her dressing room? she hinted.

Lilac took up the task with grateful fervor, rushing to her room. Eager to be sidetracked by the chore, she flung open the door to her dressing room.

And came face-to-face with her bathing husband.

Her hand seemed paralyzed on the doorknob as she took in all that sleek tawny skin. His wet hair was slicked back from his face, revealing the exquisite, classical lines of his features. Water dripped from his hair in meandering lines down his chest.

Her mouth parted at the stunningly sensual picture he made. Lilac avidly watched a drop of water trail a path down that gorgeously muscled chest, sliding lower, lower . . .

She almost stood on tiptoe to follow its course before she came to her senses.

They stared at each other in silence for several seconds.

"Come here," he said quietly.

Remembering the last time she had come upon him in this room and what had transpired between them, Lilac softly closed the door behind her. Would he want her again? She wasn't sure. He seemed remote and burning at the same time.

She approached the tub guardedly; Lilac wanted him to want her but she was leery of what he would do. With a husband like this one could never be sure.

Rejar gazed up at her. Remembering Traed's advice, he lowered his lashes to conceal the hunger in his eyes. "Would you help me rinse my hair?"

"If you wish," she whispered.

Bending down, she placed an empty basin behind the tub, then crouched on her knees next to him. She picked up a ewer of warm water.

Sliding her arm around the back on his strong neck, under his hair, she supported his head while she poured. The water gently lapped over his hair cascading into the basin.

For some reason, it seemed highly erotic to her. She watched him as she went about the task. His eyes were closed as if he, too, was aware of the sensuality of the moment. His spiky lashes were midnight crescents against his golden skin.

She was still holding him when his eyes slowly opened.

Droplets of crystal water sparkled on his long black lashes. He has never looked more sensual, she realized. The stunning blue/gold eyes captured her with a look of searing poignancy.

It was a moment of quiet intensity for both of them.

Then, as if he could not help himself, Nickolai turned his face into her bodice. He buried himself in the soft muslin of her gown, his wet arm coming around her waist to hug her tightly to him.

Lilac felt the heat of his ragged breath through the cool, damp material.

A sigh escaped her lips. There was deep emotion in him, but what was it? Guilt? Sorrow? Regret?

It didn't matter; she had to show him she . . .

Before Lilac had a chance to return his embrace, he abruptly released her.

He stared down at the water, not allowing himself to look at her. "I believe I can finish. Thank you for your help."

It was a dismissal, plain and simple.

Lilac bolted out of the room, closing the door behind her. He didn't desire her anymore. Something had died in him the previous night. He had expected something from her that she had somehow failed to give him. She would not cry again. She wouldn't!

But she already was.

Rejar closed his eyes. The calming property of water did not seem to help much.

Lilac had absolutely no feeling for him.

Yet she had ensnared him like any lured beast.

Worse, what he had feared so long ago had come to

pass. Captured, he belonged to a woman who did not love him.

It was the most terrible thing that could happen to a male Familiar.

He was enslaved by his own heart.

Chapter Seventeen

It was several days before the news of Lord Rotewick's death reached Prince Azov's household.

Everyone was sitting in the parlor since the day had turned out to be a dreary one. No one wanted to venture out. Rain sheeted down the windows and it was chilly and damp.

After luncheon they had all wandered into the parlor in search of creative pursuits.

Lady Agatha was sitting by the fire on one side, reading a cloth-covered book which Lilac suspected was on one of her favorite obscure metaphysical subjects. Probably something like "The Inexpressible Ambiguity"; she imagined the title, giggling to herself.

Seated on the opposite side of the fire, she was attempting a new sampler. Since Nickolai had praised her last effort to the point of requesting the work, she thought she might try to make him a companion piece depicting the various types of stitches in needlepoint.

Dara Joy

So far, it seemed to be coming along very nicely.

Her gaze drifted over to the men. They were seated at a table opposite each other immersed in a board game.

She smiled fondly at the sight of the two long-haired heads bending over the board in serious study as if the fate of the world resided with the next move they made. Men often gave vast importance to the silliest of things.

The game itself consisted of a checkerboard and chips that were white on one side and black on the other. The object of the game was to surround your opponent's color with your own by moving horizontally, vertically, or diagonally across the board one space at a time. If you succeeded, that chip or row of chips flipped over to your own color. The winner was the one who had the most chips of his color displayed at the end of the play.

It was a game of strategy and skill.

Both of the brothers had taken to it as soon as Auntie Whumples had explained the rules to them. In fact they had been at it for hours, completely immersed in their "battle."

Lilac frowned. It was the only thing Nickolai seemed to be immersed in lately.

Under normal circumstances the crude thought would have caused her to blush scarlet, but Lilac was very concerned about her husband's lack of interest in her in *that* way. Oh, he still left sweet little gifts here and there for her, picking places he knew she would be sure to find them, and he was still most solicitous of her welfare but . . . . he had not touched her in days.

She missed him.

Missed his kisses and hugs.

Missed his deep voice whispering in her ear as he moved seductively within her.

Lilac missed his arms about her in the night and the little lap under her ear when she fussed in her sleep.

Lilac gazed out the window morosely, the dismal day reflecting her heavy heart. Since that fateful night something had changed in Nickolai.

That night he had frightened her; he had been wild and out of control. His lovemaking seemed to be born of eroticism and fury mixed together in a potent brew. He had been more than she could handle; nevertheless, he hadn't hurt her.

Looking back on it Lilac could remember only the intense passion in him overwhelming her in his embrace; crashing over her like waves of a storm-tossed sea; pulling her under its voracious current. Nickolai had been the tempest.

Suffering a change into something rich and strange . . .

Lilac did not have a great deal of experience in this area but she suspected most men did not make love with Nickolai's intensity. It was something she had sensed when she was speaking with the women at Lady Whitney's and later, had come to believe as she got to know her husband better. Nickolai was a most passionate man.

At least he had been.

She glanced over at his brother Traed, wondering if the trait ran in the family. The ambient firelight reflecting off his strong, chiseled features cast him in a different light. For one thing, the glow softened his visage and Lilac could see at once the sensual side he tried so desperately to hide. Why? What pain was this brother running from?

Auntie shook her from her reverie by casually saying, "Did you hear about that loathsome Lord Rotewick? It seems he was killed in a duel last week. Served the rotter right, I say! Past time for the likes of him. Never could quite stand the fellow . . . something about him gave me the megrims!"

Rejar's hand stilled over the board.

"Who killed him, Auntie?" Lilac continued on with her needlework, not really interested in the topic, but knowing Auntie expected her to ask. It never ceased to amaze her how her aunt was able to obtain all her information on the ton since she rarely left the house.

"No one seems to know."

Pausing in the midst of his move, Rejar pierced Traed with a glittering glance. *[Why did you do it?]*

Traed sat back in his chair, fingers steepled under his chin. "Your move."

So his brother was not going to answer him.

Fine. If that was the way he wished it! Rejar moved his chip, overturning an entire row of Traed's. He exhaled noisily. *[He was mine to deal with! You should have left him to me.]*

Traed did not even flick an eyelash in response.

Auntie stopped reading, glancing up from her book. "Most odd that part of it . . . Neither the butler nor that fencing instructor, Herr Schimmer, could remember what the man looked like even though both had seen him."

The Familiar's eyes dilated fractionally, then veiled. He watched Traed speculatively. A vein throbbed in the other man's temple as he bent over to casually make his move.

Rejar was not fooled by the disinterested action; Traed had not wanted him to learn of his involvement in the matter. Now why was that?

"Have you heard about Madeline Fensley, Lilac?" Auntie went on with her sporadic gossip as she read. "Rumor has it she has come down with some type of ague. The servants aren't talking, of course, but—"

"Madeline Fensley? I recently saw her; it was the night we all went to Lady Harcorte's."

"Really? Well, I hear she is quite ill. Why I remember one time, back in ninety-eight when half the city fell victim to a noxious fever . . ."

Auntie rambled on about a shortage of leeches in the city. Lilac stared pensively down at her hoop. Should she add a row of purple chain stitches?

She did not notice Agatha had stopped her diatribe to train her lorgnette on the embroidery her niece held in her lap; nor did she notice the elderly woman gape at the hopelessly jumbled mass of tangled knots and stitches.

When she glanced up, her aunt's attention had quickly shifted back to her book.

Lilac decided to make the chain stitches green instead of purple. She began embroidering, her mind once again going to her dilemma with Nickolai. She sighed. If only he would—Strange; her embroidery seemed stuck.

She could not turn the hoop in her hand!

Surreptitiously, she lifted a corner of the wooden frame. Oh, no! Somehow, she had stitched the sampler to her dress!

She gave it a sharp yank.

The blighted thing wouldn't budge! It was sewn fast to her lap.

What am I going to do now?

Covertly, she scanned the room, making sure no one was watching her. How embarrassing! Here she was trying to impress Nickolai with her stitchery skill and she had gone and done this stupid thing!

It would not make a very artisanlike impression on him, she was sure.

Maybe she could snip it loose with her scissors. . . .

But if she did that, how would she explain a gaping hole in the front of her gown the size of a Portuguese cake?

Somehow she was going to have to escape the room.

Thinking quickly, she suddenly stood, grasping a corner of her skirt with the edge of the hoop in one hand. "I think I shall go up to check my stitching by the light of the window in my room, Auntie."

"Don't be silly, my dear; why not just stand by the windows in here?"

"Be-because the windows in the bedroom face the— the light better." She stumbled over the ridiculous excuse.

Agatha frowned. "Whatever are you talking about? Lilac, really—"

"I shan't be a minute, Auntie!" Lilac raced from the room.

Rejar watched her leave, wondering what was causing her strange behavior. When the game ended in the next couple of moves, he excused himself, following after her.

Lilac was just coming out of the dressing room when Nickolai entered the room.

"Is something amiss, Lilac?" He noted immediately that she had changed her dress.

Color heated her cheekbones. "No, no, everything is fine. I was a bit chilly so I decided to get my shawl."

"But you have changed your dress."

"Yes, well, that works just as well, doesn't it?" She looped her arm through his, leading him back downstairs. Away from the dressing room.

Rejar gave her an odd look.

"How did your game turn out?" She tried to sound very nonchalant.

He smiled. "I won." Rejar was very pleased with his victory; Traed was notoriously clever with games of strategy.

"Is Traed going to demand a rematch?"

"Most likely; however, I thought we might do something together."

Lilac's breath caught in her throat. Her heart speeded up. Finally. "Yes, Nickolai?"

"I want you to teach me to read in your language."

"What?"

"What part do you not understand?" He took her elbow, steering her toward the library.

"I—you mean you cannot read English?" She was appalled. And acting as if there could be no greater crime in existence.

Rejar chuckled. Surely there was no other place like Ree Gen Cee Ing Land. "I realize you are much more *civilized* than I am, Lilac. Perhaps you will have mercy on my barbarian self." He raised a mocking black eyebrow.

His pithy comment struck its mark; Lilac realized how patronizing she must have sounded. She hadn't meant to—it was just that she was so disappointed by his unexpected request. She had hoped . . .

Lilac got a sudden idea.

She would teach him to read and at the same time perhaps she could stimulate more than his mind. It was certainly worth a try. After all, her husband could be very *stimulating* around books. Look what he'd done for *The Tempest*.

"Very well, Nickolai." She walked over to the bookshelves and made her selection. Then she went over to the desk for a quill and paper.

"Let's sit here." She patted the spot next to her on the oversized chair.

He hesitated a fraction of a second before joining her, his large frame barely making the snug fit. The adjacent position put her husband in satisfying proximity. In fact, it was the closest he had come to her since that night.

Rejar glanced over at his mate and swallowed. Her flowery scent teased his nostrils. Tiny beads of sweat broke out across his brow. He was already semi-erect. *Perhaps this was not such a good idea.*

This had been the worst week of his life! He didn't know how much longer he could last. *Traed.*

Lilac seemed oblivious to his discomfit as she scribbled across the pages of paper, then tore them into smaller squares.

She placed each piece down on the table in front of him, reciting the name of the letter she had written there. "These are the letters of the alphabet; there are twenty-six all together."

"Only twenty-six?" The Aviaran language contained three hundred and thirty-three.

Thinking he was being sarcastic, she replied. "Yes; I have no doubt it will be difficult. However, you will need to memorize these letters first before—"

"A, B, C, D—" He pointed to each appropriate letter as he spoke its name.

Lilac's mouth dropped. "That's amazing! Are you sure you don't know how to read?" She looked at him suspiciously.

He shook his head. "No. I just speak this language. Did I do something wrong?"

"No . . . it's simply . . . never mind." She wiggled in the seat.

Rejar gritted his teeth.

"Now these letters are called consonants, and these over here are the vowels. . . ."

For the rest of the afternoon Lilac instructed her husband, who seemed to be vastly interested in letters and not in the least interested in his wife. Although said husband was failing miserably in the boudoir department, he was proving himself a superior student.

"Nickolai?"

"Yes?" He did not look up from the letters spread before him on the table.

Unconsciously, Lilac poked her little finger again and again through a small hole in the seat of the chair while she thought of a way to phrase what she wanted to ask him.

Rejar noted her action out of the corner of his eye. He tried not to groan.

"Do you think we shall have children soon; I mean . . . well, because of what we've done." *There! That brought the subject up.* She patted herself on the back for her cleverness.

Her unexpected question on a topic he least wanted to discuss at that moment took Rejar by surprise. His jaw clicked audibly. He was not about to discuss Familiar procreation with her. Especially not now. By *Aiyah*, she would run screaming from the room!

"No," he snapped.

No? This was not what she expected to hear. Her brow wrinkled in confusion. "But I thought—"

"I will explain it to you later, Lilac. Now what is this word you have made here?"

"Frolic," she said glumly. "The word is frolic."

Rejar studied the letters carefully.

Fretting over his lack of inclination, Lilac again poked her finger through the small hole in the fabric of the chair. Repeatedly.

Rejar abruptly stood, calling an end to the lesson.

"I wish to bathe. I will see you at the evening meal."

He stormed out of the room, leaving her sitting there by herself, staring dumbfounded at the empty door he had just walked swiftly out of.

How odd. He had been doing remarkably well; in fact, he was actually reading entire sentences. She had never heard of anyone doing that so swiftly before. Lilac had to admit that Nickolai was exceptionally bright.

Why had he left like that?

This past week it seemed as though he kept leaving her to . . . bathe. Several times a day, if she recalled. And he never requested any hot water. Why would he want to take cold baths? Over and over again? The man was decidedly strange.

Lilac's shoulders sagged. He hadn't appeared affected by her nearness. He seemed no more interested in her than he had been all week. A heavy sensation settled around her chest.

It was time to face the truth: Nickolai did not want her anymore.

A tear tracked down her face. If only she were like Leona; she would know what to do to entice him. Leona had so much experience.

Lilac's head snapped up. Of course! She would go to Leona; the woman would be sure to help her. After all, she had said they were friends.

This was the best idea she'd had all week.

Not stopping to think through her plan, she grabbed her shawl. She would go now while Nickolai was bathing.

Lilac hesitated, biting her lip.

Nickolai had told her he did not want her to leave the house without first informing him.

Well, she would be back before he finished with his bath. She wouldn't even call for a carriage; Jackie might decide to confer with "his Princeship" on the matter. Leona's house was only a few blocks away; it would be better to walk than risking discovery.

Too bad her bonnet was upstairs.

It really was raining very hard.

Still sitting in the parlor over the board game wondering how Rejar had managed that last move, Traed caught sight of Lilac leaving the house through the reflection in the foyer mirror.

He raised his eyebrows pensively.

"Lilac!" Leona held out her arms to the younger woman.

Lady Harcorte had elected to see the girl in her boudoir, thereby giving the appearance of close friendship. She was not ready to give up on her quest with the dashing prince; she had a reputation to maintain.

Still, the brother had proven incredibly satisfying. Albeit a tad domineering. Nonsense and stuff! Who was she kidding? He had been the best she had ever had; and she'd had oh-so-many. Just the memory of the incredible night was enough to—

She tried to compose herself.

"To what do I owe this charming, impromptu visit?"

"Oh, Leona!" Lilac ran into the older woman's embrace. "You must help me! You must!"

"Why, my dear, whatever is the matter?" Leona stood back while clasping Lilac's hands. A properly concerned expression displayed itself on her face.

The girl's eyes were red-rimmed as if she had been crying; her dress was damp; and her hair was covered with water-droplets.

There was only one thing that could get a young woman this upset. Lilac was having husband trouble.

Dara Joy

Leona tried not to let her excitement show.

"You're soaking wet; come sit by the fire. Did you walk all the way over here?"

"Yes." She nodded, shivering slightly. "I didn't want Nickolai to know I had come. He—" she bit her lip.

"He what?"

"He doesn't seem to delight in our friendship, Leona."

Smart man. "Nonsense! Nickolai adores me! Ask him yourself if you don't believe me." She slyly goaded her.

Lilac shook her head. "No, that wouldn't do, I'm afraid. Anyway, I don't care what Nickolai thinks of our friendship! *I* like you, Leona, and that's all that matters."

Leona Harcorte stamped out the foreign rush of affection she surprisingly felt for the girl. She hadn't gotten where she was by allowing herself to care about the feelings of anyone but herself! After all, who, except her father, had ever cared about her?

"That's very sweet of you dear." She patted Lilac's hand. "Tell me what troubles you."

"It's Nickolai!" she sobbed. "I believe he has lost interest in me! He turns from me at night . . . and he does not seem to want me anymore." She gazed up at Leona, large green eyes all brimming with tears and trust.

Here was her chance. Leona gloated on the forthcoming victory.

With her next words she could drive a wedge between Lilac and her husband so deep they would never be able to recover from it. The Prince would soon be hers.

What should it be? She tapped her delicate chin.

She could say she had seen Nickolai with another woman—that always worked. Or . . .

She could hint that he had made overtures to her,

but because of her dear friendship with Lilac she had naturally refused him—a personal favorite of hers. Or . . .

She could casually impart that he had been seen in the company of several of the lowest doxies from Covent Garden. The threat of disease worked wonders to dampen the ardor!

There were still worse insinuations she could come up with.— This was so much fun! What should it be? Leona glanced at the innocent, trusting little face next to her. Something she had though long dead in her rose to the surface.

She couldn't do it.

In that brief glimpse it was as if time had overlaid itself and she had seen herself fifteen years before, young and trusting, and so completely vulnerable. A time before that bastard Harcorte had forever destroyed something in her. A time when she was a woman who still believed there was hope and a thing called love in the world. An idealistic little fool.

The unfamiliar feeling of compassion wedged itself in Leona's throat.

Agitated, she stood, placing herself before Lilac. If she was going to be noble, she'd best do it quickly before she made herself sick.

"Don't be a pudding-head, Lilac!" Her cross voice stymied the younger woman. Lilac blinked back her tears, gaping at her.

"Wh-what do you mean, Leona?"

"Men do the most incomprehensible things at times; it is not for us—logical beings that we are—to waste our time trying to figure out their odd behavior. Nickolai *adores* you."

"How do you know?" Lilac wasn't sure she believed that.

Leona slashed her hand impatiently through the air. "If there is one thing I know in this world, it's men. Believe me, Lilac; if there is a problem between the two of you—and I don't think there is—it's temporary."

"But"—her lower lip quivered— "he doesn't . . ."

"For heaven's sake, Lilac! Use the brains you were born with! The man is probably waiting for a gesture from *you*. Men can be the oddest creatures—tell him what you want."

"You think?" A light of hope lit up her pretty face.

Leona put her hands on her hips. "Yes! Go back to him right away and stop this nonsense."

Lilac stood. "I will," she said determinedly. A bright smile etched across her mouth. "Thank you, Leona!"

Impulsively, she hugged the older woman, whispering in her ear. "You know, you're not nearly as uncaring as you want people to think."

Leona watched her race down the stairs. "Yes, I am," she whispered sadly.

Behind her, the door to her bedchamber opened.

Leona looked over her shoulder. Prince Azov's brother strolled into the room, boot heels clicking insolently on her parquet flooring. His glittering green eyes betrayed nothing as he assessed her.

The hardened mask she wore to face the world was once more firmly in place. "How long have you been there?" she demanded furiously.

He ran a knuckle down the smooth skin of her cheek, a soft caress of speculation. "Long enough."

The fact that he had witnessed her appalling display of sentiment horrified her. She twisted away from him. "Don't ever mention it to me."

"If that is your wish." Strong hands on her shoulders turned her around to face him.

352

Shocked, she started to object.

His lips silenced her.

Rejar impatiently draped his red robe over his shoulders, tying the sash with a short tug.

He was not going to be able to withstand much more of this. And what did she mean by penetrating her finger slowly through that opening in the chair! Just thinking about it caused him to grind his teeth. Did the woman *plan* to torture him?

Picturing her arousing action again, he groaned.

The chilly bath water had been punishment enough on this damp day.

He was about to walk out of the dressing room when he spotted the dress Lilac had been wearing earlier. The one she had abruptly changed. It was lying pooled on the carpet next to a stool.

He must have knocked it off in his haste to immerse himself.

Bending over to pick it up, he was about to replace it when he hesitated, frowning. *What was this?* Her project seemed to be *fastened* to the front of the outfit. Curious, Rejar examined it closer.

A huge grin spread across his face.

So that is why the little *souk-souk* left the room in such a hurry! He chuckled. Only his Lilac.

Carefully returning the dress to the stool, he strolled into the bedroom.

Before he had gone a few feet, his wife entered the room, softly closing the door behind her. Not seeing him, she started to tiptoe across the room.

Rejar crossed his arms over his chest.

What was she hiding now? He examined her closely, noting the damp dress and water droplets veiling her hair. "Have you been out?" he scowled.

"Eek!" Startled, Lilac spun around, hand to her heart. "My God, Nickolai, don't scare me like that! You move as silently as a—" Her words faltered.

He raised an eyebrow.

"I thought you were still taking a bath."

"Oh, yes? Then why were you trying to sneak into the room?" His penetrating glance slid down her body. "Was there something you did not wish me to know, hmm?"

Lilac blushed guiltily.

"I hope you were only in the garden, Lilac; although I cannot imagine why you would wish to go outside on such a day."

"Nickolai, don't be angry. I had to do . . . an errand."

"Why did you not tell me? I would have escorted you or done whatever you required. There was no need for you to get soaked like this."

"Um . . . you were bathing and I didn't want to disturb you."

He glowered at that foolishness.

"But I will next time." she quickly added.

Her concession seemed to appease him. "As long as Jackie was with you I suppose it was all right."

Uh-oh. I wonder if a man who looks like a fir tree can be bribed. Lilac plastered a reassuring smile on her face, nodding in agreement.

"Next time, I prefer if you would let me know before you decide to leave; I am concerned about your welfare, Lilac. There are dangers in this world I believe you know nothing about. I would not see any harm come to you."

Moved, Lilac blinked back the sudden tears in her eyes. How was it that Nickolai could affect her this way? She should be incensed at his overbearing attitude; yet here she was emotional because he was concerned about her. She thought about what Leona had said, wondering if the woman was right. Did he still want her?

And if he did, how was she to find out?

She suddenly realized that her husband was perfectly dressed for the job she had in mind. Her yearning gaze took in his muscular form covered in nothing but red silk. Inspiration struck! She used the opportunity to place her hand on his silk-clad forearm. "That's very sweet, Nickolai."

As experienced as he was, Rejar had no trouble deciphering the searing look his wife was giving him. *So, Traed's advice had proven true.* She wished his touch upon her once again.

He breathed a sigh of relief, his body already responding to her nearness.

Nonetheless, he wanted much more from her.

While Traed's advice was appropriate for the initial circumstances, Rejar decided he was going to follow through with his own instincts. He had an idea.

He reached over to clasp her waist with his hands.

Lifting her off the floor, he held her up to him at eye level. They gazed into each other's eyes for several tension-fraught moments.

Finally he spoke in a measured voice. "Do you desire me?"

Lilac's put her arms around his neck. "Yes, Nickolai," she whispered, admitting the truth.

"Good." His mouth brushed along her temple. "Do you want me to give you pleasure?"

"Yes," she breathed, drinking in his erotic scent, the evocation of the musky taste of him.

"Will you do something for me if I give you *everything* you desire?"

Lilac buried her face in the silky hair, nodding against the side of his face.

"Since I have come here you have read to me many stories, Lilac. Now I am going to tell you a story. It is a complicated one so it may take some time for me to tell it to you. Do you understand?"

Lilac had no trouble interpreting; Nickolai was implying that if she wanted him she was going to have to take *all* he had to give. This time she nodded her head rather shakily against him.

"You must promise me that when I start the tale, you will let me finish it and you will listen to what the story is about." He caught her earlobe in his white teeth. "Do you promise?"

"Yes, Nickolai; I promise."

"Fine. I will begin. A long time ago, there was a little girl and her name was . . . *Prunella.*" Lilac nipped his neck; Rejar smiled against her hair.

Carrying her, he walked over to the bed, positioning her in the middle of the mattress. He sat down beside the curve of her hip, placing a palm on either side of her waist.

He bent over her, his glossy hair sweeping forward with the motion. "One day Prunella looked into a pool of water and what do you think she saw?"

"Fish?"

"No, *souk-souk.*" His nimble fingers began to unbutton her dress. "She saw, much to her surprise, countless bursts of light."

"In the water?"

Rejar peeled off her sodden dress. "Yes. She did not know what the lights were . . ." her pantalettes slid down her legs. ". . . so she stooped down for a closer look and realized she was seeing millions of tiny stars in the pool."

"How pretty!"

"Very." Rejar was not responding to her comment so much as the lovely form now exposed to his view. He shed his robe, coming over her.

"Prunella continued to watch the miraculous picture before her, seeing that many of the tiny stars had even smaller specks circling around them, like so—" His tongue swirled a pattern around the curve of her aureola.

Lilac thought him a most inspiring storyteller. Her voice caught as she reacted to his apt demonstration. "Wh-what were the specks?"

Rejar smiled to himself, licking the side of her neck with a slow sweep of his tongue. *By* Aiyah, *she was listening.*

He murmured against the skin of her throat. "It suddenly occurred to Prunella that these specks were . . . worlds."

Lilac gasped. "Worlds?"

"Think of it, Lilac; a pool filled with stars, and around these stars—worlds. . . ."

He let her mull that over for a while as his mouth took hers in a devastating invasion. Lilac's fingers threaded through his hair, caressing the sides of his head as he sought to deepen his kiss.

He needed her so. There was no one that felt like this for him; no one who *tasted* like this.

A low sound of gratification rolled in his throat.

Lilac kissed him back, opening her mouth for him, letting her tongue tenderly slide along his.

"Lilac . . ." he whispered against her gentle lips.

She pressed her mouth against his closed eyes, those spiky lashes that so beguiled her; over his strong cheekbones, the bridge of that perfectly straight nose, along the sensual curve of his upper lip. Cinnamon and bayberry and that *extra* special something surrounded her, calling to her on the deepest level.

She wanted him inside her.

Feeling much the way she did, Rejar whispered, "I cannot wait, Lilac; forgive me." And he entered her in a long, endless thrust.

They both cried out.

[I love to become a part of you.]

His emotional thought only added to her desire for him. "I want you inside me, Nickolai . . . always," she murmured against his mouth.

Her responsive words made Rejar throb within her. "My heart, my heart . . ."

He took her strong and slow.

With every stroke, with every loving movement, he continued to tell her his story. "Prunella saw that these tiny specks were—ah, yes, *souk-souk* right *there*—worlds, and she soon discovered a curious thing: if she watched very closely her view seemed to magnify and she could see that on each world there were people."

"Nickolai, Nickolai, please . . ." Lilac wrapped her thighs tightly around his lean hips.

"Shh, listen . . ." He kissed her. "Not all of these people were alike; in fact, some of them were very different than what she was used to."

Exasperated with his slow torture, Lilac wiggled about, causing her husband to close his eyes in ecstasy.

Through a gargantuan effort, he regained his sensibility. There was much at stake here. "Remember your promise."

Lilac reluctantly stilled her fidgeting.

Rejar continued his slow, deep movements along with his story. "It seemed these people who lived on the worlds inside this *particular* pool lived their lives surrounded by the presence of magic."

"Magic?" This got her interest.

"Yes. Prunella soon discovered that magic was quite common on these worlds; however, not everyone had the ability to do magic and those who did often had different abilities from others." The palms of his hands slid over and down her backside, cupping her derriere to bring her up to him as he plunged wholly into her.

"*Oh!*" Lilac took a shuddering breath, trying to concentrate on what he was saying. "How did they live with this magic, Nickolai? Did it not upset their lives?"

"No, for it was natural to them, simply the way they were."

A tiny line creased her brow as she mulled this over. Rejar could not help but press his lips against the spot.

"Prunella soon found her most favorite people on one of the hidden worlds there. This was a very special place," he whispered enticingly. "These people were rare and different from all the others. Because of this, they were protected by a powerful race of magicians; for their abilities and the beauty of their spirit were highly sought after."

"They sound lovely. What were they like?"

"They were much like you or me except for one difference."

Caught up in the story, among other things, Lilac looked up at him. "What was that?"

"They could change their shape at will—into a cat-like form."

Lilac froze in his arms. "Nickolai . . ."

"You promised, Lilac."

She said nothing for a tension-fraught moment. "Very well, go on with the story."

He embraced her waist, kissing the corners of her mouth. "When they changed form it allowed them to see and experience things others could not. Prunella knew this was nothing to be afraid of because she saw that this ability was a natural trait of these people, who, in their natural form, looked much as she did."

"What did these people call themselves?"

"Familiars."

Lilac stared at his chest, not speaking.

Rejar stopped moving, remaining deeply embedded in her. "One day, in order to help his brother, one of the Familiars entered a . . . whirlpool in the water around them. The currents swirled him around and around; he had no control of his life or what happened to him as he spun about the vortex. Without warning, he was flung out of the churning spout in the water pool and he found himself—"

Lilac put her hand over his mouth. "Don't say it."

He removed her hand from his lips, kissing the palm. "He found himself falling into the air. To protect himself, he changed into his cat-form. With a burst of lightning he broke through the barrier of the universes and crashed down next to his Prunella."

Lilac threaded her fingers through the glossy hair on the sides of his head. "You can't expect me to—"

"She was riding in a coach," he continued on inexorably, "next to her aunt, who was extremely frightened of the cat. But Prunella wasn't. She was very kind to him and took him home with her."

Lilac blinked several times, clearly distressed by what she had heard. It had the disturbing ring of truth to it. "I—"

He placed his tapered finger against her mouth. "*Shh*. It is all right, Lilac. I only ask that you think on it."

She didn't want to think right now. She only wanted her husband to hold her and make love to her. The amazing story made him seem that much further removed from her; she did not want Nickolai removed from her. The strange reality of it panicked her. "Nickolai, please don't stop now!" she cried out.

Seeing how upset she was, Rejar immediately obliged her, gliding his tongue into her mouth, imitating his languid ebb and pulse below. It was time to show her that he was the same man, that she need not fear him.

His tender actions provided the reinforcement she needed; Lilac instantly relaxed under his accustomed touch. *{There is a flow to us together,* souk-souk, *like the water I spoke of. Do you feel it?}*

Lilac ran her palms down the plane of his back, letting the tips of her fingers feel every contour of rippling muscle as he advanced and retreated within her. "I do feel it, Nickolai."

{Waves . . . there is much about waves I will teach you, Lilac—waves on water, waves in moonlight, waves we create together . . . } He took her breast in his mouth, lovingly suckling on her.

"Yes . . . oh, yes . . ."

They moved together in a dance as old as time. Mimicking the resonance of life itself. They flowed into each other.

It was a marvel that spanned galaxies, planets, and, yes, even pools of star-filled water.

This time Rejar did not hold back; he joined his wife in completion.

Both of them surging, swelling, breaking.

Releasing, exchanging, and clinging . . . together.

Chapter Eighteen

"Mmmm . . ." Rejar rubbed his chin against Lilac's shoulder.

The soft nap of her cotton chemise, not the velvet skin he anticipated, brushed his jaw. He frowned. "Why are you wearing this?"

Lilac yawned sleepily, tucking her derriere closer to the warm of the male body behind her. "I'm chilly."

"With me keeping you so close?" He tease-kissed the nape of her neck, drawing her tighter into the circle of his arms.

Lilac smiled. "I suppose it was all that dampness yesterday; I feel a bit achy as well."

Concerned, Rejar raised up on one elbow. "Was I too rigorous for you?"

Lilac gazed at him over her shoulder. "No, Nickolai; not at all—you were very gentle." She patted the hand still curved around her waist.

Rejar was not convinced. He cupped her chin, examining her closely in the morning light. "You look pale, *souk-souk*. Are you sure I have not worn you out?"

Lilac giggled. She couldn't help it. Imagine a man being concerned he had been *too* satisfying! "Well, if you did, I can't think of a better way to wear oneself out, can you?"

Chagrinned, Rejar smiled softly in agreement.

She sat up in bed, stretching. "I feel deliciously weary. In fact, I think I shall go out to the garden in this glorious sunshine"—she gazed at him coyly from beneath her lashes—"unless you have something better for me to do?"

Rejar laughed. How pretty she looks, he thought, with her hair tumbling over her shoulders and those forest green, Aviaran eyes twinkling at me . . .

"Best you go out in the garden; I must be careful how 'delicious' I make you feel." He planted a smacking kiss on her shoulder, grazing her with the edge of his teeth.

"If you insist." She threw the covers back, trying not to wince as she made her way to the dressing room.

"Lilac?"

"Yes?" She paused in the doorway.

"Think about the story I told you last eve."

Her back stiffened slightly. Without responding to him, she closed the door softly behind her.

She couldn't think about anything right now; she was terribly achy. She hadn't been this sore since the morning after her wedding night. Although . . . Nickolai had been very gentle with her last evening.

Come to think of it, she wasn't at all sore down *there*. Shrugging, she decided a morning outdoors in the sunshine could only help.

It did not help.

In fact, by the afternoon, Lilac had a distinct sore

throat to go along with her sore muscles.

By evening she had taken to bed with a fever.

"What is wrong with her?" Rejar stood over the bed, a worried expression marring his sultry face.

"She seems to have an ague." Agatha fussed over her niece, lifting the covers to her chin. Lilac had fallen into a troubled sleep.

"What is that?"

"I'm afraid she is ill, my boy."

"I am too much for her," Rejar sadly said.

Agatha had a coughing fit.

Rejar lightly tapped her on the back. "Are you all right, Lady Agatha?"

"Yes, of course I am all right!" Impatiently, she waved his hand away. "This has nothing to do with you, my dear boy! Lilac has a disease of some kind."

He did not understand. "What is dis-ease?"

Lady Whumples looked at him rather strangely. "It is a sickness which is contracted in some unknown fashion."

He thought about this a minute, suddenly going pale. "This is like the pox Jackie warned me about? He said that women called doxies—"

"*Young man.*" She reached over and smartly boxed Rejar's ears.

"Ow!"

"I will not have that kind of talk in this house! This is *nothing* of the kind!"

Rejar rubbed at his stinging ears. "Lady Agatha, I do not understand."

"Lilac has a fever. We do not know what causes these sicknesses of the body. There are those who liken it to a poison in the blood."

"Is there nothing we can do? Can we not get a healer for her?"

"You mean a doctor? I must tell you, your Highness, that I am not one to subscribe to those quacks; it is my opinion that they cause more harm than good. My advice is to let Lilac try to rally on her own. We will do our best to make her comfortable, of course."

"I will take your advice, Lady Agatha."

But Lilac did not seem to rally.

Over the next several days her condition steadily worsened. Her fever rose, she went in and out of lucidity, and an ominous rattle sounded from her chest while she struggled for each breath she took.

Concerned over this strange malady which had suddenly afflicted his mate, Rejar did not leave her side.

Distraught, he sat by her, trying to get her to drink some water, to swallow some broth. He bathed her forehead with cool cloths, covered her with more and more blankets to stop her chills, and paced and paced and paced.

None of it was helping.

"You must rest or you will be no good to her." Traed rose from his chair on the other side of the bed. He had stayed close to Rejar for the past several days, his calm presence offering immeasurable support.

"I cannot." Rejar ran a weary hand through his long hair.

Agatha watched him from the corner of the room. If she had ever had any doubt as to the depth of his feelings for her niece, his behavior these past days would have laid those doubts to rest.

However, Agatha had never had that uncertainty with Prince Azov.

She, who trusted few and liked even less, had taken to this man immediately. His brother she regarded just as highly. She had always had very good intuition when it came to people. If only that same intuition

365

could be applied to help her niece. Agatha sighed mournfully; Lilac was not doing well.

"Nickolai . . . Nickolai . . ." Lilac called to her husband, her voice sounding weak and thready.

Rejar abruptly stopped his pacing to go to her. "I am here, Lilac." He smoothed back a few strands of hair which had fallen over her forehead. The skin there was dry and very, very hot.

She did not seem to hear him.

She just kept calling his name in a voice growing fainter and fainter.

He could not take anymore. "Send Emmy for a healer," he said to Agatha.

"Your Highness—"

"*Do it!*"

Against her will, Agatha went to the landing, telling Emmy to go quickly and get a doctor.

Within the half-hour the doctor arrived. He was filthy and stank of death. Under normal circumstances, Rejar would not have even let the man into his home, but he was desperate. He did not believe Lilac would last the night.

"Can you help her?" he asked him.

The doctor walked around the bed as if looking at the patient from differing angles would help him assess what was wrong with her. Then he bent over the bed, lifting her eyelid to peer into her eye.

Rejar could barely stand the sight of that filthy hand touching her. "Well?" He was losing his patience.

"Yes, I believe I can help her; although there is no guarantee."

Rejar breathed a sigh of relief.

"You must leave me alone with the patient for several hours."

Rejar hesitated. "Why?"

"The procedure can be upsetting to those of the family, I insist—"

"Ask him what he intends to do, your Highness!"

"Lady Agatha is right. I am afraid what you ask is not possible. I would never leave my wife alone in a situation such as this; she is depending on me to watch out for her."

The man drew himself up. "If you insist, that is your right. I must warn you it is not for the faint of heart. These illnesses must be tackled with vigor else they will not be driven from the body."

"I understand."

Agatha began sobbing into her handkerchief. Using the Prince's name for the first time, she implored him, "I beg you, Nickolai! Don't do this. If my niece is to die, let her go in peace."

Rejar rubbed his eyes, fatigue, sorrow, and worry claiming him equally. "What is the procedure?" he asked, resigned.

"Well, first we must bleed her, then—"

Rejar's eyes snapped open. "What do mean you 'bleed' her?"

"It is how the disease is removed from the body, through the blood. I must open a vein with this lancet," he removed a dirty knife from a case in his pocket. "Leeches"—he held up a jar of disgusting, squirming creatures—"are applied to the spot to further aid in the procedure."

Rejar staggered back, collapsing into a chair.

"If this does not work, we may try blistering. Along with purging her system, a caustic liquid is poured onto the skin in an effort to boil the illness away. As a matter of course I'm afraid her Highness will be hideously scarred."

"Get out," Rejar whispered.

"I'm sorry?"

"I believe my brother has told you to leave." Traed took the man by the collar and the seat of his pants and tossed him out the door.

"Have a spot o'this, yer Princeship." Dazed, Rejar felt Jackie tug at his sleeve. He took the glass the man gave him, gratefully swallowing the brandy.

"I could not bear it if you allowed him to continue," Agatha sniffed.

"Nor I." He pulled the chair up to the edge of the bed, preparing for a long vigil.

His gaze went to the bedside table spotting the books there. Picking one, he faced it on its side, reading the title. *Songs of Experience*, he read, by William Blake. Lilac so loved to read.

Carefully, he opened the book of poems, remembering the many times she had comforted him by reading aloud. Maybe this time he could bring a small measure of comfort to her. He began to read haltingly,

> *"Tyger, Tyger, burning bright*
> *In the forests of the night,*
> *What immortal hand or eye*
> *Could frame thy fearful symmetry?"*

Rejar took a deep breath, his emotions on the verge of spilling over, then continued:

> *"When the stars threw down their spears*
> *And watered heaven with their tears,*
> *Did he smile his work to see?*
> *Did he who made the lamb make thee?"*

Rejar threw the book aside and, placing his head on the bed, wept.

He wept for Lilac; he wept for the fear that prevented her from truly having known him; he wept for his one-sided love, and he wept for all that would never be.

After a time he felt Traed's hand on his shoulder. "I am sorry for you both, brother." This kind of pain Traed knew well.

[What kind of a world is this Ree Gen Cee Ing Land, Traed? I vow I cannot understand it. Horror and beauty . . . where a man can illuminate the soul with the gift of simple words yet an unknown illness can steal life away without warning.]

"I know not," Traed said quietly. "Surely it is a poison."

Rejar looked up at his brother, his sensitive face tear-streaked. "Poison?" he whispered. Agatha had said the same; this thing called disease was likened to a poison.

He blinked, a recollection forming in his mind.

"Traed! When we were on Ryka Twelve, on our way to Zarrain to see you, Lorgin was poisoned by a *xathu* beast."

Traed had not heard this before. "Such a poison is deadly! How did he survive?"

"Yaniff had an idea. He believed that if I passed through Lorgin in the midst of my transformation—while I was still in my energy state—I might take the poison with me."

Traed rubbed the back of his neck. "It was very risky; you could have been poisoned as well."

"Not as long as I was able to disperse the poison from myself before I imbodied."

"There was no danger to you?"

"No." Rejar did not quite meet Traed's eyes.

Nor did he tell his brother of Yaniff's prophecy to him. The wizard had warned him against it. At the time Rejar had scoffed at his words, saying he would never

369

be tempted to do such a thing again. How little he understood.

"You wish to try this with Lilac?"

"Yes." He faced Lilac's aunt. "Lady Agatha . . . Agatha. You are going to see something which might upset you; I hope you will find it in your heart to have understanding. What I am about to reveal to you, I do for Lilac's sake."

Then he began to metamorphose.

He started to glow from within. Streams of light flowed and arced around him. His form shimmered and started to melt into a gleaming phosphorescence.

"My word!" Agatha gasped.

"Blimey!" Jackie's eyes bulged as he chomped down on the stem of his pipe.

Traed stood by, an uneasy feeling settling in the pit of his stomach. Something Lorgin had said about Rejar's superior ability to defend himself teased at his mind. Suddenly, Yaniff's words came to him out of nowhere . . . *His kind heart will get him into trouble* . . .

Instantly, Traed realized *this* was where the real threat to Rejar was! Not Rotewick; it was never Rotewick. "Rejar, wait!"

It was too late.

The Familiar had already attained his energy state, a state no Familiar ever holds for more than a moment.

Traed watched transfixed as Rejar passed through the body of his wife, pausing that extra fraction of time to make sure he cleansed the "poison" from her. That extra fraction of time that would cost him dearly.

With his passing, Lilac was already breathing easier. She opened her eyes in time to see an amorphous frame of light hovering near the bed. She knew exactly what had occurred; she had felt him slide through her.

Traed observed the glowing configuration barely

pulsing, getting weaker and weaker. It was obvious Rejar could not regain his corporeal form; he did know how to draw the energy to himself. Soon his strength would wither and his life would dissipate. He would die.

Unless . . .

There was only one way to help him.

Traed would have to break a solemn oath he made to himself. An oath never to unleash the awesome power contained within him.

All his life he had seen the destruction that followed in the wake of such terrible power. His own father, Theardar, had destroyed so many lives, including his own, because he could not control the raging force in him.

It was the same power which flowed through his son, hidden all these years only by his strength of will.

The glow was very faint now; his brother was hanging on to his last shred of life.

Rejar.

There was no choice. There never had been.

Closing his eyes, Traed stood away from the walls as he called forth the latent ability that flowed through his veins.

Small arcs of lightning started to flash around the tips of his fingers, traveling up his body. Soon he was engulfed by the arcs circling around him, growing in strength and number.

Once released, the power rose up in him greedily.

"My word!" Agatha croaked.

"I'll be laying off the gin, I think." Jackie gulped.

Outside, clouds began to converge over the house; the sky blackened and thunder sounded. A howling wind shook the house. Lightning traveled all around him now, from his fingers outward.

The keening wind reached a crescendo as the energy surge amplified over the room and him. Wind swirled about; it was an uncanny storm. The crystal chandelier bounced against the ceiling, delivering eerie chimes.

Lilac would never forget the way Nickolai's brother appeared just then. His eyes were closed in concentration, his long hair, freed by the wild wind, swirled around him as he stood with clenched fists fighting to contain what he had unleashed.

With a roar of thunder and a crackle of energy, every window in the room blew out.

The chandelier crashed to the floor.

"My word!" Agatha clutched the wall for support.

The Aviaran opened his green eyes, which were now shot with sparks of incandescent lightning. Across the room the faint glow of Rejar's life force was all but dissipated.

Traed sent him a powerful burst of energy; it flowed from the center of his chest directly into the waning phosphorescence.

At first, nothing happened and Traed feared he was too late. But then, the glow grew a little brighter.

Rejar was fighting to live!

Traed was proud of the Familiar's strength of will; another would not have lasted this long. He sent him another strong jolt. The glow grew brighter still.

Stay with it, brother, do not give up. . . .

Traed drew yet more power from his seemingly unending reserves and began sending a steady flow of current directly into his brother's being. The blood-tie connecting them aided his task.

A shape began to coalesce in the pulsing phosphorescence. His brother's corporeal body was trying to form! Encouraged, he continued to send him his power.

Rejar metamorphosed out of the light.

He collapsed onto the floor, naked and barely alive.

Everyone was silent for a few seconds, obviously shocked by what they had witnessed.

Sadly comprehending the debilitated state he was in, Traed joylessly hoisted Rejar over his shoulder and lowered him onto the bed next to his wife. His brother would not last long.

Knowing none of this, Lilac bent over her husband, overcome by relief. Clutching his shoulders, she bowed her head against his chest. He did not even have the strength to embrace her.

Traed straightened, his sights meeting Jackie's. The man gave him a frightened look and bolted out to the hallway and down the stairs.

"Jackie, stop!" Traed raced after him. He caught up with him in the downstairs foyer.

"I—I think it's best I take me leave, sir."

"Wait! You do not understand, Jackie—"

"I don't want to understand!" Traed tried to interrupt but Jackie held up his hand. "Listen to me, sir. I've seen a lot in me day. I've seen things no man wants to see and I've seen things I shouldn't 'ave. But I ne'er seen nothing like that! There are some things in this life it's best not to be knowin' about. Now I like yer fine, sir, but this is one o' them times."

"I see."

Jackie nodded. He gestured up the stairs with his pipe. "Will 'is Princeship be all right?"

Traed exhaled heavily. "I do not think so."

"I'm right sorry to be 'earing that." He puffed on his unlit pipe pensively. "Is there nothing' *you* could do, sir? I mean—what with what I saw in that room . . ."

Traed stared at the floor in silence.

"I see. Well, as I said, I must be gettin' along now.

It's best I see no more o' this. A man can't speak about what he doesn't know, now can he?"

"I understand. Can we give you anything to ease your way?"

Jackie rolled his hat in his hand. "Nah, 'is Princeship 'as been more than generous wit' the likes o' me. I'm set, I am."

"Will you not stay to say goodbye to Rej—the Prince?"

"I best be goin' now." He started to leave, then stopped at the door, turning around. "Whatever the outcome, I'm sure a fine bloke such as yerself will do the right thing."

He put his pipe in his mouth and closed the door behind him.

Traed heard footsteps approaching behind him in the hall.

"Is everything all right upstairs, sir?" Emmy asked worriedly. "There was a sudden terrible storm, but it's blown over now."

"Everything is fine, Emmy."

"And Lilac, I mean, her Highn—"

"She is fully recovered." His dull response did not register on Emmy. The longtime servant was just happy the little miss was all right.

When Traed walked into the room, Lilac was leaning over Rejar anxiously. She had covered him with a blanket.

"What's happened, Traed? What's wrong with him? He can't seem to move. His mind seems clouded and his speech is all muddled." Her anxious green eyes beseeched him for reassurance.

Traed wished he did not have to tell her what was to come. However, the task fell to him. "He is weak, Lilac.

He passed his life energy through you, cleansing your spirit of the illness. He could not stand to see you suffer, could not bare to watch you perish."

"But why is he so weak? He can barely breathe."

"He has the ability but not the knowledge. Once, he saved his brother Lorgin's life with this technique—I believe he must have had the help of a powerful mystic named Yaniff." An expression of overwhelming sorrow came over him. "Yaniff tried to warn me; I did not understand what he meant."

"Wh-what do you mean?" she whispered.

"The danger to my brother was himself." Traed's face saddened. "It was his kind heart which led him to disaster."

Lilac stroked her hand gently down Nickolai's face. "When will he feel better?"

"He is not going to get better, Lilac." Traed said the words quietly.

Her head snapped up. "What?"

He could not meet her devastated look. "He is dying. He cannot maintain his life force."

"Dying?" Lilac blinked back the unacceptable truth. Nickolai could not be dying! He had . . . he had . . . *saved her life at the cost of his own.*

Lilac choked back a sob. All this time her aunt had been right; she had said he was a man who would willingly give his life for those he placed under his protection. A man of substance, she had called him.

And he was.

A man who cared enough to sacrifice his own life, who was gentle and kind, noble and honest. A man who possessed not only physical beauty but also inner strength.

The truth hit her then.

His beauty was of his entire being. What else could

he be but good? Regardless of where he came from or what special abilities he had! He was not something to be feared. . . .

He was something to be loved.

With her realization came understanding. What he must have gone through! Cast adrift in a completely foreign environment, the horror of discovering he was in a place where he would never be accepted, indeed, where he might be destroyed.

Everything had to be strange and alien to him.

She recalled when he had told her his "story" that he had mentioned something about entering the whirlpool in order to help his brother. How very like him, she acknowledged.

Oh, she had treated him so dreadfully! And still he had pursued her despite her blind resistance to him. A man of fortitude. Auntie had been right about everything. How could she have been so unaware?

A chill of foreboding raced down her spine. Her revelation came too late.

"No—no!" She grabbed her husband's hand in her own, bringing it to her lips. She spoke his name for the first time, admitting who and what he was. And more.

"Rejar, Rejar, I love you. Don't leave me!"

Rejar opened his eyes slowly. "How it pleases me to hear you speak my . . . I want you to know . . ." The hand she held weakly stroked her face.

"My heart," he whispered, "I have had many women . . . so many women . . . but you are the only . . . the only one . . ." The blue and gold eyes suddenly glazed over. "Yaniff, you must . . . tell Traed . . . there is no weakness in love; tell him . . ."

He did not seem to know where he was.

"Rejar!" Lilac shook his shoulders, willing her husband to come back.

"Yaniff rails at me so . . . He wants me to join them. . . . I vow I am tired of it. . . ." His incoherent rambling faded out along with his consciousness.

Lilac fell on top of him, sobbing.

Traed clenched his fists. *No weakness in love?* How wrong his brother was. There was every weakness in love! If there were not, would he even consider doing what he was about to do?

A weighty feeling descended upon him. Could he let his brother-of-the-line die? He had taken care of him as a child, guided him, laughed with him, watched over him. He had given his oath and even if he had not— *this was his brother*. Whom he loved.

There was someone who could possibly save him.

Yaniff.

Traed would have to call forth his old Charl master. To do so, of course, would uncloak him to the Guild; for only the highest level mystics had the ability to send an arc through time, space, and dimension.

Rejar did not have many breaths left, he knew.

There was no choice; he would expose his power and sacrifice himself so his brother might live.

There would be no escape from the High Guild after this. They would demand *him* in the name of his family honor. He was bound by the blood tie oath of *Chi'in t'se Leau*. The wizard Yaniff had cunningly said to him, '*Your life for his.*'

Well, now he had it.

Chapter Nineteen

Traed closed his eyes and clenched his fists.

With a flash of lightning, he opened a small window in the Tunnels and sent his signature arc into another universe. The call, or *arcing* as it was known on Aviara, took with it his last hope for freedom from the curse of his heritage. It would instantly alert every high mystic in the realm to the presence of his power.

It seemed as though not a moment had passed from the time the signal was sent to when a portal opened and the ancient wizard of Aviara, Yaniff, stepped through into Ree Gen Cee Ing Land.

"My word!" It was all Agatha could seem to utter. Her niece had tried to explain a little of what she knew about these strange occurrences while Traed had been downstairs with Jackie; however, this was too much to take in! None of her special books had ever mentioned this.

Yaniff did not spare time for greetings; instead he

made his way directly to the bed where Rejar lay. He already knew the gravity of the situation.

"Can you help him?" Lilac beseeched the old man, her face tear-streaked. "You are the ancient mystic Rejar and Traed have been talking about?"

Yaniff smiled slightly. "Yes, although I think I am getting tired of everyone referring to me as ancient. Move aside quickly, child, and let me see what I can do. There is not much time." Lilac scrambled out of his way.

Without hesitation the old wizard placed his palms flat on the Familiar's chest and conjured up a significant spell:

> *"My gift of life once more I lend;*
> *To renew your spirit twice again;*
> *He called Rejar come whole for me!*
> *And speak to all of your destiny."*

There were no flashing lights, no arcs of lightning, no cracks of thunder. In stillness and simplicity, the greatest wizard of Aviara brought life back to Rejar ta'al Krue with only the power of his words. Traed could not help but marvel at his mastery.

Rejar's eyelids fluttered.

The Familiar opened his eyes and, seeing Yaniff above him, clasped the old man's hand where it still rested upon his chest. A tear rolled out of the corner of his gold eye, so glad was he to see the old man.

"Oldefather," he whispered affectionately.

"Rest for a moment, Rejar." The wizard passed his hand over the Familiar's face, and Rejar closed his eyes.

"Why does he call you that, Yaniff?" Traed had overheard Rejar's remark.

Yaniff straightened and turned to face his adoptive son. "It is the weakness; he knows not what he says."

"Or his Familiar senses tell him something."

The two men stared at each other. Neither spoke.

It did not appear Traed's arc had particularly surprised this old master. *He knew,* Traed realized. He had known all along.

"Will he be all right, Mr. Yaniff?" Lilac asked hesitantly. This old man with the long white hair, crimson robes, and an odd animal perched on his shoulder evoked an air of instant respect.

"Yes; he arises now." Lilac looked over to the bed, surprised to see her husband struggling to sit up. She ran over to him.

"Rejar! Stop! You are still weak!" She tried to fix the pillows behind his back as he leaned against the headboard.

Lilac. She was recovered and he was still alive! A surge of joy rushed through him, giving him a burst of strength.

Rejar grabbed his mate about the waist and pulled her onto the bed next to him. "Not so spiritless, *souk-souk,* that I do not remember what you have said to me!" He kissed her soundly on the lips. "Make everyone leave," he whispered mischievously to her. "I want to *talk* to you."

"You must be better—you're back to your usual naughty self." She playfully punched his shoulder, then hugged him tightly to her.

Rejar embraced her as well, clasping her to him as though he would never let her go.

"She is right; you need rest, Rejar. You both do." Yaniff walked over to the bed, his warning reminding them what they had both been through recently. Rejar reluctantly released her.

Lilac took the opportunity to scoot off the bed; she needed to speak with Auntie Whumples. The poor dear had been standing frozen in the same spot with her mouth gaping open for much too long.

Rejar watched her comfort her aunt. "She has accepted me. Things will change between us now."

"Perhaps." Yaniff pulled up a chair, sitting by the bed.

"Thank you, Yaniff, for giving my life back to me."

Yaniff waved his hand as if returning life to someone were a small deed. "You realize you could have brought the forces to yourself had you been of the Charl?"

Rejar sighed in good humor. "Ah! Do not waste the opportunity, old man! I do not know why you have always wished me to join the Charl; I do not have these abilities, Yaniff."

"You have them and more. Would you yet risk the life of your wife and yourself again because you have abilities that you do not know how to use?" he slyly asked.

Rejar gave him a patented look out of the corner of his eye. "Very well. You have your wish; I will join you."

Yaniff beamed; he clapped Rejar heartily on the back. "Finally! I vow, you have been a trial to me, Rejar. For a Familiar, you are an extremely stubborn man."

At Rejar's narrowed look, he quickly added, "However, this can be a good trait. I, myself, will guide you on your journey to find the knight within. Together we shall bring him forth." His gaze went to Traed. "For both of you." he murmured.

Rejar sat up straighter, astonishment showing on his face. "It is gone!"

"What is gone, Rejar?"

Dara Joy

"The restlessness—it has completely left me. What was it, Yaniff?"

The wizard gazed at him speculatively. "Give me your hands."

Rejar did. Yaniff clasped his hands, closing his eyes. When he opened them he was smiling.

"Yes . . . I believe it does make sense."

"What, Yaniff? Tell me."

"Know you not that the restlessness was *you*, Rejar?"

"I do not understand."

"The Charl part of you that you have always tried to suppress—it spoke to you and would not be silent until you recognized it."

"I still do not understand, Yaniff."

"You will in time."

Rejar furrowed his brow. "There is not much of my father's line of power in me. I have no Charl abilities."

"You think not?" The wizard smiled mysteriously. "Well, together we will seek this hidden side that speaks to you and see what we will find."

"As you wish, Yaniff, but you waste your time."

"A wizard never wastes his time. That is your first lesson, Rejar."

The Familiar leaned back against the pillows, smiling. "Perhaps I shall be the exception," he joked.

Yaniff seemed to find his own humor in Rejar's words. He chuckled, his fingers going up to stroke his winged companion on his shoulder. "Your life will be one of many changes, my young friend. As you have the ability to transform yourself, so too, will the path of your life alter and change."

"Can you see my future then, Yaniff?"

"Some."

"What do you see?"

"I will only tell you this—you will become a man of

382

legendary power both within and without. You will be a great leader of men. However, your revelation of power will cost you dearly."

Rejar snorted. "You see wrong. I have no desire for power or greatness. I desire only to be with my wife and lead a quiet life—in love."

"Such is not your destiny, Rejar. You have already learned that you cannot deny who you are. There is greatness in you; you will become a legend among our people." He specifically gazed across the room at Traed when he said, "The time for avoidance is over. This is my prophecy."

"It is not me you speak of! I am a man whose interests lie in other directions."

Yaniff said nothing.

"Perhaps I should not return with you to Aviara after all."

"You will come; for you have already sensed you cannot remain here. You could never be your true self in this world."

Rejar inclined his head slightly, the truth of Yaniff's words evident.

"I must return now; word has been sent to me from the Familiar world that Gian Ren is missing."

Rejar was shocked. "*Taz* Gian is missing?"

"Yes. As you can imagine, there is much unrest on M'yan."

"I will not be long in coming, Yaniff. This news disturbs me."

"It disturbs us all; however, *you*"—Yaniff shook his finger at him—"will be involved in your studies."

Rejar frowned. He did not like this twist of events. "He is my blood relative, Yaniff."

"And you now belong to me. You have agreed to be my student; your allegiance is to the Charl. In time you will get used to listening to your teacher. As for Gian, the High Guild will do everything in its power to help the Familiar people; you know that."

Rejar exhaled slowly. He did not know if he was going to like this student business. He was used to making decisions solely on his own.

Yaniff approached Traed.

"Rejar has agreed to join the Charl; I have accepted his oath. You will bear witness to this. I am sure the Guild is waiting to speak with you as well."

The green eyes narrowed as they contemplated the wizard.

It suddenly occurred to Traed just how Yaniff had manipulated the situation.

The old wizard had cornered him well.

He had played his game and set his trap, garnering both Rejar and him at once. By using his power to help Rejar, Traed was forced to release the power inside him; while Rejar was made to see how dangerous it was for him not to open himself to his Charl side.

The old wizard had played each off the other, using one to bend the other. Traed had to admit it was clever of him. Clever and insidious.

"Think you I know not what you are about, Yaniff?" Traed said in a harsh tone.

Yaniff had expected this reaction from him. "It was out of love, Traed; I hope in time you realize that. You could not hide forever."

"No, I suppose not. It was a fantasy of mine, you see, which required *true* magic."

Yaniff nodded poignantly. He understood Traed's dilemma well. "I go now; stay with him. He will need you to open the Tunnel."

"Are you so sure I can?"

Yaniff raised one eyebrow. "Yes." He called forth the Tunnel.

The pulsating circle grew and grew until a maw large enough for him to enter opened in the room.

"My word!" Agatha stuttered.

Before he entered the Tunnel, Yaniff boldly eyed the elderly woman. Letting his gaze run the length of her, he winked saucily.

Then he was gone.

Agatha began fanning herself. Apparently Yaniff's brazen action was enough to snap her out of her stupor. "Did you see that? What impertinence!"

At least her aunt was speaking again. Lilac crawled back onto the bed feeling terribly downhearted. Sitting back on her haunches, her white lawn nightgown billowing around her, she suddenly looked very young.

"You are leaving us to go to your home in the pool, Rejar?" Her eyes filled with tears.

She still didn't quite understand, but she was trying. He smiled gently, thinking that she looked adorable. Especially since her lower lip couldn't decide whether to quiver or pout.

"Yes." His fingers brushed that delectable lip. "You and Agatha are coming with me."

Her mouth parted in surprise.

"Did you think I would leave you, *souk-souk*?"

"But—but I can't swim!"

Rejar roared with laughter. "You do not have to swim, Lilac. You will love Aviara! There are pretty gardens for you to enjoy, the weather is not damp or chilly like here, and everywhere it is green with many, many flowers. The air is sweet and clean. Moreover, there will not be the confines placed upon you that you have had to endure here in Ree Gen Cee Ing Land." His hand cradled her lovely face. "I think this Lilac will bloom there."

"It sounds lovely." She nuzzled against his caress.

"It is; a beautiful place where you will never have to suffer something like this again." His thumb traced the dark circle under her eye, evidence of her recent illness. "Ah, and I have a special little pet for you. Her name is Sookah. She is very sweet and affectionate—or she will be once she gets over her jealously of you."

"What kind of pet is it?" she asked warily.

His eyes twinkled. "A *souk-souk*."

Lilac hit him with a pillow.

Rejar gave her The Smile, looking much like a cat with tail feathers around his mouth.

"Agatha, when I mated with Lilac I promised you I would take care of you both. Will it upset you to leave this home?"

"I should say not! I detest the strictures that I have been forced to live under my entire life. Just think of it . . . I shall be able to explore the mysterious unknown! It is my life's dream! I am quite excited by the prospect; why, I can hardly wait!"

Rejar's blue/gold eyes flashed with humor and a good dose of Aviaran male arrogance. "That is fortunate since you *are* going." He would never leave the old woman behind.

Agatha viewed him obliquely. "I shall have to work on you, young man. I can see by that rapscallion who was here before where it is you get your arrogance."

"We shall not be returning," he added gently, letting her know all that the voyage entailed.

Agatha placed her hands on her hips. "Good. I shall simply have to decide what to take with me." No matter what the circumstances, she would be with Lilac.

"Nothing," Rejar said softly. "We should take nothing."

"I see." That made Agatha pause for a moment. She rallied quickly. "I may take my mother's locket, of course?" She fingered the one possession around her neck she truly could not bear to leave behind.

Rejar smiled. "Of course."

"What shall happen to all of this?" She gestured with her hand, indicating the property and possessions.

There was a tap at the door.

Emmy stuck her head in, eyes going wide at the broken windows and fallen chandelier. "I was just wanting to check on her Highness's health, Lady Agatha. I had to see for myself that the poor dear was all right. I hope I'm not intruding?"

Rejar eyes locked with Agatha's.

They both grinned.

Emmy was soon to become the richest maid in all of England.

"Come, Lady Agatha, Emmy," Traed took the two women's arms, "Let us leave these two to . . . recuperate." Traed walked them to the door.

[Thank you, brother. For everything. I know what this has cost you. Once again you have stood for the family of Krue.]

Traed hesitated at the door. He looked back at Rejar. "Am I not a part of this family?" his tone was very quiet.

[Yes.]

"And the *elder* brother as well?"

Rejar was slower responding this time. *[Yes . . .]*

"And you must pay heed to an elder brother, must you not?"

Rejar sulked, dreading what was coming. His experience with Lorgin told him it could be anything. Anything at all.

"Good, then stay out of my head!" A huge smile broke across Traed's face.

Rejar looked at him, shocked. *Traed was grinning? Mayhap I am still delirious!* The Familiar's lips twitched.

Raising that one mocking eyebrow, Traed closed the door behind him.

Aviara

Lorgin stood in the Hall of Tunnels, waiting.

Abruptly a portal opened and Yaniff stepped through. Alone.

Lorgin looked behind the mystic to see if the others were following, but there was no one.

The Tunnel sealed.

"Where are Rejar and Traed?" He was not a little concerned. It was past time his brothers came home. Suleila was beside herself, having not seen Rejar for so long, and Krue was threatening to go after his errant son himself.

Rejar would not be a happy Familiar if that were to occur.

"They will be along shortly."

"But who will open the Tunnel for them?"

"Traed will open the Tunnel."

Lorgin wasn't sure he had heard him correctly. "Traed? How can he . . . ?"

"I will tell you everything in good time. Ah, yes! Rejar will have a surprise for everyone, I think."

Lorgin did not like surprises. Especially from his Familiar brother. Experience had taught him that with Rejar it could be anything. Anything at all. "What kind of surprise?" he asked warily.

Yaniff's eyes glittered. "You will see when they get here."

"They?"

Yaniff chuckled. "And how are Adeeann and Melody?"

Lorgin instantly beamed like the proud father he was. "Fine. I vow she is the smartest babe! I think she will be a ruling council member."

"You can tell this?" Yaniff chided. "Truly, Lorgin, it is you who is the great seer!"

Lorgin grinned sheepishly.

"Here—a gift for Adeeann. A momento from her home world." Yaniff tossed him a curved object.

Catching it, Lorgin examined it curiously. "What is it?"

"It is called a pipe."

"What do you do with it?"

"There are those who smoke it, but I have found it works best *unlit*." The wizard's cryptic laughter echoed off the walls as they made their way back to the home of Krue.

"I did not tell you the rest of the story, souk-souk . . ."

Rejar and Lilac lay curled together on their sides, closely embracing each other. They had been through a life-affirming ordeal of discovery and were not about to let go of each other any time soon.

"Tell me how it ends, Rejar." Lilac rested her cheek against his chest.

"Well, the old wizard sends his brother to watch over him because he is concerned. You see, the Familiar would not leave this new world he had come to, even though he knew he did not belong there."

"Why wouldn't he leave?" She kissed the golden hollow at the base of his throat. Cinnamon and bayberry teased her.

"Because he had found something that was more im-

Dara Joy

portant to him than life itself. It had come to him that the 'whirlpool' must have brought him here *especially* to be with his Prunella. So he could not return with his brother; for how could he go and leave his heart behind?"

"Rejar." Lilac gazed up at him, eyes shining with all the love she felt for this exceptional man. Her own sweet Rejar.

He brought her hand to his lips, kissing her fingertips. Staring deeply into her eyes, he placed her palm over his heart. *[It beats for you.]*

"I love you so, Rejar."

A long, mellow purr of contentment followed the tender touch of his lips to hers.

The day Rejar agreed to join the Charl marked a day of awakening for him.

All that Yaniff prophesied would come to pass.

The second son of Krue would go on to become a champion of extraordinary power and strength among his people.

In the passing of time, the name Rejar, or "the Gifted," would become legend. Such a transcendent destiny, however, would demand its own price.

So begins the story of Rejar ta'al Krue.

Anne Avery, Phoebe Conn, Sandra Hill, & Dara Joy

WHERE DREAMS COME TRUE...

Do you ever awaken from a dream so delicious you can't bear for it to end? Do you ever gaze into the eyes of a lover and wish he could see your secret desires? Do you ever read the words of a stranger and feel your heart and soul respond? Then come to a place created especially for you by four of the most sensuous romance authors writing today—a place where you can explore your wildest fantasies and fulfill your deepest longings....

_4052-2 $5.99 US/$6.99 CAN

HIGH ENERGY/WHIRLWIND COURTSHIP
Dara Joy/Jayne Ann Krentz writing as Jayne Taylor

High Energy by Dara Joy. Physics. Zanita Masterson knows nothing about the subject and cares little to learn. Until a reporting job leads her to one Tyberious Augustus Evans. The rogue scientist is six feet of piercing blue eyes, rock-hard muscles, and maverick ideas, and the idea that he is seriously interested in her seems insane. But a night of monster movies, cookie-dough ice cream, and wild love is almost enough to convince Zanita that the passion-minded professor is determined to woo her—with his own masterful equation for sizzling ecstasy and high energy.

And in the same heart-stopping volume...

Whirlwind Courtship by Jayne Ann Krentz writing as Jayne Taylor. When Phoebe Hampton arrives quite by accident at the doorstep of Harlan Garand's mountain cabin, he is less than pleased. Convinced that she is another marriage-minded female sent by his matchmaking aunt, Harlan would gladly throw her out. But Phoebe is a damsel in distress, and an attractive one at that, so against Harlan's better judgment he lets her stay—even though she wishes she were a hundred miles away! Grudging host and grudging guest will just have to put up with each other for a few days. After that, they'll never see each other again—or will they?

_3932-X   **(two passionate contemporary romances in one volume)**

$5.99 US/$7.99 CAN

Dorchester Publishing Co., Inc.
65 Commerce Road
Stamford, CT 06902

Please add $1.75 for shipping and handling for the first book and $.50 for each book thereafter. NY, NYC, PA and CT residents, please add appropriate sales tax. No cash, stamps, or C.O.D.s. All orders shipped within 6 weeks via postal service book rate. Canadian orders require $2.00 extra postage and must be paid in U.S. dollars through a U.S. banking facility.

Name _____

Address _____

City _____ State _____ Zip _____

I have enclosed $_____ in payment for the checked book(s).
Payment <u>must</u> accompany all orders.☐ Please send a free catalog.

REFLECTIONS IN TIME

ELIZABETH CRANE

Bestselling Author Of *Time Remembered*

When practical-minded Renata O'Neal submits to hypnosis to cure her insomnia, she never expects to wake up in 1880s Louisiana—or in love with fiery Nathan Blue. But vicious secrets and Victorian sensibilities threaten to keep Renata and Nathan apart...until Renata vows that nothing will separate her from the most deliciously alluring man of any century.

_52089-3 $4.99 US/$6.99 CAN

TIMESWEPT

Don't miss these passionate time-travel romances, in which modern-day heroines fulfill their hearts' desires with men from different eras.

Traveler by Elaine Fox. A late-night stroll through a Civil War battlefield park leads Shelby Manning to a most intriguing stranger. Bloody, confused, and dressed in Union blue, Carter Lindsey insists he has just come from the Battle of Fredericksburg—more than one hundred years in the past. Before she knows it, Shelby finds herself swept into a passion like none she's ever known and willing to defy time itself to keep Carter at her side.

_52074-5 $4.99 US/$6.99 CAN

Passion's Timeless Hour by Vivian Knight-Jenkins. Propelled by a freak accident from the killing fields of Vietnam to a Civil War battlefield, army nurse Rebecca Ann Warren discovers long-buried desires in the arms of Confederate leader Alexander Ransom. But when Alex begins to suspect she may be a Yankee spy, Rebecca must convince him of the impossible to prove her innocence...that she is from another time, another place.

_52079-6 $4.99 US/$6.99 CAN

Dorchester Publishing Co., Inc.
65 Commerce Road
Stamford, CT 06902

Please add $1.75 for shipping and handling for the first book and $.50 for each book thereafter. NY, NYC, PA and CT residents, please add appropriate sales tax. No cash, stamps, or C.O.D.s. All orders shipped within 6 weeks via postal service book rate. Canadian orders require $2.00 extra postage and must be paid in U.S. dollars through a U.S. banking facility.

Name_____
Address_____
City _____ State_____ Zip_____
I have enclosed $_____in payment for the checked book(s).
Payment <u>must</u> accompany all orders.☐ Please send a free catalog.

A Glimpse of Forever

Linda O. Johnston

Her wagon train stranded on the Spanish Trail, pioneer Abby Wynne searches the heavens for rain. Gifted with the visionary powers, Abby senses a man in another time gazing at the same night sky. But even she cannot foresee that she will journey to the future and into the arms of her soul mate.

Widower Mike Danziger has escaped the L.A. lights for the Painted Desert, but nothing prepares him for a beauty as radiant as the doe-eyed woman he finds. His intellect can't accept her incredible story, but her warm kisses ease the longing in his heart.

Caught between two eras bridged only by their love, Mike and Abby fight to stay together, even as the past beckons Abby back to save those trapped on the trail. Is their passion a destiny written in the stars, or only a fleeting glimpse of paradise?

_52070-2 $4.99 US/$6.99 CAN

Promises from the Past

Victoria Bruce

"Victoria Bruce is a rare talent!"
—Rebecca Forster, Bestselling Author Of *Dreams*

A faint scent, a distant memory, and an age-old hurt aren't much to go on, but lovely Maggie Westshire has no other recollections of her missing father. Now she finds herself on a painful quest for answers—a journey that begins in Hot Springs, Arkansas, and leads her back through the years, into the strong arms of Shea Younger. He is from a different era, a time of danger and excitement, and he promises Maggie a passion like none she has ever known. And while she is determined, against all odds, to continue her search for her father, Maggie doesn't know how much longer she can resist Shea's considerable charms, or the sweet ecstasy she finds in his timeless embrace.

_52064-8 $4.99 US/$6.99 CAN